# SONG OF EBONY

A SNOW WHITE RETELLING

THE SINGER TALES
BOOK 1

DEBORAH GRACE WHITE

LUMINANT PUBLICATIONS

# SONG OF EBONY: A SNOW WHITE RETELLING

By Deborah Grace White

**Song of Ebony:**
**A Snow White Retelling**
The Singer Tales Book One

Copyright © 2022 by Deborah Grace White

First edition (v1.0) published in 2022
by Luminant Publications



ISBN: 978-1-922636-62-1

Luminant Publications
PO Box 305
Greenacres, South Australia 5086

http://www.deborahgracewhite.com

Cover Design by Karri Klawiter
Map illustration by Rebecca E. Paavo

*For the Brothers Grimm*
*You guys went on some crazy wild rides*

CONTINENT OF Providore
KJEMPER
(GIANTS' LAND)
BATTLEMENT WALL
TOVE
BRIARFORD
FROSSENLAND
FROSSEN MOUNTAINS
VADOLIS
TEREN
FOREST OF ILGAL
SUNNIVA
VALLEN
EAST RIVER
TERENFORD
MEDULLE
LERNVALE
PORT DULLA
REVILED LANDS
ISEL SELVANA
KORALLID

# PROLOGUE

"Where are you off to, Marisol?"

Marisol stiffened slightly at the curt voice. It was just her luck that Horace would be wandering past the royal nursery at this moment. The head of the queen's personal guard had always been a little too shrewd. More than once, Marisol had found his eyes on her, their expression too searching to be friendly.

The young nursemaid forced herself to stand straight, telling herself sternly not to be rattled. He couldn't know where she was going. There was no way he would guess—she'd been too careful for that.

"I'm taking Her Highness outside for some fresh air," Marisol said, trying to speak casually as she settled the infant in her arms more comfortably against her chest. "She often has a walk at this time."

"But it's not usually you who takes her, is it?" the guard asked, still that cool edge to his voice that Marisol didn't like.

She raised an eyebrow, trying to look confused by his questioning. "Sometimes it is. It depends who's available."

"Perhaps I should accompany you, see to Princess Bianca's safety," Horace said.

Marisol's other eyebrow went up to join the first. "I thought you'd been assigned duties elsewhere," she said tonelessly. "Since your charge is no longer in need of your protection."

A shadow crossed Horace's face at this veiled mention of Queen Gloria's death. Marisol wanted to roll her eyes. The guard certainly took his duty overly seriously, but it was time for him to stop being surly about his failure to keep the queen alive. A royal guard could do nothing against the dangers of childbirth, after all, and it had been six months since that disaster. Most likely he was just sore over the fact that he'd been forced into a less exalted role when the queen died, and was hoping to secure the post of head guard for the infant crown princess.

As if in confirmation of Marisol's words, another guard rounded the corner, hailing his fellow cheerfully.

"Horace, there you are! The captain is expecting us in five minutes. Best not be late, old fellow."

The guard nodded reluctantly, his eyes not leaving Marisol as he half-turned to face the newcomer.

"Yes, I'm coming," he said.

The other guard ambled up to them, bending into a bow when he saw Horace's companion.

Or rather, the burden carried by Horace's companion.

"Your Highness," the guard said smartly, his tone respectful as he addressed the oblivious infant. His eyes flicked across Marisol, and as men's eyes so often did, they lingered, liking what they saw.

Marisol was just summoning her most appealing smile when the guard dropped his gaze again to the princess, greeting Marisol with only a vague nod. "Ready, Horace?"

Marisol clenched her teeth as the two men walked away, irked not for the first time that her proximity to the six-month-old princess seemed to make her invisible. Before she'd become a nursemaid to Princess Bianca, she'd received plenty of admiration for her pretty face and trim figure. Not that it was the type of admiration she was interested in—she'd never intended to throw her affections away on a fellow servant, or a guard.

No, her mother had always assured her that her face was pretty enough to set her sights much higher. Although, Marisol reflected with a smirk, even her mother wouldn't have guessed just how great a match Marisol fully intended to achieve.

The wooden boards below her feet creaked as Marisol hurried around the curved corridor. The palace was built around the largest, strongest tree in the area. Possibly the largest in Selvana, for all she knew. The moss-covered giant had likely stood for hundreds of years, and would surely dominate the jungle for hundreds more.

The sheer size of the foundation tree meant that it was no short walk to reach the opposite end of the circular story on which the nursery was situated. Marisol passed window after window, but her eyes didn't flick outside. She had no interest in the familiar view of the jungle's canopy stretching away toward the sea. She'd seen it so many times from the princess's nursery that she was thoroughly bored with it.

She glanced at the intricate carving that graced the tree's trunk, which formed the corridor's inside wall. The scene was familiar, depicting the history of the city of Sel. She'd already passed the section covering the first arrival of settlers from the mainland of Providore, and the commencement of building the first elevated dwellings. The tiniest of shudders went over her as she glanced at the next images, showing how the diminutive elves had initially welcomed the arriving humans, teaching them how to forage in the lush but dangerous environment, even helping them to build homes on the ground.

It had all been a front, of course. When humans began dying

from the wild magic that saturated the jungle floor, they'd realized the elves' duplicity. Then, when the humans had been at their weakest, the elves had attacked.

Until recently, Marisol had believed like most others that the elves had all been killed in the conflict that followed. She'd thought the rumors of whole communities of them living hidden away down on the jungle floor had been a myth.

She knew otherwise now, of course.

Another shudder ran over her, but she forced down the trickle of fear. She wasn't sure if it was the unnerving elves which frightened her, or her own people. Certainly, if anyone knew what she was doing, she would be severely punished. Perhaps executed. Perhaps even banished to die down below. She couldn't entirely suppress a third shudder, and the infant in her arms squirmed uncomfortably, picking up on her tension. That would be worse than an outright execution, Marisol thought. Everyone knew that in the generations that had passed since the fight with the elves, the magic had only grown wilder and more dangerous.

There was a reason no human had set foot on the ground of Selvana for generations.

Marisol shook off these grim thoughts. No one was going to find out what she was doing. She'd be very careful today, and if her plan worked...well, she'd soon have the means to make sure no one could threaten her.

The view of the ocean had disappeared from the windows, the vista instead one of tangled vines and mossy trunks. Brightly colored birds swooped in and out of sight, and the cheeky chatter of the wild monkeys kept the heavy air from being still. Marisol picked up her pace, hurrying by the carvings showing the construction of the sprawling treetop city of Sel, the capital where the vast majority of Selvana's human population was situated.

Marisol's steps took her toward a round hole cut in the floor. Settling the baby more firmly against her shoulder, Marisol climbed down the ladder poking out of the hole, stepping off onto the wider platform of the story below. The whole building descended in that way, each story larger than the one above, so that the whole thing would look like a cone if it could be viewed from the side in its entirety. It couldn't, of course, as the jungle pressed in against it on all sides, and other buildings sprawled out from it, connected by sturdy wooden walkways. But the design of the palace was well executed, meaning that in the event of a fall, you'd never go more than one story down.

Because a fall right to the forest floor would kill you for certain—if not the fall itself, the wild magic waiting below.

Marisol only descended two more stories before hurrying along one of the walkways reaching straight out from the tree's trunk. She may not have banked on Horace noticing her leaving the nursery, but she'd still known better than to arrange the meeting place on a lower level of the palace itself.

She didn't go far, however, knowing the princess's absence would be noticed if they were gone too long. She traversed three more tree-top buildings before she began to descend. This time she was going down much less secure ladders, and she clutched the child nervously. If something happened to Princess Bianca on this outing, Horace would see her face the consequences.

The princess didn't seem to mind going down ladder after ladder after ladder. She giggled, clutching Marisol's sleeve and waving a dimpled hand. Her skin was dark enough to blend with the wood around them, and Marisol had taken care to dress both herself and the child in earthy colors, green and brown. Nothing to make them stand out. Even the baby's generous tuft of dark hair matched the gloom that grew the further down they went, away from the golden touch of the sun.

They didn't pass anyone—the route was a series of simple

access ladders, designed to allow the emptying of dirty laundry water and such things onto the forest floor below. No one would choose to go so low when not using it for refuse. Marisol had certainly never been so close to the jungle floor. Her nerves rose as it loomed into view below them, only about fifteen feet down.

She reached the platform at the end of the descent, stepping off the ladder and hastening to the center of the space. She clutched the child close, and Princess Bianca seemed to grasp her fear, because she snuggled uncertainly against the nursemaid.

Marisol felt a flash of something almost like fondness. She'd never been especially interested in babies—taking the role of nursemaid had always been a stepping stone to greater things— but after all, it was quite nice to have an infant nestle against you. She and the princess would soon be more closely tied together. Perhaps it would be fun to have a connection with a baby when it was no longer her job to do all the associated messy, unpleasant tasks. Princess Bianca was certainly a cute infant, with her enormous dark eyes and the red tint to her rounded baby lips.

A strange whistle drew Marisol's thoughts from their path. It didn't sound like any jungle animal she'd ever heard, and she moved reluctantly to the edge of the platform, her eyes searching the dark forest floor below.

Even though she was looking for them, she almost gave a shriek at the sight of the small figures weaving through the undergrowth. They were so camouflaged, she never would have spotted them if they hadn't been moving. Their greens, grays, and browns merged expertly into the jungle.

"I'm...I'm here," she called nervously, her voice quiet for fear of catching the attention of someone above.

Three of the figures stepped out into a small space of more open ground below her, where the foliage had suffered from the humans dumping their filthy water. They turned their faces up toward her, and Marisol bit her lip to keep in a gasp.

They were so eerie, their mature faces seeming out of place on their child-sized bodies. She'd expected the tapering ears, of course, but the greenish-gray color of their faces unnerved her. It made them look ill, she thought.

"Is one of you Acacius?" Marisol asked nervously.

None of them answered her question.

"Do you wish to treat with us, or not?" one of the elves asked, his voice high and cold.

"Of...of course," said Marisol. "That's why I'm here."

"We will not gaze up at you as if you were somehow elevated above us, instead of below us in both position and intelligence," another elf snapped. "If you wish to speak with us, you will descend."

"But I can't!" Marisol gasped. "I'll die if I come onto the ground."

"Perhaps," said the elf, sounding unconcerned. "Perhaps not."

"Surely you don't expect me to take that risk," Marisol argued. "What use would our deal be to me if I'm dead? Or to you, for that matter?"

The third elf sighed. "Let us not waste time on pointless displays," he told his fellows, sounding petulant. "We are here for a purpose, so let us reach it." He looked over his shoulders, snapping the fingers of one small hand. "Bring the ladder."

Several other elves trotted forward, carrying a large ladder that had—with the elves themselves—been concealed in the underbrush. They propped it up so that its end reached the platform under Marisol's feet. It was only just long enough.

"Descend," the first elf said in his cold voice.

"Can't you come up?" Marisol asked, not quite able to hide her alarm.

"We will not," growled the second elf. "We are not cowards like your kind."

"Plus the magic doesn't kill us," added one of the ladder-carrying elves fairly.

"Thank you, Lurgl, you may return to your post," the angry elf said with a touch of irritation.

With a shrug, the elf called Lurgl jogged back into the brush.

"Descend." The elf's voice was deadly now, and Marisol knew that her only options were to obey or to turn back entirely. That thought steeled her—there was no way she was backing down when she'd come so close to her goal.

She cast an uncertain glance at Princess Bianca, but concluded that it would be worse to leave her unsupervised on the open platform than to carry her down the ladder.

The princess made no objection as they once again began to move downward. She was watching the elves out of eyes that seemed entirely too curious and aware. Marisol could only be relieved that the princess was probably still a year off speaking, by which time she would have long forgotten this strange encounter.

When Marisol was only half a dozen rungs from the bottom, she stopped, clinging awkwardly to the ladder.

"This is as far as I'll go," she said firmly. "I have no desire to be killed by wild magic."

One of the elves made a scornful noise, but none of them actually protested.

"You brought your proof?" demanded the one who seemed to be the leader.

Marisol nodded, jostling Princess Bianca on her hip. "This is the princess. Surely the fact that I was able to bring her without being challenged is all the proof you could desire that I truly have the access to the king which I claimed."

"It could be any baby," said the third elf skeptically.

The first one shook his head. "No, that's the princess, all right. She has the look of her mother, and her blood smells of the crown."

"If you say so." The objecting elf dropped the matter, apparently satisfied.

But far from comforting Marisol, the assurance had left her unnerved. Just how closely did these elves watch the people of Sel? She would have to remember that potential threat when she was in charge.

"Very well," the first elf continued. "We have brought the talisman we discussed."

He moved toward the ladder with a stride which lost none of its confidence for being short. Reaching into his dull green garment, he pulled out a necklace. Marisol gasped aloud at the bright golden jewelry. She'd never owned anything half so fine.

"This is the talisman?" she asked eagerly, shifting position so that the princess was pressed against her by only one arm, that hand gripping the ladder so that the other could reach out and take the necklace.

She thought she saw a gleeful gleam flash across the elf's face, but it was gone in a second and she dismissed it, too focused on her prize. She ran a finger over the sparkling red gem which formed the necklace's pendant.

"This will make the king fall in love with me?"

"No," said the elf disdainfully. "Of course not. No talisman can create love."

"What?" Marisol's head shot up. "But that was the deal! It's no use to me if I can't make him love me—my whole plan depends on it."

"You'll have to use your natural charms," an elf voice said snidely from the bushes.

Marisol scowled, her pride stung. "It's impossible," she snapped. "He's so heartbroken over his wife's death he can still barely even look at the child, after six months. He's miserable all the time. How can I possibly make him fall in love without magical intervention? And there's no way he'll marry me without love—I'm a nursemaid, not a titled lady with connections."

She held the necklace out, reluctant as she was to part with it.

"If it doesn't make him fall in love, there's no deal. Take it back."

"I don't think so," said the leader, definitely smug now. "You took it willingly, which means our bargain is activated. You are bound to it now, as are we."

Marisol swallowed, alarm rushing over her as she remembered the vague stories she'd heard, about the distant past. Elves were dangerous to make bargains with—everyone always said never to do it. She'd disregarded those legends. They were just the sort of dire warning old stories always carried. But the glint in the elf's eyes made her wonder uneasily if there were factors at play that she was unaware of.

"The bargain," she said carefully, "was that you would give me a talisman to make the king fall in love with me, in exchange for payment once I attained the position of queen. If the talisman doesn't do what you said it would, the bargain is already void."

The elf smiled mirthlessly. "That might be what you inferred, but it is not what was said. Check the correspondence if you're uncertain. We offered a talisman that would *help* you win the king's heart. And that is what you have received."

Marisol looked down at the necklace doubtfully. Her position was growing more uncomfortable, the arm that was holding both Princess Bianca and the ladder straining painfully.

"What does it do, then?"

"It will make its subject—the king—feel happy when in

your presence," said the elf, speaking clearly and slowly, as if the exact wording was important. Marisol committed the description to memory.

"Is that all?" she asked, disappointed. Happiness was hardly the same thing as love, much as they were supposed to go together.

The elf narrowed his eyes. "You say that as if it is a small matter," he said. "To induce happiness requires powerful magic, and to narrow it to affect only one specific person, and only in specific circumstances, requires a complexity your simple mind couldn't comprehend." He sniffed. "Not to mention the skill involved in concentrating it into a talisman of such small size."

Marisol didn't much like his tone, and a retort rose to her lips at the tiny elf's mention of small size. But she bit it back, not wanting to antagonize them with the details of their pact still not finalized.

"All right," she said, not very graciously. "It's certainly something to work with. I'd be the only one he's ever happy around, so I suppose it might be possible."

*Probable*, she added internally, thinking with satisfaction of the lovely face she saw reflected in her mirror each morning. Once the king had been broken out of his sorrow, surely he wouldn't be impervious to her charms. Not when she would take such pains to please him.

"As for the payment," she went on. "We didn't specify the amount in the correspondence, but—"

"Indeed we did not," said the elf, that gleam back in his eyes.

Again, unease washed over Marisol. "Don't think you can be greedy," she said quickly. "It won't do you any good to have unrealistic expectations. I've got a pretty good insight into the state of the kingdom since I started working in the palace. There's wealth available to the crown, certainly, but not excessive piles of gold or anything like that."

The elves all laughed, even the ones hidden in the foliage joining in.

"We are not interested in gold," said the main speaker.

Marisol stared at him. "What *do* you want, then?" she pressed.

"We will notify you of the nature of our payment at a time of our choosing," the elf said smoothly.

"But when will that be? After I become queen, you mean?" Marisol asked.

"After that, certainly," the elf agreed comfortably. "Sometime after that."

Marisol didn't like the vagueness of his words, but she let the matter drop. Having gotten a taste of the elves' deviousness, she'd been half expecting them to demand payment immediately, which she couldn't have given. It would take time to win the king over, now she knew she'd have to work harder at it than she'd hoped.

"How will you tell me when you want to claim it?" she asked, a sudden doubt occurring to her.

"We will communicate with you through this." At another click of the fingers, the elf summoned an underling from the tree line. The new elf trotted all the way to the base of the ladder, holding out a silver hand mirror.

"A mirror?" Marisol asked blankly. She stared at it. "Is it another talisman?"

"It is," the lead elf confirmed. "You may use it to communicate with us at any time, and you can be certain we will be keeping an eye on you by means of its magic. And do not think to deceive us with your reports through the mirror. It will display only the truth, regardless of what question is asked. Keep it on you at all times during daylight, or we will come looking to discover why you have discarded it. Understand?"

His voice was threatening, and it sent a flash of annoyance

through Marisol. But she swallowed it, reflecting that the time would soon come when she would hold the position to deal with anyone who tried to push her around like this. After all, what did she care if the elves watched her activities? They had no interest in the politics of the human kingdom, and were unlikely to interfere.

Marisol nodded, hesitating as the elf before her held out the mirror.

"Can you put it in the pocket of my gown?" she asked.

"No," he said shortly.

With another scowl, Marisol pulled herself and the baby more tightly against the ladder, reaching up to slip the necklace over her head. One hand now free, she grasped the mirror. The elf immediately retreated, and they all began to move back into the undergrowth.

As Marisol maneuvered herself, trying awkwardly to get the mirror into her pocket, the unthinkable happened. Princess Bianca, leaning forward to watch the disappearing elves, gave an unpredictable squirm, the movement dislodging her from the nursemaid's grip.

Time seemed to expand, each second a lifetime of terror as the princess slid down and fell unhampered to the jungle floor below.

Marisol's scream was quickly stifled as she remembered what would happen to her if she was found in that position. The child hit the ground, instantly sending up a ferocious wail.

For a moment, Marisol was paralyzed with horror. If only Horace hadn't seen her, there might have been a way to hide her involvement in the tragic accident. But then her mind caught up. The baby was still crying, which meant she was still alive. Whatever the stories said, contact with the jungle floor hadn't killed Princess Bianca instantly.

"Help!" Marisol cried, not loudly enough to reach up

through the empty stories above her, but certainly loud enough to penetrate into the underbrush. She couldn't see a hint of any elves, but the tingling on the back of her neck told her they were still watching. Not to mention the ladder she was standing on, which they would surely collect once she was gone.

"Please!" she cried. "Can't someone pass me the baby?"

But there was no answer.

Stifling an oath, Marisol slipped the mirror into her pocket and descended the last few rungs. With her feet on the bottom one, only inches from the deadly dirt below, she reached down, her arm straining with the effort.

The baby princess was still crying with gusto, her arms flailing in the air as she lay on her back. Seizing one of the child's fists, Marisol eased her up until she could grasp at her little gown. With difficulty, she managed to haul Princess Bianca up and into her arms without ever touching the dirt herself.

The infant didn't still at the contact, continuing to weep as Marisol hastened back up the ladder. She ascended a few stories before stopping to look the princess over. A quick examination convinced Marisol that the baby had received more fright than actual hurt, and she breathed a sigh of relief. The consequences to herself if the crown princess had been killed while in her care didn't bear thinking about. She didn't think any magic-induced happiness could overcome that.

She brushed the child off, smoothing out her little gown and righting a bootie which had come loose. It was as she was using her sleeve to make sure there was no dirt in the princess's hair that she made an alarming discovery.

There, among the child's dark tresses, was one streak of shocking, stark white. Marisol stared at it, horrified by this evidence of the princess's misadventure. Had she sustained some hurt after all? Had the magic affected her in some way that wasn't immediately obvious?

Her heart racing, she put the baby down. Princess Bianca had stopped crying, but at being placed on the wooden platform, she let out a renewed whimper.

"It's all right," Marisol soothed her anxiously. "You're all right."

She rearranged the girl's hair, trying to cover up the white streak. Not quite satisfied with the effect, she pulled a ribbon from around the baby's tiny waist, tying it instead around her head. The effect was very pretty, and the white hair was now covered.

"There you go," she said placatingly. "As good as new."

Princess Bianca hiccuped, staring up at Marisol out of wide, teary eyes. Again that almost-fondness tugged at the nursemaid, but it was quickly turned back by the fear now brought on at the very sight of the infant. Marisol had known there were risks associated with taking the princess on this errand, but she'd never dreamed the child would carry a physical mark of Marisol's clandestine deal. She just had to hope that no one would know what it meant. Perhaps once it grew out, the hair would all come back in as it was before, dark and natural.

The whole exercise had taken longer than Marisol had planned, and she hurried back to the palace, afraid they would be missed. Sure enough, she hadn't quite made it to the nursery when she was waylaid by another nursemaid.

"There you are, Marisol, how long a walk did you take?"

"Is everything all right?" Marisol asked warily.

"Yes, of course," the other girl said impatiently. "But the king is sitting down to dinner and wishes to bid the princess goodnight."

The girl rolled her eyes, although she didn't speak aloud the gossip they'd all shared many times. The nightly ritual was often the only point of contact the king had with his daughter in a day, and it wasn't even near her bedtime. But by wishing her goodnight as he sat down to eat, he was saved the need to seek her out at a separate time.

"I'll take her," the other girl said, holding out her arms. "You've got a meal waiting for you."

"No, I'm happy to go," Marisol said, pleased at this opportunity to start working on the king. She resisted the urge to pat the gem now hidden under her simple servant's gown.

"Very well, it's all the same to me," shrugged the other nursemaid, chivvying her along. "Don't be long, or your dinner will be given away."

Marisol ignored her, climbing the extra ladder to the story above. When she reached the curved dining hall, she checked on the threshold to admire its size and general grandeur. It wrapped around half the tree, positioned so as to command a view of both sunrise and sunset. Even in the early evening the space was flooded with light thanks to the low wall which only stretched up half the story, periodic beams connecting it to the roof. Marisol had only been in there a handful of times, and a thrill went through her at the thought that she might soon eat every meal at that long, curved, polished table.

The food on top of it was also tantalizing, all kinds of smells wafting to her nose as she made her way across the room to the king's solitary seat. He looked dwarfed by the huge surface, like an elf sitting down to eat at a human table.

The thought made Marisol nervous, and she had to remind herself that no one could read the guilty secret in her mind. Still, the mirror felt unnaturally heavy in her pocket as she neared the king.

"Your Majesty," she said, dropping into a curtsy. "You requested to see Her Highness?"

"Ah yes," the king said, trying valiantly to smile at his infant daughter, but not quite managing it. "Good night, child. Sleep well."

He pressed a kiss to Princess Bianca's forehead, and to Marisol's surprise, the infant suddenly lurched forward, seizing her father's tunic in a firm grip. She made an inarticulate baby noise that was clearly a plea.

For a moment, the king just looked stunned. Then his face softened, and he reached out as tentatively as if he'd never held a baby before. Maybe he never had, Marisol didn't know. She surrendered the princess, and the king settled the child on his lap. He certainly did look happier than Marisol had seen him since his wife's death, and she knew a flash of annoyance. Was the infant princess going to get the credit for her efforts? Would her presence make King Octavio associate his happiness with her rather than with Marisol?

She schooled her features into a smile as the king raised his glance to her, a look of wonder on his face. "She's a striking little thing, isn't she?" he asked.

Marisol nodded. "Without a doubt, Your Majesty. A little beauty."

The king's eyes moved over Marisol's own lovely face, and his smile grew. Marisol knew a surge of satisfaction.

"May I say, Your Majesty," she said deferentially, "how wonderful it is to see you smile? It's been too long."

A shadow passed across his face, but it was gone in a moment, its rapid departure seeming to surprise even the king.

"It has, hasn't it?" he said. He looked at her again. "You're very kind. What's your name?"

"Marisol, Your Majesty," she said quickly, dropping into a curtsy.

"Marisol," he repeated. "A lovely name. And you're one of Bianca's nursemaids?"

Marisol hid a flicker of annoyance at being forced to articulate the yawning chasm between their stations.

"I am, Your Majesty," she said warmly. "But the sweet little thing is so dear to me, I think of her as much more than a charge."

"How lovely," said the king, clearly pleased. "She is fortunate to have such carers around her." He sighed. "I'm afraid I haven't given her much attention." He hesitated for a moment, then gestured at the long, nearly empty table, laden with enough food for ten people. "Perhaps you and Bianca can stay to dine with me tonight. She ought to eat with her father, oughtn't she? And I'm sure I couldn't manage without you."

"Your Majesty is very kind," said Marisol. Her voice was calm, although inside she was squealing with delight. The elves had not exaggerated the power of the talisman.

Her smile as she settled into place, to the obvious disapproval of the attending servers, whose opinion she cared nothing about, was as broad as the king's.

Everything was progressing perfectly to plan.

FIFTEEN AND A HALF YEARS LATER...

## CHAPTER ONE

# *Bianca*

Bianca skipped a little as she hurried across the familiar wooden boards. If she'd suspected for a moment that there might be a change in her father's condition, she never would have let her governess take her so far away. Honestly, did the woman really think Bianca had never watched a paradise nut harvest before? She'd been tagging along with the harvesters on such expeditions since she was a small child.

She sighed, knowing a moment of wistfulness for the days of her childhood, when she'd been allowed to more or less run wild. It was different now she was a young lady, or at least according to the queen. Not that her stepmother had showed any interest in her before she'd turned sixteen.

Bianca chastised herself for the uncharitable flavor of her thoughts toward the queen. She knew it wasn't just her age that had brought new restrictions to palace life. Her father's ailing health had cast a pall over everything. He'd been growing steadily weaker for the last year, and had been bedridden for weeks now.

But not today, Bianca reminded herself, once again skipping a little as her boots clacked against the floorboards. A familiar scent wafted past her, from the incense that burned at regular intervals in every building in Sel, keeping the mosquitoes at bay. It was so universal in the treetop city that she made no conscious note of it.

However, she did notice the heat that radiated toward her as she passed the doorway to the cookhouses. These rooms were suspended out on a massive branch rather than in toward the tree's center. Bianca spared a glance for the place where the palace's hot food was prepared. In an attempt to protect against the fire escaping, stone slabs lined the reinforced wooden structure, cut from enormous boulders salvaged from the jungle floor long ago. The heat from the stone fireplace emanated out, and Bianca hurried on, glad to leave the area behind. She had no idea how the cooks stood it.

A sly breeze curled through the open windows that lined the rounded corridor, cutting through the otherwise stifling heat and sending wisps of Bianca's long hair dancing. It had been particularly humid this season. Bianca longed for it to rain, to clear some of the moisture in the air. But the clouds, although constantly threatening a downpour, had yet to break.

Her thoughts returning to her father, Bianca redoubled her pace. She'd entered the palace from a walkway on the southern side, leading from one of the smaller storehouses. But that building didn't extend as high as the palace, so to reach her father's rooms, Bianca had to ascend several more stories.

Hurrying toward the ladder ahead, she ran a hand along the carvings that scored the trunk of the foundation tree. She'd walked this corridor many times, and she was familiar with each portrait there. Her touch lingered for a moment on her father's likeness—the deep brown of the wood actually an excellent match for the rich warmth of his face—then grasped the ladder.

Pulling herself up hand over hand, Bianca quickly reached the next story. The ascension points were lined up in this part of the building, so she was able to climb three more immediately. Hurrying along the royal level, she found her voice rising, coming out of her throat without conscious thought. She was so used to the way her words swayed and swirled, she didn't pause to reflect on the strangeness of it. Others did plenty of that for her.

Her words danced around her, a celebration of hope and excitement at the news about her father. She spoke to no one in particular, just enjoying the sound of her own happiness.

She'd almost reached the royal dining room now, and her hand was once again trailing along the trunk that formed the inner wall. On this level, there were no carvings, but trailing creepers had been trained to grow decoratively along the wall. It was across these vines that Bianca's fingers ran, the lush green life pleasant under her touch.

As she rounded the corridor, the guards at the door to the dining room came into view. The fond smiles on their faces told her they'd heard her approach before they'd seen her, and she beamed back at them.

With a final flourish of her words, Bianca lifted her hand from the wall. Something caught her eye, and she looked back at the trunk. With a gasp, she came to a stop, right next to the doorway. Small red blossoms had erupted from the vine, growing and opening with impossible speed. A glance back showed the same phenomenon all the way along her path.

"Beautiful," declared one of the guards, delight in his voice. He hesitated. "My daughter would love those flowers."

"Of course you can pick some for her," Bianca said at once. "They won't be missed." She gave a laugh. "How can they be, when they weren't expected?"

"Thank you, Your Highness," said the guard, bowing to her. "My daughter will be thrilled to have blossoms made by the voice of our Snow Princess."

Bianca was in the act of picking a blossom herself, but she laughed again, a little self-conscious this time. "I don't think my voice made them," she said, tucking the flower into her hair. "They must have been in there before. I'm not sure why my words help bring things out like that."

"It's because our Snow Princess is lovely in every way," said the guard loyally, dipping his head once more. "Even the jungle appreciates your beauty."

"You are much too kind," Bianca protested.

It was true. She knew she didn't deserve the credit for the strange things that often happened around her. But she was glad everyone seemed to take such delight from it. And of course she knew that her unique abilities could have made her a despised oddity—they probably would have if she'd been a peasant rather than a princess, she had the honesty to acknowledge. Still, she greatly appreciated the fact that everyone was so kind about her strange voice, and had been for as long as she could remember.

Happy words rose in her throat again, spilling out as she entered the dining hall that led into her father's rooms. She'd expected the space to be empty, so pulled up short at sight of the two figures enjoying bowls of what appeared to be armadillo stew.

"Stop that awful yelling, please, Bianca," said the older of the two women curtly. "You'll give us headaches."

Bianca fell silent at the queen's rebuke, holding in a sigh. *Nearly* everyone was so kind about her strange voice.

"To be fair, Mama," chimed in the younger of the two, Princess Ilse, "I don't think you could call it yelling. She was actually speaking very quietly."

Bianca sent her half-sister a tight smile. She appreciated the fourteen-year-old princess's desire to be just, but there was nothing to be gained from contradicting her mother. Any disagreement on Ilse's behalf—however slight—regarding Bianca's failings always seemed to make the queen more determined to find fault with her stepdaughter.

"It isn't normal behavior to speak aloud to yourself," Queen Marisol said with dignity. "You must rid yourself of the habit, Bianca."

"Of course she's not going to stop making her words dance," Ilse said, sounding scandalized. "It's her signature!" She glanced at her sister thoughtfully. "Well, that and the hair." She ran a hand down her own dark locks as if to reassure herself they were still where they should be.

Bianca had to hide a smile. Her little sister certainly did have beautiful raven hair, but the effect was a little spoiled by how vain she was about it.

Ilse tilted her head toward Bianca's own tresses. "Do you really not mind being called the Snow Princess? I think I'd be offended."

Bianca shook her head, strolling forward until she stood next to Ilse's chair. "It's said with affection. One of my tutors started calling me that when we studied about the mainland of Providore, and I was so fascinated by the concept of snow. He said it was as white as my hair, and it stuck. It's a nickname, not an insult."

"Well, I suppose there's something to be said for standing out," Ilse said doubtfully. "I'd like to be known for something so striking, but I can't think of anything about myself that's half as interesting as either your voice or your hair."

Bianca shook her head indulgently. "I'm sure you'll find your *signature* with time," she said, borrowing her sister's own term.

"Hopefully," Ilse agreed. She thought for a moment, then returned to her food with a nod. "Yes, all things considered, I still think I wouldn't want people commenting on something unnatural about me."

In spite of her words, Bianca's hand crept to the ends of her unrestrained hair, rubbing a snow-white strand between her fingers. She had once been very self-conscious of her colorless tresses. But she'd made her peace with it now—even come to like it, especially given most of her father's subjects looked at her with admiration rather than ridicule.

"Nonsense, Ilse." Queen Marisol's voice was sharp as she chastised her daughter. "Just because Bianca's hair is an unusual color doesn't make it unnatural. Such a vulgar insult should never come from a princess's mouth."

Bianca raised an eyebrow. Unusual? More like unheard of. She'd never seen anyone other than herself and the elderly with white hair. And no one knew where it had come from. Apparently her mother's hair had been nearly as dark as Marisol's own.

Regardless, her stepmother's response was predictable. For some reason, the queen was more defensive of Bianca's unusual hair than the princess had ever been herself. The older woman always rushed to put anyone in their place who showed their astonishment too plainly.

Bianca would be warmed by the support if she could shake the rankling feeling that the matter had more to do with her stepmother's pride than anything. Queen Marisol may not be Bianca's birth mother, but she'd been the queen since Bianca was an infant, and she was the one who'd raised the crown princess. Theoretically, that was. Bianca had very few memories of her stepmother taking an active hand in her upbringing.

"Bianca." The queen's disapproving voice was directed at her stepdaughter, now. "Speaking of the proper decorum expected from a princess, what *have* you done with your dress?"

Bianca wanted to roll her eyes as she followed the queen's gaze down to the embroidered strap that hung from a belt at the waist of her dress. She'd drawn it back between her legs, securing it on the back of her belt so that her skirts had become two ballooning pant legs.

"It's what everyone does, Mama. It's too impractical to be clambering up and down ladders and across branches in a full skirt."

"*Everyone* does not do it," the queen contradicted. "A princess certainly shouldn't."

Bianca and Ilse exchanged glances. It was absurd for the queen to pretend she was unfamiliar with the custom practiced by almost all the women of Sel. The belts were an almost universal feature of dresses designed in the city. Even the wealthiest and best connected of families didn't expect their daughters to risk breaking their necks—or worse, falling to the deadly ground below—because their movements were hampered by voluminous skirts.

Except in the palace, apparently.

Letting it go as she always did, Bianca turned around, mutely requesting her sister's help in untying the strap from the back of her belt.

Ilse complied readily, making no comment on her mother's rebuke. She was as inured as Bianca was both to the queen's defensiveness about her stepdaughter's hair and to her strict notions of proper conduct.

It was all ridiculous, Bianca reflected mutinously, her stepmother putting on such airs. Bianca was old enough now to hear the gossip that spread inevitably around the palace. How the queen could know what was expected of a princess, Bianca couldn't imagine, given she'd been a nursemaid prior to marrying the king. It was hard to picture her in such a nurturing role.

When the servants spoke of the story, the words sounded like a fabulous romance, but the emotion was never quite there. As if they, like Bianca, were a little perplexed at what had made the king fall so hard for someone so far below his station. And so soon after the death of a wife whom, by all accounts, he'd loved dearly.

But then, Bianca reflected with a dash of bitterness, Marisol was very pretty. She tried to push these unkind thoughts away. It wasn't just about that, surely not. Her father was certainly prone to melancholy, but he always seemed happy when he was with Marisol. And that was surely worth a great deal.

"There," said Ilse, when the fabric of Bianca's gown had fallen into place, the strap itself dangling down the front of the skirts decoratively. The younger princess gave Bianca a little push, spinning her back around.

"I heard what the guards were saying," she said, her eyes now on the blossom in Bianca's hair. "Did your words really grow the flower somehow?"

Bianca shrugged, uncomfortable under her stepmother's scrutiny. The older woman looked even more disapproving than before, if that were possible. "I don't know. Perhaps it was there already and I just hadn't noticed."

"Not likely," scoffed Ilse. Her eyes passed over her sister's face, and a sigh escaped her. "It matches your lips, you know. They're as red as blood, just about."

"What a thing to say!" Bianca laughed. "Blood? Is that supposed to be a compliment?"

"Of course it is!" Ilse protested. Another sigh slipped out. "I wish I was half as beautiful as you."

Bianca fidgeted uncomfortably. She hated it when Ilse said things like that, not least because it clearly infuriated her step-mother. It wasn't that her sister was resentful—Ilse spoke without rancor. But it was a sign of vanity, all the same. And Bianca always felt awkward at the reminder of how much Ilse defined herself both by her beauty and by comparison with her older sister.

Queen Marisol's influence, all of it. There was no doubt in Bianca's mind. She knew no one else so focused on physical beauty, a fact that rendered the queen's own good looks unappealing, at least in Bianca's mind. But she kept the angry thoughts to herself.

"*You* are beautiful, Ilse," she said firmly. "And," her tone turned teasing as she tried to lighten the moment, "your hair is beautiful without being *unnatural*."

Ilse chuckled, once again running a hand over her braid. "True," she agreed comfortably. "But it's very difficult to be noticed when you're just passably beautiful. People expect that as a minimum from a princess."

"I'm not sure where you get such ridiculous ideas," Bianca said laughingly—and entirely untruthfully, her gaze flicking to her stepmother. "There are many other ways—better ways—to earn admiration than being pretty."

"Maybe." Ilse didn't sound convinced. She nudged a bowl toward her sister. "Are you going to eat?"

Bianca shook her head. "No, I'm just here to see Father. Someone brought word to me that he's up! I came at once!"

"Yes, isn't it wonderful?" Ilse agreed, dipping into her stew again. "I was just in there with him before, but the physician said he shouldn't overdo it, so Mama called me out here to eat with her."

"I hope he's still awake," said Bianca, anxious that she might have missed her window.

"I'll come with you," said the queen, rising.

Bianca bit the inside of her cheek, wishing she could think of a way to exclude her stepmother. For some reason Bianca couldn't fathom, the queen had seemed determined to be present whenever Bianca was with her father, for as long as she could remember. She didn't hover around Ilse like that. It was most unfair, and the last thing Bianca wanted right now.

"Your Majesty."

The words came from the head of the queen's personal guard, who stepped forward from his place against the wall to capture Queen Marisol's attention.

"I apologize, Your Majesty, but I forgot to report to you the situation on the fourth level. Some of the wooden railings have begun to rot, and it has compromised the integrity of the whole section. It needs urgent attention, and given the king is still recovering, the head of the maintenance workers seeks your approval to rebuild the entire area."

The queen frowned. "That sounds like unnecessary expense."

"The report led me to believe it is quite necessary, Your Majesty," said the guard emotionlessly. "It's a routine matter, merely requiring confirmation. I believe the king would normally take the head's recommendation on approving such requests."

The queen didn't like that. "You are not asking the king," she said smoothly. "You are asking me. And I am not willing to simply trust that a bunch of common woodworkers are telling the truth about the extent of work necessary. Likely they've overstated the damage in order to gain more work and thus more gold. Do I need to remind you that some of the supplies required for that type of maintenance are finite? It's been generations since we could replenish anything that requires work on the ground to make. Once the items run out, they're gone."

Bianca frowned, hovering. Her stepmother was right about the supplies—so many items were scarce, from clothing to metal and many things in between, what they had used and reused from the ground-dwelling days. But that wasn't what Marisol cared about. It wasn't the first time Bianca had heard her use that argument—which no one needed to be reminded of—to justify her more frequent complaint that someone was trying to swindle the crown. For her part, Bianca could never understand her stepmother's determination to suspect everyone of greed and other ulterior motives. The king certainly didn't seem to share the entrenched suspicion, and his calm authority had once prevented any harm from coming from the queen's attitude. But it had been some time now since he'd been able to effectively rule, and in that time Bianca had listened to many conversations such as this one.

It was on the tip of her tongue to intervene, to back up the head guard. The palace's team of woodworkers were an efficient and hardworking bunch, and Bianca had never heard anyone but her stepmother accuse them of dishonesty.

But she held in the words. Surely Horace could give a more convincing argument than she could, and in any event it was too good an opportunity to pass up. The stern old guard likely had no idea of it, but he'd provided Bianca with exactly what she'd been craving.

Silently thanking Horace for his excellent timing, Bianca slipped past the dining table, heading for her father's door.

She was delighted to see upon entering that the reports hadn't lied. Her father really was up and about, looking more cheerful than she'd seen him in months. He was still very thin, and she didn't like the dark circles under his eyes. But he was upright, standing beside the window and looking over the canopy.

"Father," she greeted him delightedly.

The king turned, a smile lighting his face at the sight of his oldest daughter.

"Bianca, my child. Let me look at you." He held out his hand, and Bianca hurried forward, slipping hers into it. Her father searched her face, his gaze a little piercing. "When did you become a woman, little Bianca?"

She laughed. "I'm only sixteen, Father," she protested.

Still smiling, he shook his head. "But I swear yesterday you were six." He reached out a thin hand and patted her cheek fondly. "You look very like your mother, you know."

"Do I?" Bianca asked, pleased.

The servants had told her as much, but it was pleasant to hear it from her father. She couldn't recall him saying it before. He didn't speak much about her mother, probably because Marisol was usually in the room, and she clearly didn't like it.

The king nodded solemnly. "Your eyes are very like hers, and your face." He smiled softly in memory. "Her skin wasn't as dark as yours, but she would have been delighted to see that her wish came true."

"What wish?" Bianca prompted.

His gaze returned to her from across the years. "Oh, she told me when she was expecting that she hoped the baby would have skin as dark as ebony, like mine. She was just being sentimental and romantic, I suppose. But then, we were very young then, and very much in love."

Bianca found she had no words, or at least none that could get around the lump in her throat. She'd never heard her father say such things, and the picture his words conjured was painfully beautiful. She wished so fiercely that she could have known her mother. Surely she had been a warmer person than Bianca's stepmother.

"The hair would have surprised her, however," continued King Octavio in a rallying tone. "Neither of us expected a Snow Princess." His eyes danced a little as he used the nickname, the smile in them robbing the words of any potential for criticism.

"Are you truly well, Father?" Bianca asked, gripping his arm. "Do you feel better?"

"Much better," he said brightly. "I can't quite believe it. I haven't felt this much myself in weeks. Months, even."

"I'm so glad," Bianca said delightedly.

Before she could say more, the door opened, and her step-mother came in. The look she cast at Bianca was as suspicious as her words about the maintenance workers, as if she knew Bianca had tried to lose her, and resented it.

But, as always, the king shared none of his daughter's disappointment at the arrival of his wife. His face lit up at once, his features lightening further as the queen came toward him.

"My dear," he said, reaching out his free hand to her, so that he held both his wife's and his daughter's hands. "How spoiled I am, surrounded by such an array of kind and beautiful women. We just need Ilse to complete the effect."

"I'm afraid not, Your Majesty." The physician bustled in, looking disapproving. "You need rest, not excitement."

He chivvied the two women out as if they were erring children rather than royalty. Bianca cast a regretful look back at her father, but he just smiled at her. As soon as they were back in the dining hall, the physician spoke again.

"I need a word with you, Your Majesty. About His Majesty's condition."

"But he's getting better, isn't he?" Bianca demanded, alarmed by his somber tone. "He's up."

"He is up," the physician agreed, sounding hesitant. But before he could elaborate, the queen jumped in.

"You and Ilse should resume your studies," she said curtly. "The physician is speaking to me, Bianca, not you."

Bianca hesitated, wrestling with her frustration. What did her stepmother gain from excluding her? She wasn't a child anymore—surely she had as much right as anyone to know about her father's health. It was absurd how the queen was looking at her, with that edge of suspicion. She was paranoid if she saw a threat in Bianca. What mischief could the princess possibly do with information about the king? She'd never dream of taking advantage of her father's illness, or spreading the royal family's private information around the city.

"Bianca."

The queen's voice was as hard as steel, and Bianca let out a sigh, moving back to join her sister. Half of her was furious with her own spinelessness in not insisting on being included, and the other half was congratulating her restraint in avoiding conflict.

She wished she knew which half had the right of it, because they couldn't both be the voice of wisdom—they were too often at war with one another.

# CHAPTER TWO

# Bianca

Ilse seemed to feel no such frustration at being excluded from the physician's report. She chattered cheerfully as the sisters made their way out of the dining hall and along the corridor.

"Let's not go back to the governess," said Bianca suddenly, interrupting whatever tale she hadn't been listening to. "Let's go up to the tower."

"All right!" agreed Ilse, predictably delighted to throw off their lessons.

The pair cast a look around, making sure their mother wasn't in sight, then looped their belts between their legs before hurrying to the closest ladder. By the time they reached the palace's topmost level, they were both giggling. Nodding to the lone guard on duty, they hurried across the narrow platform. It was the smallest story of the whole palace, and the ladder where they'd entered wasn't much more than an arm's length away as they leaned on the chest-high balustrade.

"It's beautiful, isn't it?" said Bianca, gazing out over the treetops.

"Mm," Ilse agreed contentedly.

The platform sat at the very top of the tree, commanding a view in all directions. The sea was behind them as they looked southward, across the sprawling expanse of Sel. Most of the city was hidden by the canopy, but here and there a building poked through, and Bianca could picture it all with ease. The familiar walkways running high above the ground, the layered buildings full of the constant bustle of life. It wasn't a large city, not as large as it had once been, apparently. She'd seen the rotting ruins of buildings on the outskirts of the capital herself. But it was still busy enough to constantly hum with motion, and it still contained the vast majority of Selvana's residents.

She wondered idly what life must be like in the few outlying settlements. The journey there was hazardous, through treetops only sporadically lined with decent walkways. Apparently it involved a fair amount of free climbing, something which terrified most residents of Sel. It terrified Bianca a little, too, although there was a part of her which thought it might be exhilarating to pit herself against the jungle that way.

It was the same part of her which wanted so much to push back against her stepmother's exclusion and criticism, and she silenced it now as she had earlier.

She dismissed the villages from her mind, sparing only one more thought for how isolated and difficult their lives must be. It wasn't the easiest life even in the capital, of course. Held captive in the air as they were, unable to descend to the ground, they were limited in what they could eat, what resources they could access. According to the history Bianca studied, the kingdoms on the mainland had no such restrictions.

It would be nice to be able to roam the jungle floor, she thought, not for the first time. What treasures might be hidden down there, blocked from view by the jungle's lush growth? But it was impossible, and she let the thought drift away in the still, heavy air.

"It's fascinating to think there were once so many more people living in Sel, isn't it?" Bianca asked her sister.

"Is it?" Ilse didn't sound at all fascinated.

"Well," Bianca reasoned, "surely the population should grow, not shrink."

"Well, I'm sure it would have if not for the war with the elves," Ilse pointed out.

Bianca frowned, picturing the scale of the damage she'd seen on some of the outlying buildings. It was hard to believe the elves—who had supposedly been only the size of human children when fully grown—had caused that. What kind of weapons had they used?

She frowned to herself as she cast another look over the mostly hidden city. Her sister was right that the fight with the elves had reduced the population of the human settlement. But it had been such a long time since then. Much as she didn't like to think badly of the only way of life she'd ever known—not to mention the culture she loved—she had to acknowledge the truth. The true cause of their waning population wasn't a long-ago war. It was the rigors of living in the trees, barred from the security and resources the land would offer if it wasn't rendered uninhabitable by wild magic.

She couldn't help but feel that more could be done to expand their options, but all anyone seemed interested in doing was patching up the treetop world they were confined to.

*If even that*, Bianca thought, her frown deepening as she remembered her stepmother's reaction to Horace's very reasonable report.

"Do you think Father will be able to take over running things again soon?" Bianca asked abruptly, turning to Ilse. "Now he's getting back on his feet?"

"Probably," Ilse said, unconcerned. "But he can take his time. I mean, Mama has been managing fine while he's been unwell."

Bianca pressed her lips together to keep in the criticism bubbling up. Ilse had always been more tolerant of the queen's more frustrating ways. Understandable, of course. Not just because Marisol was Ilse's mother by birth. But because she'd always treated the younger princess with much more patience.

"What is it?" Ilse asked, picking up on her silence more shrewdly than Bianca had expected.

"Well..." Bianca shrugged. "I thought she was harsh, and overly suspicious. Do you really think the woodworkers were trying to exploit the crown? I mean, I've never heard of any problems like that with the palace maintenance crew before."

Ilse frowned, her tone taking on a defensive edge. "I'm sure Mama would know better than we do, Bianca. She's the queen, after all. She knows how things work. Just because she isn't high-born doesn't mean she isn't a good ruler."

"I wasn't talking about her birth," Bianca protested. "I was talking about her choices. It just seems to me like she's determined to think everyone is untrustworthy, when from what I can see—"

"Your Highnesses?"

The familiar voice of their governess drifting up from the story below made both girls cringe. It seemed they'd been run to ground, so to speak.

"Yes, we're up here," Bianca called, resigning herself to a scold.

But when the older woman emerged at the top of the ladder, there was no reproach on her pale face. She looked, most uncharacteristically, like she was struggling to find words.

"What is it?" Bianca asked, alarmed. "What's happened?"

"It's His Majesty," the governess said, and Bianca's breathing hitched. "You're to come straight away."

Their tension of a moment before forgotten, the sisters exchanged a fearful glance. Then they both raced for the ladder, half falling down the rungs in their haste. The trip back to their father's rooms felt interminable, and yet when Bianca reached the door, she hesitated. Some formless fear rose up in her, making it nearly impossible to get her legs to move.

Ilse clearly didn't suffer the same limitation because she rushed straight past her sister. Bianca followed haltingly, her heart sinking at the sight before her eyes. It was a familiar scene from recent weeks, with her father stretched out on his enormous bed. The queen's presence in a chair beside him was less common, but the hovering physician was what told Bianca this time was different. The man's face was very grave as he took the king's pulse. Bianca's father didn't seem to be conscious.

"What happened?" Bianca demanded, throwing herself to her knees beside the bed. "He was so well half an hour ago!"

The physician gave a heavy sigh. "It is as I reported to Her Majesty," he said sadly. "I had concerns about the suddenness of his recovery. Sometimes, with this type of illness, the patient can rally right before the end. But it is not a true recovery, alas."

Bianca stared at her stepmother. "That's what he reported to you earlier? Why didn't you tell us?"

The queen met her eyes unflinchingly. "You are told what you need to know, Bianca. Any other burdens are mine to bear."

"What do you mean, the end?" Ilse asked the physician, horrified. "What are you saying?"

Queen Marisol cleared her throat quietly. "The physician does not believe your father will live through the night," she said, her voice unnatural although quite calm. "Or that he is likely to wake again."

"No!" Bianca wailed, refusing to believe it. "That can't be true!"

"I will leave you for now," the physician said softly, bowing himself toward the door. "Although I will return soon to check on His Majesty's condition."

Bianca's gaze passed to her sister, seeing her own shock and terror reflected in Ilse's eyes.

No, perhaps not quite. The sisters would feel the shock and grief in equal measure, of course. But to Bianca, the death of their father meant a burden Ilse would never have to worry about.

In spite of the privacy, the royal family said little to one another as the afternoon melted into evening. The king continued to breathe, but it was a raspy, labored sound. Bianca's mind was numb, unable to comprehend the sudden deterioration of everything. She'd been so happy such a short time before, sure that her father was past the worst of the lingering illness.

"It's living in the trees," Bianca whispered into the stillness, after at least two hours.

"What?" Ilse turned tear-filled eyes to her. "What are you talking about?"

"Our supplies are so limited up here," Bianca insisted. "What if there are remedies on the ground that could have helped him?"

"That's nonsense," snapped the queen. "We can't go on the ground, Bianca. No one can survive it."

She tugged the gauzy sleeves of her dress down a little, the movement uneasy.

"But when's the last time we tried?" Bianca pressed. "What if things have changed? My history tutor made it sound like not everyone died when the elves convinced the humans to build homes on the ground. He said some could withstand it, but the risk was too high."

"No one can withstand it," the queen said angrily. She narrowed her eyes. "It sounds like that tutor is teaching you tall tales, and dangerous ones at that. I'll have him removed from the position."

"No, don't do that!" Bianca protested.

But she could see from her stepmother's face that it was already too late. Frustration welled up inside her once again at the queen's heavy-handed ways, but she pushed it down, ashamed of herself for nursing her grudge while her father lay dying before her.

Dying. Could it be true? It didn't feel real.

The hours crawled by. The physician came and went, and eventually the queen and Ilse both sank into uneasy sleep in their chairs. But Bianca's mind remained wakeful. She leaned forward, placing her hand on her father's head and letting her words flow fluidly, making them dance, as Ilse put it. They were words of hope, of fear, of love. She might have been imagining it, but it seemed as though her father relaxed, his brow smoothing out a little.

It was less than an hour later that she heard him take one great rattling breath, and then he fell still.

Bianca's little cry brought the physician bustling over from his position in the corner. He took his time examining the king, but when he lifted his head, he didn't even need to speak for Bianca to understand.

She let out an involuntary wail, throwing herself across the covers and weeping onto her father's still hand. The sound woke her stepmother and her sister, and soon Ilse was weeping as well. Bianca could hear no sound from the queen, but perhaps she was crying silently. Bianca didn't turn her head to look.

When she could bear it no longer, she pushed herself away from the bed, racing to the window and throwing wide the wooden casement to expose the dark jungle beyond. Normally the view would include the star-strewn sky, but no light was visible now, the air still thick and heavy with the threatening clouds which refused to drop their load.

Only the faintest glow of muted moonlight identified the sea beyond the jungle, and it was toward that Bianca's soul seemed to reach. She longed for the open space, the freedom. She wished she could fly away, both from her grief and from her responsibilities.

Without thinking about it, she let her words tumble out, the audible dance one of desperate lament. As the sound poured out into the jungle, Bianca could almost feel something else going with it, some tangible but invisible force that seemed to be carried on her words.

All at once, the clouds broke. In timing that seemed perfectly to reflect the tragedy of the moment, the skies split open, and the torrent began. In a matter of seconds, the gentle patter of the first few drops on the leaves became a relentless downpour, water falling in sheets and drenching every surface of the jungle.

Bianca embraced the intensity of it, glad in an agonizing way to have the very skies reflect her emotions.

A frantic knock at the door was followed by the guard whom Bianca and Ilse had greeted up in the tower. He all but fell through the doorway, bowing deeply when he saw the assembled royals.

"Forgive the intrusion, Your Majesty," he said, his eyes flying to the bed, "but I have an urgent—"

His words cut off abruptly as his senses caught up.

"King Octavio has passed away," said Queen Marisol, still speaking evenly.

The guard looked horrified, and he sank into another bow. "That is terrible news, Your Majesty."

"I assume there is a reason you were barging into His Majesty's rooms at this time of night," the queen said, her tone frigid.

"Yes, what was so urgent?" Bianca asked, worry coloring her words. The guard had seemed worked up when he entered.

"Perhaps we can assist."

The guard swallowed. "My apologies, Your Highness. Of course, I wouldn't normally...but protocol is to report directly to the king, because he's the only one with authority to order..."

He floundered for a moment, clearly unsure who to report to. His eyes slid to Bianca, and she realized that he was waiting for some encouragement, some sign of her willingness to hear the report.

She cleared her throat, but before she could speak, the queen interjected smoothly.

"You may make the report to me."

"Yes, Your Majesty," said the guard, bowing again. "A ship has been spotted attempting to make anchor in the harbor. A ship flying no flag."

Queen Marisol made an angry noise in her throat. "Are we to deal with pirates at this moment?"

The guard said nothing, looking nervous.

"We don't know they're pirates," Bianca reasoned. "What if it's a genuine contact from the mainland?"

"The mainland has made no attempt to contact us since we confirmed that the magic on Selvana has grown too wild for the land to be inhabitable," the queen rapped out. "They are pirates, like the rest of the ships, coming in hopes of mining the magic for profit."

"Mining the magic?" Ilse repeated, looking confused. "Like the elves used to do, back when they still existed?"

"Yes," said the queen shortly. She rubbed her chest in an uncomfortable gesture Bianca had seen before. "A despicable practice."

"I didn't know ships came from the mainland for that purpose," said Ilse.

"It's been years since the last such attempt, Your Highness," said the guard. "King Octavio," his gaze flicked to the bed then quickly away, "ordered warning shots be fired. The ship turned back without landfall."

"I suppose if we want to be rid of them, all we need to do is let them land," said Ilse dully. "None of them will survive."

"No," said the queen, still sounding irate. "I intend to act more decisively than that. Anyone from the mainland who thinks they can breach our sovereignty will learn their mistake. Sink the ship."

"Sink it, Your Majesty?" the guard repeated, eyes wide.

"At once," the queen confirmed.

"Sink it?" Bianca stepped forward. "But what if they're genuinely trying to communicate with us? Contact with the mainland can only benefit us, surely!"

"This ship is not a legitimate envoy," said the queen impatiently. "If it was, it would be flying the flag of its kingdom, in honest display. They are pirates."

"Even if you're right, surely it's not necessary to sink the ship!" Bianca insisted. "Can't you fire a warning shot, like Father did?"

The queen ignored her, turning back to the guard. "Sink it."

"But that's such a waste of supplies," Bianca said desperately, trying a different approach. "It's like you always say, the supplies are finite. We have such a limited number of cannon balls, and no way to acquire more, since we no longer have operations on the ground or trade with the mainland. To sink the ship will take many more than just one warning shot. Surely we don't want to use up so many supplies."

"If we send a clear enough message, we won't need more," said her stepmother dismissively. "No more will come. We will send these pirates to the bottom of the ocean."

"No." Bianca's fists were clenched. "Do I have no say? You're no longer queen, Mama, not with Father gone."

Queen Marisol froze in her seat, turning slowly to stare Bianca down with a frigid gaze. "What did you say?"

Bianca swallowed, regretting the unfeeling words at once. "I know we're all reeling from his loss," she tried again. "But we have to remember that things have changed now."

"You are barely sixteen," Queen Marisol reminded her. "You cannot assume the throne until you reach eighteen years of age. Until which time, I remain queen of Selvana."

Bianca bit her lip. She wasn't entirely sure that was correct—the part about the dowager queen retaining the rule, that was. She knew the law about needing to reach majority before ascending. But she recognized that she was in no position to argue, and that it would be better for the gawking guard not to witness any family conflict anyway.

"Please, Mama," she tried again, speaking more calmly this time. "Please reconsider your command. I don't see any necessity to sink the ship."

"I will not reconsider," the queen said shortly. She turned to the guard, raising an eyebrow as if surprised by his presence. "Why are you still here? You have your orders."

With a swift bow, the guard ran from the room. A short time later, the sound of the cannons could be heard, even over the downpour. Bianca drew in a sharp breath, her fists clenched.

To her surprise, there were only two explosions. They waited in strained silence for more to follow, but instead the guard came sprinting back.

"They've raised a flag, Your Majesty," he said, his attention wholly on the queen now. "It's the flag of Medulle."

"They're not pirates!" Bianca cried. "They must be a genuine Medullan envoy!"

"Nonsense," said the queen, irritated. "If they were, they would have been flying the flag at the beginning. This is a trick, designed to stop the shelling. Resume fire, and do not stop until the ship is at the bottom of the ocean."

"But you'll kill them all!" Bianca cried.

"I expect so," her stepmother agreed, her face unyielding. "The magic will deal with any survivors who make it to shore."

Furious frustration rose up in Bianca, but the guard had already left to carry out his orders. She stumbled from the room, abandoning her father's form as she ran after him. She climbed up to the tower in a daze, disregarding her instantly sopping clothes as her eyes frantically searched the downpour. She could dimly make out the shape of the ship on the water, and tears clogged her throat as the cannons sounded again, and again.

It was unbearable, knowing the wrong thing was being done, and being powerless to stop it.

*Worse than that*, whispered a voice in her head. *You* do *have the power, you just don't know how to wield it.*

She sank to her knees, horrified both by the death that lay in the royal rooms behind her, and that being meted out before her. And no less horrified by the prospect of what was to come.

Because Bianca had seen her stepmother's face when she'd openly defied her, claiming in front of others that the queen had no more right to her crown.

Bianca had crossed a line, and the queen wasn't going to let her forget it.

# CHAPTER THREE

# FARRIN

Farrin leaned against the railing of the ship, excitement and nerves jostling for position inside him as his eyes searched the island looming into view. He patted the rucksack over his shoulder, reassuring himself that he had all his possessions on his person, where they were ready for arrival. And where they couldn't be pilfered from below deck in his absence.

The afternoon was growing late, but there was no yellow cast to the sky, like there would be on a clear night. Everything was gray, muted by the thick, dark clouds hanging low in the sky. It would surely rain soon, and he hoped they'd be safely anchored by then.

He glanced back, sparing a thought for his home, far across the expanse of unbroken water. His mind turned fleetingly to the strange, mute girl who'd been washed up near his home city of Port Dulla not long before. He hoped his parents and brother would be kind to her in his absence. He felt a little bad for the way he'd given her the slip in his flight to the harbor. But honestly, it was a relief to be away. He had nothing against her—in fact he felt very sorry for her, and wanted to help her, in a general sort of way. But it was a little more than he could take, being constantly followed even in his own castle, watched adoringly by a silent, hopeful girl who was barely older than a child.

He put the girl from his thoughts, trusting in his family to take care of her needs. Thoughts of his family didn't lighten his heart, however. His parents would have discovered his flight long before now, although it was possible they hadn't figured out his destination. He winced. If they had, they would be beyond furious. But after all, he was eighteen now. He didn't need their permission to go on a voyage.

The argument was absurdly weak, even in his own head. He knew perfectly well that princes couldn't just traipse blithely around the continent, consulting no one's pleasure but their own. Especially given the danger of his chosen destination.

Still, if there was even the slimmest chance of his voyage being successful, he would gladly take whatever recriminations his parents unleashed on him. As long as they didn't take it out on his brother. Poor Emmett wasn't to blame. He'd had no idea what Farrin was planning.

But Farrin had explained in the note he'd left that his unsanctioned journey was purely for the purpose of trying to find a solution to Emmett's...condition. So it was plausible that King Johannes and Queen Sula might think their older son had a hand in the escape. That hadn't been Farrin's intention. He'd just thought it the only possible excuse that might soften his parents to his flight, even the tiniest bit. They were as devastated by the blight afflicting their heir as Farrin was.

Familiar guilt washed over Farrin at the memory of how his brother had gotten into the state he was in. What utter fools they'd both been, to toy with things they didn't understand. How could they have thought they could wield magic that powerful, that wild?

A soft groan escaped Farrin. If only he'd been the one struck by the rebounding magic. It didn't matter so much for a second-born prince to be...well, to be what Emmett was. But of course his pigheaded big brother had to get all protective, shoving Farrin out of the way and taking the full blast himself.

"That's what I get for having slower reflexes," Farrin mumbled into the wind.

"What? Wha's that ye're muttering, me fine fellow?"

"Nothing."

Farrin turned to look at the crew member who was striding past, his arms full of rope and his gaze suspicious. The sailors didn't know who Farrin was, or at least he was fairly sure they didn't. But perhaps the captain had told them the exorbitant sum Farrin had paid for inclusion in this clandestine voyage. Because the sailors all seemed perfectly aware of how wealthy Farrin was, and he'd gotten the impression during the voyage that they looked on him none too kindly as a result.

Sailors, he scoffed to himself. That wasn't quite the word. Pirates, more like. But he supposed he shouldn't complain, not after he'd waited months for such an opportunity. He'd been searching desperately for a solution ever since Emmett was afflicted a year before. But his research had only turned up the fables about aconitum about six months prior. When he'd first learned that the rare plant grew only on the inaccessible island kingdom of Selvana, he'd despaired. But some surreptitious investigation had revealed that there were those willing to attempt the dangerous journey for the illicit treasures to be found on the island.

He'd been fortunate to learn of this particular voyage, truth be told, and to barter his way aboard. And now he was going to learn whether his gamble had paid off, or whether the dire warnings he'd grown up with were true, and venturing onto Selvanan soil was nothing but a death wish.

The wind was against them, and they made slow progress

toward the island. Through the dim light of evening, Farrin could barely make out the shoreline. It looked rocky, harsh cliffs giving way to the jungle which crowded every visible inch of the island kingdom.

As the darkness fell, the wind rose. Farrin noticed a palpable change in the mood of the crew. Before they'd been efficient but calm. Now there was a frantic edge to the way they raced around, securing things on deck, and manipulating the sails in ways Farrin's untrained mind couldn't decipher.

"Where are we going?" he demanded, gesturing toward the shore. "Shouldn't we be keeping course?"

The moon momentarily broke from the heavy clouds, and by its light Farrin could see a harbor up ahead. Except the ship wasn't heading for it, the crew apparently trying everything they could to redirect away from the natural landing place.

"Sure, if ye wish fer the locals ter see us and ward us orf afore we can get a sniff o' the land's magic," grunted one sailor, as he lashed a rope to one of the ship's smaller masts. "Our suppliers don' meet us in the main royal 'arbor."

Farrin was about to retort that he hadn't come to plunder Selvana's magic, but he realized before the words escaped that it wasn't entirely true. Aconitum was a plant with highly magical properties, and his sole intention was to harvest it and carry it home, right out from under the Selvanans' noses if necessary. He didn't know the identity of the *suppliers* several crew members had mentioned, but he realized he may well have to rely on their cooperation to find his quarry. He had no idea where to search, and he couldn't exactly wander over the land.

"I'd suggest ye get below deck," the sailor called to him over the noise of the wind and the waves. "Things'll get real rough when them clouds break."

Farrin shook his head. "No, thanks." He'd much rather see what was going on than be trapped below deck.

The words were barely out of his mouth when he felt a drop of water fall on his nose. At first he thought it was spray from the ocean, but a moment later the heavens opened, and rain began to fall in earnest. Farrin was used to downpours—the western part of his kingdom was similar in climate to Selvana, and even Port Dulla received its share of heavy rain.

But this torrent was like nothing he'd witnessed before. Within moments the deck was flooded, streams pouring over the side into the ocean below. The rain was almost violent in its relentlessness, and Farrin couldn't help the fear that flashed instinctively through him.

The deck lurched violently, and Farrin was thrown from his feet, although fortunately not over the edge. The experience was frighteningly reminiscent of his last voyage, which had ended in disaster. His heart was pounding as he scrambled up, casting his eyes around to see the helmsman struggling up from a similar position. The wheel spun wildly, and the oaths of the crew around him alerted him to their defeat—the ship careened back onto the resisted course, heading straight for the harbor. For a fleeting moment, Farrin was glad. He wasn't knowledgeable in such matters, but even to him the main harbor looked like the only vaguely safe landing place on the shoreline.

That consideration suddenly held much less weight a moment later, when a muffled boom reached Farrin's ears. Another followed soon after, this one mere moments before something blasted a hole in the railing only two yards from where he gripped it.

With a cry, he threw himself backward, scrambling away from the jagged wood. The shouts of the pirates surrounded him, as everyone raced across the deck, responding to orders from the captain which Farrin couldn't catch over the pounding rain. His mind coming back to life, Farrin pushed himself to his feet, stumbling in his haste to cross the slippery deck and reach the captain. He'd been aware that the Selvanans might be hostile to the pirates, and had come prepared.

"Here!" he cried, pulling something from his sodden rucksack. "If we raise this, will they stop firing?"

The captain paused his frenzied instructions long enough to stare at the dripping Medullan flag. "Where did you get that, lad?"

"From the palace," said Farrin shortly. "I'm Prince Farrin."

The captain's mouth fell open, fear flashing across his face. "There goes my incentive to survive," he growled. "They'd hang me for coming back without ye."

"What?" Farrin asked, his heart picking up speed. "What do you mean?"

"Prince or sailor, we're all about to meet our maker," the captain rapped out gruffly. "I suggest ye prepare yerself for it. If the sea doesn't claim ye, the land will."

"I don't accept that," Farrin cried, shaking the fabric in his hand. "Isn't this worth a try?"

"I suppose anything is worth a try," the captain agreed.

At his curt order, one of the crew members seized the flag and ran to the main mast. Soon the Medullan colors were waving wildly in the wind above the beleaguered ship.

Whether anyone would be able to see it from shore was another question, but Farrin was encouraged to hope when no more cannonballs followed the first. They all waited in tense silence for the longest fifteen minutes of Farrin's life.

Then the boom rang out again, and the captain cursed, resuming his frantic commands. The next two cannonballs hit the water. But at the third, the sound of splintering wood heralded the collapse of the main mast.

The captain was still screaming orders to his crew, but Farrin heard none of it, his ears ringing as a potent mix of fear and determination seized him. He'd come here for Emmett, and he hadn't gotten this far only to die before he even set foot on the island.

He threw himself alongside the nearest sailor, copying the man's motions as he tipped cargo off one side of the boat, through a gash in the ruined balustrade. Farrin flinched as a cannonball missed its mark by mere feet, falling into the water close by, but he kept at his task. The last of the crates splashed into the rain-lashed water below, and the ship lurched the other way. Farrin's companion grunted in satisfaction as the wind caught at a sail suspended from the ship's smaller mast. But the relief was short-lived. Another cannonball came flying from the shore, and this time the aim was true. It slammed straight into a lifeboat that was halfway through being lowered into the ocean, rendering the smaller vessel unusable.

Farrin's eyes had barely taken in the damage when another cannonball struck. It tore through the bowels of the ship, eliciting screams from those working below, and sending water pouring into the vessel's midsection.

"Abandon ship!" The captain's order shocked Farrin out of his momentary stupor. He may not be a sailor, but he'd lived all his life in a coastal city. He knew no captain gave that order lightly.

Around him, men began vaulting over the railings. Mastering his terror, Farrin followed them, thrown to the mercy of the ocean for the second time in as many voyages. It seemed too much to hope for another miraculous rescue this time, but he didn't let himself dwell on his chances. He hit the surface hard, for a moment unable to find which way was up in the churning, pitch-black chaos. The water was cold, but far from frigid in the humidity. It was just enough to send a jolt of clarity through his mind.

Someone thrashed near him, the sailor's leg catching Farrin in the side and forcing him away from the surface. Farrin was fairly certain it hadn't been intentional—he doubted the other man had even noticed the contact—but he still kicked away, trying to put some distance between himself and the panicked sailor.

When his head finally broke the surface, he could barely gasp in air, thanks to the rain pouring in sheets into the ocean. Farrin trod water with his legs, lifting one hand to clear his eyes of moisture. With a gasp, he realized that the listing ship was nearly on top of him, and he struck out blindly, trying to get away from it.

Another boom shook the heavy air as a new cannonball sliced through the already floundering ship. It hit so close to Farrin's position that a splintered shard of wood struck him, lodging itself in his leg.

With a cry, he temporarily lost the battle with the surging swells, his head going back under.

*No*, he told himself furiously, as his mind began to panic. *I am* not *dying here.*

Using his uninjured leg, he kicked back above the waterline. He let out a breath of relief when he got his bearings. He was on the landward side of the wreck, at least.

He was aware of the ship sinking rapidly behind him, but he didn't look back. He struck out for shore, moving with the sure strokes of a seaside prince who'd learned to swim as early as walk.

The rest of the crew didn't seem to be doing the same. Farrin passed a few who were clinging to bits of the wreckage, attempting to propel themselves back out to sea.

"What are you doing?" he shouted, over the roar of the rain and the waves, and the continued booming of the cannons. "The ship's done for, and none of the lifeboats made it! If you stay in the ocean, you'll die for sure. At least on land you might have a chance!"

One of the men shook his head vehemently. "You've got it the wrong way, lad! Don't set foot on that shore!"

Farrin ignored the dire words, knowing it was no time to listen to sailors' superstitions. The pirates would be warning him about mermaids, next. His heart sank for the inevitable fate of all those staying in the water. There was no other land nearby, nothing closer than the mainland. And that was much too far to make it on what was little more than a piece of driftwood.

His strength was nearly spent when the rocky shore finally loomed within reach, but Farrin didn't slow his pace. He saw, too, that he wasn't totally alone in his course, as he'd thought. Two other heads bobbed in the water before him, the pirates gazing doubtfully at the rocky cliffs, and the small sandy cove that broke the daunting natural barrier.

"What are you waiting for?" Farrin yelled, as he drew alongside them.

One of the men glanced at him, fear in his eyes. "The magic is too wild. It'll kill us the moment we set foot ashore."

"Surely there must be ways to avoid it!" Farrin argued, spluttering as he received a face full of water. "The Selvanans live here, don't they?"

"They don't touch the ground—they live in the trees!" the other sailor snapped. "Only we can't get to 'em, can we?"

Following his gaze, Farrin saw what he meant. Even in the muted darkness he could see that the jungle dominated the landscape before them. But it didn't begin at the water's edge— there was a substantial distance of sand and rock before the tree line. There was simply no way to reach the trees without crossing the land itself. And even if they managed that, the trees didn't look as though they'd be easy to climb or travel through.

"We'll simply have to risk it," Farrin said, steeling his resolve.

"Speak fer yerself!" growled the pirate, still moving only

with the rise and fall of the swells, making no attempt to approach the shore.

Farrin ignored him, swimming forward again and wincing as pain shot through his skewered leg. He didn't feel as confident as he might have seemed, but the simple truth was that while the sailors might have some doubt, he had none whatsoever about his fate if he stayed in the water. His only hope for survival was land under his feet.

His boots hit the sand at last, just as a big wave took him from behind, tumbling him forward and onto the beach. He scrambled out of the impact zone, and for the briefest of moments, he thought he'd escaped. Then he felt it—the magic gone wild.

Power seemed to flow steadily from the jungle, making the air doubly thick and heavy. But that wasn't what caused him to cry out. He'd felt such a phenomenon before, in the deeper parts of the Forest of Ilgal, in Medulle's far west.

No, it was the sharp surge of magic that rushed up through the ground itself that jolted him. He felt its vicious force as it seized hold of his body and sent pain lancing through every inch of his awareness. It didn't feel aggressive, as he'd expected, however. He had the impression that it wasn't dark so much as it was just...powerful. Much too powerful for his frail human frame to endure.

# CHAPTER FOUR

# FARRIN

And yet, he wasn't dead.

The pain of the magic's contact began to ebb as Farrin felt some other force flare to life inside him, pushing steadily back against the unbearable pressure. He could still feel the assault of the magic, and it was still wildly uncomfortable. But there was equilibrium between the two powers, and the magic of Selvana no longer threatened to crush him.

Lifting his head slowly from the sand, Farrin squinted up at the jungle. It was forbidding in the darkness, rain dripping steadily from every layer of foliage. But at least it was now within his reach. He'd felt the power of the wild magic, without a doubt. But it hadn't killed him.

He struggled to his feet, looking over his shoulder in time to see the other two men swimming uncertainly toward shore. Clearly they'd been emboldened by his survival. As soon as the first man touched the sand, he let out a panicked cry, apparently seized as powerfully as Farrin had been by the magic running rampant in the land.

Farrin opened his mouth to reassure him, to tell him to hold on a minute longer, but the words died in his throat. Before his eyes, the man keeled over, his final shout cut off as he fell, lifeless, into the shallows.

Farrin's eyes, wide with shock, passed to the man still bobbing in the water. He could see the suspicion on the sailor's face, but he had no answers about how he'd survived when the other man hadn't. The relentless waves carried the body of the first sailor back out toward his fellow, and the man lost his nerve entirely. With splashing haste, he retreated, swimming back out toward the open ocean. Farrin's gaze went ahead of him, searching the darkness in time to see the ship slip at last completely below the waves. The Medullan flag, limp against the broken mast, was visible until the end.

Shaken to his core, the young prince turned away from the scene of death and destruction on the water, his attention shifting to the jungle before him. What did he do now? The magic of Selvana hadn't killed him on impact, but the land itself still might. He didn't know the first thing about surviving on this island. And he now had no way of getting back to Medulle. No one was even going to come looking for him, because like a dolt he hadn't told his family where he was sneaking off to.

He contemplated searching for the ship's intended landing point. He didn't know where to go, but the crew had definitely talked about suppliers set to meet them. Whether they were meeting them on arrival or at a future date, he didn't know. Whether they would look kindly on him, an unexpected addition to the ship's crew with no knowledge of the underhanded plan, he also didn't know. It was clear that these suppliers, whoever they were, didn't have the sanction of the crown here in Selvana, or they wouldn't have to meet the incoming ship clandestinely. But it was also clear that whoever was in charge in Sel wasn't inclined to look favorably upon the ship's arrival, even with the Medullan flag flying from the mast.

In short, there were far too many unknowns, and very little that Farrin actually did know. He cast another look back at the writhing ocean, shuddering. No one else had attempted to make land, but he could see no lifeboats on the water. Every one of his former companions was at the mercy of the ocean, and he could see no hope for either them or himself in that direction.

He paused to check his injured leg. The small shaft of wood had come out in his desperate swim, and the wound was bleeding, although not too freely. Seeing nothing else for it, Farrin ripped a length of fabric from his tunic, wrapping it as tightly as he could around the wounded limb.

Then, taking a deep breath, he turned his back on the beach and plunged into the darkness of the jungle. The air was so heavy, he found himself swatting a hand in front of his face, his overwrought mind thinking for a moment that he could clear the thickness a little. He had to almost climb across the ground, the undergrowth was so thick. Insects buzzed past his ears, and his eyes kept catching flashes of movement. It was probably his mind playing tricks, he tried to convince himself. The rain was still pouring down, its impact causing leaves to jump on all sides, giving the impression that the jungle was constantly in motion.

The chattering of a monkey made him whip his head to the side, but the creature couldn't be seen. Farrin blundered on, with no idea of direction, and no goal in mind. His only thought was survival, and for that he would surely have to keep moving.

His thoughts flew inevitably to the ill-fated expedition he and Emmett had taken into the deepest parts of the Forest of Ilgal. The outcome of this journey could hardly be worse than that disaster. He glanced at the foliage around him, willing a sprig of aconitum to leap out at him from the darkness.

But of course, even if he did find the elusive plant—even if it turned out not to be a legend—how could he carry it back to Medulle? He had no ship, and from all he'd heard, the Selvanans no longer had a fleet. It had been generations since they'd been in a position to embark from the harbor.

That was a problem for the future, he told himself, as panic threatened to rise. For now, surviving until daylight was enough of a challenge. He continued to fight his way through the jungle, with no concept of how far he'd come. His leg ached like a dull flame as he limped along, and the wild magic of Selvana pressed relentlessly against him. It was a constant discomfort— like pressure on his chest—even though it didn't seem to be any immediate threat. It made it even harder to draw breath in the heavy air.

It was hard to judge, but he would guess it had been about two hours since he'd left the beach when he suddenly froze. He couldn't have said what made him stop. He hadn't heard or seen anything he could identify as alarming. But some instinct told him that he was in deadly danger, for the first time since he'd entered the trees.

Farrin turned slowly on the spot, trying to locate the source of his unease. The rain had slackened considerably, and although it still fell in a steady patter, he'd been hearing the sounds of the jungle for some time. All at once, he realized that he no longer heard any other creatures, either in the trees or on the ground.

Cold fear shot down his spine. What had silenced them? If the other creatures of the jungle were scared of it, he surely should be, too.

Moving slowly, he reached for his hip, drawing out the sword he always wore. The sound of ringing steel was deafening in the unnatural stillness, and he winced as he kept pivoting.

He'd just completed a full circle when a sudden flash of movement gave him a bare moment's warning.

With a cry, he brought his sword up in front of him, dodging nimbly to the side in the same movement.

It was only just enough. Thanks to his sidestep, the leaping jaguar missed its mark, sailing past Farrin by inches in the darkness. The jungle cat landed lightly on its feet, crouching again as Farrin once more raised his sword, hating the way his arms trembled.

*What a way to die*, was the only coherent thought in his head.

"Did you hear someone call out? I think someone's over there."

The voice was so carrying, both Farrin and the jaguar paused, momentarily united in surprise. Farrin hadn't heard anything else approaching. That was hardly shocking, of course, but he got the sense the predator hadn't either. The jaguar spun its head, its golden eyes searching the darkness for the source of the voice, recalculating. Was the newcomer a threat, or merely a welcome additional course to the feast?

"HELP!" Farrin bellowed, startling the jaguar yet again. "I'm over here!"

"Who's that, then?" The voice sounded amazed. "Not one of us, is it?"

"I don't know who it is, Lurgl," sighed a new voice. "It clearly can't be one of us, because the rest are all back home, aren't they?"

The voices were closer now, almost upon them. There was something off about their trajectory—it almost sounded as if the speakers were crawling through the underbrush rather than walking. Maintaining his stance, Farrin turned his head a little in search of them.

That was a mistake. Seizing the opening, the jaguar lunged

again, teeth bared and claws outstretched. Farrin had let his guard down, and he knew as he tried clumsily to raise his sword that it wouldn't be enough.

But then, astonishingly, something blasted out of the foliage, an invisible explosion that only seemed to target the jaguar. The jungle cat fell backward with a snarl, landing winded on its side. For a moment it lay stunned, then it picked itself up and, to Farrin's immense relief, limped away into the darkness.

"What did you do that for?" grumbled the second voice.

"You must have heard the cry for help," scolded the first. "Someone was being attacked by a jaguar."

"Sure, but not one of us," said the other curtly. "You wasted a lot of magic, flashing that counterattack around."

"Oh, for shame, Dionysius," said the more cheerful of the two. "So we're too selfish to help anyone but ourselves, even in a matter of life and death?"

"Not *my* life and death," muttered the one called Dionysius.

"Hello?" Farrin called, squinting into the darkness. "Where are you?"

"He's probably one of the smugglers," grumbled Dionysius. "Off to meet that ship Dakarai saw earlier. Why else would he be crashing through the jungle at this time of night?"

"Please," Farrin tried again. "I can't see you. Won't you come out so I can thank you for saving my life?"

"Of course." The bright voice was followed by movement as a nearby plant rustled and a small figure emerged.

Farrin's jaw dropped, and he stared at the miniature man in complete astonishment.

"But...you're an elf," he said stupidly, his gaze passing over the man's pale face and tapered ears.

"Yes, last I checked," laughed his rescuer. "What were you expecting, a—" His words cut off as his eyes went wide in amazement. "You're a human!" He hollered over his shoulder. "Dionysius! It's a human!"

"All right, all right, it's not like I've never seen a human before." The other elf's words were muffled by foliage as he approached. "No need to shout about it," he added, as he emerged into sight. He was even smaller than the first elf. "You'll rouse half the predators in the—" He also broke off as he caught sight of Farrin, looking like he was impressed, and resented it. "You're on the ground."

"Yes, that's what I'm saying," Lurgl said excitedly. "A human *on the ground*." He looked eagerly up at Farrin. "Are you a singer, then?"

Farrin shook his head. "No, I'm not. And I don't know how I've survived contact with the magic in the land, I really don't. The other man didn't."

"Other man?" growled Dionysius, his eyes narrowed in suspicion. "What other man?"

"I'm from the mainland," said Farrin. "I just arrived here on a ship, but—"

"I *said* he was involved with the smugglers," protested Dionysius, sounding outraged. "And you helped him, Lurgl!"

"I'm not part of the crew," Farrin cut in quickly. "I purchased a place on the ship for my own purposes. But the ship was sunk by cannons from Sel."

Lurgl gave a low whistle. "Bad business, that."

Farrin nodded, swallowing thickly. "I think I'm the only survivor," he said. "I certainly didn't see anyone else successfully make land."

"Hm." The one called Lurgl looked him over. "You're in a spot of trouble, then, aren't you?"

"I really am," Farrin agreed, making no attempt to sound either more confident or more competent than he was. "As you just saw, my chances of surviving this place alone aren't good.

And I'm not sure if it would be better or worse to try to make contact with the humans of Sel."

Lurgl clucked his tongue. "No, wouldn't do that, if I were you. Not if they fired on your ship, and not after you've been skipping around the ground like this. They wouldn't take well to that." He shook his head. "No, there's only one thing for it, then. You'd best come home with us, see if we can get you patched up."

"Lurgl," complained Dionysius. "He's a *human*. And a smuggler. We're not taking him home."

"Of course we are," said Lurgl brightly.

"You've got to stop taking in strays," said Dionysius through gritted teeth. "Or the place will be overrun."

"I seem to recall you were a stray once," Lurgl pointed out, unperturbed. He jerked his head back the way he'd appeared. "Come on then—what's your name?"

"Farrin," Farrin replied, wondering too late if he should have given a false name. But neither elf showed any sign of suspecting his royal status, and he was soon stumping through the trees after them.

"Not far now," Lurgl said happily, after about half an hour.

Farrin could only hope the elf was telling the truth, because he felt almost dead on his feet. Just when he thought he couldn't go on any longer, he heard the sound of rushing water up ahead. A moment later, they broke out of the trees and into a small clearing. Even bathed in the sporadic moonlight visible through the shifting clouds, Farrin could tell it was a beautiful spot.

The clearing wasn't large, most of it taken up by a forest pool pressed against a cliff. A thin waterfall cascaded down the stony face of the cliff, tinkling into the water below. The elves skirted the pool, heading straight for a cave on the far side of the clearing. Farrin was limping gratefully in their wake, too weary and frazzled to even care about their intentions anymore, when something detached itself from a nearby tree and launched onto him.

Farrin gave a cry, his arms raised in a futile attempt to ward off the feline. For a terrifying moment he thought it was another jaguar, but the form that landed gracefully on his shoulders was much too small.

"Hey there, cut it out," said Lurgl, sounding irritated. "He's a guest."

The creature ignored the elf completely, holding its precarious position as it kneaded its claws lightly in Farrin's tunic.

Lurgl sighed, clearly unsurprised by the animal's defiance. "She doesn't usually listen to any of us much," he informed Farrin. "She's not really anyone's especial companion. She just likes to sort of hang around us."

"What is she?" asked Farrin, too embarrassed to voice the question he really wanted to ask: *will she eat me?*

"She's an ocelot, dummy," scoffed Dionysius. "You really are new to the jungle, aren't you?"

"Oh, lay off," said Lurgl reproachfully. "The poor child could do with a little kindness, not ridicule."

Farrin opened his mouth to protest that he was eighteen, not a child, but realized in time that such a declaration would only make him sound as young and raw as Lurgl clearly thought him. He was painfully aware of not having shown himself to best advantage that night.

But he promised himself, as his rescuer gestured for him to follow into the cave, that he would prove he was stronger and more capable than he'd so far shown. Not to the elves, to whom, after all, he had nothing to prove. But to himself. He was a prince of Medulle, not a frightened child cast adrift in a hostile world. He'd come to Selvana for a purpose, and he was going to achieve it. He was going to find the aconitum, and find a way to carry it back to Emmett. And if doing that meant first learning to survive in this strange and terrifying place, then so be it.

Whatever the cost, it would be worth it. He wouldn't waste the unexpected gift of being able to survive the deadly land. He would embrace that advantage, and master every aspect of life on Selvanan soil.

No matter how long it took.

# TWO YEARS LATER...

# CHAPTER FIVE

# Bianca

Bianca's boots clipped against the wooden boards as she hurried along the royal wing. She made no other sound, not even tempted to make her words dance today.

It should be a happy day, of course. Tomorrow she would turn eighteen, and that was surely cause for celebration. Not just because she always enjoyed the fuss of a birthday, but because of what this particular birthday represented.

Tomorrow she would come of age, and claim her position as Selvana's queen.

It was a terrifying thought, but at the same time, exhilarating. She'd been waiting for this moment for two years, and she was eager to make some substantial changes in the treetop city. She didn't like the way her stepmother was running things, but any time she tried to say so, the queen was quick to cut her off before she could build any momentum. Several times a day Bianca reminded herself to keep her peace, to wait just a short while longer, until she would have the authority to put things back on track.

When her father had died, she'd been afraid of her responsibilities, sure that she had neither the confidence nor the expertise to successfully steer a kingdom, sixteen-year-old that she was.

But watching Queen Marisol's reign had changed her attitude. Bianca didn't think herself especially wise. But she trusted her instincts much more than she trusted those of the older woman. So many times she'd felt uneasy about the queen's decisions—sometimes without being able to articulate the reasons even to herself—and the outcome had proved her concerns well-founded. It was a promising sign of her own capacity.

And, of course, a ruler wasn't supposed to rule alone. Young as Bianca might be, she was surrounded by older, more experienced advisors whose wisdom she could draw on. Already, as her birthday drew nearer, she'd noticed some of the senior advisors looking to her when her stepmother made increasingly unreasonable decisions, and beginning to discuss policy with Bianca when the queen wasn't around. Bianca certainly had no intention of following her stepmother's lead in refusing to take advice, assuming that everyone had some sinister motive.

The worst part was that Marisol seemed unable to recognize it when her decisions led to disaster. She was quick to blame mishaps on someone else, some other factor. Bianca frowned as she remembered the incident, only a few months before, when the queen had become convinced that the paradise nut harvesters were plotting to steal their gleanings from the crown, and had insisted that their number be halved to allow the guards accompanying the group to outnumber the harvesters. Of course the harvest was correspondingly poor, leading to a minor crisis in the paradise nut industry. Anyone willing to raise their voice had protested the smaller number of harvesters, but even then Queen Marisol hadn't acknowledged that her own commands had been responsible. In fact, she'd been hardened in her suspicions, sure that the harvest was smaller because some of the produce had been stolen, right out from under the guards' noses. The head guards had been demoted, and much less competent—but more biddable—ones elevated to fill their positions.

The whole thing had been beyond frustrating to witness, and Bianca had held in her disapproval with superhuman effort, reminding herself yet again that it was only a few more months. She just had to hope that Marisol hadn't turned the people against the crown too drastically in that time.

Bianca's frown deepened as she passed the entrance to one of the walkways that connected the palace to a nearby building. There were four armed guards manning the opening, as there were on every such entrance. It had never been that way in her father's day—Sel was a cheerful, sprawling mass of a community, the culture informal, and people's lives linked together as necessarily as their homes were joined by the vast wooden walkways. The palace had been the same prior to Marisol's rule, as relaxed as the rest of the city, and not much more grand, except for the scale of the building. The royal family was usually guarded, as were their private rooms. But the rest of the building was open, any resident of Sel allowed to wander through if they wished, to admire the carvings that told their history, or enjoy the view from the top of the tower.

Marisol had changed that. It hadn't happened all at once. It had been so gradual that it was easy to miss, until Bianca suddenly realized that she could hardly make it down a corridor without passing a dozen armed guards. Marisol had even wanted to change some of the historical records, declaring such a hatred of the elves that she wished to have the carvings depicting their time in Selvana stripped away. Bianca didn't think she'd ever seen her stepmother so livid as when one of the advisors dug up a law stating that no permanent records could be altered or removed by an acting regent. Marisol hadn't pushed the point, but she had ordered for the carvings to be covered with woven tapestries.

And her increased guards made sure no one's curiosity led them to peek underneath, to remind themselves of a history it seemed their queen would rather forget.

The change made no sense to Bianca. She hadn't heard of a single instance of someone trying to breach the palace with ill intent that might have sparked the tightening of security.

But it was so like Queen Marisol. She saw enemies where there were none, too wrapped up in her own suspicions to make a fair assessment of those around her. No amount of honest dealings from others would change her belief that the majority of people wanted to swindle the crown.

In her less generous moments, Bianca found herself wondering just where that suspicion came from, and what Marisol's attitude had been toward the crown when she had been a regular member of the populace herself.

But anytime she thought that way, Bianca felt a surge of guilt that had nothing to do with Marisol and everything to do with Ilse. In spite of never knowing another, Bianca had never been able to think of Marisol as her mother. Perhaps because she had no memories of the older woman showing her warmth or affection. But she loved her sister dearly, and knew that Ilse considered her mother deserving of her position.

Bianca had noticed her sister growing more uncomfortable the more Bianca challenged the queen, and hated the distance it was creating between them. Her fear over how her ascension to the throne would affect the relationship between them—especially once Ilse saw that Bianca intended to overturn most of her stepmother's decisions—was one of the dark clouds hovering over the whole idea of the following day's coronation.

The other was the worrying behavior of the queen herself. Shortly after the king's death, Marisol had often invoked the law regarding ascension, and reminded Bianca any time she was too outspoken in her opinions that she was unable to take the throne and wield its authority until she was eighteen.

After those early months, however, she'd stopped talking about Bianca's eighteenth birthday. It took Bianca months more to realize it, but her stepmother hadn't mentioned Bianca's future as monarch in more than a year. She'd certainly never encouraged Bianca to get a feel for the role, or attempted to train her. When one of her advisors had suggested, a couple of months before, that Bianca begin to take over some non-essential duties as a way to ease her into the role she would soon be assuming, Marisol had responded with instant anger and suspicion.

The word treason had been muttered, and the advisor had soon after been sent to fill an unpopular position in one of the outlying settlements.

Bianca didn't need any great wisdom or experience to recognize that these were incredibly worrying signs. But much as she knew her stepmother wasn't excited about handing over control, Bianca didn't really think the other woman would actually refuse to recognize Bianca's right to rule. She'd have no grounds whatsoever once Bianca turned eighteen, and the rest of the kingdom wouldn't just stand by and let her cut out the rightful queen.

Would they?

It was a disquieting thought, and Bianca's skin crawled a little as she reached her stepmother's suite. There were two guards at the door. One of them was Horace, the queen's head guard, well known to Bianca. The other, however, was a more recent appointee, who'd only just become a guard. Prior to that he was a huntsman, part of one of the palace's official hunting parties. From what Bianca could tell, he'd risen to such an elevated position among the royal guards less from actual skill and more from a willingness to do whatever Queen Marisol asked of him.

He wasn't the only one, and this fact contributed significantly to the feeling of being watched that now seemed to follow Bianca everywhere in the palace.

"I need to speak to my stepmother," she said, drawing herself up.

"Her Majesty is not to be disturbed at present," the unknown guard told her curtly. "Your Highness," he added as an afterthought.

Bianca chewed on the inside of her cheek, trying not to let her irritation show. She could feel Horace's eyes on her, although the head guard said nothing. She met his gaze, addressing her words to him.

"I need to speak with her," she said calmly. "It's a personal matter, and it can't wait."

The guard studied her for a silent moment, his expression hard to read. Bianca had always struggled to guess what was happening inside the older man's mind. He'd been her stepmother's head guard for as long as she could remember, and yet she'd never had the sense the queen fully trusted him.

Although that wasn't saying much, given Queen Marisol seemed to trust no one.

"Of course, Your Highness," he said at last, unbending as he gestured to the door.

Ignoring the other guard's scowl, Bianca stepped forward, pausing when Horace spoke again.

"May I say, Your Highness, that we all look forward to a joyous celebration tomorrow, and anticipate a long and fruitful reign."

"Thank you," said Bianca, surprised and a little moved. "I will endeavor to live up to the trust my people will place in me."

Without another word she moved into her stepmother's

suite, dismissing the guards from her mind and once again steeling herself for the conversation to come. She still wasn't sure whether she was making the right decision, to broach the touchy subject of her coronation openly with the acting queen. As always, the voice of restraint argued in her mind with the impatient voice which told her to fight back against her stepmother's heavy-handed ways.

Well, this time she was letting the more insistent voice win, and time alone would show the wisdom or otherwise of that course.

"Stepmother?"

Bianca spoke softly, surprised to find the queen's personal receiving room empty. The older woman must be in her sleeping chamber. It was surprising at this time of day, and even so, Bianca would have expected an attendant maid or lady-in-waiting to have been hovering in the receiving room, ready to respond to the queen's any whim.

No such person appeared, however, and Bianca hesitated. Were the guards wrong? Was her stepmother not even in here? But surely not. Whatever his silences meant, Horace was diligent as the queen's head guard. He wouldn't be guarding an empty room due to some careless error.

Bianca moved forward uncertainly, heading toward her stepmother's sleeping chamber. A familiar voice—laced with even more familiar impatience—stopped her in her tracks.

"What do you mean, *people*? The arrangement was for gold."

As silently as she could, Bianca inched toward the door, which stood ajar.

"As I told you over seventeen years ago, the arrangement was most certainly not for gold," replied a cold voice. "The arrangement was for payment."

*Arrangement? Payment?* A chill passed over Bianca. Who was

her stepmother talking to, and in her own sleeping chamber? She didn't dare go close enough to peek.

"But people can't be payment," the queen argued. "I never dreamed you intended for me to send you people to die!"

"As for what will happen to them once they come to us, that is not your concern," said the voice. "And I am not to be blamed for the fact that your imagination was insufficient to encompass the full potential of our bargain."

"I can't force families to sacrifice their members to whatever mad cause you have in mind," Queen Marisol insisted.

"You can't, or you won't?" came the answer. "Are you the queen or not?"

"Of course I am," Bianca's stepmother stormed. "But that's more than my subjects would swallow." Her voice turned wheedling. "Can't we discuss this at a later time, perhaps in a month or two?"

The voice was hard and unyielding. "You are bound by our bargain, and if you fail to meet its terms, you will unleash something even worse."

"I'm not refusing," said Marisol quickly, sounding uneasy. "I'm just asking for more time. I need to think of a way for it not to look suspicious."

Bianca's breath caught in her throat. She'd never really trusted her stepmother, but even she hadn't thought Marisol was this bad. Would she really hand her people over to this unknown group to be killed, once she could make it look like an accident?

"This isn't the best moment for me to undertake something so sensitive," Marisol blundered on. "Tomorrow is—"

"The timing is no accident," the voice cut her off. "Do you think we don't know what's going on in the palace? We told you we'd be watching."

Bianca could hear the scowl in her stepmother's voice. "What you ask is too high a price. That number of people—"

"Well," the voice once again interrupted, "if you think it too many, we might be willing to consider a lesser substitute, as an interim measure."

"What lesser substitute?" asked the queen, her voice laced with that familiar suspicion.

"The princess."

A cold chill went over Bianca's body at the emotionless reply, and she realized she was trembling.

"The princess?" Marisol responded sharply. "Ilse? There's no way in the world I would ever consider—"

"We're not interested in your brat," said the queen's companion. "We want the older princess. Princess Bianca."

There was a long and painful silence, each second of which sent a fresh shard through Bianca's heart. She didn't need to be in the room to know that her stepmother was considering it.

"Why do you want Bianca?" she asked at last.

"If you had even the barest hint of intelligence, you would already know the answer to that question." The speaker sounded bored now.

Predictably, Queen Marisol bristled. "You will not speak to me that way," she snapped. "I am the *queen* of this kingdom, and I will have the respect due to my position."

"Queen?" scoffed the cold voice. "A false queen, who's set herself up in place of the rightful ruler, whom everyone would prefer to see on the throne."

"That's not true!" snarled Marisol.

"Of course it is," the voice replied calmly. "I told you that this mirror would display only the truth. I cannot lie to you when communicating through it."

Bianca's frown deepened. Communicating through a mirror? What did that mean?

"Were you under the illusion that you are popular among your stolen subjects?" the voice taunted. "If so, you have not been paying half as close attention as we have. Everywhere the whispers are the same...you are not as legitimate as Princess Bianca, not as capable..." The voice took on a cunning edge. "Not as beautiful."

"What nonsense," raged Marisol, sounding angrier now than Bianca had ever heard her. "She's a *child*. She knows nothing of how to rule a kingdom, and could never hope to match a grown woman's beauty."

"She is a child no longer," scoffed the queen's companion. "She is a fully grown woman, whereas you are growing old. Everyone but you acknowledges her remarkable beauty."

"Beauty?" laughed Marisol, sounding almost deranged. "With that unnatural, ghastly hair?"

Bianca stood rooted to the spot, terror rushing over her. She'd known her stepmother too long not to recognize that she was speeding toward disaster.

"Ah yes, how you hate that hair," crooned the queen's tormentor. "But it does nothing to detract from Bianca's beauty. On the contrary, its striking contrast against her ebony skin ensures she is seen and admired everywhere she goes."

Bianca had a mad urge to dash into the room and slap her hand over the speaker's mouth to silence him. She didn't know what his intention was, but she had no doubt it was something evil.

"But if your affection for her is such that you wish to protect her," the voice said carelessly, "so be it. If you prefer to withhold her from us, and unleash the consequences of the broken bargain instead—"

"Affection! For that little snake!" shrieked the queen, enraged beyond reason now. "She is nothing to me. Preening her way around the palace, when anyone with sense can see she is not fit to rule." There was a moment's trembling silence. "I am queen here," Bianca's stepmother said at last, her voice hard and calm now. "If Princess Bianca is your price, then name the time and location, and she will be delivered to you. What happens to her after she is released onto the ground is, as you say, no affair of mine."

"Very good," said the cold voice, once again sounding bored.

*Onto the ground?* Bianca's blood was pounding in her ears, but she forced her legs to move. She had to get a look at whoever was with the queen, to know who she was dealing with. She inched her way toward the door, trying to place as little of herself as possible in the opening.

Thankfully her stepmother stood with her back mostly to the entrance. But to Bianca's confusion, she could see no sign of anyone else. And, as the unseen speaker had said, her step-mother was holding a mirror up, as if admiring her appearance.

Bianca pulled back, afraid the other woman would see her reflection. Although if she was truly speaking to someone through the mirror, presumably by way of magic, perhaps there would be no reflection.

It made no sense. No one in Selvana wielded magic. They hadn't been able to ever since the magic went wild, too powerful to be harnessed. The elves had been able to do it, apparently, just as they'd been able to survive on the ground. But they were all long gone.

Her stepmother was speaking again, but Bianca couldn't hear the words. Her mind was too clouded by panic, and her only thought was that she needed to escape the room before she was discovered.

# CHAPTER SIX

# *Bianca*

Bianca fled across the room, trying to calm her racing heart as she slipped back into the corridor.

"Your Highness?" Horace's voice was calm, but the inflection told Bianca he knew something was amiss.

For a moment she just stared blindly up at his face, her tale on the tip of her tongue. But she bit back the words. She may have wondered at times whether the queen fully trusted the guard, but Bianca had no particular reason to trust him herself. He was, after all, her stepmother's head guard. And she'd just been reflecting that the other guard likely only achieved his position through unquestioning and unscrupulous loyalty to Queen Marisol. If she told them what she'd overheard—even if they believed her—how could she be sure they'd act against her stepmother? Would they be just as likely to assist the queen in disposing of her unwanted extra daughter?

The thought chilled Bianca to the core. It had never occurred to her that her stepmother's actions in filling the royal guard with unqualified sycophants might actually be a barrier to Bianca claiming her throne. She'd tolerated what she considered unwise appointments by reminding herself that she could dismiss them all when she was crowned, if she so desired.

But had this been Marisol's plan all along? Had she intended to keep Bianca from ever being crowned, through force if necessary? Was that why she'd been dodging the topic of the upcoming coronation?

Surely not. The queen had seemed stunned by the demand for Bianca to form the payment for whatever unsavory bargain she'd struck.

That, of course, was a matter of equal concern. Who outside the palace wanted Bianca dead, and why did they want to achieve it by throwing her to the jungle floor? She supposed it was the best way to make it look an accident.

"Your Highness?" Horace tried again. "Is all well?"

Bianca pulled herself together, giving him a curt nod. "It wasn't a good moment to speak," she said. "My stepmother seemed occupied, so I didn't stay to interrupt her. I'll have to come back later."

The lie fell awkwardly from her lips, and she cursed her own transparency. She'd never had cause to hone the skill of deception. In her blissful ignorance, she hadn't thought she needed such a talent.

"I see." Horace looked like he saw more than Bianca wanted him to, although that could just be her fear painting an ominous hue on his words. "If you find yourself in need of any further assistance, Your Highness, do not hesitate to seek me out."

Bianca blinked in surprise at his words. She'd barely exchanged any conversation with the man before today, and she wasn't sure what to make of the offer. Was he trying to trap her? To convince her to give him her confidence so he could carry the information back to her stepmother?

How she hated these mind games! It wasn't like her to look

for ulterior motives in those around her—that was Marisol's way, not Bianca's.

Unable to muster any response to Horace's words, Bianca took off down the corridor, wishing her haste didn't look so much like a flight.

Flight. The thought flitted across her mind, unbidden. She could flee. Try to get some distance between her and the stepmother who was apparently willing to sacrifice Bianca's life to save her own skin.

Bianca pushed the thought away, ashamed. This was her kingdom—she was the rightful queen, as of midnight. Even if she had somewhere to go, which of course she didn't, she couldn't run out on her people, flee her responsibilities. Especially not when doing so left them in the hands of a paranoid, scheming, false ruler.

With no clear aim in her mind, she found herself hurrying back to her own room. All was quiet inside, her maids having already laid out her elaborate gown for the next day and withdrawn, not expecting to be needed until after the evening meal.

Bianca found herself at the window, looking out at the familiar and beloved view of the jungle and the ocean beyond. The light alerted her to the advanced hour—she hadn't realized how late it was. Her room looked east, so she couldn't see the setting sun, but it was casting a net of vivid colors across the whole sky, and the clouds over the sea were a riot of pink and orange.

To claim such a view, her room was necessarily near the top level of the palace. Below her was layer upon layer of canopy, hiding the lethal forest floor below. Was she really in danger of being thrown down there to die?

"What am I going to do?" she whispered to the tranquil scene, horror threatening to overcome her. How could she protect herself against her stepmother's plans? Whom could she trust, and what would the queen's mysterious companion do if their demands weren't met?

"Bianca?"

Bianca whirled at the bright voice, relief flooding through her as she saw her sister coming through the doorway with her usual exuberance.

"There you are!" said Ilse, catching sight of her. "It's almost dinner. Your last night as a princess! I feel we should make a fuss."

"Ilse." Bianca's throat was so dry, the name came out a croak.

"What's wrong?" her sister asked, frowning as she took in Bianca's expression. "Are you nervous about tomorrow? I thought it was going to be a pretty relaxed affair."

Bianca shook her head frantically. "Not tomorrow. Ilse... Mama. She..." Bianca swallowed, struggling to find the words. "I went to see her just now, and...and she..."

"Have you been fighting with Mama again?" Ilse scolded, sounding suddenly too weary for her sixteen years. "When will you two learn to get along? I know you don't see eye to eye on everything, but surely you must realize she's your best resource for learning to be a good monarch. She's the only person you know who's actually done it!"

"A good monarch?" Bianca gave a hollow laugh. "Is that what you think she's been these past two years?"

Ilse's eyes narrowed, offense creeping into her tone. "Of course she has. And if she doesn't have everyone's confidence, whose fault is that? You could give her your support every now and again, instead of always undermining her with your—"

"Ilse, I don't have time for whatever bitter seeds she's planted in your mind right now," Bianca cut her sister off brutally. "She's planning to kill me, and keep my throne!"

There was a moment of total silence, and the look on Ilse's face was possibly the most horrible thing Bianca had ever seen.

"That's a terrible thing to say," Ilse said, her voice now quiet. "The worst thing you've ever said, Bianca. Whatever you think of her policies, how could you be so spiteful?"

"Ilse, you don't understand!" Bianca surged forward, gripping her sister's shoulders in her desperation to make Ilse believe her. "It's not spite! I was just in her rooms. I *heard* her!"

Ilse's forehead creased in a frown. "I don't know what you heard, Bianca, but it sounds like you weren't supposed to be listening. I'm not going to pretend she's perfect. I can easily imagine her saying something when she's letting off steam that would sound bad out of context. But of course she would never mean you any real harm."

Bianca shook her head frantically, almost crying with frustration. "No, it wasn't like that. She was using *magic*, Ilse. She was speaking to someone in this mirror, and they said that she owed them payment for a bargain, and they named *me* as the price, and she said she'd send me onto the ground!"

Ilse just stared back at her. "Bianca," she said slowly. "That makes no sense. Mama can't use magic. *No one* in Selvana can. And she'd never let either of us anywhere near the ground!"

"That's what I thought, too," said Bianca, releasing her sister and gripping her head in her hands. "But I know what I heard. Ilse, I don't know what to do. I don't know who to trust."

"Well, I like that!" Ilse protested. "Thanks, Bianca. Why should you trust me? I'm only your sister!"

"I do trust you," Bianca protested. "You know I do—I'm telling you this, aren't I? But even you don't believe me!"

Ilse frowned at her. "I'm not accusing you of lying, Bianca. But you've misunderstood. There's just no way you heard what you think you did. It's impossible on so many levels. We're all highly strung, with tomorrow's big events. But you can trust me, and you can trust Mama. No one's trying to do you any harm."

She looked concerned, clearly wondering where her sister's uncharacteristic suspicion had sprung from. Bianca couldn't hold in a groan.

"That's exactly the problem," she said bitterly. "I trust your intentions, Ilse, without a doubt. But you're blinded when it comes to Mama. You always have been."

She turned back to the window, ignoring her sister's protests as her mind raced through her options. They felt alarmingly few. She was a queen by birth, about to turn eighteen. And yet she felt like a small, frightened child, alone in a world that had suddenly turned hostile.

"Just...just stay with me, all right?" she said, still not looking at her sister. "If we're together, surely nothing too terrible can happen to me. She'd never hurt you, after all."

"That's right," said Ilse soothingly. "No one's going to hurt you, Bianca. We can stay together all evening, if it will make you feel more relaxed." Her voice turned businesslike. "Now, let's get you presentable for dinner."

She spun Bianca around, marching her to the looking glass and beginning to tie back her snow-white hair.

"You really shouldn't wear it down so often," she scolded.

"Why not?" Bianca asked dully, unable to muster any enthusiasm for the topic of hairstyles.

"Because it's how the common people wear their hair," Ilse said matter-of-factly. "You're a princess—almost a queen—and your hair should be styled as befits your station. Especially since it's your most striking feature, so you know everyone will always be looking at it," she added artlessly. She coiled a colorless strand around her own dark finger. "It's certainly a statement, isn't it?"

Bianca gave no reply, her mind full of the memory of her

stepmother's rage when the unknown speaker told her that everyone admired Bianca's unusual hair.

"Are you done?" she asked, seeing that Ilse had stopped her task, her satisfied gaze fixed instead on the reflection of her own —elaborately dressed—dark hair.

"Almost," Ilse said, jumping slightly and giving Bianca's hair a final twist. Her eyes lingered on her sister's face in the mirror. "How do you get your lips to stay so red?" she asked wistfully. "I put crushed berries on mine every morning, but it never lasts more than an hour or two. I'd kill for color like that."

"Don't say that," Bianca said sharply, her tone so fierce it made her sister start.

"It's only a figure of speech," Ilse said mildly. "I was just trying to compliment your features."

Bianca tried to soften her words. "It's not a good figure of speech." She spun in her seat, seizing Ilse's hands. "Ilse, your face is lovely, at least as lovely as mine, if not more. But even if it wasn't..." She shook her head, struggling for the words. "It's not good to want what others have."

*It leads to treason and murder and illicit deals to do away with the rightful ruler who stands between you and a stolen throne*, she added silently. But she couldn't say the words to Ilse, not when her sister was so incapable of believing her mother at fault. And Bianca didn't want to say it, either. She didn't want to believe her beloved sister could ever grow to be as warped as her mother.

"Don't scold, Bianca," said Ilse, irritated. "It's all well and good for you to say that when you're the one about to take your throne, the one who can make your words dance, the one everyone says is beautiful and sweet and—"

A knock at the door interrupted Ilse's rising complaint. Both girls turned, Bianca tightening her grip on her sister's hands convulsively.

"Enter," Bianca called, annoyed to hear the waver in her voice.

The door swung open to reveal the guard who'd stood outside Queen Marisol's chambers a short time before. Not Horace, the other one. The one who had been a huntsman until recently.

Bianca's heart beat wildly as his eyes settled on her. "What is it?" she asked, trying to sound regal this time.

His expression remained emotionless, almost unnatural. "You're needed for a final discussion with the steward regarding tomorrow's ceremony, Your Highness."

Fear shot through Bianca, every instinct warning her against going with this man. "It can surely wait until after dinner."

"No, Your Highness," he said. "The steward says it can't. He assured me it wouldn't take long."

"Go ahead, Bianca," said Ilse lightly. "I'll tell Mama that you've been delayed, and we can wait for you before we eat."

Bianca met her sister's eyes, trying to convey a silent message. "You said you'd stay with me," she muttered.

For a moment Ilse just looked confused, then she rolled her eyes. "Bianca, don't be absurd. It's not like you to be so suspicious—I heard the steward asking for you earlier."

"Did you really?" Bianca asked, doubt creeping in.

Ilse looked put out. "Would I lie to you? Now go. I'll see you at dinner soon."

She bustled out of the room, leaving Bianca to rise and move slowly toward the guard.

"Where does the steward wish to meet me?" she asked warily.

"On the platform where the coronation is to take place," he said.

Bianca hesitated, wondering if she really was being paranoid. It was a public enough location. She gestured for the guard to precede her, following him down several levels to the large open platform where seats had already been set up. When she saw that the steward was indeed waiting for her, she let out a relieved breath. It seemed her fear that the guard had reported her eavesdropping to her stepmother had been unfounded.

The conversation with the steward was longer than promised, and by the time Bianca was released, darkness had almost completely fallen. Through the branches above, she caught the odd streak of red in the sky, but the lanterns were all lit, and in the treetop palace, night had come.

"I'm so late for dinner," she muttered, hurrying across the platform to the nearest ladder.

"Wait, Your Highness," the guard said, moving out of the shadows where he'd awaited the end of her meeting with the steward. "I'm to take you this way." He gestured to a ladder on the other side of the platform, going downward.

Bianca hesitated, her foot already on the bottom rung of the ladder. She glanced around for the steward, but he'd already left, descending to a lower level.

"What do you mean?" she asked, all her wariness returning. "My family is waiting for me at dinner."

He shook his head. "No, Your Highness. They're waiting for you this way. And we're later than expected."

Bianca pulled herself up one step, her forehead creasing. "I think you're confused," she said flatly. "My sister expected me at dinner half an hour ago."

The guard glanced around, his expression suddenly uncertain. "I'm not supposed to tell you this," he said, "but your sister isn't waiting for you up there. She's the one who organized the surprise. They've set up an early birthday celebration, since tomorrow will be focused on the coronation." He bit his lip. "I wasn't supposed to tell you—it's meant to be a surprise. But...I don't know if you know this, Your Highness, but I'm new to the guards. I used to be a huntsman. I really want to make a good impression, and I'm worried we're already so late the surprise might be ruined."

Bianca hesitated, lowering herself back onto the platform. She was disarmed by the guard's vulnerability. She'd been so quick to judge him, to assume he'd gained his position dishonestly, when in fact she had no concrete reason for thinking ill of him. Was she becoming her stepmother, to see threats and enemies everywhere? He'd told the truth about the steward—perhaps it was the simple truth that Ilse had organized a surprise birthday celebration for her. Her sister had certainly been at pains to make sure Bianca looked presentable.

"Where is this celebration?" Bianca asked, moving toward the guard but still leaving a sizable gap between them.

"This way," he said, sounding relieved. "They'll be wondering what's kept us." He led Bianca down the ladder and across a hall. When they entered a passageway she'd never been into before, she stopped.

"Wait, where is this?" she demanded. "I don't know this place."

"Servants' passage," the guard explained. "It will get us there more quickly."

Bianca drew back, alarm racing through her as she realized that the area was deserted but for them. "I don't think so," she said.

"It's not much further, Your Highness," the guard said, looking perplexed.

But Bianca was already regretting following him even this far. She shook her head firmly. "No. I'm going to the normal dining hall."

She reached behind her, turning slightly. But her hand had

barely found the latch of the nearest door when a flash of movement brought her head whipping back around.

Too late, she realized the guard's intent, and she was still drawing in breath for a scream when his hand closed over her mouth. Swift as a pouncing tiger, he had his other arm around her, holding her in a viselike grip.

# CHAPTER SEVEN

# *Bianca*

Bianca couldn't even scream around the guard's hand. She tried to lash out, but he was much stronger than her, and she'd never learned to fight.

His hand dropped suddenly from her mouth, but before she could make a sound, he'd drawn a length of fabric into its place, tying it firmly. She kicked back at him, but he didn't even grunt when her boot connected with his shin. Moving efficiently, he bound her hands behind her back, and bound her feet. She didn't see where he produced the rope from, but there could be no doubt he'd come prepared for resistance.

Before she could fully grasp her disastrous situation, Bianca found herself being dragged down another ladder, helpless and silenced. The guard paused at the next level to retrieve a cloak he must have left there earlier. The fabric was dark, and once he'd thrown it around Bianca's shoulders and tied it, not only were her bound hands hidden, but the hood covered her distinctive hair.

As he hauled her back up again and threw her over his shoulder, Bianca cursed her own foolishness. Out of a childish need to prove she wasn't like her stepmother, she'd given trust so easily, even with cause to be suspicious. She raged silently against the evil of this man who had so expertly exploited her impulse toward kindness.

Her hope that they'd pass a helpful servant quickly dwindled. The whole section of the palace seemed to be deserted. For the next couple of levels, Bianca was mystified by it, but as they descended further, she began to catch sight of rotting boards and broken balustrades. There was a whole section of steps which her captor had to leap over, bruising her in the process.

Memory flickered at the edge of Bianca's panicked awareness. Several months ago, a group of servants had approached Queen Marisol about the state of the servants' passages on the western side of the palace. Bianca had gotten the impression that it was a last, desperate effort—likely there had been many complaints preceding it, which she hadn't been present for. But of course the queen had refused to address the issue, insisting that the servants were exaggerating the danger. It seemed the whole passage had subsequently been deserted in favor of the less practical main thoroughfare.

How convenient, Bianca thought in a detached manner. Her stepmother's unreasonable response back then had paved the way for her much more insidious scheme tonight. It was curious how numb Bianca felt, hardly able to muster emotion as they traveled lower and lower. She just couldn't bring herself to believe she was heading for her death. It was too surreal, too impossible.

When they left the palace, Bianca began to struggle again, hopeful of making some sound to attract passers-by. But they encountered no one on the short journey which took them across three more buildings.

Panic truly set in as the guard began to descend another ladder, this one less maintained than the palace ones. She kicked wildly against his chest, but it made no difference. They were below the level of most dwellings, now, and Bianca no longer had much hope of being spotted.

When they reached a platform from which no further ladder descended, Bianca dared to hope she might have misunderstood their ultimate destination. They were still a fair way off the toxic ground. But then the guard retrieved a rope that had been left looped over a nearby post, and began to bind it around Bianca's middle.

She fought against him, grunting as she tried to plead through her gag. The guard's expression remained stony as he completed his task. When he stepped back, Bianca was bound so tightly she could already sense her hands losing feeling.

"It's not personal, Your Highness," said the huntsman-turned-guard, not meeting her eye. "I'm following the commands of my sovereign."

*I'm your sovereign!* Bianca wanted to scream. *In a few short hours it will be official!*

Would have been official, she realized. Without her presence, there would be no coronation. She was a crown princess who would never be queen. The thought made her feel cold, and not because she coveted the power of a crown. All her life she'd known that she had one responsibility—one huge, all-consuming responsibility—to her people, her family, herself. And she'd failed it. Failed before she ever properly began. Selvana would be at Marisol's mercy now, and even if she did cede the throne to Ilse, Bianca's rightful heir, how distant in the future would that time be? And how much would she have twisted Ilse's attitude by then, without the influence of her father or sister to soften the suspicion Marisol lived by? Would Ilse be as hard and untrusting as the current queen before long?

The thought was almost worse than all the rest.

Bianca was powerless as the guard secured the loose end of

the rope to a wooden beam. Looping it around a post, he kept hold of it, striding back to Bianca. With only a moment's hesitation, he kicked her, his boot sending her off the edge of the platform.

With a horrible lurch in her stomach, Bianca fell, only to be pulled up short by the rope. The rope burned her as it pulled tight, her midriff bruising, and the pressure knocked the air from her lungs. She gasped, struggling to draw in breath through the gag. The air was so heavy down near the ground, so humid and still and menacing. Everything was menacing. The lush foliage around her dripped steadily, although there had been no rain for hours. She could feel tiny eyes watching her, and hear the soft chirps of unseen creatures. None of this would have unnerved her up in the canopy, but down here it all reeked of fear and death.

The guard began to lower her more slowly, the ride rough and full of jerks as she tried fruitlessly to free her hands. How could she have gotten here? How could Marisol have done this? How could Bianca have allowed it?

And why put her through this particular ordeal, she thought bitterly. Why tie her up and lower her instead of just pushing her straight off? The result would be the same when she touched the ground.

But she didn't touch the ground. Just as the earth rose below her and her panic reached a crescendo, the slow descent stopped. She was dangling, suspended painfully in the air but not actually touching the jungle floor. She stared up at the guard, confused and breathless. Was it possible he'd had a change of heart? Was he going to relent and pull her up after all?

He was far above her, but not so far she couldn't make out his face. She saw no indecision there. So why hadn't he lowered her all the way to the ground? As she watched, the guard's eyes scanned the area around them, both the undergrowth and the nearest buildings. He didn't seem afraid of detection. It was more like he was...waiting for someone.

Bianca's bewilderment momentarily overtook her fear. Who could he be waiting for? Was someone coming to collect her? But how could anyone reach her here, unless they were on the ground? And no one could be on the ground...could they?

She could see the same confusion in the guard's eyes above her. He had no answers, either. He didn't really understand what he was taking part in, but was just following orders in the hope of securing his own advancement.

Bianca kicked hopelessly, achieving nothing but making herself spin, the ropes merciless as they dug into her. Everything was spinning. Her whole world was on end, and nothing was as she'd thought. Her future was being snatched away, her stepmother was using magic, someone was apparently traversing the forest floor, on their way right now to get her. To do what to her? None of it made any sense.

She was far from any mosquito-repelling incense now, and already the insects were landing on every bit of exposed skin, taking full advantage of her incapacitated state. Of course she could do nothing to swat them away, although the motion of the rope helped a little. Bianca's stomach churned, and she closed her eyes, going still in an effort to stop the spinning. As her body slowed, however, her mind seemed to speed up. She could see so many details now that she hadn't been able to see before, like threads connecting so many incidents to this one terrible moment.

So many times she'd failed to stand up to her stepmother, but the memory that stood out most clearly was the night her father died. She remembered in perfect detail how that guard had run in, with news of a ship fighting against the weather in the harbor. There had been that moment of uncertainty after he realized the king was dead, when he hadn't known whether to turn to the crown princess or the widowed queen for directions.

And Bianca had been too slow, too uncertain to put herself forward. If she'd been more confident, she could have jumped in with a different order regarding the ship. Perhaps the lives of those poor men would have been saved. A shudder went over her as she remembered the reports that had come in soon after, of bodies washed up on the shore. No one had retrieved them or buried them, of course. The Selvanans had observed them from the trees, unable to reach them even if they'd wanted to.

Bianca was hanging limply now, but her thoughts spun on. She couldn't help but wonder if her failure to claim that guard's obedience had led to much more than the old tragedy with the sailors. Was it her imagination that made that moment so crucial in hindsight? Or had it really all stemmed from that decision? Had that been the moment she allowed her stepmother to take this path, to begin to cut her out of her rightful place? Had that past moment of weakness, in the fresh grief of her father's sudden death, led to this terrible present, where she dangled helplessly in anticipation of death, like a fly caught in a spider's web?

The thought sparked another memory in Bianca, this one nothing to do with big decisions or matters of state. She'd been a small child, watching in horrified fascination as a large blowfly struggled frantically in the web of an enormous jungle spider. Normally Bianca hated the noisy creatures, but she'd felt so sorry for it, she'd wanted to free it. She wouldn't have thought twice about it if the fly had already been dead—such scenes were a common part of jungle life. But she couldn't stand to see it fighting so desperately, helpless as it waited for the spider to approach.

She'd already been hanging half out of the window ledge

when her father entered the room and panicked at seeing her balanced so precariously over the massive drop below.

When he'd grasped her intention, he'd shaken his head, his voice gentle as he explained it to her.

"I know it's hard to watch," he'd said. "But there's a natural order to these things. It's not our job to interfere in the rhythms of the jungle, and we'll do more harm than good if we do. If the spider has spun his web well, he deserves to catch his fly. Otherwise he'll go hungry. If you free this fly, will you find the spider a new meal? And what about that victim?"

Bianca had understood his point, but she still hadn't liked it. And although she kept the promise he extracted from her—that she wouldn't climb out the window and interfere—she'd lingered after he left, watching miserably as the fly continued to fight with steadily decreasing energy.

She couldn't have explained it, but she had this horrible sense of watching her own approaching fate, watching herself lose strength the longer she fought.

And then the spider had shown himself. Moving steadily across his web with that unnerving gait of arachnids, he'd come to claim his meal. Bianca had almost broken her promise then, tears standing in her eyes as she watched the miniature play of life and death. But then something incredible had happened. As the spider approached, the fly had gone berserk. It had fought with a renewed strength, and before Bianca's astonished eyes, it had broken free, ridding itself of the web that had ensnared it, and flying away, albeit a little drunkenly.

When Bianca, overjoyed, had run to tell her father, he'd laughed. "Well, it seems the spider didn't spin his web well after all," he said. "Maybe it was an old spider, or maybe it was careless in maintaining its web. Poor hungry spider. Bit of a waste, when the fly probably won't survive long like that anyway."

But Bianca hadn't agreed. She'd been jubilant, painting a

picture in her childish mind of the fly making it home to his fly wife and fly family, living a long and restful life. She felt no pity for the spider, who was surely master of his own fate already, unlike a lowly fly.

With the memory came a rush of fierce determination. Bianca wasn't going to give up fighting. She didn't accept that Marisol had spun her web well enough to make it unbreakable, and she certainly didn't accept that such a feat meant the false queen deserved her prize. Bianca had allowed herself to be caught in this web with shameful ease, but that didn't mean it was over. She would fight to the bitter end, no matter how poor her life expectancy might be, no matter how strong the web seemed.

She thrashed wildly, moving every inch of her that she could. Her bound feet kicked against the ropes there, her hands jerked furiously against one another, over and over again. The strands rubbed her wrists raw, and tears sprang to her eyes, but she didn't let up. She heard a cry from the guard above, but she ignored him, still flailing with everything she had. To her amazement, her feet suddenly sprung apart. The bonds must have loosened as the guard hauled her through the treetops.

Encouraged, Bianca struggled even harder. If she could just get her hands free, she might be able to climb the rope, get back to the platform. Her wrists felt as securely tied as ever, but an ominous groaning from above told her a moment too late that something else was about to give.

With a crack, the rotten old post she was tied to toppled, sending Bianca jolting downward. Her cry was muffled by her gag as she fell, and she hit the ground with a soft thump.

But the death she expected didn't come. On the contrary, the moment she made impact, she felt a surge of energy rush into her, so powerful it temporarily erased all the pain from the ropes. It was so intense that every nerve felt on fire, and she half expected to hear her body humming. The power seemed to come from the ground itself, pouring into every inch of body where she lay motionless against the earth.

Bianca lifted her head, gazing around her in a daze. It all felt like some bizarre dream. Had she dozed off, nervous about the upcoming coronation, and fallen into a highly realistic tale of her mind's construction?

But no. Already the pain where the rope had chafed her wrists was reasserting itself, and her shoulder ached from landing so awkwardly, with her arms still tied behind her back. Bianca struggled onto her knees, shuffling strangely with her restricted arms. She peered upward, to see the shocked and horrified face of the guard on the platform above.

"You...you're alive," he said, his voice carrying down as the faintest whisper. "How are you alive?"

The gag was still in place around Bianca's mouth, but she wouldn't have answered him even if she could. She had no more idea than he did how she was still breathing, and she didn't intend to hang about for him—or whomever he'd been meeting here—to change that.

Her eyes darted around the small clearing, and identified the weakest patch of undergrowth. She blundered toward it, her steps hampered not only by her bound hands, but by the rope still tied around her midriff, and the broken chunk of wood trailing at the end of it.

She heard the guard cry out, but she ignored him. She had no idea what he would do next, but she doubted her unexpected survival would be enough to make him risk his own life following her onto the ground. For the moment, at least, she was more worried about whoever had been going to meet him here.

Bianca glanced up as she crashed through the foliage, but no walkways appeared in the canopy above. The route she'd taken led her away from Sel, into the depths of the untamed jungle.

The thought was terrifying, but she didn't turn around. Where would she go in Sel? Whom could she trust to take her part against her stepmother's schemes? She remembered the guard's words about Ilse having planned the whole *surprise* for her. She'd assumed it was just a lie, designed to keep her malleable until the moment brute force took over from persuasion. But now there was a seed of doubt. Ilse had been the one to seek her out, after she'd eavesdropped on her stepmother, and had been quick to assure Bianca that she was exaggerating the importance of whatever she'd heard. She said she'd kill for Bianca's appearance. Would she kill for her title as well?

Was it possible even her sister had already been turned against her, and she'd just been too naive, too trusting to realize it?

It was a truly horrible thought, and Bianca refused to accept it. But neither did she consider for a moment trying to find her sister now.

Her progress into the trees was absurdly slow, the wooden anchor making it impossible to properly flee as it crashed against everything in its path. She wouldn't get far like this. Stopping, Bianca turned back and strode to the end of her leash. Denied the use of her hands, she kicked furiously at the rotting chunk of wood, venting her fear and anger. It splintered under her boots, and soon she was able to kick it free of the rope altogether.

Better. She was still trailing a length of rope, but at least there was nothing on the end of it. She resumed her awkward, shuffling run, clambering over fallen logs and blundering through ferns. Her feet slipped on the moss, and more than once she fell flat on her face, but she hastened to struggle back to her feet, determined to keep moving. The hood of the cloak the guard had forced onto her fell, and her hair flowed around her, well and truly loose from Ilse's styling now. Her gown billowed around her, catching on brambles and getting in the way. She longed to be able to tie it back between her legs with the sash dangling down her front, but without her hands, she had no hope of securing it.

Darkness had fully descended now, and Bianca could see little in her path. She winced as vines brushed her face, terrified they might be snakes. Several times she caught the eerie glow of eyes in the darkness, watching her. A sob rose up in her throat, although the gag kept it from escaping. The worst of it was, she knew she must be leaving a trail that even the most inexperienced of huntsmen would be able to follow. Whoever had been coming to claim her would have no difficulty catching up to her.

With each extra step, the pain of her wounds grew, until her wrists felt like they were on fire, and she could barely draw breath from the tightness of the ropes around her middle. And to make matters worse, the power that had felt so exhilarating on first contact was beginning to build to an unbearable pressure. Each touch of her feet on the ground sent more jolting into her, and she could feel the weight of it building on her very bones. It seemed she wasn't fully immune to the wild magic, after all. She felt like she was being slowly suffocated, and she knew she couldn't go on much longer.

At last, her fire ran out. Exhausted and alone, she sank to her knees, pain overwhelming her senses.

Her father had been right. Escaping from the spider's web was nothing but a waste. In the end, it didn't matter whether the fly fought or submitted. It had no hope of survival.

# CHAPTER EIGHT

# FARRIN

Farrin slung his bow over his back, a little disappointed by the results of his hunt. The brocket deer was smaller than he'd normally hunt. It would still make a reasonable meal, of course, especially for the smaller elves. The others would probably appreciate the contribution. But he'd hoped for something larger.

A glance up at the canopy above told him that the sun would soon be setting in the sky beyond. He'd better call it a day.

"Come on, Lottie," he called softly to the apparently empty jungle. "Time to be on our way."

The lithe form of the ocelot slunk out of the undergrowth. Lottie rubbed her cheek along Farrin's leg, purring at sight of his catch.

Farrin just grunted. No doubt she would expect to share in the spoils, in spite of providing no assistance whatsoever in the hunt. Still, he liked to have her company when he was out this deep in the jungle.

Securing the carcass over his shoulders, Farrin set off at a lopsided jog, eager to reach more familiar ground before darkness fully fell. If he'd had more success with his hunting, he wouldn't have stayed out this long. He was far from the lost, frightened castaway he'd been two years ago, but the jungle was still a dangerous place at night. He'd probably need to sleep at the cottage tonight. By the time he'd prepared his kill and they'd eaten, it would be much too late to safely travel to his current camp.

And if Dionysius was inclined to complain, Farrin could always set the night's lodging as the price of the meal he was providing. He smiled at the thought of the irritable elf. Elves weren't common in Port Dulla, but like most humans, Farrin had still grown up with a basic understanding of the danger of making bargains with the crafty creatures. And he'd never felt any real desire to bargain with the others at the cottage. He was glad to give his assistance freely any time it was sought, knowing that they'd saved his life in more ways than one.

But sometimes, just for fun, he couldn't help responding to Dionysius's grumbling by offering him a very reasonable deal for something the elf knew Farrin would have happily given for free if he'd kept his complaints to himself. It enraged Dionysius, but it entertained the rest of them hugely.

Farrin didn't bother searching the undergrowth for the aconitum flower as he moved silently through the jungle. He'd scoured this route on his way out earlier that day, and had only begun his hunt when he was convinced there was no sign of the elusive plant.

Elusive was right, he thought, scowling to himself in a sudden and uncharacteristic burst of frustration. Two years he'd been searching this blasted jungle, looking high and low and everywhere in between. He'd found no sign of his prize, and it was growing harder not to lose hope. The idea of making it home at all, let alone with a cure for Emmett's condition, seemed less likely by the day.

Farrin pushed down the unpleasant thought, pulling his usual detachment around him like a cloak. He couldn't afford to dwell on any emotion associated with his situation. When he'd first braved the jungle, determined to learn its ways and achieve his mission by sheer force of will, he'd thought of himself as a resilient person. It was embarrassing to remember how quickly the hardships of the land—not to mention the isolation—had worn away at his strength. He still clung to his determination, but he'd learned the hard way that he could only do so by removing emotion from the picture altogether. He couldn't even afford hope—opening that floodgate would leave him vulnerable to the despair that was always just below the surface, threatening to overwhelm him.

If he allowed himself to really feel any of it, it would crush him...his own longings, his own fears...worse, the clawing guilt that came from imagining what his family must be suffering, surely believing him long dead. The physical results of his folly were dire enough—he couldn't afford to grapple with the emotional consequences as well.

No, his task was what kept him sane, not any thought of returning home. He'd learned to survive out here, that much he'd achieved. He would continue to follow his routine, day in and day out, and eventually, he would find the aconitum. At least, that was the belief he hung his sanity on.

Lottie ran sleekly ahead of Farrin, leaping from log to tree and back to the ground, frolicking as only a feline could. Once or twice she paused, listening for a moment then running on, apparently satisfied that whatever sound her superior ears had detected was no threat. Farrin caught her eyeing off his load, and clucked his tongue admonishingly.

"Don't even think about it," he told the ocelot gruffly. "You can have some when the rest of us do, but you're not getting first pickings. This is for the others, at the cottage."

She looked a little sulky, but gave no response beyond the flick of one silky ear.

They continued in silence for over an hour, moving steadily northward. Farrin was now in familiar territory, and he knew the human city of Sel wasn't far ahead. He skirted westward, giving it a wide berth. It was unlikely any hunting or harvesting parties would be out this late, but it didn't hurt to be safe.

It was Lottie who heard it first, the ocelot's sudden stillness alerting Farrin to the proximity of another creature. The jungle cat's ears flicked, her head spinning toward the city, which was now to the east of them.

"What is it, Lottie?" Farrin breathed. "What do you hear?"

It was an unnecessary question because a moment later, he heard it, too. Something was blundering through the undergrowth, the movements loud and clumsy.

Farrin frowned. He'd never heard anything in the jungle travel that conspicuously, with the exception of wounded creatures. His eyes searched the darkness, uncertain. It was coming from the direction of the city. Had some poor beast been injured by a hunting party, but gotten away? He knew their archers were often impeded by their inability to descend low enough for a proper shot, and sometimes the grappling hooks they used in order to retrieve their prey failed to properly latch.

Lottie slunk behind a moss-covered stump, apparently deciding to remove herself from sight. She didn't seem especially concerned, though. Listening to the sound, Farrin thought he also could probably evade notice easily. The creature didn't appear to be on a collision course with them.

But he hesitated. His curiosity was roused by the unusual sound. If it was a large, injured animal, perhaps he could bring a proper feast to the cottage, as he'd hoped. And even if it wasn't something he could eat, he felt he should perhaps put the poor creature out of its misery.

Reaching a sudden decision, Farrin scaled the nearest tree, vaulting from a sturdy branch into the next tree along. He moved swiftly through the lower branches, in spite of the slight limp he had long since grown used to. He'd set his course to hopefully intersect with the traveling animal, but found no sign of it. After a moment's listening, he realized he could no longer hear its movement. Checking that his kill was still secure, he tested a few trailing vines before finding one strong enough. Using it to move silently to another tree, he ran on nimble feet along one branch then another, back toward where he'd last heard the sound.

A low moan caught his ears, and he dropped into a crouch on the branch, peering down cautiously through the leaves.

What he saw almost made him topple out of the tree.

It was a woman! A human woman!

Farrin could hardly believe his eyes. He'd spotted plenty of elves in his endless traipsing through the jungle, and had spied on human hunting parties up in the trees many a time. But in two years in Selvana, he'd never once seen another human on the ground.

Until now.

He blinked several times, but no matter how much he told himself it was impossible for a human to be alive down there, the human-sized figure didn't shrink to the form of an elf.

And it wasn't impossible, was it? He was proof of that. He'd been living mostly on the ground for two years, with no sign of being struck down by the wild magic yet.

Farrin ran a hand over the short beard he now sported, his eyes silently raking the woman below him for any indication as to her identity. It was fully dark now, with only small slivers of moonlight slanting down through the canopy, but his nighttime vision was much better than it had been when he'd first arrived on the island.

By his estimation, the woman's gown was costly. Her head was bowed in grief as silent sobs rocked her. She seemed to be elderly, her white hair glowing in the darkness. Although, he reflected irrelevantly, it was surprisingly long and thick for a woman of that age.

His heart stirred a little at her despairing posture, and he tried to push the emotion back, a desperate edge to his efforts. He couldn't afford to let himself feel her pain, whatever its cause. That would give his own pain too great a foothold.

Besides, he told himself prosaically, he should reserve sympathy until he knew who she was. She must surely come from the nearby city, and he had no reason to love the residents of Sel. Had she been banished down here? And why?

Farrin was still motionless and silent, but the woman suddenly looked up, giving him a second shock. She wasn't elderly at all. She was young, younger even than him by the looks. Her milky hair was a striking contrast against her dark skin, but the effect was certainly not unpleasant. He had no doubt she turned heads wherever she went. Her huge, dark eyes searched the rustling jungle fearfully, tears glistening in the silvery light. Her face looked round and pleasant, but he couldn't get a proper look at her. Not with the gag secured around her mouth.

Again, his sympathy stirred, demanding to be heard, and again he pushed it back, his eyes refusing to linger on the painful-looking gag. Instead, he glanced over the rest of the form kneeling below him.

He had no idea why her hair was as white as snow—he hadn't observed the phenomenon in any other Selvanans—but she was undoubtedly young. Young and beautiful.

Farrin drew in a breath in spite of himself as he realized that, in addition to the gag, her hands were bound. A rope trailed away from her form, back through the foliage. Moving silently, Farrin followed it, still keeping to the branches above the girl's head. Was she tied up to something? Or was someone at the other end, holding her like an animal on a lead?

But when Farrin found the end of the rope—far enough away from her that he felt safe to drop down and investigate on the ground—it just trailed loosely. There was nothing there.

It was all extremely peculiar, and he had no idea what to make of it. For a moment he hovered, the hardest part of his emotion-starved mind telling him to fade off into the trees as he knew well how to do, and not get involved in whatever was happening here.

But not for a moment did he really believe that part of him would win. Dulling emotion for the sake of his own preservation was one thing, but he hadn't fallen so far from who he used to be that he would turn his back on someone else in need simply to avoid feeling.

He couldn't just leave this girl to her fate. A fate which could be in no question if she remained in her current situation.

For one thing, he wanted answers regarding the incredible phenomenon of another human surviving contact with the lethal Selvanan ground. But more compellingly, he knew exactly how it felt to be vulnerable and alone, stranded in the dangerous jungle at night. The stranger's plight brought up memories that battered dangerously against his artificial detachment—he forced himself not to turn away from them, but to remember what it had truly been like. Lurgl and Dionysius could so easily have left him to fend for himself the night they found him, and if they had, he would certainly be dead.

Paying the favor forward to this girl seemed like the least he should expect from himself as a human being.

Nevertheless, she was from Sel, she must be. And Farrin felt reluctant to reveal himself. He slipped back up into the trees, whistling softly for Lottie with the bird call he'd long since memorized.

The ocelot slunk through the branches, appearing so quickly she startled Farrin.

"Lottie," he murmured. "I'm going to help her."

The jungle cat settled back on her haunches, lifting one paw to lick lazily at a bramble.

"Lottie," said Farrin sternly. "*We* are going to help her."

The ocelot raised an insolent face toward her human friend, her expression bored.

"Can you get the rope off her?" Farrin asked, choosing to ignore her open disdain for his plan. "Do you understand, Lottie?" He spoke slowly and clearly. "I want you to bite—off—the rope." He mimed what he meant, gesturing at his own midriff.

Lottie yawned.

"So help me, Lottie," hissed Farrin. "If you don't do this, I'm never catching you fresh meat again. You'll have to hunt for yourself, like a *real* wild cat."

Lottie turned reproachful eyes on him, but seemed to realize he meant business. With an offended flip of her tail—catching Farrin full in the face so that he again had to fight to keep his balance on the branch—she leaped nimbly to the ground below.

Farrin heard the girl's muffled grunt as the ocelot came into sight. She struggled to her feet, staring warily at Lottie. With total disregard for the stranger's reaction, Lottie crouched then sprang onto the girl, claws digging into her gown for purchase.

The girl struggled, trying to throw off the large cat. Lottie hissed, but clung on tenaciously, already biting at the rope where it emerged from the girl's waist. Farrin wanted to throttle the ocelot—was it possible to make the assistance seem more like an attack? But after a minute, the rope fell away. Half of it was still wound around the girl's middle, but she was no longer trailing any length. That was an improvement.

Lottie looked up from her position on the girl's gown, her amber eyes searching the canopy for Farrin. Fortunately the stranger didn't seem to realize the ocelot wasn't alone, and she didn't search the trees herself. When Lottie's eyes latched on to him, Farrin gestured at his mouth, trying to point to the gag.

He didn't think the ocelot understood, but all at once Lottie swiveled, one paw reaching up and slashing at the girl's cheek.

Farrin's hiss of annoyance was hidden by the girl's own cry. She recoiled, a shoulder tilting up to cradle her bleeding face. But then she seemed to suddenly realize that she *could* cry out, and she drew in a shuddering breath. Blood trickled down her cheek from the superficial scratches, but the gag was gone.

"Thank...you?" she said, staring uncertainly at the ocelot.

Her voice was full and soft, and Farrin found himself unexpectedly mesmerized. It had been a while since he'd heard a human voice, far from the city as he'd been these last two months.

The girl spoke again, humor creeping into her words as she added, "I don't suppose you can get the ropes around my wrists?"

Farrin could only hope Lottie didn't understand. After the performance with the gag, he didn't trust the ocelot's sharp claws anywhere near the girl's wrists.

Lottie, of course, gave no answer. Pushing off the girl's legs with a force that made the stranger wince, Lottie sprang up into the tree, wending her way quickly to Farrin's side. Farrin considered the situation, only able to think of one solution. It was a good thing they were so close already.

"Time to go home," he whispered to Lottie. "Lead her to the cottage."

This time he knew Lottie understood—she'd found her way

back to the cottage without him many a time, more than once fetching help when Farrin had been injured. But she clearly didn't like the idea, because she turned her nose in the air.

But Farrin didn't back down, staring unblinkingly at the cat for so long his eyes began to sting.

With a bad grace, Lottie gave in, dropping to the jungle floor again. She let out a disgruntled hiss, then loped off into the trees.

"Wait!" called the girl. "Do you...do I..." Her voice dropped to a confused mutter. "Do I follow it?"

*Yes,* Farrin said silently, *follow the ocelot!* Almost as if she could hear him, the girl took a tentative step forward, and then another. She started when Lottie's face thrust suddenly back through the undergrowth, letting out a disgruntled yowl.

This time the girl followed more quickly, soon disappearing from sight.

As soon as he was sure she was gone, Farrin dropped to the ground himself. He frowned back at the very obvious trail she'd left. She'd clearly been running from someone, and it seemed likely they'd track her with ease. Rubbing his hand over his beard again, he gathered up the end of the rope and the bloodied gag. He could only think of one idea, and he sighed. Such a waste of his efforts. The elves at the cottage wouldn't be pleased.

He detached the deer from his shoulders, laying it down on the jungle floor and untying his rope from around it. Then he pulled out his knife, his nose wrinkled in distaste for his task as he tried to make it look like the carcass had been partially consumed by a predator. He left the severed rope and the gag nearby, smearing a bit of the deer's blood on it for good measure. With any luck, it would look like the unfortunate girl had stumbled on a jaguar eating its kill and been carried off in the deer's place.

His task complete, Farrin set about obscuring the trail the girl had left as she followed Lottie. Once he'd done so for a decent distance, he took to the trees again, careful not to leave a track of his own. He caught up to the pair easily, seeing with approval that Lottie was doing as she'd been told. Farrin saw them as far as the clearing before giving a low whistle.

Lottie stilled, her head swiveling back toward him before she jumped into the trees again.

"Wait!" the girl called after her, but Lottie didn't pause.

After a moment, the girl turned back around, her eyes searching the clearing. Farrin frowned as he realized only a thin light was coming from the cottage hidden inside the cave, like the lantern the others usually left burning when they expected to be home after dark. Were they out, then? It was a little late to be mining. What unlucky timing that they'd worked late on this particular night.

"Perhaps we'd better not try to return to our camp," Farrin muttered to Lottie, as she reappeared beside him. "We'll obscure the tracks she left on her way into the clearing—clumsy thing, isn't she?—then find a spot to camp nearby. We might have some explaining to do come morning."

The ocelot made no reply. By now she'd spotted the loss of Farrin's delicious load, and realized the extent to which she'd been betrayed. Tail in the air, she stalked away from him, giving him an excellent view of her rear.

Farrin rolled his eyes, a smile tugging at his lips. It really wouldn't kill her to hunt for herself for a change. As he set about trying to hide the tracks, his thoughts were full of the girl who'd made them. Who was she? Where had she come from?

And why did he feel like she was about to change everything?

# CHAPTER NINE

# Bianca

Bianca stared in confusion around her, wondering where the ocelot had gone. Fear stirred. Was this some kind of trap? But if the plan was to lure her to her death, why bother to remove her gag, and cut off the trailing end of the rope around her waist?

More unanswerable, why would an *ocelot* bother to do any of that, or know it needed to be done?

It was all very strange, but she wasn't about to say no to the reprieve. It was certainly a lovely spot. She wandered forward, taking in the dark clearing and listening to the tinkling of the nearby waterfall which broke the stillness of the night. Even the pressure of the wild magic had eased in this more open space, as if the clearing wasn't as suffocated with it as the heavy jungle.

As Bianca moved around the edge of the water, she realized there was a cave yawning ahead. Her steps faltered, unnerved by the deeper darkness. Then her eyes caught a thin beam of golden light, and she hurried forward. It truly didn't occur to her until she'd already entered the cave to question whether the source of the light was friend or foe. She felt so horribly alone since the ocelot left that her whole being yearned for the sight of another creature.

The light wasn't strong, and it took a minute for Bianca's eyes to adjust enough to make out the shape looming ahead inside the cave. When she did, she came to a sudden stop, drawing in a gasp.

It was a house. Not a wooden dwelling fallen from the tree-tops, but a house built of stone, clearly intended to be on the ground. She'd seen pictures of such dwellings in the history books, relating to the brief period when humans had lived on the ground alongside the elves. This building must be a relic of that time, and it must have belonged to humans—it certainly looked human-sized. But how was it so well-maintained? And who had left a light burning inside?

Belatedly, Bianca's fear trickled back in. Who or what might be waiting for her in there? Why had that ocelot led her here?

But the light was too inviting, as was the prospect of shelter from the dangers of the jungle. Bianca's bound wrists were so painful that every movement brought forth a whimper, and her breath was labored, both from the tightness of the rope still around her middle and the constant pressure of the wild magic. She would drop soon either way, so it may as well be inside the building as in front of it.

Her gait still awkward because of her bound hands, she shuffled up to the door.

"Hello?" she called nervously. "Is anyone here?"

There was no reply. She lifted one boot, using it as best she could to knock tentatively on the door. Still nothing.

The door didn't seem to be locked, but Bianca still had diffi-culty manipulating the latch without proper use of her hands. Eventually she managed it, however, using her shoulder to push it wide. She peered uncertainly inside, but it really did seem to be deserted.

As she moved properly into the simple stone dwelling, she saw that the light came from a lantern positioned just inside a window, to one side of the only door. It seemed like a beacon, and she so wanted to believe its purpose was to welcome, not to trap. But that kind of trusting attitude had landed her in this mess.

She shivered, reminding herself that she really had no other options. Her eyes passed over the small space, and she realized that the size was off. The doorway she'd entered had been plenty taller than her height, but the furniture inside seemed too small. There was a table, with plates laid out as if in readiness for a late supper. There was even a plate of flat bread in the center of the table, like the hardy food the hunting parties took on longer trips. The place was clearly not abandoned. Someone was coming back to eat that food, and probably soon. Seven someones, she amended, counting the plates.

Another shudder went over her. In her current state, she'd be powerless to defend herself against one stranger, let alone seven. But then, they couldn't be too fearsome, she thought doubtfully. Not if they were small enough to sit at that low table. Her eyes traveled to the other end of the space, where four small beds sat beneath two hammocks. Curiously, another hammock was hung by itself in the opposite corner of the room.

The beds were too short even for her frame, and she was no giant. Bianca frowned. Did children live here? Surely not. It was awful to think of seven children living in this place all alone. And how could *anyone* live here, down on the ground? How was she here, still alive after hours out of the trees?

Bianca let out a soft moan, unable to grapple any longer with the impossibilities of this horrible night. Her stomach ached, reminding her of the dinner she'd been prevented from attending. Where were Ilse and her stepmother now? Were they frantic with worry at her failure to appear for the meal?

Ilse might be worried and confused, but her stepmother wasn't, Bianca reminded herself. Although no doubt she was feigning it convincingly. Bianca spared a thought for the guard who'd dragged her out of the palace, wondering what he'd reported to his mistress. Had he told the queen that Bianca had escaped, and had survived the first impact with the ground? Or had he hidden the truth, afraid of the consequences to himself? Both options seemed equally likely.

There would be no coronation tomorrow, that much was certain. And what would the populace think? Would they believe her dead? Would they think she'd run away, overwhelmed by her responsibilities?

She knew she should be angry, but she was too exhausted for anger. And too overwhelmed, although not by her royal duties. She knew it was a risk to stay where she was, with the identity and intentions of the dwelling's inhabitants unknown. But it was surely a bigger risk to venture back into the jungle alone at night.

Disregarding both dignity and the evils of theft, Bianca waddled to the table. She dropped to her knees and bent over the wooden surface, grabbing some of the flat bread with her mouth. She made a mess of it, leaving crumbs all over the place, but the food was enough to soothe her protesting stomach.

She struggled back to her feet with an effort, moving now toward the beds. She considered trying to clamber up into one of the hammocks, but it was too hard without her hands for balance. So she threw herself down, stretching sideways across all four of the beds. An involuntary cry escaped her as she chafed her raw wrists, but the pain wasn't enough to keep her from drifting down and away.

<><><>

"Who ate the bread?"

The angry voice startled Bianca from her sleep, pain instantly assaulting her awareness. She'd rolled onto her bound hands and seemed to have lost feeling below the wrists.

"I didn't work all night to come home to no food! Ulmer, wasn't it your turn to set the table? What do you call this?"

"Hush, Dionysius!"

The second voice was sharp, and Bianca held herself tensely, keeping her eyes screwed shut out of an instinct of self-preservation. She heard footsteps approaching, and drew in a shaky breath.

"I don't think Ulmer ate the food, somehow," said the second voice mildly. "It seems we have a guest."

Bianca heard several sharp gasps, then another set of footsteps pattered up. "It's a human! How's she alive, though?"

"Just because she's old doesn't mean she's at death's door," cut in another voice.

"Oh, go shove your head in an anthill, Dakarai," came the irate reply. "I wasn't talking about her being old. I was talking about her being on the ground. She should be dead."

"Oh." Dakarai seemed struck by this point. "So she should. Are we sure she isn't?"

Someone prodded Bianca hard, and she judged it time to stop pretending to be asleep. Struggling upward, she summoned her most regal voice.

"I'm definitely alive, and I'm *not* old, thank you very—"

Her words cut off as she shuffled around and caught sight of her audience. For a moment she thought she must still be dreaming, but the pain in her wrists suggested otherwise. Her eyes traveled slowly over the forms before her—each of them fully mature, in spite of being the size of children—landing finally on the closest pair of pointed ears.

"But...you're elves," she whispered.

"Good work, halfwit," said the nearest elf, his voice identifying him as the one who'd told Dakarai to go stick his head in an anthill.

"You're supposed to be dead," Bianca said blankly.

"So are you, oldie," said another elf with a grin. Dakarai, she was pretty sure. "And yet here we all are."

"I'm not old," Bianca said, mustering what dignity she could. "My hair has always been like this."

"Has it now?" The elf who spoke was elbowing his way to the front, and Bianca noticed that he was the tallest of the group by a decent margin. His eyes—the same piercing green as all the others—were thoughtful as they rested on Bianca's hair. If her hands had been free, she would have smoothed it self-consciously, but as it was, she could do nothing but sit and endure the scrutiny.

"No, Lurgl." The angry elf's voice was flat.

The elf—Lurgl, apparently, although it was hard to believe that could be his actual name—turned from his contemplation of Bianca, his expression mild.

"No what, Dionysius? I didn't say anything."

"You didn't need to," Dionysius growled. "I could see it in your face. You want to adopt her. But we're *not* taking in any more strays!"

Bianca wanted to protest at this description of herself, but a moment's contemplation forced her to acknowledge that he wasn't too far off.

"What would you do, throw her out into the jungle?" Lurgl asked.

Dionysius's answer was instant. "Absolutely! We don't need or want any women fussing around in here."

"Oi!" came a shout from the back of the group.

Dionysius paused, glancing behind him. "No offense, Raella."

"I very much *am* offended," said the new voice, as its owner shoved forward through the ranks. Bianca saw Raella emerge, looking irate and very clearly female. "I, for one, wouldn't mind having another girl around to keep you all in order." She gave Bianca a knowing look. "They live like pigs, the lot of them."

Bianca saw several of the other elves roll their eyes, exchanging long-suffering glances. Lurgl, the tall one who had apparently wanted to adopt her, seemed to be trying to hold back a chuckle, his expression indulgent.

"Don't stray from the point," snapped Dionysius. "You can't seriously be considering taking in another human? May as well start taking in giants!"

Several voices tutted at him, and the female elf scowled openly. "Bite your tongue, Dionysius. That's out of order. We're elves—we'd never have dealings with giants. Humans aren't the same at all." She turned back to Bianca. "And it's not just up to us whether she stays. Where are you from, child? Do you have somewhere to go, someone expecting you?"

Bianca hesitated, unsure what was safe to tell them.

"I'm from Sel," she said at last. "I was attacked yesterday. Someone pushed me down, I think trying to kill me. I thought I'd die when I touched the ground. I truly don't know why I didn't."

They all looked her over thoughtfully, no one speaking for a moment. It was the irritable Dionysius who broke the silence.

"This is the huntsman's doing, just wait."

"He has a name, Dion," said one of the others reproachfully. "And I don't see you rejecting the meat from his hunting. Would it really kill you to show him a little respect?"

"Yes," said Dionysius shortly. "It would. And he sent this waif here, I bet you my best ax."

"Done," said another voice, the speaker hidden in the general clump.

Dionysius turned, his manner suddenly businesslike. "My best ax for yours," he said formally, and the two elves shook hands.

"Witnessed," chorused the other five, most of them sounding bored.

Bianca blinked in confusion, struggling to keep up with the various threads.

"The huntsman?" she repeated faintly. "Who's that?"

"Oh, he's all right," said Raella, adding loftily, "for a human. He doesn't live here, but he's here a lot. Brings us meat, sometimes, although he's not actually a huntsman, properly speaking. He's on a different kind of search."

Bianca stared at the elf, a horrible suspicion growing inside her. She knew someone who was no longer a huntsman, who lived somewhere other than this clearing, and who might have had the capacity to lead her here. Was this a trap after all? Had this been where the huntsman-turned-guard had been intending her to end up all along?

She drew back, looking at the elves with fresh suspicion. Their manner didn't seem at all sinister, but could she trust her own judgment? Clearly not.

"Where is this huntsman now?" she asked warily. "What does he look like?"

"He's human," said Dakarai dismissively. "How should we know what he looks like? He's tall, and his limbs are all too long."

Bianca nearly groaned. That didn't really help her narrow things down.

"We won't keep you here if you don't want to stay," said

Lurgl, taking control of the conversation. "But we also don't want to just set you loose and risk you exposing our haven here." He frowned. "How did you find it, incidentally? *Did* the huntsman lead you here?"

"I don't know," said Bianca helplessly. "I don't know who that is. I followed an ocelot. I know it sounds crazy, but it...it seemed to be telling me to come."

A chorus of understanding murmurs passed around the small group, several little heads nodding.

"So it *was* him," said one, and the elf who had made the bargain with Dionysius visibly deflated.

"We don't know that," he chimed in. "Not yet proven."

Dionysius rolled his eyes, but several other elves nodded their heads sagely.

"True. Not yet proven."

"Well, if he sent you here, it was no doubt in the belief we'd take you in if you needed shelter," Lurgl said, cutting off the murmurs. "Which of course we will. If you want to stay, you're welcome. But we'll expect you to do your part around the place. Do you know how to cook and clean? Because you'll have to learn if you don't. We all take our turns."

"I can learn," Bianca said with determination. "You called this place a haven. Does that mean others don't know you're here? Meaning the one who attacked me won't be able to find me if I stay here?"

"Of course humans can't find this place," scoffed Raella. "They can't come on the ground, can they?" She hesitated. "Well, most of them can't."

Bianca bit her lip. Her mind was slowly catching up with all the bewildering revelations. If there were still elves alive down here, then it may well have been some of their kind who were supposed to collect her from the guard. But she didn't know whether she wanted to reveal that speculation to the elves in front of her. Not without more information.

"You can join me in the ladies' corner, I suppose," said Raella grandly. She gestured toward the lone hammock. "We'll have a time making a bed big enough for you, but we can string you up a hammock easily enough."

"A hammock is fine," said Bianca quickly. "Thank you."

"All right, then," said Lurgl. "It's decided." He turned around, clearly intending to address the group, when a new voice spoke.

"There's something not right about her."

Everyone looked surprised, their heads swiveling to a lone figure standing slightly back from the group.

"It speaks," muttered Dionysius, but Lurgl sent him a warning look, and he fell silent.

"What do you mean, Ulmer?" Lurgl asked patiently. "If you have concerns about letting her stay here, speak freely."

"Something not right," Ulmer repeated stubbornly. He eyed Bianca darkly. "She didn't say her name."

"That's true," Lurgl said, turning back to Bianca. Strangely, his eyes seemed to dance as he addressed her. "What is your name, child?"

She hesitated, wondering if she should be honest, or if her identity might put her in danger.

"Bee," she said, settling for an old nickname.

The quiet elf, Ulmer, looked unconvinced. His eyes narrowed as they roamed up to her hair. "How are you alive on the ground? Why's your hair like that?"

Bianca squirmed under his gaze. "I don't know," she acknowledged. "I truly don't have an answer for either of those questions."

"That's enough, Ulmer," Lurgl said authoritatively. "Leave her be. There'll be time enough for questions later. For now, everyone has work to do." He glanced out the window toward the mouth of the cave. The sun was properly up now, and Bianca could hear the cheerful calls of birds alongside the musical patter of the waterfall. "I know everyone's eager to sleep after doing night work, but let's get a meal on the table first."

The group scattered with such speed, Bianca was left blinking. As unimposing as his manner might be, Lurgl clearly wielded authority in the group. And he wore it with a casual unconcern.

The elf smiled at her, his forest-green eyes sparkling in his pale face. Like the others, he was dressed in the colors of the jungle—green, brown, and gray. He was wearing a waterproof poncho, but she could see that underneath it, his clothes were closely fitted. She opened her mouth to ask for his help with her bindings—which none of the elves seemed to have even noticed under the cloak still fastened about her shoulders—but he spoke before she could, his voice low and soft.

"I know who you are, Princess." His eyes passed up to her hair, then back to her face. "Perhaps better than you do."

# CHAPTER TEN

# Bianca

Bianca stared at the elf, no words coming to her rescue. Lurgl seemed to see her shock, because he backed off a little, chuckling.

"We'll speak more later," he said. "For now, you can relax. You're safe here."

And with that, he trotted out of the room, leaving Bianca open-mouthed and still bound. The whole dwelling was deserted, everyone having dispersed to their tasks according to some pre-arranged schedule. Bianca struggled to her feet and drew in as deep a breath as she could around the constriction on her waist.

She staggered out of the hut, her muscles screaming in protest at being trapped in the unnatural position for so many hours. She was grateful she'd been able to sleep, but she'd never woken feeling less rested. She spotted one of the elves by the water, a fair way around the pool. It was Raella, collecting water in a cauldron.

But Bianca had only made it halfway around the water's edge when the female elf stood, whistling cheerfully, and abandoned her full cauldron to zip into the tree line.

With a groan, Bianca came to a stop. Her hands were in such a bad way, she was starting to have concerns about lasting injury. She half-turned, looking for another elf who might be willing to help, when something dropped suddenly from the trees in front of her.

She couldn't stop the shriek that slipped out as she whirled back around. She stumbled back, almost falling over in shock at the sight of a man—an actual, full-sized, human man—rising from the crouch into which he'd fallen. He held a bow in one hand, but it wasn't strung. He seemed to have been binding it with twine, reinforcing a damaged section.

"Where...where did you come from?" Bianca asked stupidly.

He didn't answer, his face marred in a frown as he looked her over. He was considerably taller than her, although that was the least of their contrasts. His skin was as pale as hers was dark, and his hair was a golden color, its near-shoulder length showing off a tendency to curl. He sported a rugged beard, and his dark eyes—their brown a striking combination with his tawny hair—looked heavy, as if he hadn't slept much the night before.

Was this the huntsman the elves had spoken about? If so, he certainly wasn't the same man who'd pushed her from the platform. She remembered Dakarai's description of this huntsman as tall with limbs that were too long.

The elf had undersold him.

The huntsman, if this was him, was as perfectly proportioned as he was handsome—albeit in a rugged, woodsy sort of way, nothing like the well-groomed attractiveness of the young men in the upper ranks of Sel's society.

"They didn't even untie your hands," the man said, his voice as scratchy as his chin. He sighed. "Typical elves."

Leaning the half-mended bow against a nearby trunk, he stepped forward, moving with a slight limp. Stranger though he was, Bianca felt no inclination to shrink away from him. She knew, somewhere in her mind, that her tendency to be too trusting had led her into this mess. But she just couldn't deny the instinct that told her he was no threat.

He lifted the cloak the guard had placed around her, tossing it over one of her shoulders to better access her bound hands. The action seemed to bring his attention to the rope still around her waist, and his frown deepened. Reaching into his belt, he pulled out a small but lethal-looking hunting knife.

Bianca flinched in spite of herself as he raised it, and he paused.

"May I?" he asked, his voice abrupt, sounding like it wasn't used very often. "I won't hurt you."

She nodded, feeling foolish. Of course she'd guessed his intention, but she hadn't been able to help the flash of alarm after the events of the previous twelve hours.

The huntsman slipped the knife under the rope, slicing it in one clean motion. Bianca pulled in a deep lungful of air, her heart soaring with gratitude. The pressure of the wild magic was still a discomfort, but it was manageable now she could properly draw breath.

Her liberator's face didn't change at all as he spun her half around. His movements were slower and more careful this time, but Bianca still let out an involuntary whimper as he made contact with her chafed wrists.

She heard his small intake of breath, and his hands paused for a moment.

"I'm all right," she gasped out. "Please don't stop. I'm desperate to be free of the bindings."

After another moment he resumed his work. His voice sounded gruffer as he spoke again.

"I should have realized the fool elves wouldn't think to cut you free. They're not a bad bunch, as elves go. But they're not the most compassionate of creatures. Not practiced at thinking of the needs or desires of others than their kind."

"I don't think they even saw the bindings," Bianca said softly. "I should have asked for help, but I was too overwhelmed by… everything…to gather my thoughts."

"Ah, Farrin!" It was Raella who spoke, emerging from the trees ahead, her arms full of kindling.

"Morning, Raella," the huntsman said curtly.

"You've met the new girl, have you?" said the elf, trotting up to them. She wrinkled her nose in thought. "Or did you already know her? Was it you who sent Lottie to lead her here last night?"

At her words, a small, furry shape dropped from a nearby tree, the ocelot slinking up to the huntsman and wending between his legs.

The man grunted in apparent affirmation of Raella's guess.

"Was that a yes?" she asked officiously. "We're going to need a more decisive answer, with more witnesses than just myself."

The huntsman paused his work. "Did someone strike a wager over it?" he demanded.

Raella nodded, and he rolled his eyes.

"Elves," he muttered. "Bargains and wagers. They're incorrigible."

With the words, he finished his task, the severed bindings falling away from Bianca's hands at last. She brought her arms around to the front, stretching them and flexing her still-numb fingers. The freedom of movement was such a relief, tears sprang to her eyes.

"Thank you!" she gasped. "Did Raella call you Farrin?"

He nodded. "That's my name."

"Thank you, Farrin," she repeated, her words fervent. "A thousand times thank you, and may every task of your hands prosper!" She was so grateful for the simple act of kindness, her words began to dance of their own accord as she recited the traditional Selvanan blessing.

The effect of her word dance was instant and unnerving. Firstly, both Farrin and Raella froze in place, and two more heads popped out of nearby foliage, although Bianca hadn't realized other elves were within hearing range.

Secondly, there was a loud crack, and Farrin's half-bound bow slid from its position against the tree to lie on the mossy ground. Moving as if in a daze, the young man picked it up, pulling off the twine.

"It's fixed," he said quietly, lifting it up for everyone's inspection. "The crack is fully sealed again." His eyes rose to Bianca's. "As good as new."

She stared from the bow to him, confused and once more fearful. His tone was almost ominous.

"You're a singer," Farrin said, the words a statement rather than a question. "And a powerful one."

"She's a *singer*?" Raella repeated. Her voice was shrill and carrying, and three more elves appeared, as if from nowhere.

"A singer?" they chorused, a host of emerald-green eyes piercing Bianca.

Ulmer—the one who'd challenged her in the cottage—stepped forward. "I said there was something off about her. Why keep that to yourself, eh?"

"But that's a good thing, isn't it?" asked an elf whose name Bianca hadn't caught yet. "If she's a singer, and she's here on the ground, that's good, yes?"

"No, Eason, you daft beetle, it's not a good thing," growled Dionysius. "It means we're caught up in something that could destroy everything we've built here." He rounded on Bianca, his expression fierce. "Where did you really come from? How did you end up on the ground?"

"I told you the truth," she protested. "I'm from Sel, and yesterday evening someone pushed me from a platform."

"Who pushed you?" demanded Dionysius, his green eyes narrowed and the tips of his ears quivering in his displeasure.

Bianca squirmed a little. "I don't know his name." She saw the elf's expression, and her tone turned defensive. "I really don't know his name!"

"Who is he, though?" Raella pressed, seeming no more convinced than Dionysius.

"He's a guard," said Bianca.

"A guard?" The elf called Dakarai looked confused. "Aren't they supposed to protect people, not try to kill them? Are you sure it wasn't an accident?"

"Don't be a fool, Dakarai," snapped Dionysius. "She's the first singer Selvana's seen in generations, and you think someone got her onto the ground by accident? This is the others' doing, no doubt about it."

"There's certainly no question of it being an accident." Farrin's voice—so much deeper than the elves'—caused everyone to look at him. "You lot should work on looking at what's above your noses. This poor girl was bound at the wrists and the waist until five minutes ago, and when I found her blundering through the jungle, she was in an even worse state. Someone tied her up and threw her to her fate."

Bianca bit her lip as she regarded the tall young man. She wasn't quite sure how to feel about his words. Much as she could find no good reason for it, and was embarrassed to acknowledge it to herself, she felt warmth spread through her at his concern. But he was so tense, not just as if he was irked at the elves, but as if his own words made him angry and uncomfortable. Besides which, she didn't altogether like being called "this poor girl" and generally being cast as a helpless victim.

Even if that was what she'd so far shown herself to be.

"So you admit it!" Dionysius cried, a triumphant gleam in his eyes. "You're the one who led her here!"

"Of course," said Farrin. "Where else could I have taken her?"

"Arbor," said Dionysius commandingly, holding his hand out to another elf. "You heard him."

The elf—whom Bianca recognized as the one who'd made the wager, sagged. "I'll get my ax," he said glumly.

Dionysius's face hardened again as he turned back to Farrin. "But why did you lead her here? What were you thinking, landing us in this?"

"I did it for you, Dion," said Farrin, his voice suddenly pleasant instead of clipped. "Because I know how much you enjoy taking in lost souls. I thought of you especially when I asked Lottie to lead her here."

A titter went around the other elves, and Raella leaned in helpfully to explain to Bianca. "He can never resist baiting Dionysius. Now poor old Dion can't decide whether to be pleased he's won the bargain with Arbor, or angry about Farrin leading you here."

"I see," said Bianca, not at all truthfully.

"Never mind all that," said Dionysius, turning abruptly back to Bianca, although he continued to speak as if she wasn't present. "If she was really tied up, that settles it." The elf's alabaster skin was wrinkled so ferociously across his forehead, it brought his hairline closer to his brows. "No one would bother to tie her up that securely if they thought she'd die on impact with the ground. She was being sent down here because she's a singer."

"Hold on," protested Bianca, feeling that she'd been much too passive in the conversation so far. "The man who pushed me was as stunned as I was that I didn't die on impact. I could see it on his face. And what in the world is a *singer*? I've never even heard that word before, so I don't see how I can be one."

"You've never heard of a singer?" Farrin asked blankly. The ocelot, Lottie, leaped nimbly up onto his back and draped herself around his shoulders as he spoke. He reached up an absent hand to scratch her chin, all the while continuing to stare at Bianca. "How is that possible when you are one? And there's no doubt you are. We all heard you sing."

"You mean when I made my words dance?" she asked curiously. "Is that what it's called? Singing?"

He nodded slowly. "You didn't know that? I had no idea Selvana had so completely lost its knowledge of magic." He frowned. "But you can't be totally uneducated in the ways of magic—you just used your voice to channel magic and mend my bow."

Bianca's mouth fell open. "I mended your bow with my words? How is that possible? No one can channel the magic of this land. It's gone too wild."

"So I thought," said Farrin, his eyes studying her face. "But the enchantment was very clear. You sang *may every task of your hands prosper*, and instantly my most recent task completed itself to a standard only attainable by magic."

Bianca opened her mouth, then closed it, completely at a loss for what to say. Was it possible he was right? But what did that mean? That would change...everything.

"How did you say your hair went white?" demanded the elf who'd lost the wager with Dionysius. He'd returned with his ax, which he moodily handed over to the other elf.

"Where are your manners, Arbor? There's no need to interrogate our guest."

Lurgl appeared from the trees on the other side of the dwelling, a basket of eggs over one arm.

"Lurgl, she's a singer!" Raella announced, a hint of accusation in her voice.

"Oh." Lurgl's posture drooped a little. "You've figured that out already? I was hoping she could settle in before everyone started losing their minds over that."

"You knew?" Dionysius exploded.

"Of course," said Lurgl calmly. "I know why her hair's like that, too. I was present when it happened."

It was Bianca's turn to exclaim. "You can't have been! It's been like this since I was a baby."

Lurgl chuckled, offering an egg to Lottie, who clawed her way halfway down Farrin's chest to swipe it up.

"Elves age very gracefully, my dear. I'm older than I look. I was an adult when you were an infant."

"But..." Bianca's mind was spinning. "I thought I was born with white hair."

"You weren't," Lurgl said decisively. "When I first saw you, you were a wee cute little thing with a tuft of dark hair and plump little cheeks." He paused, studying her face dispassionately. "Your lips were as red as they are now, though. Like blood." His refined features took on a dreamlike look. "A creature of contrasts, from birth...and even more so now."

"Ugh," complained Raella. "Don't put on your mystical blue-blooded elf voice, Lurgl. We're not interested in your predictions about the future. You have plenty of explaining to do regarding the here and now!"

A chorus of elven voices echoed the sentiment, and Lurgl sighed, raising his hands in an acknowledging gesture. But when he spoke, he addressed himself to Bianca, not his brethren.

"Last night was not your first time touching the ground, Bee," he said.

Bianca felt a flash of relief at his use of her nickname.

Apparently he didn't intend to tell the other elves her identity, at least not yet. Then his words caught up with her, and she forgot all about such trivialities.

"Wait, what?" she demanded. "Of course it was! No one from Sel touches the ground. No one! Don't you think I'd remember if I'd been down here before?"

"No," said Lurgl patiently, "I don't. Because you were too young to remember." He held her gaze. "You were only about six months old, I believe. The queen dropped you by accident. I have no doubt it was after that incident that your hair turned white. Singer or not, the magic in the ground was too potent for your young form to handle. You're lucky it affected no more than your hair."

"The queen?" repeated Dakarai, looking bewildered. "Why would the queen be carrying Bee around?"

Lurgl sighed. "She wasn't the queen back then. The king hadn't even begun courting her yet. She was just a nursemaid, and Bee was her charge."

"That can't be true," said Bianca through numb lips.

In spite of what she said, she was rattled by the accuracy of the details. She knew that when she'd been six months old, Marisol really had been her nursemaid. Hopefully the other elves wouldn't figure out what that meant. She wasn't quite ready for them to know that she was supposed to be crowned as Selvana's queen that morning. Shaking off that bitter thought, she frowned at Lurgl.

"If I'd been dropped from the trees as a baby, I would certainly have died, whether or not I could survive the wild magic."

"The queen wasn't up in the trees," Lurgl said simply. "She'd descended almost to the jungle floor on a ladder we provided. She came to meet with us, you see. She made a bargain with our illustrious leader."

The group went unnaturally still, every eye fixed on Lurgl. All but Farrin's brown ones, that was. The other human was looking between the elves, apparently as confused as Bianca by their sudden change in manner.

"The human queen had a bargain with the elves?" Dionysius said, his high voice quavering.

"Has," Lurgl corrected calmly. "It's still active. Like I said, she wasn't queen then. She wanted our help to become queen, and the absolute fool made the bargain without first settling on the terms."

"Did she know nothing about elves?" demanded Farrin incredulously, over the top of the elves' chokes of disbelief.

Lurgl shrugged. "I guess not."

"That's who she was speaking to," whispered Bianca, horror washing over her.

What had her stepmother done? Bianca had no training in the ways of elves, but in the space of half a morning, she'd grasped that they weren't to be bargained with lightly. What had Marisol involved Selvana in?

"What do you mean?" Lurgl asked, his eyes drilling into her. "What did you hear?"

Bianca swallowed, her eyes finding his. "She was speaking to someone in her room. But there was no one there, just...just a mirror. She was arguing that she'd promised gold, but they disagreed. They were demanding *people* as payment."

Lurgl sighed. "Yes, that was their intention, right from the start. Although of course they took care not to let her know that. Go on," he encouraged. "What else did you hear?"

Bianca tried to remember. "She said she couldn't send people to the ground to die, and then...then they agreed to take me instead." She hesitated, not letting her gaze stray to anyone but Lurgl. "They...they asked for me by name."

"And did they say that would satisfy the agreement?" the elf asked sharply. "What was their exact wording?"

"I—I don't remember," Bianca admitted. "I was too busy panicking over what to do."

"Typical human folly," muttered Dionysius.

Farrin turned, scowling at the cantankerous elf. "You could show a little compassion, Dionysius."

"You're one to talk!" the elf exploded. "Where was your compassion for us when you sent her blundering in here? Don't you realize what this means?" He pointed a furious finger at Bianca. "The elves asked for her by name, so they clearly knew she's a singer, and that she'd survive down here. She's payment for a bargain between them and the human queen! You think the elves will just let that go? They'll tear the jungle down to claim her if that's what it takes, and you've ensured they'll follow her straight here!"

An uneasy murmuring went around the group, a couple of the elves actually edging back from Bianca.

"I...I'll leave if I'm not welcome," Bianca choked out. "I don't mean to put anyone in danger. It's just that I have nowhere else to go."

"If you kick her out," Farrin said, his voice low and rougher than ever, "I'll never bring you another kill again. And that's a promise."

Bianca couldn't quite meet his eye, heat rising up her cheeks at his defense.

"No one is kicking anyone out," Lurgl said soothingly. He shot Dionysius a reproving look. "And there's no need to be dramatic. We each have our own reasons why it would be unpleasant for us to be discovered here, but none of us would be in true danger. Whereas Bee would definitely die if we turned her loose in the jungle on her own."

"That's true," Raella said, nodding sagely.

Bianca sighed, but didn't attempt to argue.

"*You* might be in actual danger if we were discovered, Lurgl," said Arbor doubtfully.

Lurgl just shrugged. "I'm not concerned about that."

"They may not be able to track her here," Farrin interjected. Dionysius gave a disbelieving snort, but Farrin ignored him. "I tried to cover her tracks on the final approach."

"Oh, good, you covered her tracks," said Dionysius sarcastically. "That will make sure they stop looking for her. They'll just let the unfulfilled bargain go, no doubt."

Farrin shot him an irritated look. "I wasn't finished. I was bringing you a deer last night, and after I found...Bee, is it? When she followed Lottie, I left the deer behind after, well, mutilating it. I tried to make it look like Bee had interrupted a jaguar feeding on the deer and been carried off herself instead."

Bianca stared at him, not sure whether to be grateful or disturbed by this forethought.

"Great!" exploded Dionysius. "So not only has this waif deprived us of our security, but she also cost us a hot meal!"

"Mind who you're calling a waif," snapped Bianca, reaching her limit with the inhospitable elf.

Lurgl's eyes were once again sparkling as he gave her an approving nod, but it didn't mollify her. She wished the elf didn't know she was a princess. It made her feel more ridiculous to have a witness to just how far she'd fallen in the last twelve hours. Metaphorically as well as literally.

The other elves ignored the interaction, muttering amongst themselves as to whether Farrin's misdirection would work.

"That was clever, Farrin," Raella said in undisguised amazement. "Very clever for a human."

Farrin gave a long-suffering sigh, but made no comment.

"Definitely a good thought," Lurgl agreed firmly. "We can hope it worked, but we should still set up a protective ward."

"You want to waste our stores on this girl?" Dionysius demanded.

"She's sought shelter here, just like each of us did before her. Including you," Lurgl reminded him sternly. "And it's not just about her. As you've pointed out, we don't especially want to be found, either."

"If they're looking for her because she's a singer, I for one want to protect her," said Raella stoutly. "I never agreed with the strategy, and I know I'm not the only one. Isn't that why half of us are exiled here?"

"Strategy?" Bianca asked warily. "What strategy are you talking about? Why exactly would the elves want my—the queen to send people down to the ground? How does it benefit them if a bunch of humans die?"

"It doesn't benefit them for humans to die," said Arbor curtly. "It benefits them for humans to *live*."

Bianca waited, but no one expanded. "I don't understand," she said blankly.

"No doubt," Arbor responded. "But if you want information, you'll have to make us an offer. We don't give things away for free. We're elves."

"Oh, Arbor, it's too early in the morning for that," complained Raella. "Especially when we haven't slept yet."

"That's right," Lurgl said firmly. "Let's set up the ward, then we can eat and sleep for a few hours. Any further plans can wait that long."

With a chorus of assenting murmurs, the elves trotted off again, leaving the two humans standing alone by the pool.

Bianca turned slowly to face Farrin, trying and failing to read his unexpressive face.

"If I ask you a question," she said slowly, "will you give me an honest answer?"

He took a moment to reply. "I don't know," he said, in the same scratchy voice. "That depends on the question."

Bianca let out a soft sigh, rolling her still-stiff shoulders. "That's fair, I suppose," she acknowledged.

"What do you want to know?" he pressed, his curiosity apparently getting the better of him.

Bianca let her shoulders drop, meeting his eyes. "Do you think I'm going to die down here?"

# CHAPTER ELEVEN

# FARRIN

Farrin went still, mesmerized by the calm intensity in those dark eyes. He knew a strange impulse to shelter the girl, reassure her with soothing lies. But he pushed it aside. Quite apart from the fact that he had no reason to coddle her, it wouldn't really be kindness. The jungle wasn't gentle on the underprepared, or the overly optimistic.

"Your odds are better than they were when I found you last night, but it's still very possible," he said bluntly. "If the wild magic hasn't killed you by now, I doubt it will without intervention. But there are plenty of other things that can kill you down here. Staying here with the others is your best chance, I would say."

She frowned slightly, her lips puckering at one corner. Lurgl had been right, Farrin reflected irrelevantly. They really were unusually red and full. Actually, come to think of it, the elf hadn't said anything about them being full.

"So they won't kill me?" she asked doubtfully, waving one arm toward the cottage hidden in the cave. "Not even the angry one?"

"No, I don't think so," said Farrin. "Lurgl might seem relaxed, but he runs a pretty tight ship. He won't tolerate any violence against you, not if he's given you leave to stay."

She nodded slowly. "So he's the leader, is he? I got that impression." She cast a searching look over Farrin, and he suddenly had to fight the urge to fidget. "Thank you for helping me last night. Why did you do it?"

"I could see you were in desperate need of someone's help," he said simply. "And there was no one but me to help you."

She seemed stumped by this prosaic reply, but after a moment, her forehead creased again. "But why didn't you reveal yourself?"

"I didn't know who you were, or whether to trust you," he said.

She looked like she wasn't sure whether to be amused or offended. "You really thought I looked like a threat?"

Farrin shrugged, unashamed of his caution. "In the jungle, the apparent absence of a threat can be very deceptive. I haven't survived this long by making assumptions, or rushing in when a more careful approach was available. You were unknown, and therefore potentially dangerous. In the two years I've been here, I've never seen another human on the ground."

"Two years?" she repeated, clearly startled. "You mean you've been on the ground for two years?"

"I mean I've been in Selvana for two years," he said.

"But...how did you get here?" she asked. Before Farrin could answer, her eyes went wide. "You're from that ship?" Her voice had dropped to a whisper. "The one which flew the Medullan flag?"

"But which was sunk anyway," Farrin said, his voice hard. "Yes."

The girl bit her lip, looking suddenly—and inexplicably—close to tears. "I'm sorry," she whispered.

Farrin regarded her, surprised by her reaction. For his part, it was strangely easy not to indulge in the emotions that usually accompanied the memory of that night. He had other things to occupy his mind in this moment.

"It's not your fault," he said evenly. "I assume you didn't load the cannons."

She kept her eyes lowered, making no response for a long moment. When she looked up, her expression was still heavy.

"Were there any other survivors?"

"I don't think so," Farrin said.

She nodded. "What did you mean before, when you said the wild magic wouldn't kill me without intervention?"

Farrin shrugged, slinging his perfectly mended bow over his shoulder. "Just that while you're clearly able to survive contact with the magic-soaked ground, someone—the elves, for example—could still use magic to attack you."

She frowned. "The stories do say that the elves could wield the magic. But I never understood how it worked."

"They can't channel it through themselves like singers can," Farrin said. "Their bodies aren't susceptible to it in the same way, which is why the wild magic doesn't overwhelm their senses and kill them. But they can mine it, and store it in talismans, which they can then use for specified purposes."

"Talismans?" the girl repeated, looking lost.

Farrin let out a breath. She really knew nothing, it seemed. Astounding for a singer.

"Magical objects," he explained, clearing his throat. He couldn't remember the last time he'd spoken this much in one go. "Enchanted to perform magical functions."

"The mirror," she muttered. "It must have been a talisman."

Farrin said nothing, watching her as she thought. After a moment, she looked up.

"You said singers can channel magic through themselves? How can you be sure I am one of these singers?"

"Because you can sing," he said incredulously. "That's what a singer is. Anyone born with the ability to sing *is* a singer. They can draw the magic up from the land and channel it for all kinds of purposes, according to their training. Anyone who can't sing...can't do that. And can't learn. You have it or you don't."

He frowned. "Surely you know your singing—making your words dance, you called it—is unusual. Or can lots of other people do that up there in Sel?" He waved a hand in the general direction of the canopy city.

She shook her head. "I've never heard of anyone but me doing it. Everyone's always seemed so astonished by it—I don't think anyone in Sel knows what *singing* is. Maybe we did once, but..."

She trailed off, looking troubled. "So that's why strange things have often happened when I make my words dance?" she asked.

In spite of the heavy heat of the jungle, she shivered, bringing her raw, bleeding hands up to rub along her arms. In the process, she scratched absently at one of the many mosquito bites he'd noticed dotting her skin. Those must have been driving her crazy when her hands were bound.

"Is that why the elves want me?" she asked. "Do you think Dionysius is right, and they knew I'd survive being on the ground?"

"Most likely," Farrin told her honestly. "It's like Dionysius said. There would be no point tying you up if you were being pushed to your death."

The girl frowned. "So is that the reason I survived, then? Because I'm one of these singers?"

"I think so," Farrin said slowly. "I don't pretend to be any authority. But since you can channel the magic, you're probably not at risk of being overwhelmed by it, like most people would be. I suppose it must pass through your body rather than destroying it."

She blinked, looking so confused he couldn't help but feel sorry for her.

"Is that why you can survive down here?" she asked. "Are you a singer, too?"

Farrin shook his head. "I'm definitely not a singer. I've never been able to sing a word in my life." He frowned as he wrestled with the old question, seeing again in his mind's eye the confronting sight of the sailor who'd followed him from the water that awful night. "I don't know why I can survive on the Selvanan ground. It's not what I expected."

"That makes two of us," the girl said faintly.

Her forehead creased in thought as she ran a hand through her glowing, colorless hair. Farrin's eyes followed the gesture.

"But the elves apparently *did* expect it," she mused. "Was it just because they saw me survive being dropped onto the ground when I was a baby? Did my survival tell them I'd be a singer? Either way, they obviously had a purpose in mind when they orchestrated my abduction. What exactly would they do with me if they got their hands on me?"

"That I can't answer," said Farrin shortly. "But I doubt you want to find out."

She groaned, running both hands over her face, the movement not quite steady. "This is not how I expected my birthday to go," she muttered.

Farrin paused. "Today is your birthday?"

She lowered her hands quickly, looking flustered. "Never mind that," she said. "Do you think the other elves will find me here? The ones who made the deal with my—with the queen?"

Farrin took note of her stumble. He wasn't sure what she was hiding, but there was definitely something. And he had no doubt it would come out soon enough. This girl wasn't practiced at deception, that much was certain.

"It's possible they'll find you here," he told her matter-of-factly. "But it's more likely they'd find you if you wandered out into the jungle. If you want my advice, I would say your safest course is to stay here." He glanced at her hands, which were once again scratching, trying to think just of the practicalities, not of the sympathy that still threatened his much-needed detachment.

"You shouldn't scratch your bites," he said abruptly. "I know it's maddening, but they'll go down more quickly if you leave them."

"I know that," she sighed. "I just can't help myself."

"Take this," he said, pulling a wad of leaves from one pocket of his breeches. "Crush it up and rub it on the bites. It'll help. There are other plants you can use to repel them, as well. You'll need it down here, trust me."

"Thank you," she said.

He nodded. "Your wrists need attention, too, although I don't have anything for those. I know Eason has some healing salve. See if you can get him to give you some." He frowned, remembering how utterly inexperienced she was with elves. "But don't make a bargain with him for it if you can help it. Try to trick him into giving it to you for free."

"Trick him?" she repeated, sounding a little scandalized. "That seems underhanded."

Farrin chuckled. "If you're worried he'd resent it, don't be. They'll put on outrage or offense if they think they can use it to manipulate you, but the truth is that any elf would respect you more for managing to hoodwink them into giving you something. If he insists on a bargain, make sure the terms are very clear, and the cost to you isn't unreasonably high." He frowned.

"You know what, maybe I'd better speak to him for you before I go."

"No." The girl surprised him with the strength of her reply. "I don't need anyone to speak for me. I can handle myself."

Farrin regarded her with some amusement, although he tried to hide it for the sake of her dignity. Clearly, he'd ruffled her feathers.

"All right," he said. "If you say so. I have no desire to interfere."

"Wait," she said, reaching out and grabbing his arm as he turned away.

Farrin stilled, completely thrown by the touch. Elves weren't demonstrative by nature, to say the least. It had been two years since he'd been willingly touched by any creature other than Lottie. A storm of emotions, long held down, surged toward the surface of his awareness, almost breaking free of his control. For a moment he teetered, right on the edge of a terrifyingly bottomless well of loneliness that seemed to be waiting to suck him down and under. He mastered the feeling with an effort, raising his eyes to meet the girl's pleading ones.

"I didn't mean to offend you," she said, sounding anxious. "I don't want you to think I don't appreciate your help. I do." Her grip tightened on his arm, and her voice clogged a little. "You saved my life," she added earnestly. "I'm in your debt forever."

Farrin chuckled, as much to hide his embarrassing rush of emotions as anything. "For the love of all you hold dear, don't ever say anything like that to an elf." His smile grew more natural as he looked down into her undeniably beautiful face. He never would have thought white hair would be attractive on someone so young, but stars above, the contrast was breathtaking. "I'm not offended," he assured her. "I just have places I need to be."

She nodded, releasing his arm and looking—if he wasn't mistaken—a little forlorn.

"Of course. I shouldn't keep you."

"I'll return," he promised, then paused. Two years in close proximity with elves had taught him to be very cautious when making anything resembling a promise. "Well, provided the jungle doesn't swallow me up. Which is always a possibility." He gave her another smile, the expression not as familiar to his face as it once was. "Until then, look after yourself, Bee."

She hesitated, her eyes searching his face. "You're from Medulle?"

He nodded, tensing a little. He didn't want to answer any searching questions about his identity, not when he'd gone two years without the elves even suspecting who he was.

"Do you know much of the Selvanans?" Bee asked tentatively.

"The humans, you mean?" Farrin asked. He shook his head. "Almost nothing. I took the cannon fire as a sign it was best not to climb up and knock on any doors."

She hung her head, nodding in acknowledgment. "That's fair," she said, her voice soft and sad. Forcing a smile, she looked up at him. "Well, thank you again, Farrin," she said. "And Bee is just a nickname. My name is Bianca."

"Bianca," he repeated, finding that he liked the way it rolled from his mouth. It was musical, like her. A good name for a singer. "Well met. And happy birthday."

With a final nod, he grabbed hold of the closest branch, swinging himself up into the tree and ascending toward the canopy with light steps. Instantly the pressure from the wild magic lessened, and he breathed a little more freely. Lottie leaped up beside him, keeping pace with ease as they moved away from the clearing.

They traveled quickly through the jungle, but Farrin's thoughts stayed behind, dwelling obsessively on the girl.

Bianca.

Whatever he'd said about having places he needed to be, he had nothing to do which took precedence over her dramatic arrival. He wasn't going to be searching for aconitum today. He was going to find out what was happening in Sel.

The ocelot stayed with him as he moved southward. He kept running through Bianca's revelations in his mind. Even more astonishing than the fact that she was a singer was how little she knew about her own capacity for magic. Had it really been so long since Selvana had seen any singers? She hadn't even recognized the word, let alone understood how to channel magic through her song. It was a shame for her to go through so much of her life without learning her craft at all. Not that it was too late to learn, of course. She'd said it was her birthday today. How old was she? Not more than eighteen or nineteen, surely.

Farrin's pace slowed as he moved further south. The thought of approaching the human city made him nervous. He'd been careful to avoid it for two years. But he needed answers. Something was definitely going on, something very different from the status quo he'd seen since arriving on the island. And although Bianca might be keeping some details to herself, it seemed highly unlikely that she had the explanations. Not when she knew so little about the basic realities of her own situation.

The morning was advanced when Farrin reached the outskirts of the human city. He'd traveled in the trees when he could, and the rest of the time on the ground. As always, he'd been careful not to descend until he was far from the clearing with the cottage. The elves would never let him come back if he left tracks that might betray their location. And he had a new, and incredibly compelling, reason to want to return.

Again, Bianca's striking face filled his mind, her expression uncertain but her eyes determined as she said she could handle herself. Farrin tried to shake the image off—it wasn't the time to get distracted. He'd slept little in his makeshift camp near the clearing, and his head felt heavy and sluggish. But he kept his eyes and ears open, knowing he couldn't afford to let his guard down. Lottie helped on that front—if danger was approaching, she would alert him long before his dull human senses would.

Not that he especially needed the ocelot's help to identify the group moving westward through the trees. Their voices were loud, and they displayed no signs of stealth as they trudged across the wooden walkway above. Farrin slipped into a hollowed-out trunk, going still and trusting his earthy garb to disguise him. It was a far cry from the embroidered tunic he'd worn when he first set foot on Selvanan soil.

As he expected, none of the passing group even glanced down as they moved overhead. Harvesters, he decided, after a moment's cursory observation. This was a well-used route, and Farrin knew of a natural grove not far away, with a thickly clustered concentration of sapucaia trees. He'd stolen the odd paradise nut from the grove in passing himself. The area was also richly crowded with passionfruit vines, so perhaps the fruit was the true target of the harvest.

"Thought you weren't coming on today's harvest?" one voice carried down to Farrin's hiding place.

The man's companion grunted. "I promised to take me daughter to watch the coronation. But that's neither 'ere nor there now, is it?"

Coronation? Farrin frowned, slipping from his hiding place and moving through the undergrowth on silent feet, following the progress of the conversation above.

"Terrible business," said a third voice, this one belonging to a woman. "It's years since we've had anyone fall. How it could happen to a princess beats me!"

# CHAPTER TWELVE

# FARRIN

Farrin drew in a sharp breath. Princess? Bianca was a princess. So that was what she'd been hiding so inexpertly.

It took him a moment to process the rest of the harvesters' words. His mind was too caught on a detail which was trivial in light of everything, but which his thoughts couldn't seem to move past. He was a prince in hiding, and she was a princess attempting to hide. He wasn't sure whether it was humorous or tragic.

Eventually he caught up with the conversation. The harvesters had spoken of a canceled coronation. He frowned as he remembered what Bianca had let slip. Today must be her eighteenth birthday, the date she was supposed to be crowned. He'd been truthful when he told her he didn't know much of the people who lived in Sel. But the elves at the cottage knew more than he did, and they discussed the human city occasionally. He'd heard Lurgl speak of the widowed queen, with her two daughters, only the younger of whom shared her blood. The elf had never seemed overly invested in the situation, but Farrin had heard him call the queen an imposter once, because she was ruling in her dead husband's place instead of handing control to the young crown princess.

And now, on the eve of her coronation, that princess had been pushed to the jungle floor, given to the merciless elves as some kind of sacrifice to satisfy a bargain made long ago by the imposter queen.

Farrin's face hardened. It was increasingly difficult not to let the sympathy overwhelm his tight hold on his emotions.

At least the information regarding Bianca's identity answered the question of how the queen's attention had been drawn to her when she was an infant. No wonder the poor girl was so unprepared to be turned loose all on her own. He remembered Lurgl's words about the queen dropping Bianca as a baby...the elf knew who Bianca was. He must do. And yet he hadn't shared that information. Farrin pursed his lips in thought. Lurgl must have his reasons.

"She was so young," the woman above was saying mournfully. "And so very beautiful. Such a tragic end to her life."

"Aye," agreed the man who'd spoken of the coronation. "Me little girl is heartbroken. Princess Bianca was her hero. She met her last year—me lass was crying over an unripe mango. I'd told her it was too soon to pick it, but she didn't listen. She's only three, you know. Well, our Snow Princess was passing by and heard her crying. She knelt to comfort her, and put a hand on the mango, and it ripened right before our eyes!"

Farrin barely heard the sorrowful murmurs of the man's companions, too caught on the nickname. What did these Selvanans know of snow? If he'd had any doubt the supposedly dead princess was Bianca—which he hadn't—it would have disappeared on hearing that description. She'd said herself she didn't know how her hair was like that. It must be as unusual here as it would be in Medulle.

"We'll miss those dancing words, no question," said the

woman sadly. "It was almost like a kind of magic, the touch she had. We'll probably never see her like again. Terrible to have a funeral in place of a coronation."

"When is the funeral to be?" asked one of the others.

"I heard they still haven't found her body," responded the first.

"Really?" The woman sounded surprised. "I thought she'd already been recovered by use of the hooks."

The man grunted in contradiction. "They're keeping it pretty hush, but I overheard it on my way through the palace. Guards are out now looking, combing the area as best they can from the canopy."

The walkway was passing over a sparse section of undergrowth, and Farrin paused. It wasn't worth the risk of being seen. He'd heard all he needed to.

He waited until the voices had faded away, then slipped back the way he'd come, taking to the trees at the earliest opportunity. Banking on the fact that another group wouldn't follow the last so closely, he padded softly across the walkway, his gait uneven thanks to his limp. Lottie loped beside him most of the way.

When she suddenly leaped softly from the wooden railing to a nearby branch, the movement alerted Farrin to someone's approach. He followed, not quite as nimble as the jungle cat. Shortly after he'd reached the safety of a nearby tree and inched around its trunk out of sight, he heard it himself. Heavy footfalls and quiet voices. A guard patrol. He must be very near the city now.

It took only a moment to ascertain that this was a regular patrol, not a special search party. If the harvesters were right, and a search was underway for Bianca's body, it wasn't happening in this part of the jungle. Farrin eased down the trunk, dropping from branch to branch and gritting his teeth as the pressure of the wild magic pushed harder on him the further he descended.

At last, he lowered himself lightly to the ground, feeling the wave of pressure—uncomfortable almost to the point of pain—that rushed forward to meet him, as always.

In two years of exposure, he'd grown used to the presence of the wild magic. But that didn't mean it was gone, and it didn't mean he couldn't feel it anymore. It was always harder to breathe, harder to find energy when he was on the ground. Whatever force had woken in him when he first made landfall on the island lived still, pushing back constantly against the wild magic's assault. But it could only hold it at bay. It could never actually drive it off.

Sometimes Farrin wondered whether the air would feel disconcertingly thin and empty if he ever made it back to Medulle. Perhaps he'd lose his balance as he found himself moving with the expectation of resistance which didn't come.

He repelled the image violently. It was exactly the type of thought he couldn't indulge in, not if he was going to cope with his present situation. Deep within himself, he understood that his continued determination to find the aconitum meant that he was still trying to make it home and rescue Emmett from the nightmare he must be living. But he didn't let himself think about that eventual goal—he only allowed himself to focus on the troubles of the day.

Making it to another nightfall, keeping the rhythm of this life going.

Time seemed different now from what it used to be. Even if he hadn't become stranded here, he would still have been forced to acknowledge the childishness of his intentions when he set sail from Port Dulla. Like a fool, he'd expected to find the aconitum within days and head straight home. He'd been searching for two years, and there was still plenty of jungle to cover. Perhaps it would take him a decade.

He shrugged off the thought as he moved quietly through the undergrowth, heading for the place where he'd found Bianca the night before. If he was going to be in Selvana for years more, it was all the more reason to spend his energy learning to better navigate the environment rather than dreaming of ways to get home. In itself, the idea of a prolonged residence on the island didn't even daunt him anymore. There was a beauty to the place, as wild as the magic that made it largely uninhabitable. He'd come to appreciate it in spite of himself.

The sound of voices brought Farrin to a stop shortly before he reached the place in question. He took shelter behind the covering nook of a kapok tree, listening to the speakers, who were of course up in the canopy.

"There." The voice was commanding and certain, nothing like the subdued mutterings of the harvesters. "Is that a rope down there?"

"I can't tell from up here," responded another voice, sounding much less confident. "It's probably a vine."

"I don't think so," the first man replied.

His eyes searching the undergrowth, Farrin caught a glimpse of the very rope he'd watched Lottie gnaw from Bianca's waist hours before. They'd found the right place, at any rate.

Farrin shifted position, trying to catch a glimpse of the speakers without exposing too much of himself to view. He saw a flash of movement in the trees high above. There were no walkways here—the men must be climbing free across the canopy. It was a skill cultivated by fewer of the Selvanans than Farrin had at first expected. Perhaps that was why the second speaker sounded nervous.

"Come on, Horace, there's nothing to find," the man in question said. "I don't like it any more than you do, but the princess is long gone by now."

"Long gone where?" barked the deeper voice. "You said you saw her fall. So where's the body?"

"I told you, she fell into dense foliage," said his companion, sounding petulant.

"My own squadron searched that patch of foliage with the grappling hooks," the man called Horace replied. "They pulled up nothing but plants. They had huntsmen among them, skilled with retrieving catches. If her body was there, they would have found her."

"What are you suggesting?" the other man said, exasperated. "I saw her fall, Horace. She's dead. You have to accept it."

"I'll accept it when I see the body," said Horace curtly. "Are you blind, man? You think I'm wandering aimlessly? There was a clear trail back there, and it led to that rope. How do you think it got there?"

"Firstly, it's a vine," said his companion. "Secondly..." He hesitated. "Well, isn't it obvious? I'd rather not dwell on it, but surely you realize what happened. A predator found the body before your men ever got to it, and dragged it off. What else could cause the tracks?"

Horace was silent for a moment. "Maybe that's what happened," he said flatly. "Maybe it isn't." Farrin heard a hard note creep into the older man's voice. "Maybe there's more to this tale than I've been told."

"I don't know what you mean by that." The other man was clearly hedging.

"You hold yourself mighty smugly for a man who failed in his most primary duty," Horace snapped back. "You clearly don't grasp what it means to be a guard. But I've been guarding Selvana's queen since before you learned to hold a bow, *huntsman*, and I would sooner die than let our crown princess fall to her death. How is it you saw her fall and did nothing? And no one even alerted me to search for the body until this morning!"

"I'm not smug," said the other guard, outraged. "I'm as devastated as anyone about what happened to Princess Bianca. If I could have gotten to her in time, I would have. And I don't know why you think anyone should have alerted *you*. You were never on the princess's detail. Your job is to guard the queen."

"Exactly." Horace's reply was so quiet, Farrin couldn't be sure he heard it right.

"It sounds to me like your loyalty is in question." There was a dangerous edge to the younger guard's voice now.

"My loyalty has *never* been questioned," growled the one called Horace. "And my orders come from Queen Marisol directly. I'm to search for the princess's body. If you intend to get in my way, you can feel free to return to the city right now."

Farrin couldn't make out the other guard's resentful mutters, but he did hear Horace's voice once again ring out.

"I'm going lower."

Judging it time to be gone, Farrin detached himself from the trunk of the kapok tree, trying to move as stealthily as Lottie. The last thing he wanted was for these two guards to see him. He'd certainly been given plenty to think about.

The younger guard was clearly hiding something, but what? Was it only his own incompetence in failing to keep the princess safe? But if he truly had seen her fall, he must have seen that she was bound. Was he the one who'd bound her?

Farrin felt his teeth clench together at the thought, the strength of the reaction frightening him as his own emotions once again threatened to break free. But he couldn't deny the outrage he felt on Bianca's behalf. Perhaps it was because, while he had grown up surrounded by guards of his own, he'd always been encouraged to train, to be able to defend himself if necessary. Bianca clearly hadn't been given the same opportunity. And the idea of a guard—a man chosen for his strength, and trained to have the power that came from skill with weapons and combat—would not only fail to protect his charge, but actually turn his strength and training against her, intent on bringing about her gruesome death...

Every instinct within Farrin rebelled against such repulsive conduct.

But of course, it was entirely possible that the guard hadn't actually seen what had happened. Perhaps he was covering for himself. He certainly seemed the more suspicious, but it was the older one—Horace, he'd been called—who had explicitly stated that he acted on Queen Marisol's orders. If the queen had intended Bianca to be handed to the elves, and if she had a way of communicating with the elves, she must know they'd never received the prisoner. Perhaps the queen really did want confirmation of whether Bianca had been killed by the jungle.

And what would she do if she couldn't find that confirmation?

What would she do—what would either of those guards do —if they found Bianca herself?

Farrin's unease only grew as he took a circuitous route away from the site. Afraid of being seen, he hadn't even gone on to check whether the mutilated deer was still there to be found, or whether a predator had come and finished the task he'd framed such a creature for starting. He didn't know which, if either, of those guards was being honest with the other.

But he did know one thing—he wouldn't trust either of them for a moment. Not with Bianca's life.

And why was her life suddenly so precious in his estimation? The thought was more troubling than all the rest. He'd never wanted to see anyone killed, but it was more than that. He felt almost panicked at the thought of the hesitant young princess in the hands of these potentially unscrupulous men. And he couldn't afford that kind of investment in a stranger, over whose fate he had no control.

There was a lot to get his head around. Calling Lottie with a soft whistle, he turned southward, away from the cottage in the cave. He'd told Bianca he'd return, but he hadn't committed himself to any specific time. If he didn't give himself space to recalibrate, the emotions he'd held at bay for two long years would rise up and claim him the next time those trusting brown eyes met his appealingly.

He needed to think things through, and nothing would aid that process like solitude.

# CHAPTER THIRTEEN

# Bianca

Bianca stared into the trees where Farrin had disappeared, feeling foolishly lost without him. He hadn't exactly been warm, but he had been...well, human. Much less daunting than the seven elves now bustling about the clearing. A few hours before, she'd thought elves little more than a legend, creatures lost in the past, at least as far as Selvana was concerned.

Now, she seemed to be living with a bevy of them. And she had no idea how to navigate their peculiar ways.

Her chafed wrists throbbed viciously, the sensation reminding her of Farrin's words about the elf called Eason having healing salve. Suddenly, she remembered her own words when Farrin had offered to speak to the elf on her behalf.

*I don't need anyone to speak for me. I can handle myself.*

Well, she'd best prove that true, for her own peace of mind if nothing else. She marched back toward the cottage, relishing the freedom of movement that came from her hands being loose. She didn't feel she'd sufficiently thanked Farrin for that service. Her expression of gratitude had been a little lost in the subsequent uproar over her *singing*, as he'd called it.

A shiver went over Bianca, half fear, half excitement. It hardly seemed possible that Farrin could be right, but it made no sense to doubt his words. He must be telling the truth.

But how? It was so impossible, so absurd. She couldn't wield the magic of this land. No one could. They hadn't been able to in generations. The magic was simply too wild, too powerful to be harnessed. Of course, they supposedly hadn't been able to safely descend to the ground in generations either, yet here she was. The pressure remained steady, but already she was adjusting to it. With the removal of the rope from around her waist, she could breathe again, and she found the intensity of the wild magic's press was considerably lessened.

She was fairly sure she knew which elf was Eason, and she didn't spot him outside the cottage. Entering the dwelling with a show of boldness she was far from feeling, she scanned the room.

There he was, bending low over a cauldron which bubbled over the fire in the corner. Bianca strode up to the small figure, noting with interest that when he threw a pinch of some kind of powder into the cauldron, there was a definite glow to the puff of smoke which billowed out and up the small chimney.

"Did you just use magic in that stew?" she asked curiously.

Eason looked up, sending her the ghost of a wink. "Don't tell Lurgl. He doesn't like us wasting our stores on matters relating purely to comfort, but I have no interest in eating flavorless stew. And flavorless is all I can achieve without magic."

Bianca peered into the cauldron, fascinated. "So the magic makes it taste better? How?"

"Well, it's not exactly the magic that makes it taste better," Eason said matter-of-factly. "It's the cinnamon. But we don't harvest it for cooking. We mine it for magic. These plants are highly imbued with the stuff. They're not intended for eating."

Bianca stared at him. "Cinnamon has magic in it? Is that why it's so rare?"

Eason snorted. "It's not rare. Your people might be too afraid to harvest it because the trees don't grow far above the ground, but it's everywhere down here." He shook his head. "And if the plant has grown high enough for your lot to reach it, I doubt there's any magic left in it."

There was a definite edge of condescension to his words, and Bianca decided to move on from the topic.

"Farrin told me you might have healing salve," she said. It was probably too abrupt, but her wrists were stinging furiously. "Did he mean salve with some kind of healing magic in it? Or just soothing?"

"How should I know what he meant?" Eason said shortly. "I didn't place the thoughts in his head, or pull the words from his mouth."

Bianca tried to keep her patience. "And yet, I feel sure you have an educated guess."

Eason flashed her a grin, as if he'd warmed to her in spite of himself. "I do," he confirmed.

Bianca waited, but he said no more. She remembered Arbor's earlier comment about elves not giving information away for free, and gave up on getting a straight answer from Eason. Honestly, at this point it didn't matter whether there was magic in the salve. She'd take it either way.

"Can I please have some of the salve?" she asked, getting the words out as politely as she could around her teeth, which were gritted in pain.

"In exchange for what?" Eason asked, the words almost lazy, like they were a reflex rather than a specific thought.

Bianca hesitated, thrown. What could she offer him? "I have gold, back in Sel," she said uncertainly. "But I don't know if and when I'll be able to access it again. So I don't think I can offer to pay for the salve."

"Not interested in gold," said Eason dismissively. His attention was back on the cauldron, and Bianca could tell that he felt confident he held the upper hand.

She scowled, watching him add another liberal pinch of cinnamon, which sent a small puff of purple smoke upward. A thought tickled her mind. Farrin had said she should try to avoid making a bargain for the salve, but that ship had clearly sailed. He'd also said to trick Eason if she could. She hadn't liked the idea, but she was fast getting the sense that a dash of deviousness was a necessity for survival among elves.

"Your salve for my silence regarding your use of the cinnamon," she said curtly. "If you let me apply a liberal amount of salve to my wrists..." She paused, remembering that Farrin had said to make the terms clear. "By liberal, I mean enough salve to cover every visibly chafed section of my skin," she amended. "If you let me apply that much salve to my wrists right now, I won't mention to Lurgl or any of the other five elves who live here, either now or in the future, that you used cinnamon harvested for its magic in the cooking of this morning's stew."

Eason had stopped cooking now, his full attention on Bianca, and his eyes narrowed. "Are you threatening me?" he demanded. "Blackmailing me?"

Bianca forced herself to stay still, fighting the urge to squirm under those hard, calculating eyes.

"Not at all," she said stoutly. "I'm offering you an exchange. A reasonable one, in my opinion."

She thought she saw a flicker of amusement in Eason's eyes, but his frigid tone didn't support the idea. "Reasonable, you call it?" the elf repeated, the tips of his ears wiggling in his indignation. "I gave you that information from the goodness of my heart, as a gesture of goodwill. And now you seek to use it against me?"

"I appreciate the gesture," Bianca said evenly, again remembering Farrin's comments. He'd said the elves would use offense to manipulate her if she let them. "And I would like to stay silent on the matter as a sign of my goodwill," she saw Eason's eyes light up, and hastened to finish, "as generated by your agreement to let me use your salve in exchange, as discussed."

Eason regarded her for a moment, his startlingly green eyes so narrowed she could barely see the color. Then he relaxed, all at once breaking into a grin.

"You learn quickly, Bee, I'll give you that." He held out his hand, and his voice took on a formal, slightly pompous tone. "Due to the nature of the bargain—that is, involving an exchange of silence—witnesses would invalidate our agreement. But I will trust your honor."

"You can safely do that," Bianca assured him, shaking the offered hand. Her own hand, which she generally thought of as slender, dwarfed the elf's. The motion caused her billowing sleeves—not as white as they'd been when she donned the gown—to rub against her chafed wrists, and she winced.

"The salve," said Eason in a businesslike voice. "I will fetch it."

He did so efficiently, and watched meticulously as Bianca applied it. She took care to follow her own parameters exactly, applying no more salve than she'd described. To her immense relief, the effects were almost instantaneous. She'd barely handed the jar back to Eason—who immediately sealed it again and stashed it out of sight—when she began to feel the pain ease.

"It does have some kind of healing magic in it, doesn't it?" she breathed, gratitude coursing through her.

"Yep," Eason said cheerfully, his attention back on his stew. "So you see, you got an absolute bargain."

Bianca just gave a contented sigh, not sure whether agreeing verbally would obligate her to pay extra. It was exhausting, all the deals and the careful phrasing. It was going to take some getting used to if she was really staying here.

The thought sobered her. Was she really staying here? It seemed ridiculous, but what other option did she have? She could return to Sel, of course, and take her chances. But she was no wiser than she had been the night before about whom she could trust.

"You said Farrin told you I had the salve?" Eason asked abruptly.

Bianca nodded, wary once again.

"Did he coach you on how to ask me for it?" the elf demanded.

Bianca let out a sigh, too weary to be careful with every word. "Only a little," she said.

Eason muttered to himself for a moment, then gave a sigh of his own. "Typical human behavior. Always poking their noses in, trying to help people who they've no business helping. As bad as Lurgl, honestly."

He cast her an appraising look, a smile once again lurking in his eyes in spite of his severe tone.

"No, what am I saying? The huntsman is worse than Lurgl, no question. Trying to help someone else is what's gotten him into this whole mess, isn't it?"

"I don't know," said Bianca, unable to keep the avid curiosity from her voice. "Is it? What brought him to Selvana, anyway?"

"Ah ah ah." The elf held up an admonitory finger. "No more information for free."

With a laugh, Bianca gave up on him, wandering across the room toward the lone hammock she'd noticed the night before.

Raella had seemed a little more sympathetic when Bianca's unsuspected magic was revealed, even going so far as to say that she wanted to protect her. Perhaps she would be more willing to answer questions without tedious bargaining.

The female elf was crouched below her hammock, disemboweling a bag with astonishing ferocity as she searched for something.

"Where *is* that brush?" she demanded of no one in particular.

Bianca picked her way through the mess that now formed a sizable ring around Raella's sleeping quarters.

"Can I help with something?" she asked politely.

Raella's head shot up at the simple words. "In exchange for what?"

Bianca sighed at the familiar phrase. "Is that really necessary?"

Raella shrugged, sticking her head back into the bag so that her voice came out muffled. "I imagine your people have many practices that seem foolish to us, but which you consider necessary."

"Probably true," acknowledged Bianca, quite struck by this perspective on the matter.

"I wasn't asking something of you," Raella reminded her, emerging again. "You offered to help, and I was rescuing you from giving your assistance for free instead of negotiating a reasonable exchange." She grinned as her hand closed over something in the bag. "It's irrelevant now, anyway. I found it."

She pulled out a hairbrush, much smaller than the one on Bianca's dresser at home. An unexpected pang went through Bianca at the thought of her familiar room. Would she ever see it again? Was Ilse even now wandering in from her own adjoining room, her heart breaking over her sister's disappearance?

Unless Ilse had been part of the plot.

*No!* Bianca silenced that suspicious voice, unable to bear living alongside it in her head.

"So you're a singer."

Raella stated the words as fact, sitting back against a chest as she ran the brush through her hair, which Bianca noticed was dotted with twigs. What had the elves been doing all night, anyway?

"Apparently," said Bianca wearily. "Although I have no more idea than you do, really. I'm just taking Farrin's word for it."

"Well, Farrin would know, wouldn't he?" Raella said, her tone skeptical in spite of the confidence of her words. "He comes from the mainland, where there are singers everywhere, aren't there?"

"Are there?" Bianca asked faintly. It was a tantalizing image, but also a little overwhelming.

"Don't you know your own history, girl?" Raella asked impatiently. "That's why the elves wanted humans to come to Selvana in the first place."

"Stop giving important information away for free," Arbor barked as he trotted past.

Raella rolled her eyes, but she fell silent. Bianca didn't push her. She wasn't sure how many big revelations she could handle in one morning. She searched her mind for questions which were of interest to her, but might not be considered big enough to barter for.

"What's the story with Farrin's ocelot?"

"Lottie doesn't belong to Farrin," grunted Raella. "She was hanging around here long before he showed up. She liked to beg for scraps and such, but she hadn't really attached herself to anyone in particular. Then Farrin shows up, and she's smitten after one glance at those big brown eyes." She cast an appraising look at Bianca. "Just like you, eh?"

To her intense irritation, Bianca felt heat rising up her face. "Nonsense," she said flatly.

Raella just grunted again, although her eyes held the same humor Eason's had. "Well, Lottie's been stuck to his side ever since." She struggled to her feet, tromping straight over the items she'd discarded from her bag. "I suppose you want your hammock set up, do you? Well, we have a few spares."

Bianca leaped up, thanks rising to her lips, but Raella waved her off. "No need for thanks and exchanges," she said impatiently. "You don't have to barter for a simple hammock string-up. Not with me."

Bianca said nothing, taken aback by the suggestion that an expression of thanks was in the same category as an exchange. Such curious creatures these mythical elves were.

She hadn't slept in a hammock since she'd been a child, when she and Ilse had done so as a game, pretending to be harvesters on exploratory trips, or messengers traveling the dangerous route through the unbroken canopy to the southern settlement. But she knew how to set them up safely. She helped Raella string it across the space, just next to hers.

"There we go, that's nicely inside the ward," said the female elf with satisfaction.

"Inside the ward?" Bianca repeated.

Raella nodded. "We don't just mine magic for communal uses, Bee. We all search for our own stores, too. I keep a steady supply of the stuff for my own privacy wards. How else could I live with a bunch of slobs in a single room dwelling? When we're in this corner, we can activate it with a word, and then they can't see us. We can change clothes, the works, no one would be any the wiser."

"Well, that's reassuring," said Bianca politely.

"Speaking of wards, let's see how Lurgl's getting on," Raella said, traipsing away from their hammocks and toward the cottage's door.

Bianca followed, casting a glance between the tidy and well-kept space around the hammocks and beds of the other elves—the so-called slobs—and the disaster that was Raella's sleeping area, still littered with the discarded belongings she'd shown no sign of picking up. Perhaps there was a reason Lurgl had been holding back laughter at Raella's claim that the other elves all lived like pigs, with only her to keep them in line.

"So you mine magic from the ground?" Bianca asked, catching up with Raella.

The elf grunted. "In a nutshell, yes."

"Could I do it, too, if I came with you?"

Another grunt. "No."

Bianca frowned. "No, I can't come with you, or no, I couldn't do it even if I did come?"

"Both," said Raella. "I don't want responsibility for you out there, and humans can't mine magic. Your bodies are too susceptible to it. To mine it, you have to drill down until you reach it in its raw form. If a human touches magic in that form, it enters their body. Singers can channel it and release it immediately as power, but other humans...well, it messes them up. In neither case can they mine it for storage and later use."

She increased her speed, as if to leave Bianca and her pesky questions behind. But of course, Bianca just lengthened her stride, keeping up with the diminutive elf with ease.

"How you gettin' on, Lurgl?" Raella asked, as they drew close to the other elf.

He stood halfway across the clearing, his small frame braced in a determined stance as he looked out toward the jungle.

"Good," he said distractedly, reaching into a jar in his hand and grasping some kind of fine dust. "Almost done."

He threw the dust up in front of him, and to Bianca's fascination, it didn't fall to the ground as she would expect. It spread through the air, hanging impossibly in position in a shimmering formation, almost like a web. Glinting in the morning light, it slowly faded from view, but it didn't fall. In fact, she could sense it. Impossible to explain how, but she could feel that it was still hovering there.

"There," said Lurgl in satisfaction. "No one untrustworthy will be able to come through it."

Raella looked much less impressed than Bianca felt. The elf sighed as she eyed the collection of empty tubes and pots at Lurgl's feet. "Dionysius is right, you know. It does seem a bit of a waste of so much of our stores."

"It's not a waste of them," said Lurgl calmly, dropping the final container and turning to face them. His eyes lingered on Bianca, a cheerful smile curving his lips. "It's a use of them, and in my opinion, a very worthwhile one."

"Thank you," said Bianca, her voice a little choked. "I'm—"

"Don't say in my debt," Lurgl cut her off, looking pained. "It's much too early for bartering, not when I've had no sleep at all."

"For shame, Lurgl," Raella scolded. "Throwing away an opportunity like that."

"It wouldn't be appropriate to the situation," said Lurgl with dignity. "The ward is for all of us, Raella, not just for Bee. None of us want to be found here."

"True enough," she agreed begrudgingly.

"Come," said Lurgl, the note of command apparently uncon-scious, but nevertheless compelling. "Let's see if the meal is ready. I for one am desperate to reach my bed."

The three of them went back inside, to find Eason ladling out the stew. It had a definite scent of cinnamon, but no one else commented. Perhaps it was Bianca's heightened awareness of her own bargain that made the flavor stand out so much.

The meal was short and silent, everyone focused on their

stomachs alone. No one offered Bianca anything particularly, but neither did anyone challenge her helping herself to a generous serve of the delicious-smelling warm broth.

"Well," said Lurgl, rising from the table. "I'm for sleep." His eyes found Bianca. "Bee, you actually slept last night, unlike the rest of us. Perhaps you can take a turn on clean up while we all snatch a few hours." His eyes passed over the group, a stern note entering his voice. "Only a few hours, everyone. We want to return to nighttime sleeping tonight."

There were some grumbles, but no one actually protested.

"We don't usually mine at night," Raella told Bianca helpfully. "It's much more dangerous than during the day, which is why we have to do it all together, for best safety. But there are some plants that are most magical when harvested by moonlight, and every now and then we spend a night that way. We won't need to again for months, though, so it's best to get back into normal rhythms of sleep at once."

Bianca nodded, grateful for the explanation but already shrewd enough not to say so. In spite of her few hours of sleep and her healing wrists, she was wearier than she could ever remember being before. Cleaning up the mess from the meal would be task enough before collapsing into her own hammock. She didn't want to accidentally sign up to tidy Raella's belongings as well, or anything of that nature.

The elves had all dispersed with their usual rapidity, and Bianca was left with an almighty mess. Raella might be the only one who kept her personal space messy, but none of them seemed to eat neatly.

Bianca refused to be daunted, however. She didn't want any of them to know that she'd never had to clean up a meal before, and not just because she wanted to keep her identity quiet. It was surely well past time she learned to fend for herself. A shudder went over her at the memory of the guard's restraining grip. She should learn to fend for herself with more than just food, if it came to that.

A doubtful glance at the seven elves in the room—all of whom seemed to have gone instantly from wakefulness to slumber—didn't give her any reason to think they would be either willing or able to teach her to fight.

That left only one other option. Would Farrin be open to the idea? Impossible to tell. And yet, Bianca found to her own embarrassment as she performed the slowest clean up in history, it was equally impossible not to dwell on the missing human. Raella had accused her of being besotted, and that really was ridiculous. But she couldn't deny to herself that she was intrigued by the Medullan.

He'd promised he would come back. She could only hope it would be soon.

# CHAPTER FOURTEEN

## *Bianca*

By the time Bianca had been at the cottage for a week, she'd just about lost hope that Farrin would return at all. Perhaps he really had been swallowed by the jungle, as he'd told her was possible.

None of the elves seemed concerned by his absence, although she couldn't tell if that was because they thought he was fine, or because they didn't especially care. Elves were hard to read like that.

They were also inflexible, she'd quickly discovered. Raella's refusal to take her on a mining expedition was echoed by each of the other six, and no persuasions had softened them. Lurgl seemed the least irritated by her repeated requests, but he remained firm. He explained to her that she was safe within his ward, but if she left the clearing, she would be at risk not only from the jungle but from the rest of the elves, whom he suspected would still be seeking her. And it seemed none of the elves, not even Lurgl, were willing to take responsibility for her safety while they were mining.

Princess though she was, Bianca wasn't used to such a level of restriction. She'd always been allowed to roam fairly free, at least within certain boundaries. And those boundaries had always been bigger than a small jungle clearing.

Still, she was determined not to focus on the negative. Instead, she reminded herself daily that she was lucky to be alive, and threw herself into her chores. There was certainly plenty to be learned in that arena. When she was first told how many tasks would be required of her, she'd wondered if the elves were trying to exploit her, and whether she should be bartering with them. But she quickly observed all of them taking their turns at the cooking, the cleaning, the mending, and all the other domestic chores that were apparently necessary to run a household.

Of course, she suspected that most of them would have been only too pleased to exploit her for the tasks if they could get away with it. But Lurgl ran a tight operation, and he expected everyone to contribute. Bianca respected him all the more for it. In fact, with each day that passed, her respect for the placid elf grew. She wasn't sure how the elves had all come to be here, but she got the impression he'd been the first to seek refuge in the cottage. They all deferred to him, at any rate, even the irascible Dionysius.

Lurgl might be unwilling to take her out into the jungle to mine magic, but he was at least receptive to her questions about her own apparently magical abilities. Even if he often didn't have the answers.

"So how do I pull magic out of the ground?" Bianca asked him, as she followed him across the cottage one morning.

All seven of the elves were on their way out for a day of mining in the jungle, each wearing a rucksack full of containers and specimen jars of all shapes and sizes, with a variety of tools strapped to their belts.

"I don't know the mechanics of it," Lurgl told her calmly.

"Elves aren't singers. We don't have the capacity to draw magic from the ground into ourselves."

"Well, neither do I, as far as I know," Bianca said frankly. "I mean, the magic definitely rushes on me when I touch the ground, but I don't know how to call more or less of it at will, or what to do with it as it passes into me. Is that just because it's wild, or is it that I have no training? Would I be able to shape it to tasks of my choosing if I was on the mainland, where the magic isn't out of control?"

"Not sure," said Lurgl, pausing to pull on a pair of heavy boots over his usual shoes. "Probably."

Bianca gave a despairing sigh. "How am I supposed to learn to use it with no one to teach me?"

"I don't know," Lurgl said reasonably. "But if you want it badly enough, you'll figure out a way."

With those words, he trotted out the door, joining the others who were already disappearing into the trees.

Bianca groaned, leaning back against the doorpost. That advice was no help at all. She stood there for a long time, with nothing better to do than stoke her frustration. However, as minutes passed, the irritation ebbed, and she wondered if Lurgl was right after all. Perhaps it was as simple as finding a way.

*If you want it badly enough*, he'd said. But did she want it? Did she want to be one of these so-called singers? Did she want to have the ability to channel magic—even the wild magic of Selvana—through her body and out into the world in the form of impossible feats? It seemed likely that her ability to wield magic, unconscious though it had been, had cost her everything she'd ever known.

Slowly the answer grew inside her, surprising her with its certainty. Yes, she did want to wield her magic. When she'd first come to the cottage, she hadn't been able to think of anything beyond the danger and the betrayal. But as her initial shock and fear about being attacked and abandoned to the jungle subsided, she'd gradually become aware of excitement growing within her. At last she had an answer, not only about her strange hair, but about the amazing things that sometimes happened when she made her words dance. And if the others were to be believed, she could actually learn to channel it, to mold the power to her own purposes.

It was probably true that if she hadn't been a singer, the elves wouldn't have claimed her as payment from Marisol, leading to her near-fatal adventure. But on the other hand, from what Lurgl said, if she hadn't been a singer, she would have died as a baby, when Marisol accidentally dropped her on the jungle floor.

Instead, she'd walked away with no effect beyond her unnaturally white hair.

Yes, she was glad to be a singer. And she wanted to make use of her gift to its full extent. Perhaps it would be good for Selvana to have a monarch who could reclaim some of the currently unharnessed magic that overwhelmed their land. She deflated slightly. Not that she was exactly on track for claiming her position as monarch. But another thought followed that depressing one. Perhaps her aptitude for magic could help there, as well.

Bianca wandered back into the cottage, her mind far away as she completed the now-familiar chore of clearing up the morning meal. The elves had decided that she should do this task each day, as the only one not leaving the clearing to go mining. She acknowledged it made sense, and she didn't mind the work itself. It was the reminder of her restricted movement that irked her.

She was alone all day in the cottage, and it was perhaps a good thing she had so many hours of solitude in which to complete her share of the household responsibilities. She was slow at every one of them, given she'd never had to do so much as wash a dish before leaving the palace.

But even she couldn't take all day to clear up breakfast, clean one room, and collect eggs from the small kitchen garden behind the cottage. She was therefore left with plenty of time in which to stew over her situation, and her powerlessness to change it. Over the course of the first few days, she took to working on other tasks she spotted around the cottage. Raella's area, in particular, often needed a lot of attention.

At first the elves were suspicious on their return, more than one of them making a point to inform her that she hadn't negotiated an exchange prior to undertaking the extra work, and they were therefore under no obligation to make any payment for it. She assured them all, with as much patience as she could muster, that she had no expectation of anything in return. Soon they stopped complaining, apparently pleased to have her tidy up after them and mend torn garments, however inexpertly. Especially Raella, whose area was always in absolute chaos by the time the elf left in the morning.

By the end of a week, Bianca was in the habit of doing considerably more chores than were strictly required of her. But as she finished the breakfast clean up that morning, Lurgl and the others long gone into the foliage, she decided there were better uses of her time.

She needed to use the magic she'd been given, but where did she start? Casting a cursory glance across the room, she frowned at a spoon which had fallen on the floor and therefore escaped her notice.

Bianca cleared her throat and looked self-consciously toward the door, making sure she really was alone.

"Up you get," she sang to the spoon, making her voice as commanding as she could while focused on getting the words to dance. The spoon wobbled slightly, but didn't lift.

"Hmm." Bianca twisted a strand of white hair around her fingers absently. "Not enough magic? Or not enough control?"

She closed her eyes. Thinking of what Farrin had said about singers being able to channel the magic in the ground, she crouched down, pressing her hands into the packed earth which formed the cottage's floor. She could feel the magic pouring into her, like she'd told Lurgl. The increased contact with the ground only heightened that unbearable pressure she'd been struggling with since the moment she hit the jungle floor. But how did she channel it?

Bianca focused on the sensation of pressure, the invisible force that rushed overwhelmingly over her body from each point of contact. One by one, she forced her muscles to relax, trying to lower the instinctive defense that sprang up in response to the pressure.

At once, she felt an absolute flood of some tingly and intangible substance move up her body. She tried to imagine it building in her throat, then gasped out the command again.

"Up you get, spoon!" Her words weren't very melodious, but she did sing them. She heard a dull thud, and her eyes flew open. There was no sign of the spoon on the floor, and it took her a while to locate it. It was above her head, apparently having flown upward so forcefully that it had become embedded, its rounded bowl downward, in the wooden beam.

Bianca grimaced at it. The elves were going to complain about the damage. Dionysius especially.

"But I did it," she muttered aloud, elation flooding over her. "I harnessed it on purpose!" She'd overshot her intention, but it was still a good start.

Her attempts to recreate the experience weren't as successful, however. The mental energy required to focus so intensively on the magic left her exhausted in a very short time. She could only hope she would gain stamina with practice, or she'd never be able to achieve much. And even when she had successfully used her song, the results had been patchy at best. Arbor wasn't likely to be impressed at the shoddy mending her magic had achieved in place of needlework, for example.

She would need to work on finesse, as well.

Weary, Bianca flopped into her hammock, letting the gentle swaying motion lull her. It also helped relieve the pressure of the wild magic. Sleep tugged at her, even though it was only mid-afternoon. But she resisted it, attempting to get her sluggish brain to grind back into action.

Learning to mend and cook and clean was all well and good—learning to use her magic for those purposes was even better. But it wasn't a solution to anything. As grateful as she was for the sanctuary, she had no intention of living out her life in this cottage. She needed to get back to Sel and claim her throne. She thought of her stepmother's excessive suspicion and harsh atti-tude to her subjects. Bianca needed to assume her rightful posi-tion for the city's sake as well as her own. Marisol shouldn't be queen—if her previous conduct hadn't confirmed it, her attack on Bianca did. Not to mention that she apparently only became queen through some kind of magic from the elves, for which she'd bargained Selvana's future.

A cold rush went over Bianca, but she pushed the thought away. She didn't want to know by what means Marisol had ensnared her father. It would help nothing now.

As they had many times before, Bianca's thoughts turned uncomfortably to the night her father had died, and the inci-dent with the ship.

Farrin's ship, she reminded herself, her discomfort increas-ing. If only she'd been more confident. If only she'd pushed back against Marisol's decision to—

But no. She cut off the thought. There was nothing to be gained from *if only*. She'd made a mistake that night, set herself on a path that had led here. And although the decision had been hers, the whole kingdom was suffering for it. She had a responsibility to her people to fix it. But if she wanted to claw her way back up into the canopy, she needed to understand what was really going on with Marisol and the elves. And she needed to be more capable than she'd so far proven.

If developing her magic helped achieve that, so much the better.

But her options for improvement were much too limited if she couldn't leave the clearing. And the elves clearly weren't interested in providing either information or training. Which left Bianca with only one other source.

If he'd show up, that was.

She sighed, rolling onto her side, and allowing her eyes to drift closed at last. It had been a week since Farrin said he'd come back, and she had no way to contact him. Even if he was willing to help her, she might not be able to afford to wait for him.

Her mind wandered, not quite in sleep, but on the edge of it. She wasn't in contact with the ground anymore, but she still had a hazy sense of magic floating up from the floor, from the cave outside the walls, from the nearby trees of the jungle...all around her. It wasn't difficult to drop her defenses this time, given she was too weary to mount any. The magic seemed to trickle into her and through her, and she made no attempt to stop the current or bottle it up. She just let it flow through, finding the sensation almost as pleasant as the rocking of her hammock.

*"Flower of the vine, branches of the fruitful tree,"* she sang, the words of the Selvanan proverb springing randomly to mind. *"Drumming of the endless rain, bring my heart's desire to me."*

A pattering sound reached her ears, and she screwed up her still-closed eyes in confusion at the feel of water on her face.

Then someone cleared their throat nearby, and she flew upright with a gasp.

Her abrupt motion sent her hammock rocking wildly back and forth, and Farrin's image swung into view. The young man stepped forward as he reached out to steady it, the movement seeming instinctive.

Bianca's hammock stopped, the fabric held firmly in Farrin's grip, and she caught her breath to find his face only inches from hers.

"Farrin," she said, annoyed at the breathlessness of her voice.

She half wished she'd activated Raella's ward before lying down, so that Farrin wouldn't have been able to see her consternation. But maybe he would have left if he'd found the place apparently empty.

Her struggle to find words ceased abruptly as she raised an absent hand to wipe the water from her eyes.

Water?

"Good afternoon, Bianca," Farrin said in his deep, uneven voice. "Care to explain why and how it's raining in here?"

Bianca followed his gaze around the room, her mouth falling open as she realized he was right. A small cloud had formed just above her hammock, dropping a light but steady rainfall on the sleeping area she shared with Raella.

"Raella will kill me," she moaned, looking at the elf's saturated belongings.

"I heard you singing," Farrin said, observing the rain with interest. "Did you make it rain with your song?

"I must have," Bianca said helplessly. "Although I definitely didn't mean to." Her eyes widened as she got a better look at her surroundings. "And I think I made those vines grow as well. They certainly weren't there when I lay down."

Farrin nodded, looking at the passionfruit vines now

growing in from the doorway. A tree branch was also protruding through a window near Arbor's bed, something the picky elf would never have allowed to occur naturally.

"But I wasn't even touching the ground," Bianca muttered, amazed by these signs of the power of her magic. "It was only a trickle, not that flood I felt earlier."

Farrin looked at her, clearly confused, but she didn't explain. She was thinking back over what she'd sung.

Flower of the vine. The passionfruit vine had grown right into the cottage.

Branches of the fruitful tree. She could see a ripe mango dangling from the tree branch over Arbor's bed.

And the endless rain was drumming on her face even now.

Her eyes passed to Farrin, heat rising up her cheeks as she remembered the last line of the proverb.

"Did you, um...where did you come from?" she asked awkwardly. "I mean...why are you here? I didn't...I didn't somehow..."

"Would you prefer me to leave?" Farrin asked, looking surprised.

"No, of course not," Bianca said hastily, scrambling down from her hammock without much grace. At least she'd secured the decorative sash of her crimson gown between her legs that morning, and could move her limbs freely. "I've been hoping you'd come. I just...wondered what brought you here at this precise moment."

"My own two legs, I suppose," Farrin said, still seeming confused. He gestured behind him, and Bianca saw the body of an armadillo, strung from a sturdy branch which he must have been carrying on his shoulders. "I find I'm generally received better if I don't come empty-handed, and I caught that this morning. It's not a big kill, but the elves don't eat much. I think they'll be glad of it."

Bianca nodded, feeling both relieved and foolish. Relieved at the evidence that her song hadn't magically summoned him. Foolish that the thought had even occurred to her.

"So you've been experimenting with your magic," Farrin commented, squinting up into the rain. "That's a good thing, I think." He stepped back several paces, taking him out of range of the small cloud. "It looks like you've got plenty of power. Can you make it stop raining, though?"

"I don't know," said Bianca, not sure whether to laugh or groan. "I didn't mean to make it *start* raining." She screwed up her eyes, again crouching to make contact with the ground, which was muddy now. Another Selvanan saying sprung to mind, and she latched on to it eagerly, singing it without thought. "Enough rain for today, come, wind, send heavy clouds away."

Farrin made a noise of protest, and Bianca suddenly realized how much more havoc a strong wind would wreak inside the cottage. But, to her relief, her own wielding of the magic seemed much weaker this time, in spite of the flood of raw power washing over her from the ground. The most half-hearted of breezes wafted past her, thankfully enough to disperse the unnatural cloud.

The pattering stilled, and Bianca stood again. She found herself face to face with Farrin, both of them drenched and dripping. Lifting a limp strand of hair from her cheek, Bianca couldn't quite keep in a chuckle.

An answering smile crept onto Farrin's lips, his expression suggesting he was surprised by how it felt. It was such an entertaining sight that Bianca's laughter bubbled up even more. The next moment, they were both laughing in earnest, wringing water from their clothes and shaking their heads over the absurdity of it all.

"This place is a mess," Bianca moaned, when they at last

subsided. She cast a glance from the muddy patch of floor to the vine still covered in passionfruit blossoms. "It's going to take forever to clear it all up."

"I'll help," Farrin offered.

Bianca looked at his face, seized by a sudden desire to make him laugh again. She made her voice as solemn as she could as she responded. "In exchange for what?"

Farrin stared at her for a stunned moment, then seemed to catch the twinkle in her eye. As she'd hoped, that deep laugh burst out of him again.

"You're learning quickly."

"I have to in order to survive in this household," Bianca said ruefully. But she couldn't keep in her grin. It felt so good to speak with another human again, after a whole week with only elves. She could only imagine how it felt for Farrin, living down here for two years.

"Well, come on," said Farrin, still smiling slightly. "You *won't* survive in this household if they all come home to this mess in their sacred space. Let's get it cleaned up."

Bianca sighed. "It's kind of you to offer to help, but I'm sure you intended to spend your time preparing that meat."

Farrin shrugged, moving over to the vine and beginning to pull it up. "It won't kill them to wait a little longer for their dinner."

"True," said Bianca, striding over to the door and seizing a shovel. "See how they like being thwarted for once." She ducked outside, filling the shovel with dry dirt which she brought back inside to try to cover the muddy patch of floor.

"Who's being thwarted?" Farrin demanded, a frown creasing his forehead. He'd reached the door in his removal of the vine, but he paused, looking back at her. "Have they been plaguing you with their bargains?"

Bianca shook her head quickly. "No, they've been good to me. I shouldn't complain. I'm just feeling...cooped up."

Farrin's frown lingered, but he disappeared through the doorway, returning once the vine was gone. To Bianca's surprise, he'd removed about a dozen of the passionfruit's striking white and purple flowers, which he spilled onto the large wooden table. He saw her watching and shrugged.

"Beautiful things shouldn't be wasted."

Bianca wasn't entirely sure how to respond to that comment, so she said nothing.

"Elves aren't altruistic," said Farrin abruptly. "Well, Lurgl is more than most, but even he has his limits. My point is, if they're being good to you, they have their own reasons for it. Just be wary. There's no telling what they might ultimately expect in return."

Bianca frowned slightly, wondering what experiences were behind the words. "Did they expect something unreasonable of you?"

"Nothing specific," he said. "But although they live here together, community doesn't look the same to them as it does to humans. It seemed more prudent to me not to live here permanently." He hacked away at the intruding branch, throwing his words over his shoulder. "I don't mean to speak against them. I have no reason to criticize any of them. I'm just warning you not to expect warmth."

Bianca nodded slowly. "I think I know what you mean. Their minds aren't geared toward doing favors." She sighed. "I want to join them on their mining trips, but they all say no. Lurgl says I'm only safe inside his ward, but to tell the truth, I'm desperate to get out of this clearing."

"I see." Farrin considered her in silence. "Is your freedom worth your life?"

"Maybe," said Bianca, a touch defensively. "What would you say in answer to that question?"

Farrin paused, looking taken aback. "I'd say...maybe," he admitted after a moment.

"Besides, I don't feel safer," Bianca said in a rush. "Left behind while the others are working, I mean. I'm all alone here every day. How can I be sure Lurgl's ward will hold?"

"Lurgl is highly skilled," Farrin reassured her. "And his understanding of the magic of this place is almost unparalleled. If he says the ward will hold, it'll hold."

Bianca made a noise in the back of her throat. "If his understanding of magic is unparalleled, why can't he tell me a thing about how to use it?"

Farrin's lips pulled up on one side. "Well, he probably doesn't know much about how humans can use magic. To be fair, you're the first singer in Selvana for generations. At least, the first one recorded."

"I've been thinking about that," Bianca mused. "It doesn't make sense to me. Why would I be so different? I come from Sel— both of my parents come from families who've lived here for a long time. If I was born with the capacity to sing, why weren't others?"

Farrin shrugged, taking the shovel from her hand and heading outside for another load. When he returned, Bianca kept talking.

"Do you think maybe I'm not the only one?"

Farrin frowned. "You mean others might be hiding an ability to sing? Why would they keep it a secret, though?"

"Not intentionally," Bianca corrected. She hesitated. "When I touch the ground, I can feel the magic—powerful and out of control—surging up into me. It pushes its way through, like this unbearable pressure. Do you feel that?"

Farrin straightened slowly, taking a moment to answer. "Sort of," he said at last. "I do feel a constant pressure." He laid one hand on his chest, and Bianca's eyes followed the gesture of their own accord. "Here. It's uncomfortable every moment I'm on the ground, although I'm used to it now. But I don't feel anything surging into me. The first time I touched the land here, though, it was a little like that."

Bianca thought this over. "Maybe I'm way off," she acknowledged. "But from what Lurgl said, it sounds like my first contact with the magic on the ground—when I was a baby—had a permanent effect on my hair. I just wondered if that wasn't the only effect. If maybe the contact somehow triggered my body's receptiveness to magic. Like I would never have known that I was a singer if I hadn't been exposed to the magic...meaning there might be others like me, and they wouldn't even realize."

"Congratulations," said a sour voice from the doorway. They both turned to see Dionysius hovering there. "You've figured out why Acacius and the others want you."

# CHAPTER FIFTEEN

# FARRIN

Farrin shot the elf an irritated look. Dionysius was clearly in a foul mood, and that never boded well. He would probably try to wring some kind of payment from Bianca for the damage to the cottage. Farrin would just have to make sure she didn't fall into any such trap.

"Acacius?" Bianca repeated, sounding apprehensive. "Who's Acacius, and why does he want me?"

Dakarai strolled in behind Dionysius, his eyes passing curiously over the lingering signs of Bianca's magic. Mercifully, the damage was mostly righted. "What happened in here? And do you really not know who Acacius is? He's—"

"The leader of the elves." Lurgl's voice cut across Dakarai's words with its usual calm, its owner strolling through the doorway. His green eyes fixed on Dakarai's face. "And why should she know of him? Do you know the names of the leaders of the human settlement?"

Farrin felt Bianca tense beside him, and he hid a smile. Even without what he'd overheard, he didn't think it would have taken him long to figure out her identity.

"No," Dakarai acknowledged, conceding Lurgl's point. "I don't know or care, you're right."

Apparently satisfied, he trotted off toward his own store cupboard, clutching a jar filled with wriggling worms.

It seemed Bianca, on the other hand, was far from satisfied. She addressed the room at large, her voice exasperated.

"Can someone please explain to me what Dionysius meant when he said I'd figured out why this Acacius wants me?"

"In exchange for what?" chorused five separate voices.

Bianca shot a long-suffering look at Farrin, and he gave her a smile that was half grimace. A thrill went through him at the moment of shared irritation. Such a simple thing, but so powerful after his prolonged isolation from his own kind.

"Fine," Bianca said, sounding a little petulant. "Tell me or don't, as you please. I'm not giving anyone anything for the information."

Most of the elves lost interest at once, wandering away to their various tasks. But Dionysius still stood before them.

"It's not really why he wants *you*, I suppose," he said shortly. "It's why he wants your queen to send down droves of others."

Farrin frowned, catching the elf's meaning. "You mean the object of the elves' bargain with the queen was to get people on the ground in order to see if they could identify more singers based on who survives the wild magic?"

"Basically," chimed in Lurgl, divesting himself of a rucksack that looked too large for his miniature frame.

"So they don't care how many non-singers die on impact, just as long as they identify a few singers in the mix?" Bianca demanded, outraged.

"Of course they don't care," said Lurgl shortly. "Why should they care about that? Elves don't concern themselves with human lives."

Bianca made an offended noise, but Farrin's attention stayed on Lurgl. The princess likely couldn't tell, but Farrin knew the elf well enough to realize that his voice was a little too hard to be natural. The statement was fully in line with what Farrin had told Bianca about elves mere minutes before, but something was off in Lurgl's delivery. There was something lurking behind his words, something personal.

Farrin didn't know Lurgl's story—he'd never tried to pry into it, appreciating that every member of this group of outcasts had their own secrets to preserve, himself included. But now curiosity stirred. Did the elf's history connect somehow to Bianca's situation? Lurgl had told them he was present when the princess was dropped onto the ground as a baby, after all.

"I won't allow it," said Bianca curtly. "No humans are going to be sacrificed for the elves' research."

"Well, well," said Dionysius, sounding grimly amused. "Aren't we high and mighty for a vagabond waif? What power do you think you have to stop Acacius doing whatever he wants? Particularly given your queen has given him the right with her addlepated bargaining."

"I have the power of Selvana's first singer in generations, for one thing," said Bianca, her chin lifted defiantly.

Farrin felt approval surge inside him. He was glad she was going to fight back, not just against Dionysius's barbs, but against the situation she'd been forced into.

"She has a point there," commented Eason, moving past on his way to the door.

Bianca ignored the elf, turning a determined face to Farrin. "I can't let this happen. Queen Marisol won't stand up for her people. The elves clearly have a hold on her—if they push hard enough, she'll give them whatever it takes to protect herself, even if it means people will die. I have to find a way to stop this."

"Aha!" Dakarai's head popped out from behind the door of his cupboard. "Typical humans, giving away information for free. Marisol. *Now* I know the name of the leader of the human settlement."

"Do you, though?" Bianca's mutter clearly wasn't meant to be heard, but Farrin caught it, another smile curving his lips at the fire in the exiled crown princess's eyes.

The girl looked up suddenly, and he tried to school his features. But apparently she had other things on her mind.

"Will you take me?"

Farrin stared at her, taken aback. "Will I...take you?" he repeated. "Take you where?"

"Anywhere," she said impatiently. She waved a hand toward the entrance to the cave. "Out there. If I'm going to fix what's happening, I need to be more prepared. The trouble is, I'm not going to learn what I need to in here. And this lot won't let me go on their mining trips."

"I've explained it to you," Lurgl cut in patiently. "We don't wish to take responsibility for your safety out there, past the ward."

Bianca ignored the elf, her eyes remaining fixed on Farrin with an intensity he found unsettling. "What about you, Farrin? I know it's a lot to ask, but I don't have anyone else to turn to. Are you willing?"

He hesitated, equally alarmed by how much he wanted to help her and how much he wanted her to stay in the safety of the ward. Neither impulse made much sense, not when she was basically a stranger, and he was supposed to be remaining emotionally detached from her.

"I have my own tasks to undertake out there," he said gruffly. "I didn't come to Selvana for fun."

"I'm not asking you to stop doing whatever it is you do," Bianca said quickly. "Just let me tag along. Show me how you survive out there in the jungle. Maybe answer some questions about magic, if opportunity arises?"

Farrin kept his face impassive, but inside he was groaning. What mess was he about to get himself into? Because there was no doubt about his answer. Whatever his instincts of self-preservation told him, he simply couldn't refuse the hopefulness in those dark eyes. Even after the devastating betrayal she'd suffered, she was still so trusting.

Too trusting, probably.

"All right," he said, half-resigned, half-exhilarated at the thought of human company. "Tomorrow morning. Be ready an hour after sunrise."

<><><>

Farrin woke with the dawn the following morning, his mind instantly springing to full awareness of what the day was to hold. After sharing the meal he'd provided with the elves, he'd spent the night in the cottage, something he hadn't done in a while. It seemed most efficient.

He cast a glance toward the sleeping area occupied by Raella and Bianca, but there was nothing to be seen. No sign of the hammocks he knew held the two of them, or of their belongings. It just looked like an empty corner, thanks to Raella's ward.

He pushed himself out of the simple bedroll on the floor next to Arbor's bed. Stretching, he strode for the door, eager to be out of the crowded room. He'd become used to sleeping outdoors in the last two years, and he preferred open spaces. Or at least, as open as the heavy jungle could ever be.

Lottie—who'd shown nothing but disdain for the idea of sleeping in the cottage—appeared from nowhere as Farrin entered the tree line. The jungle cat showed no inclination to make herself scarce as he found a place to relieve himself.

"A lady should have more respect for a man's privacy," Farrin told her sternly, although there was no heat in the words.

She ignored him, as usual, leaping lightly onto his shoulders as he turned back toward the cottage. The air shimmered visibly as he passed through Lurgl's ward, back into the protected bubble now surrounding the clearing.

"We're going to have proper company on our travels today," he told Lottie. "And I don't want to scare her off with our hermit ways. So best behavior, got it?"

Lottie kneaded her paws painfully into his shoulder, the rumble in her throat more growl than purr.

Farrin rolled his eyes at the feline's sulkiness. When he reached the edge of the clearing, he paused. The light was still low, but he could make out the structure situated just inside the cave, and his attention was caught by a figure in the doorway.

Bianca stood silently, gazing out at the stillness of the clearing in the early morning. Following the trajectory of her sight, Farrin tried to see it all with fresh eyes.

The clearing barely deserved the name—the break in the dense foliage of this part of the jungle was primarily thanks to the pool, and the rocky cliff that rose above it. The cave in which the cottage had been built was part of this cliff. The trees grew almost up to the water's edge, and the undergrowth was only absent along a broad strip next to the pool because of the constant tramping of the cottage's inhabitants.

Farrin knew there were fish in the pool—enough to provide a steady source of food for the elves, who carefully monitored the levels, and never over-fished. The moisture also attracted all manner of insects, their steady hum already filling the morning air. As he watched, a pair of colorful macaws swooped over the water, adding their song to the gentle patter of the waterfall. It had been a few days since the last heavy rain, and the water was consequently not much more than a trickle. But Farrin knew it would swell to a proper cascade with the next downpour.

He swatted an insect away from his face, relishing the rapidly disappearing coolness of the dawn air. He'd grown accustomed to the intensity of the humidity here in Selvana, although he did miss the feeling of being clean. It was impossible to maintain it in the jungle, and not just because of the ever-present mud. Washing in a pool such as this one was refreshing, but the moisture in the air meant he could never get properly dry afterward, and by the time he was done trying, he was already overheated and sweaty again. Even now he could feel sweat beading on his neck, and the sun had barely risen.

Bianca shifted, the movement suggesting she intended to go back inside, and Farrin stepped forward. Her eyes flicked instantly to him, and she bit her lip.

"Good morning," she said, her voice musical even when she wasn't singing.

"Morning," said Farrin. He winced a little at how rough his own voice sounded in contrast. He didn't think it had always been that way. But he spent most of his time in solitude now, and there was only so much one-sided conversation you could hold with an ocelot.

Speaking of ocelots, Lottie made her views clear as Farrin strode toward Bianca, once again digging her claws into him.

"Get off if you don't like it," Farrin muttered, shoving the cat unceremoniously from his shoulders. She landed nimbly on the ground, hissing in irritation, and Farrin straightened in relief. She was heavier than she thought she was.

"It's so beautiful down here," Bianca said, her eyes lingering on Lottie as she slunk away. "I often wondered what it was like, and wished I could explore." She shook her head. "I've seen waterfalls, of course. There are a few walkways leading to scenic spots like this. But it's different looking down from above, or even from halfway up. Down here I'm...in it."

Farrin nodded. "I know what you mean. There's something both alarming and intoxicating about being in the midst of the jungle, so lost among the foliage that you have no idea where you are in the scheme of it all." His own words took him by surprise. When had he decided to be so expansive with the princess?

Bianca knelt, digging one hand into the ground at her feet, her expression intent for a moment. "It's a lot, though," she muttered, a shudder going over her.

Farrin could only assume she was talking about the potency of the untamed magic, so different from the magic permeating the mainland, where Farrin came from.

Bianca's eyes opened, her gaze passing over the red flowers blooming all around their feet. "These are beautiful," she said softly. "I'm pretty sure I've never seen them before."

"They only grow on the ground," Farrin commented. "I don't think I've seen them climbing up the trees."

Bianca nodded, straightening. "If you give me ten minutes, I'll be ready to go." She sent a mischievous grin back into the cottage. "Preferably before everyone's up. I'm ready to give someone else a turn clearing up breakfast."

Farrin's smile felt a little stiff. "Are they making you do an unreasonable amount? I didn't really think about that when I had Lottie lead you here. It wasn't my intention to offer you to the elves as a servant."

Bianca's light laugh was so melodic, Farrin was half surprised it didn't cause magic to swirl through the air.

"I'm only doing my share," she assured him. "And I'm hardly going to complain about you bringing me here when it's the only reason I'm alive."

Farrin searched her eyes, trying to tell whether she was

being truthful, or downplaying any ill treatment from the elves. She seemed the type to do that.

"Ten minutes," he said. "I'll meet you around the other side of the pool."

With a nod, Bianca took off into the trees, still within the boundaries of the ward. Farrin slipped into the cottage, moving quietly as he rolled up his bedroll and secured it to his rucksack, so as not to wake the others.

In spite of his determination to remain detached, he couldn't suppress the jittery thrill that passed over him at the reminder that Bianca was not only willing but eager to be alone with him, away from the elves who'd been sheltering her.

Did she feel it, too? The comfort, the indefinable release that came from being with someone of your own kind, who understood your basic ways without needing explanation. Perhaps she didn't feel the loneliness so keenly, after only a week with the elves. But for Farrin, two years into his isolated and nomadic new life, being around Bianca felt almost like waking from a prolonged dream.

And he couldn't afford to wake up all the way, he reminded himself sternly. Too much would be unleashed within him. He'd agreed to help Bianca, and he couldn't bring himself to regret it. But if he wanted to keep his own head above the surface of his encroaching despair, he would have to find a way to keep her at arm's length.

# CHAPTER SIXTEEN

# FARRIN

Farrin didn't have long to wait at the designated meeting place. Bianca hurried toward him with a pack of her own, borrowed from an elf, judging by its size. She'd secured her skirts with the strap that dangled from her belt, so that they now formed a pair of ballooning pants. Farrin felt an absurd stab of disappointment. It was foolish, he knew—the style she'd adopted was more practical. But he'd been captivated by her flowing gown. Elves never wore dresses, and it had reminded him of home, where the girls always wore their skirts free like that.

"Ready?" he asked curtly, embarrassed by his own thoughts. *Arm's length*, he reminded himself. *Don't think about home.*

Bianca nodded, hoisting her small bag up her back.

Farrin frowned at it, making no move to start walking. "Where did you get that? From one of the elves?"

Bianca nodded. "Dakarai," she confirmed. "It was an old one he didn't want, which I think must be why I was able to persuade him to give it to me in exchange for me taking his turn cooking last night."

Farrin grunted, thinking privately that she'd paid too high a price. But at least she was getting the hang of the bartering that was a necessary part of interaction with elves. He turned away from the pool, his eyes falling on the point not far away where the air shimmered slightly from the ward.

Bianca followed his gaze, and her expression sobered. "Is it very dangerous out there? Lurgl seems to think I'll die for sure if I go outside the ward."

Farrin shrugged. "That sounds like an exaggeration to me, which probably means he has his own reasons for wanting you to stay inside the ward." He glanced at her, not willing to make any promises he couldn't keep. "It's definitely true that there's always the risk of death in the jungle. But you'll be with me, and this place hasn't managed to finish me off yet."

She gave a thoughtful nod, looking him up and down in a way that made him wish he was wearing a cleaner tunic. Not that she looked disapproving. Far from it.

The princess stepped closer, her eyes a little shy as they lifted to his. "Thank you," she said. "For letting me come with you. I will try to keep up, and not get in your way, but I know I'm going to slow you down."

Farrin's voice came out husky, and he had to clear his throat to try again. "I don't mind," he said. His thoughts screamed at him to remain detached, but the next words tumbled out anyway. "To tell the truth, I'm a little desperate for the company."

Bianca's smile grew, her cheeks looking a little warm. Farrin seemed to have moved a little closer to her, although he didn't remember shifting. Bianca was clearly on the point of saying something more when a shape launched itself from the branch of a nearby tree, landing on top of her head and causing her to let out an unladylike shriek as she raised her hands in defense.

"Lottie!" Farrin roared, grabbing the jungle cat by the scruff of her neck and pulling her off Bianca. "Leave her be!"

Lottie landed in the undergrowth, baring her teeth at Farrin in a menacing grimace that left him entirely unmoved—even as he acknowledged to himself that her intervention had been timely for his peace of mind.

"Best behavior, I said," he scolded her. "If you're not going to play nice, I won't take you with us!"

Lottie let out a light growl, putting her nose in the air and sauntering through the ward with her tail raised in an offensively revealing position.

Farrin sighed as he watched her go. "It's an empty threat, and she knows it," he admitted to Bianca. "I can no more stop her from following me through the jungle than I can fly."

Bianca laughed softly. "I don't blame her for being distrustful of me. I'm just an interfering stranger, after all." She patted her snowy hair in a self-conscious gesture, trying to salvage a disarranged braid. "Do I need to be careful? Will she actually hurt me?"

"Of course not," said Farrin quickly. "I won't let her."

Bianca didn't look entirely convinced, but she said no more as she followed Farrin into the trees.

He stopped before the ward, looking back at her. "Can you climb trees?"

She shrugged. "Reasonably well."

Farrin nodded. "We need to travel through the trees until we're far enough away from the clearing that we won't leave tracks leading there." He raised an eyebrow. "No walkways here."

"I understand," said Bianca quickly. "I'll keep up."

Thinking privately that she certainly would keep up, but only because he intended to go as slowly as necessary, Farrin reached for the nearest branch. Once he'd pulled himself from the ground, he turned to offer Bianca his hand, only to find her already swinging nimbly up via another branch.

She caught his expression, and it was her turn to raise an eyebrow. "I am a daughter of the jungle, you know," she told him. "We don't only travel on the walkways."

He nodded, relieved and disappointed in equal measure that there had been no need for her to grasp his hand. The part of him that was always trying to break free of his rigid control seemed to be craving another instance of physical touch from another human being. The other part of him was afraid that such a touch would undo him completely.

In any event, her capability was certainly a relief. Perhaps progress wouldn't be as slow as he'd feared.

Bianca let out an audible breath as she climbed up through the branches beside him. "It's so much less pressure off the ground, isn't it?" she said. "I can breathe now."

Farrin nodded again, most of his focus on moving safely across a sturdy branch, his eyes on the next tree over. Bianca followed more slowly, the distance between them making conversation impractical.

Farrin quickly lost his fear that Bianca was about to fall, and by the time he deemed it safe to descend to the ground again, he was barely watching her anymore.

For some time, they continued through the undergrowth without speaking, moving at a pace that was manageable for Bianca's inexperience. Even with his limp, Farrin could have gone much faster if he'd been alone.

But he didn't mind the slower pace. He even found the silence companionable, glad that the girl didn't seem to expect him to fill the space between them with chatter. If he'd ever had that capacity, he'd lost it long ago.

"We're going southwest, right?" Bianca asked, squinting up at the canopy above.

Farrin nodded.

"Where are we headed?" she asked curiously. "What is it

that you do out here? Raella said that hunting is only secondary for you, that you're on a different kind of search. What are you looking for?"

Farrin glanced at her as he stepped over a mossy log. "Have you ever heard of aconitum?"

"Aconitum?" Bianca repeated. She shook her head. "I haven't. What is it?"

Farrin let out a breath, once more torn between relief and disappointment. If she didn't know what it was, discussion of it wouldn't put Emmett's secret at risk. But then, if someone who'd grown up in Selvana had never even heard of it, what hope did he have of finding it?

"It's a plant," he told her. "It's supposed to have a very specific magical property, and no one's quite sure whether it's real or a myth. But I need it. That's why I came to Selvana."

"What's the specific magical property?"

Farrin hesitated, glancing at her again.

One of Bianca's dark eyebrows went up. "You look like you're about to say, *in exchange for what*. And we were doing so well."

Farrin gave a throaty chuckle. "No exchange," he assured her. "I'd just rather not tell you."

"Fair enough," Bianca said amicably, surprising him by how readily she dropped the matter. "What does the plant look like?"

"Small clusters of white flowers with pale purple leaves," Farrin said. "Supposedly."

Bianca nodded slowly. "Sounds unusual." She cast a look at the undergrowth around her. "Shouldn't we slow down if we want to properly look for it?"

"I've searched this area very thoroughly," Farrin assured her. "I'm working my way across the whole island. Before I stumbled across you, I was on my way back from two months of being based on the western shoreline. I'm planning to move further south for my next base. But we won't go as far today. I'll just give you a feel for it."

"I *am* holding your plans back," Bianca said, sounding guilty. "I'm sorry."

Farrin just shook his head. It always made him feel foolish, how much her friendliness rattled his long-deadened emotions. She was just so open, always ready to give, expecting nothing.

"How far south have you been?" Bianca asked curiously, after a few minutes' silence. "There's a settlement down there, you know. Very remote."

"I've heard as much, although I haven't been that far yet," said Farrin. "To be honest, it's the apple grove that interests me more than the human settlement."

"Apple grove?" Bianca repeated. "What's that?"

Farrin raised an eyebrow. "Have you never had an apple? It's a type of fruit. They're very common where I come from, but I haven't tasted one in two years." A pang of homesickness made an attempt against his self-imposed shield. "I'm very fond of them. But I guess they're not as suited to this climate. They don't actually grow all that well in Medulle either. We mainly import them from southern Frossenland."

"So how do you know there's a grove of them in Selvana?" Bianca asked.

"Lurgl told me," said Farrin. "He's been just about everywhere on this island, by the sounds of it. He said the apple grove isn't far from the human settlement, although he doesn't think they access it anymore. It must have been planted a long time ago, when the humans first came from the mainland."

"What are apples like?" Bianca asked, sounding fascinated by this simple topic.

"They're delicious," said Farrin. "Some are red, and those ones are juicy and sweet. Some are green, and they're often a little more sour. But still good to eat. I'm not sure what type are in the grove down south."

"I'd love to try one some day," said Bianca.

"I'll bring one back for you," Farrin promised, then bit his lip. Why was he making promises to this girl, no matter how trivial the subject? He knew better than that.

Bianca didn't respond, and a glance at her face showed her cheeks appealingly tinged with pink.

"So if we're not actually looking for this mystery plant today," said Bianca after a while, "what are we doing out here?"

"Careful," said Farrin curtly, nodding to the ground ahead of them. "Sinking mud." He seized a branch above his head, using it to swing himself lightly over the treacherous patch, and watching critically as Bianca did the same.

"You said you want to be more prepared," he said, once she was safely across. "I see you can handle yourself in the trees—that's good. But I thought we could get some practice in on how to navigate the jungle floor. Plus, we should try to work on your magic abilities. I'm far from the ideal teacher, but we could always do trial and error."

He grimaced as he remembered the last time he'd experimented with raw magic.

"*You* could do trial and error," he corrected himself. "I don't have the capacity to channel magic, wild or otherwise, and I won't be attempting it."

"Do you mean it?"

Bianca's voice was so eager, Farrin turned to her in surprise. "Mean what?"

"That you're going to focus your energy on helping me!"

"Of course," said Farrin blankly.

Bianca shook her head. "Don't think I don't realize how kind you're being. I've been with elves for a week, remember. I know how to recognize altruism when I see it. And you said yourself you have things to do. But if you help me find my feet down here, I might actually have a hope of fighting back and fixing this." She gave an incredulous laugh. "It's ridiculous, isn't it, that I don't know if I can trust any of the people I've known all my life, only to find my most trustworthy friend in a total stranger."

Farrin stared at her, not sure whether to be amazed that she would choose to focus on the positive in that sequence of events or alarmed that she was still so trusting. What was wrong with her, that she was so ready to put her faith in him? After all, how did she know he wasn't luring her to her death, or using her for some scheme of his own? But before he could decide whether to say any of that, Bianca surprised him still further.

"Thank you," she said again, her voice earnest. Stepping forward, she threw her arms impulsively around his waist and squeezed tightly.

Farrin went completely still, utterly undone by the contact. It was the type of hug one might give a brother, but it still sent something as potent as magic crashing over him. He hadn't been held in so long, not in any form. The desire to put his arms around her in turn, to cling to her like an anchor in storm-tossed seas, was almost overpowering.

He forced it back, holding his body stiff and unyielding. But on the inside, it was too late. The colder, more sensible part of him had been right—letting her touch him again had finished him. His frozen emotions had burst out of their bounds in a violent explosion, the warmth that only human interaction could awaken roaring to life inside him. He knew—with a half-sinking, half-soaring certainty—that it would be impossible to put it out again.

And when he was alone, all the things he'd been keeping down would come, ready to take full advantage of his tattered defenses. But for now, he had to maintain the appearance of normality, or Bianca would think he'd lost his mind.

"You're welcome," he said, his voice stilted. "But you should probably step back."

"Sorry," said Bianca, her voice breathless as she hastily let go of him. "I didn't mean to overstep."

"No need to apologize," Farrin said, still speaking in a carefully emotionless voice that was completely unrepresentative of the storm raging inside him. "It's just that you're standing at the edge of an army anthill. They'll swarm you if you give them a chance."

"Oh," said Bianca, still not quite steady as she hastened away from the innocuous-looking mound. "We don't get anthills up in the trees. Thanks for...for the warning."

Farrin just nodded. "Let me show you how to forage down here," he said, turning away from the anthill. Bianca followed meekly, the poor girl totally unaware of the tidal wave of emotion she'd started inside him.

She didn't need to be aware. In fact, it was better if she wasn't. Her ignorance wouldn't change Farrin's new reality. For better or worse, he had another human being in his world again, and one thing was certain.

He wasn't going to let anyone hurt her, whether wild animal or treacherous royalty. Not unless it was over his cold, dead body.

# CHAPTER SEVENTEEN

# Bianca

Bianca hummed quietly to herself as she stirred the porridge for the others' breakfast. Without realizing it, she added words to the simple melody, her song wafting cheerfully through the cottage.

"Oi!" Raella's outraged cry reached Bianca from the doorway, where the elf was chivvying a curious rabbit out the door. "We'll be overrun in a minute! That rabbit was practically dancing. Stop singing that nonsense about bringing joy to every animal of the jungle."

"Sorry," said Bianca repentantly. "I wasn't thinking about my words. It's just an old nursery rhyme which went well with the melody."

Raella shook her head. "Why is it you're much more effective at wielding magic when you're *not* trying to than when you are trying to?"

Bianca sighed. "I wish I knew," she said, a moment of gloom settling over her. "When I try to use it on purpose, it fights me so intensely. But I wasn't even trying just then! Was the rabbit really responding to my words, do you think?"

"Definitely," said Raella, clearly not impressed by the

unplanned display of skill. "So stop singing. Do whatever you like when you're out in the jungle with your huntsman, but in here, we don't want any funny business."

Eason gave a snigger as he rolled from his hammock, and Raella rolled her eyes. "You know what I mean," she said. "I was talking about the magic, not the mooning and the doe eyes."

"Hey!" Bianca protested, her face heating, but Raella had already moved on, intent on her morning preparations.

Bianca shook her head, but she found herself smiling again. Not at the elf's words, which were of course absurd, but at the reminder that Farrin would be arriving any minute.

It had been two weeks since her first foray into the jungle with the Medullan, and she'd already learned so much about surviving on the ground. More slowly, she was also learning about Farrin. He was always reluctant to talk about himself, but a little persistence was gradually yielding results. Besides, he didn't need to talk about himself for her to see who he was. His actions spoke volumes, from the way he scanned the ground before her feet for any possible hazard as they walked, to his patience with her clumsy attempts to channel Selvana's magic.

He had a kind heart, Bianca had well and truly decided.

What better evidence of it than his continued willingness to put up with her? With the exception of the day before, Farrin had faithfully taken her with him each morning, and let her follow him. He was sleeping at the cottage each night, not venturing too far during the days. He said he was performing what he called a seasonal search—doing a cursory hunt for the aconitum in areas he'd only checked at a different time of year, in case the season made a difference. Bianca wasn't fooled, though. He was helping her, even if two years of proximity with elves had made him too cautious to openly acknowledge his altruism.

He hadn't slept at the cottage the last two nights, however.

When he'd led her safely back to the elves the afternoon before last, he hadn't even stayed for the evening meal. He'd told her that he needed to attend to matters of his own the next day, but he would return for another expedition the day after that.

Which meant he would be there any minute. Bianca didn't doubt his promise, and she could barely keep from bouncing on her feet with anticipation, not just of his arrival, but of once again getting out into the jungle. She was almost embarrassed by how much she'd missed Farrin's company the day before—a single day had never felt so long. But she wasn't at all reluctant to acknowledge the delight she found in being able to roam free, away from the clearing.

The jungle was a treacherous place, no doubt—just a few days before, they'd only just managed to avoid catching the attention of a jaguar, and only because Farrin's reflexes were quicker than hers, and Lottie's senses were sharper than either human's. Bianca had also sustained a nasty sting from some kind of enormous black bee she'd never seen up in the canopy.

But none of that dimmed Bianca's enthusiasm. She'd always loved Selvana—it wasn't just her home, it was her responsibility. And on some level, being on the jungle floor felt like properly seeing her kingdom for the first time.

Logical or not, she loved every bit of it, even the various bits that seemed intent on killing her.

"What's wrong with the huntsman?" Ulmer's gruff words startled Bianca. The reclusive elf rarely spoke.

She followed his gaze to the doorway, her eyes lighting up at the sight of the man framed there.

"Farrin!"

Abandoning the porridge, she moved toward him, a smile on her face. But as she drew closer, she realized what Ulmer had meant by his question. Farrin didn't look well at all. There were dark circles under his eyes, and his beard was a little scruffy.

Neither of those things were what caused Bianca to draw in a sharp breath, however. It was the look in his eyes, like he was being steadily crushed. It reminded her of the night her father died, for some reason.

"Farrin, what's wrong?" she demanded, hurrying forward to meet him.

"Nothing," he said, his voice once again the scratchy sound it had been when she'd first met him. "What do you mean?"

"You look terrible," she told him frankly. "Like you're in pain. Did something happen yesterday, while you were alone? Did you get injured?"

"No," he said shortly. "Nothing happened. And I wasn't alone. Lottie was with me."

Bianca bit her lip, at a loss for what to say. It was clear he wasn't being entirely honest with her, but it was also clear he didn't want to tell her whatever was troubling him. She had no right to pry.

"Are you ready to go?" Farrin asked. "Assuming you still want to, that is."

"Of course I want to," she assured him quickly. "And yes, let's go straight away."

"Oi, what about the porridge?" demanded Dionysius.

"I'm not hungry," Bianca informed him cheerfully. She knew exactly what he was saying, but she couldn't help goading him a little. "I've got a plantain to take with me, and that will be plenty."

"I don't care if you never eat again," the elf exploded. "I meant what about *our* porridge?"

"Someone else can serve it up," said Bianca impatiently. "It's not even my turn this morning."

The elves instantly started bickering, trying to figure out who was exploiting Bianca's industrious ways to shirk their duties. Bianca turned back to Farrin, speaking softly now.

"Come on. Let's leave them to it."

He nodded, slipping out the door without another word. Predictably, Lottie appeared as soon as they reached the tree line. They walked in silence through the ward, taking to the trees as usual. This time, Farrin led her due east.

When they'd been climbing through the trees for almost half an hour without a word being spoken, Bianca reached her limit.

"Farrin," she panted, balancing herself on a branch with the help of a sturdy vine. "If you really think I can't tell something's different compared to two days ago, you must think me an imbecile."

Farrin stopped moving abruptly, his own balance perfect as he crouched on another branch of the same tree. He swiveled to face her, his brown eyes penetrating and unusually intense.

"I won't press you to tell me about it," Bianca assured him, still catching her breath from the arduous climb. "But I'm here if you want to. I just wanted you to know that."

Farrin stared at her, his own breathlessness seeming disproportionate to his level of activity. She had the sense his exertion was purely internal.

"The truth is," he murmured, "I've lost the skill of talking to people about what I'm feeling."

Bianca tilted her head encouragingly. "It's never too late to learn new skills."

To her surprise, Farrin's face hardened, and he gave a bitter laugh. "New skills? I said I've lost the ability, not that I never had it." He straightened, the movement abrupt. "Is this who you think I am?" he asked, gesturing around at the jungle. "Some hermit huntsman, incapable of connection with anyone but an ocelot?"

Moving so fluidly Bianca had barely a moment's warning, he seized a branch above his head and swung himself over to her own branch. She swallowed at his proximity, raising her eyes to look into the face glowering above her. She felt no fear of him, but her heart was racing all the same.

"I had a life back in Medulle, Bianca," he said, the words seeming wrenched from him. "People who cared about me, a kingdom which—" He cut himself off, giving his head a little shake. "I was never supposed to be stranded here—this was never the life I was supposed to live. I threw it all away like the abject fool I am, and there's about as much chance of me getting home as there is of me finding that blasted flower. So don't give me some trite speech about how everything will be better if I just talk about it!"

Bianca recoiled a little at the hardness in his voice, and Farrin turned half away from her, one rough hand flying up to cover his face.

"I'm sorry," he said, his voice a little muffled. "I told you I've lost the skill of talking to people. But that's no excuse. I have no right to take it out on you."

Bianca shifted back toward him, her heart instantly going out to the anguished man. She placed a hand on his arm, the movement tentative out of fear of intruding when he might wish for privacy.

"It's all right," she said softly. "I shouldn't have pushed you. I...I didn't realize you were so disheartened. But of course you must miss your home. It was thoughtless of me to forget what a terrible disaster it must feel to you, being stranded here, alone."

Farrin gave a hollow laugh, raising his face again. There was a look in his eyes that tugged at her heart. It was like a desperate hunger.

"You can't possibly believe yourself thoughtless, Bianca," he said quietly. "That's the last thing you are."

"That's kind of you to say," she replied. "But I have been thoughtless. I knew it was hugely inconvenient for you to take me on like this, but I pushed for it anyway, because the truth is I'm completely lost without your help."

Farrin sighed. "It wasn't the inconvenience that made me hesitate." He considered her for a moment, a wry smile tugging at his lips. "You're not entirely blameless in my troubles, though, if you're determined to make me acknowledge your culpability."

She cocked her head, startled, as her eyes flew to his. Surely he couldn't possibly know about her cowardice the night his ship was sunk. Could he?

But there was no anger whatsoever in Farrin's lopsided smile. "You can't be blamed for not realizing I was disheartened," he said. "I refused to acknowledge it myself. The truth is, I've been surviving only by refusing to think about any of it, convincing myself I didn't care about anything but my search."

He shifted a little closer, his footing sure on the broad branch. He didn't even seem conscious of the movement.

"Your only blame lies in being the one to destroy that illusion. I couldn't pretend not to care, not when I saw your plight."

Bianca stared back at him, a little hypnotized by the intensity of his focus. He was the first to break eye contact, his gaze traveling down to where her hand still rested gently on his arm.

"It was never that I didn't want to help you. It was that I was frightened by how much I did. I don't think you can imagine how desperately I've been longing for human company. How *could* you imagine it, when even I didn't realize how much I needed it?" He shook his head. "I'm not suited to a hermit's life by nature."

Bianca swallowed, struggling for words. She was the one who held his arm, but he had her utterly in his grip, his unexpected display of vulnerability completely melting her.

"I'm not sure whether to say I'm sorry or you're welcome," she managed, lowering her hand at last.

Farrin's crooked smile was back. "I'm sure I'll thank you in the long run," he told her, his voice already growing more natural. "But I'm certainly paying the price for trying to outrun the consequences of my idiocy for so long." He shook his head again, his next words a little husky. "When I think what my family must have suffered...must still be suffering, with me supposedly dead, and my brother—"

He cut himself off, and Bianca saw a little shudder go down his frame.

"You're not the only one who's made some foolish decisions," she reminded him. "My family must think I'm dead as well. At least you're thinking of them, while I've been selfishly lost in the excitement of exploring the ground."

Farrin looked faintly amused as his eyes traveled back to hers. "First thoughtless, now selfish," he said. He raised a hand, tugging a leaf from her snowy hair with strong fingers. "You don't seem to know yourself at all, Bianca."

She bit her lip, wishing she could stop the heat from rising up her cheeks at the implied praise. But as she searched his face, all thoughts of herself were lost at the ghosts she saw in his eyes.

"That's what you were doing yesterday," she realized, her voice soft. "You were wrestling with everything you've been bottling up all this time."

He sighed, moving back a little as he searched for a good handhold. "No one can outrun their demons forever. I just needed some time to...think."

*To torture yourself, more like*, Bianca thought, her heart once again wrenched.

Farrin had found a good purchase, but he paused, glancing over his shoulder. "I'm sorry I abandoned you for the day," he said. "Lottie and I went for a wander where we knew we could get some space."

He swung himself to the next branch in an agile movement.

Lottie ran sleekly along a limb above his head, and Bianca found herself fighting an utterly foolish stab of jealousy. Her sense told her that Farrin wouldn't have welcomed the presence of someone he knew so little when he was in the grip of strong emotion. But she still wished she could have been the one to be with him, to comfort him, to listen, perhaps just to sit with him in silence. How much comfort could an ocelot really provide?

Pushing aside the pointless regret, she inched along her branch, making for the spot where it intersected with another tree. Her movement was hampered by the billowing pants her dress had become, and she was relieved when Farrin dropped to the ground soon after.

"What was it like sailing here?" she asked, as they traipsed through a patch of relatively clear undergrowth. She figured since he was apparently willing to talk about his past now, she may as well ask some questions. "I've never been on a ship, of course."

Farrin made an amused noise in his throat. "I suppose you haven't. I've been around the ocean a lot—I come from Port Dulla, which is a coastal city. But I'll admit I've usually sailed along the coastline. I haven't actually been on many true ocean voyages."

"Were you nervous?" Bianca pressed.

Farrin hesitated, then nodded. "I was, a little," he admitted.

"About coming to Selvana, or the voyage?"

"Both," he said with a grim smile. "Events have justified my nerves about the first, but in terms of the second, I didn't need to worry. The voyage itself was uneventful." He grimaced. "Not like the previous time."

"The previous time?" Bianca repeated, feeling a small surge of pride as she navigated around a patch of sinking mud without needing to be directed.

Farrin nodded. "Not too long before I came here, I went sailing further out from the mainland than I'd ever been."

"Where were you going?" Bianca asked.

"Nowhere," said Farrin, sounding as if he felt foolish to admit it. "The journey was the activity. It was a celebration." He glanced sideways at her. "For my eighteenth birthday, actually."

Bianca raised an eyebrow. "You must have been wealthy back in Medulle, to afford something like that."

Farrin just shrugged. "Money can't buy sense, I suppose, because I didn't listen to the crew at all when a freak summer storm broke as we sailed homeward. We'd been on the water for the whole day, and we were supposed to be home by sunset, but the storm delayed our progress substantially. It was already dark when they told us to get below deck, and I was fascinated by the chaos of it all. I ignored them and stayed above, and I let myself get much too close to the railing."

"What happened?" Bianca demanded.

Farrin shook his head in apparent disbelief at his former foolishness. "The ship pitched violently, and I fell in."

"That must have been terrifying!" she cried.

"It was," Farrin acknowledged. "I thought I would fall forever into that icy darkness. I was being tossed about, my air was running out, and everything started going black." He frowned slightly. "I don't really know what happened next. I have this elusive memory of rising rapidly toward the surface, but then I blacked out. I think I must have dreamed it. It makes no sense—I'm not a cork, to float up with that much force." He let out a sigh. "The next thing I remember was waking up on the beach. Everyone agreed I was incredibly lucky to be washed to shore, rather than drowned in the deep."

"Incredibly," Bianca agreed. "After that experience, I'm amazed your family let you get on another ship."

Farrin's pained silence spoke volumes, and remembering

what he'd said about his guilt over what his family was suffering, Bianca hastily changed the subject.

"I had some time to think yesterday as well," she told him.

Before Farrin could respond, Lottie dropped from the trees above, landing on his shoulders with enough force to make him grunt. Farrin waved a hand to Bianca for silence, and she stopped moving at once. She strained her ears with all her might, but could hear nothing.

Farrin crept forward, his movements as stealthy as a jungle cat, in spite of the slight limp with which he always walked. He disappeared behind an enormous fern, and Bianca hesitated. Was she supposed to follow, or stay back? Not liking the idea of being left behind, she moved forward as silently as she could manage. Farrin quickly came into view, crouched behind a moss-covered log from which a profusion of fern fronds sprouted.

He glanced back at her approach, and gestured for her to join him.

"Through there, see?" he breathed, when she was on her knees beside him.

Magic coursed up into her from the mossy soil, overwhelming and unharnessed. She had to clamp her mouth shut to quell an instinctive desire to sing. Following Farrin's gaze, she saw a deer, grazing quietly a stone's throw away.

"It's a red brocket. There are several of them." In an apparent attempt not to scare the creature away, Farrin had leaned so close that his breath tickled her ear, his words less than a whisper.

The air was already thick and warm, as it always was, but extra heat bloomed along Bianca's neck, where her hair curled against her skin in the moist air.

She nodded stupidly, not taking in the substance of his words. After a moment, the deer looked up, apparently spooked by something, then moved away slowly through the trees.

Farrin let out a sigh, his voice still quiet, although he no longer leaned toward her.

"If it was later in the day, I'd say it might be a good opportunity to teach you the basics of hunting, but I don't want to lug a deer around all day."

"We could leave it to collect later," Bianca suggested.

But Farrin shook his head. "I don't want to risk attracting predators right into our homeward path."

"Good point," Bianca acknowledged.

Farrin eased himself to his feet, his limp more pronounced as he maneuvered over the log behind which they'd been crouched.

"Does it hurt?" Bianca asked abruptly.

He looked at her, confused, then followed her gaze to his leg.

"No," he said, thankfully not seeming bothered by the impolite question. "Not usually. I'm used to it now."

"So it hasn't always been like that?" Bianca asked. "How did it happen?"

"During the shipwreck," Farrin told her. "I was in the water, and a cannon hit the ship near me. Some wood exploded into my leg, and the wound was never properly treated."

For a moment, Bianca was silent, trying to master her voice. Farrin had already turned away when she blurted out, "I'm so sorry that happened to you."

He turned to look at her, seeming surprised.

"I mean, of course anyone would be sorry you were injured," said Bianca hastily. "But it's more than that. I...I deeply regret that being your first impression of this kingdom."

Farrin stared at her for another moment before his confusion suddenly turned to comprehension of some kind. Not knowing what was in his thoughts, it made Bianca nervous.

"Of course, I would feel the same way." He shook his head, his eyes friendly. His anger before might be a contrast to his previous unemotional calm, but so was the new warmth he was showing her. She liked this less filtered version of him better. "Don't apologize, Bianca," he said lightly. "There's no need for you to carry that."

Bianca bit her lip. If he knew her identity and her role in the incident—or rather, her spineless lack of a role—he might feel differently. But guilty as she felt about her omissions, she was still nervous of the consequences of revealing her identity.

"Come on," said Farrin, moving away from where the deer had been grazing, once again heading eastward. After a couple of minutes, he glanced at Bianca. "I was a little intense before, up in the trees. I'm sorry if I frightened you."

"Oh, no, of course not," she said brightly. "I could never be scared of you. I know you wouldn't hurt me."

Farrin frowned at her, for some reason not pleased with what she'd intended to be an encouraging answer.

"Look at that!" Bianca said, pointing to a spot of vibrant blue on a nearby rock. "It's a poison arrow frog. They're rare up in the canopy—incredibly rare. Did you know they're toxic if you—"

Her words were cut off by Lottie. This time the ocelot didn't emerge from the foliage, just hissed sharply. Farrin froze at once, his eyes narrowing as he inclined his head, clearly listening hard.

"What is it?" Bianca breathed, as soundlessly as she could. "More deer?"

He shook his head, then turned abruptly toward her. Moving so quickly she hardly comprehended what he was doing, he seized her around the waist with both hands. Bianca's breath left her in a gasp as he lifted her bodily from her feet and shoved her up toward an overhanging branch.

# CHAPTER EIGHTEEN

## *Bianca*

Her mind catching up, Bianca grabbed at the branch, grateful for Farrin's assistance as she scrabbled her way up. The next moment, he'd sprung up beside her, his silent gestures urging her to climb higher.

They scaled the tree in record time, neither speaking. Only when the jungle floor below was fully hidden by foliage did Farrin signal for her to stop. Obediently, Bianca held as still as she could, resisting the urge to twist around and try to peer at the ground.

For a few moments there was total stillness, no sound stirring the heavy air except the hum of insects. Then Bianca's ears caught it...stealthy movements below.

She turned wide eyes to Farrin, and he gave her a reassuring nod. He looked tense but not afraid, and Bianca's racing heart calmed slightly. He didn't seem to expect them to be torn to shreds, at least not imminently.

Just as whatever it was passed directly below them, Bianca heard something else, something which made her gasp in shock.

Voices. And not the chattering of monkeys, or the call of a bird. Voices speaking actual words.

Farrin shot her a sharp look, and she clamped her mouth shut again, straining to hear.

"Oi, look there. A poison arrow frog. That could be handy. Got a specimen jar?"

"Course I do. Where are your wits, to be out in the jungle without one?"

"We're not on a mining expedition, are we?" snapped the first voice. "Just give me the jar."

"In exchange for what?"

Bianca's eyes flew to Farrin's. The grim expression on his face showed no surprise. He'd already known the party was made up of elves.

She shifted at last, eager to see the group for herself. She'd never seen any elves beyond the seven at the cottage. Would these ones look different?

A leaf drifted down from her movement, and Farrin's hand shot out, his grip like iron as he grabbed her wrist admonishingly. She frowned slightly at him, but subsided. In another minute, the elves had moved out of the clearing where they'd seen the same frog that had caught Bianca's eye.

Farrin didn't relax, however, his hand still tight around Bianca's wrist. And a moment later, his caution was validated.

"Are these tracks?" The voice was muffled by the increased distance, but Bianca could still hear the excitement in the elf's words. "Could be human, do you think?"

"Maybe," mused a new voice, as high and cool as the other two had been. "It looks like something large."

"Let's investigate," said another voice eagerly. "Maybe this isn't a waste of time after all."

Bianca held her breath, her hand flying to cover Farrin's where it still clutched her wrist. His knuckles were as hard as stone, and she could see the muscles standing out in his arms as he held himself ready for action. But, to her immense relief, the elves followed the trail back the way the humans had come.

A full minute passed before Farrin released his grip.

"Come on," he said tensely. "We need to get away from here as quickly as we can. And we shouldn't use the ground if we can avoid it."

Bianca nodded, although her gaze was thoughtful as it followed the elves.

Because of the direction the elves had chosen, their route through the trees took them further from the cottage. By the time Farrin seemed relaxed enough to suggest he would tolerate Bianca speaking, she thought she could smell salt in the air.

"Are we near the ocean?" she asked, amazed.

Farrin gave a terse nod. "I didn't intend to come this far," he said. "I should never have brought you this way. But the elves shouldn't be out here. We're nowhere near their settlement."

Bianca frowned. "I do wonder if we were too hasty, running from them. Maybe we should have followed them—they might have information we could use. Or they might have been friendly. They didn't say anything to suggest they're the ones working with the queen."

"Bianca!" Farrin came to an abrupt stop, his face horrified. "What are you saying? You think we should have followed them...spoken to them...tried to *befriend* them? Are you mad?"

"No need to be so dramatic," said Bianca, irked. "I only said that they *might* have been friendly. What if they could have told us what the other elves want with me? What if—"

"Do you honestly not understand the danger you're in?" Farrin took hold of the branch above him, steadying himself while he gripped Bianca's shoulder with the other hand. "Bianca, you cannot let the elves catch you. I know the ones at the cottage seem all right, but the others are not like them! If they get their hands on you, they'll exploit you for whatever purpose best serves them, without an ounce of compassion for whether it kills you or not!"

He stopped, breathing hard. His alarm and frustration were written clearly across his face as he gave a disbelieving shake of his head.

"No wonder you're in this fix. You're absurdly trusting. How have you survived this long?"

"It's not bad to be trusting," Bianca shot back, stung. "I've survived just fine because whatever you might think of this place, most people truly don't want to hurt me! Most people are kind. Like you."

Farrin let go of her shoulder, a groan escaping him.

"Bianca, that's exactly what I mean. All that talk before about being sure I'd never hurt you. How could you possibly know that for certain? From the moment we met, you've been ready to blindly follow me out into the jungle, with no guarantee that—"

"Well, was I wrong?" Bianca interrupted. "*Are* you going to hurt me?"

"Of course not," said Farrin impatiently. "But the point is, you can't know that for sure."

"Farrin." Bianca paused, not sure whether she wanted to rage at him or reassure him. "I know you better than you seem to think. I'm confident that you're trustworthy."

Farrin was silent for a moment. "Were you confident that the guard who pushed you to your supposed death was trustworthy?"

Bianca flushed in spite of herself. "No, I wasn't," she said defensively. "I know I was foolish to follow him—I don't deny it. I *wanted* to trust him, but I wasn't sure. I didn't know him."

Farrin's words took on an incredulous note. "And you think

you know everything there is to know about me after three weeks?"

"Of course not," Bianca argued. "We're not talking about knowing everything there is to know. But I know enough."

"Even if that were true," said Farrin, "that's now, when we've spent every day of the last two weeks together. What about the first day you followed me into the jungle, when we'd met only twice? Did you think then that you knew me enough to trust me with your life? For all you know, I could be luring you out here to kill you, or for some sinister purpose of my own."

Bianca scowled back at him, unimpressed. "Well, if you are, I wish you'd get on with it," she said shortly. She nodded toward the sound of water. "The ocean isn't far. I don't know how to swim—it shouldn't be too hard to push me in and get rid of me."

"Don't be ridiculous," snapped Farrin.

"I thought it was ridiculous *not* to suspect you of trying to kill me," Bianca retorted. "If the idea is so absurd, why am I being chastised for trusting you?"

Not giving him a chance to answer, she swung her way down to a lower branch. She ignored his sounds of protest as she descended all the way to the ground. They'd left the elves far behind by now, and she needed some distance. She'd turned his criticisms away as if they were simply foolish, but the truth was, they burned. Rightly or wrongly, she'd come to respect Farrin enormously, and she valued his good opinion. She'd thought it was a good thing to look for the best in others—it was painful to realize that he saw it as a shortcoming...that he thought her weak and foolish, like a child who couldn't be trusted to take care of herself.

She could hear Farrin following her, and she didn't try to lose him. She wasn't foolhardy—she knew she'd be lost on her own. She just didn't want to argue with him anymore. A drop on her face was followed by another, and another. Bianca sighed, bracing herself for the inevitable. Sure enough, a moment later the clouds opened in earnest, and rain poured down in sheets. The canopy above, seeming so impenetrable a moment before, offered little protection. In no time at all, Bianca was soaked.

With a few quick strides, Farrin caught up to her, and she flashed him a tight smile.

"At least we don't have to worry about our tracks," she said.

He nodded, his eyes searching her face carefully, but he said nothing.

Bianca turned away from him, focusing instead on the ground in front of her feet. It was a necessary shift. In a remarkably short time, the rain turned the ground to sloshy mud. Her boots were soon coated, and it was increasingly harder to keep her footing as she clambered over mossy logs and pushed her way through foliage.

"We shouldn't go any further," Farrin said abruptly. "The elves should be far enough ahead. We can turn back to the cottage now."

Bianca shook her head, continuing forward. "It's so early in the day to go back. The rain might pass quickly, you never know."

"No, Bianca, I don't know this area as well," said Farrin. "We should stop. I can't remember exactly where, but somewhere out this way there's a—"

Bianca never heard the end of his sentence. As she placed one boot on the ground in front of her—her eyes on Farrin instead of on her feet—she felt the earth give way. The ground seemed to disappear beneath her as she fell, arms flailing in a desperate attempt to grab hold of something.

"Bianca!"

Farrin's horrified cry reached her ears just as she thudded to a painful stop. She rolled to the side and stifled a scream. She was on a tiny ledge of rock, a massive drop below her. The rain fell relentlessly onto the rocky slope, sending mud sliding down its surface.

Shifting as minimally as she could, Bianca looked up the way she'd fallen. The jungle floor was visible above, Farrin's pale face thrust over the edge. He looked absolutely terrified.

"Bianca, are you all right?"

"I think so," she said, not daring to stretch any of her limbs to check. Her heart was racing frantically, her mind so clouded by panic it was hard to find words. "It's...precarious."

She swiveled slightly, and a small chunk of rock came loose from underneath her shoulder.

"Don't move!" Farrin shouted. "I'll get something to pull you up!"

Bianca was too frightened even to nod—who knew how small a movement would send her plummeting to her death? Farrin's head disappeared, and for an agonizing few minutes, she felt just as alone as she had the night she'd first blundered through the jungle.

But she wasn't alone. Farrin's head reappeared, a length of thick vine draping over the edge of the cliff.

"Can you grab it?" he called.

Bianca reached out tentatively, but the movement again caused some of her ledge to dislodge, and she froze with her arm half out.

"I don't know if I can," she gasped.

"Don't risk it," he said. "Hang on."

He disappeared again, but this time only for a few moments. When he came back into view, his form blurred by the torrential downpour around him, he was holding the vine. Evidently he'd secured it to something out of Bianca's sight.

"What are you doing?" she cried, as he started walking backward down the treacherous slope. "It's too unstable—you'll be swept down!"

She had to really shout to make herself heard over the rain, which was growing increasingly more violent. But she may as well have saved her breath for all the notice Farrin took of her words. He continued to move steadily down the cliff face, stopping only once he'd gone a little way past her. There wasn't much of the vine left.

"Don't move," he instructed her, his voice also raised above the din. "I'll tie it onto your belt. If the ledge starts to give way before I'm done, try to grab it with your hands before you fall."

Bianca swallowed nervously, but made no argument. Farrin must have found some kind of foothold, because his hands didn't seem to be taking all his weight as he leaned toward her. His face was now level with hers where she lay prone across the rock. Farrin gripped the vine higher up with one hand, releasing the other. With deft fingers, he slid the end of the vine through Bianca's belt, his hands barely brushing her. Mercifully, the movement didn't trigger any further rock slides. Bianca held as still as a statue as Farrin pulled the vine's end—now looped through her belt—up to where his other hand still gripped the vine. Somehow, he managed to tie a knot without plummeting down himself. Bianca was now attached to the vine, although it wasn't taut. It hung slack above her, meaning that if she were to fall, the knot would be brutally tested by gravity.

"Don't move if you can help it, but be ready to grab hold," Farrin called, yelling even though his face was close to hers. "I don't know how much I can avoid disturbing your end of it while I climb."

Bianca nodded, and Farrin wasted no time beginning his ascent. Hand over hand, he pulled himself up the slope, his feet on the rock, and his hands gripping the vine. Amazingly, he made it to the top without Bianca's miniature ledge giving way.

"Now grab hold!" he called, once he'd braced himself on the jungle floor above.

Bianca tried to move carefully, but even so, the motion instantly caused the rocks on which she was lying to come loose. She barely grabbed the vine in time, her hands sliding painfully along it as she scrambled to get her feet under her.

"Are you all right?" Farrin shouted frantically.

"Yes!" she called back. "I have it."

She started walking up the slope as Farrin had done, but she didn't need to pull herself hand over hand. Farrin did that for her, reeling the vine in as she walked, his grip steady and unwavering. In only a few tense minutes, Bianca reached the top of the ledge, where Farrin's hand shot out to grab hold of her arm. He hauled her the last distance up, and they both stumbled several steps from the edge before collapsing, exhausted, into the undergrowth.

"Thank you," Bianca managed to gasp out.

Farrin didn't speak, but his hand shifted on the muddy ground, searching until it found hers. He squeezed, the gesture managing to communicate both his earlier fear and his current relief.

When she'd caught her breath, Bianca pushed herself up on her elbows.

"You saved my life," she commented. "At risk of your own." She pretended to search her memory. "Now what were we speaking of before?" she asked innocently. "Tell me again how I shouldn't trust you, because you might have lured me out here to kill me?"

Farrin gave a weak laugh, releasing her hand to place his own over his eyes for a brief moment. Then he seemed to shake off his residual tension, pushing himself to his feet.

Bianca followed, glancing over the mud-spattered Medullan. "You're a mess," she told him frankly.

He looked down at himself, his eyes laughing a little as they scanned her. "I'd give the obvious reply, but it wouldn't be very chivalrous."

Bianca laughed, lifting a limp strand of wet, white hair from her face. "I've changed my mind," she said ruefully. "I think we should go back to the cottage after all. If we can find our way."

Farrin nodded. "We're not lost. I couldn't remember the exact location of that quarry, more's the pity, but I know how to get home."

Bianca nodded gratefully. "I'm sorry I wasn't paying better attention when you told me to stop."

"It's not your fault," said Farrin heavily. "I was so rattled by the elves being where I never imagined we'd find them, I lost track of how far we'd come."

"Why do you think they were out here?" Bianca asked. "If it's so far from their settlement? One of them said they weren't mining, didn't he?"

Farrin gave her a look. "They weren't hunting, either. They weren't equipped for it. I can only think of one reason they'd be combing an unfamiliar part of the jungle, looking for large tracks."

It took Bianca a moment to take his meaning, and when she did, her eyes widened. "You think they were looking for me?"

"I'm almost sure of it," Farrin said grimly. "So you see why it would be such a terrible idea to take even the smallest risk of them seeing you."

Bianca frowned, not appreciating the reminder of their previous argument. "Let's go," she said, attempting with no success to wipe off her muddy hands on her sopping gown.

Farrin led the way through the jungle, moving much less cautiously now that the downpour provided so much protection from being seen or heard by anything. Bianca followed silently, her thoughts jumbled from the various misadventures of the morning. Plus, it wasn't practical to chat over the rain, which continued to saturate them all the way back to the cottage.

When they were just outside the protective ring of the ward —not that it was visible from the outside by even the faintest shimmer—Bianca turned to face Farrin.

"Thank you," she said. "For saving my life, of course, but also for taking me with you today. But you don't need to come back for me tomorrow."

"What?" Farrin took a step toward her. "Bianca, what do you mean? You don't want to go out into the jungle anymore?" He bit his lip. "What happened back there, Bianca, it—"

She shook her head, cutting him off. "It's not just that. This is what I was going to say earlier, when I said I did some thinking of my own yesterday." She lowered her eyes, more rattled by his evident disappointment than she cared to let on. The change in him since he'd given in to his emotions was certainly noticeable. "And it's not that I don't want to go into the jungle with you. It's that I have to stop dodging my responsibilities."

Farrin frowned. "The elves can cook and clean for themselves, Bianca. They were managing fine before you arrived."

"I'm not talking about them," Bianca said, half laughing at the absurdity of the idea. "I'm talking about me." She gestured toward the hidden cottage. "What am I doing here, Farrin? What's my plan? It's been three weeks, and I'm just...hanging about. I need to go home, to Sel."

"What?" Farrin's alarm was as clear as his disappointment had been. "Bianca, you can't just stroll back in there. The queen tried to have you killed, remember?"

"She tried to have me handed to the elves," Bianca corrected. "Whatever she did or didn't know, they seem to have realized that the ground wouldn't kill me."

"So you think she'll just leave you be if you magically reappear three weeks after she's told everyone you're dead?" Farrin asked sarcastically.

Bianca rolled her eyes. "Of course not. But I can't let her just get away with it. Especially not if this is the beginning of some campaign by the elves to get humans on the ground, never mind how many of them die from it. I have a responsibility to the people of Sel. Because I'm the only one who knows they're in danger," she added hastily.

For a moment, Farrin surprised her by looking faintly amused. But the expression quickly faded as he studied her earnest features.

"You really mean it," he said quietly, the words not a question. He shook his head. "It's too dangerous, Bianca. It's not worth risking your life."

Bianca gave a twisted smile. "You're very protective, aren't you? I think you can't help yourself." It was true. Even though he thought her little better than a naive child, he still wanted to keep her safe.

Farrin's laugh was a touch bitter. "It must run in the family, then. I'm nothing compared to my brother. It's an impulse with him—he doesn't even know he's doing it." He ran a hand down his face, water flicking from his beard.

"You mentioned your brother earlier," Bianca said, distracted by the emotion on Farrin's face. "He...he wasn't on that ship, was he?"

Farrin shook his head. "No, thank heavens," he said fervently. He sighed. "But he's in trouble, and it's because of me. Well," he amended, "because of both of us, really. It's not *all* my fault. It was definitely joint stupidity."

Bianca waited for him to expand, but he didn't. "That's who you're trying to help, isn't it?" she said, comprehension dawning. "That's who you need the aconitum for."

Farrin nodded slowly. "He's suffering from a terrible affliction," he said. "One that started because of something we meddled in. And I found an old record claiming that aconitum might be a remedy for it."

"What's the nature of the affliction?" Bianca asked.

Farrin didn't reply this time, his expression shrouded once again in the old wariness.

It was Bianca's turn to sigh. "No need to tell me all your secrets," she said without heat. "I think we've both had enough honesty for today."

"Bianca..." Farrin hesitated. "About what I said earlier...I didn't mean to hurt your feelings."

Bianca shrugged, and Farrin's brow creased.

"I did mean what I said, though," he added. "You need to be careful—more careful than you are being."

She just shrugged again, feeling weary and defeated.

"Don't do anything rash," Farrin pressed. "Just...give me another day to see what I can find out. I'll come and speak to you tomorrow night, the next day at the latest. Promise to wait until then at least?"

"If you insist," said Bianca dully. One day wasn't likely to make much difference, after all.

She took a few steps toward the ward, turning back just before she entered it.

"You know," she told him softly, "when I was trapped on that ledge, and you were out of my sight, I had no way to know you weren't going to just leave me there."

"I know," said Farrin quickly, "and I'm sorry you—"

"No." Bianca cut him off with a gesture. "You didn't let me finish. What I was going to say is that I had no way to know you would come back, and yet it didn't occur to me to wonder, even for a moment, whether you would abandon me. I knew you wouldn't. I just...knew. Without having to consider it." She searched his face. "That's what I meant before. I do know you, Farrin. And whether you think it foolhardy or not, I trust you."

Which was why his criticism hurt so much. She didn't add that thought aloud, however. Turning away, she plunged through the ward without giving him a chance to reply.

# CHAPTER NINETEEN

# FARRIN

Farrin stared after Bianca, his thoughts conflicted. He wanted to be grateful for her words, for her trust. Warmth rushed over him at the thought of her good opinion. But it was tempered with fear. She was so innocent, and so determined to think well of everyone. Perhaps he'd been so inclined once himself. But, confronting as it was to acknowledge, his two years of struggle had made him too embittered to so readily give others the benefit of the doubt. And that was in spite of the fact that his sufferings were almost entirely the result of his own folly. Bianca's had been caused by the malice of others, and she still didn't seem to have learned the lesson of mistrust.

Another emotion vied with his gratitude and fear. Regret. He'd clearly hurt her, and he hadn't meant to do that. But he couldn't take back his words, not when he'd spoken only truth, and only out of concern for her.

She was right about him, of course. He'd rather die than hurt her. The strength of the thought drew him up short, but he didn't try to dig into it. It was certainly true that he'd been willing to risk his own life for hers when she'd fallen into the quarry. She said she hadn't considered the possibility that he might abandon her to her fate...well, neither had he considered it. The thought had never occurred to him.

And now she was determined to go back to Sel.

Farrin's face hardened as he remembered what he'd overheard from the guards. He couldn't let Bianca blindly skip back into the treetop city. Not when he couldn't trust her to adequately consider her own preservation. If one of those guards intercepted her, would she follow them willingly? Would her generous heart get her killed?

Reaching a decision, Farrin set off through the jungle, around the edge of the ward. He didn't even need to keep to the trees this time. The rain still poured in sheets from above, obscuring any sign of his passage as he moved southwest. He knew where the others were mining at the moment, and he needed to speak to Lurgl.

He understood Bianca's feelings, of course. She didn't realize he was aware of her identity, but he perfectly comprehended why an exiled crown princess would feel a burning responsibility to return to her throne and right the wrongs that had driven her from it. But if she went in without a plan, he could only see one outcome.

And he found himself entirely unable to live with that particular outcome.

It took him almost two hours to find the elves, but he didn't begrudge the time. At least the rain had slackened off enough to make speech possible, although it still fell steadily.

When he emerged into a large clearing halfway to the western coast, it was Ulmer he first stumbled into. No one else was in sight, but Farrin had no doubt the others were nearby. The seven elves usually worked in the same area for safety.

"Huntsman." The reticent old elf looked up at Farrin through narrowed eyes. *He* certainly didn't suffer from an excess of trust. The thought almost made Farrin smile. Ulmer's manner was about as far removed from Bianca's as possible.

"Ulmer," Farrin greeted him. "I'm looking for Lurgl. Can you tell me where he is?"

"In exchange for what, huntsman?" Ulmer asked, his voice unusually low for his kind. In an elf, it was almost a growl.

Farrin stared emotionlessly back. "I offer nothing and expect nothing. Only ask."

Ulmer's eyes narrowed further at the traditional reply, then he sighed. With a jerk of his head, he indicated behind him.

"Last I saw him, he was mining magic from a rockfall through the trees there. But I wouldn't swear to it."

"Thank you for a gift freely given," said Farrin formally, striding past Ulmer.

It didn't take him long to find Lurgl. The elf was whistling cheerfully as he worked, using a small stone tool to chip away at a pile of rocks left by the collapse of a nearby boulder.

"Farrin," he said, his voice friendly enough. "What brings you here? I thought you'd be out gallivanting with Bianca all day."

"We had a little too much adventure, and I've taken her back to the cottage early," said Farrin curtly. "She's what I want to speak to you about."

"Oh?" Lurgl straightened, leaning his elbow against a nearby tree. "Seeking permission to pay your addresses, are you? I'm aware of human conventions, of course, but I'm flattered you consider me enough of a surrogate father for her that you would approach me about it."

"Very funny," growled Farrin, not amused by the wicked glint of humor in Lurgl's green eyes.

"You would be setting your sights a little high," Lurgl said with unconvincing solemnity. "But then, she clearly likes you, so that has to count for something."

Farrin searched the elf's face shrewdly. "So you do know who she is? I thought you must."

Lurgl raised an eyebrow. "Did you? Then you've outdone me, and I congratulate you. I had no suspicion that you knew her identity."

"I did some investigating after she first arrived," Farrin said, waving a dismissive hand. "But that's all neither here nor there."

"Maybe not to you," Lurgl said mildly. "But her identity is of great significance to me."

Farrin narrowed his eyes, trying to read the elf's calm expression. "What does that mean?" he asked, a growl in the words. "What's your purpose in harboring her?"

"My counsel is my own, I believe," said Lurgl, unperturbed by Farrin's menacing demeanor.

After a moment's consideration, Farrin let the matter drop. If Lurgl didn't want to tell him, there was no way he could change that. And it wasn't exactly a shocking revelation to him that the elf must have some ulterior motive in giving Bianca shelter. Lurgl was a good elf, even kind, in his way. But he was still an elf.

"Well, I suppose her identity is relevant to my issue as well, now I think about it," he said gruffly. "Because I'm pretty sure that's why she feels compelled to go back and call the queen to account for her dealings with the elves. And with Bianca herself, of course," he added as an afterthought.

Lurgl raised an eyebrow. "Does she, now? Well, it's a sensible idea."

"It's not sensible!" Farrin exploded. "She has no plan, and no ability to defend herself! She'll be going to her death!"

"No ability to defend herself?" Lurgl repeated incredulously. "Farrin, she's a singer! The first this island has seen in generations! Do you have any concept of the amount of power accessible to her in this land?"

"But it's not accessible to her," Farrin argued. "Yes, she's a singer, but she has no idea how to practice her craft. We've been trying, Lurgl, every day. And on the times she gets anything to happen, she has so little control over it. When she actually tries to channel magic, usually it's very weak, or nothing at all."

Lurgl frowned. "Yes, it is surprising," he agreed. "I confess, I thought that if a singer got onto the ground, he or she would release fabulous power with every note. I'm sure that's what the rest of the elves think, too. That's why they wanted her so badly."

"And what will they do with her when they find out she's useless to them?" Farrin asked darkly.

Lurgl raised an amused eyebrow. "Useless? You don't think creatively enough, my dear boy. Even without her magic, there are many uses for an ensnared queen."

"Princess," Farrin corrected. "She's the crown princess, at least for now. She hasn't been crowned queen yet."

Lurgl shrugged. "Human ceremonies mean little to us. She was the heir of the previous king, and he has been dead for some time. She is Selvana's queen, whatever the vain and self-serving woman sitting on her throne might wish."

Farrin ran a hand down the side of his face. "Be that as it may, I still think it would be foolhardy of her to just go back, without some kind of protection."

"Are you offering yourself as that protection?" Lurgl asked, intrigued. "Do you intend to come out of hiding and show yourself to the humans at last?"

"If I have to, I will," Farrin said shortly. "But that wouldn't be enough. What we need is information. We still have no real idea what's going on." He shot the elf a sharp look. "Or at least, I don't. You said the elves always planned to demand people as payment from Queen Marisol."

Lurgl nodded slowly. "Yes, on the understanding that there would surely be at least some singers among them, and they would be able to channel magic once on the ground. I understand Acacius's purposes in that. But what use one singer would be to him all on her own is hard to imagine. I suppose he hopes she'll be the first of many."

"We need to ascertain what they want with her," Farrin said. "I'd also like to know exactly what's in Queen Marisol's mind, but I can't think of a way to find that out. With the elves, however, I might have a chance." He met Lurgl's eye. "If you're willing to help me."

Lurgl propped his stone chisel on a low-hanging branch, resting his chin on top of his hands as he considered Farrin.

"What exactly is it you're asking for?" he prompted.

"I'm asking you to come with me and help me spy on the elves' settlement," Farrin said. "Tomorrow. To see if we can overhear anything useful relating to Bianca's situation."

Lurgl straightened, his eyes staring into the distance as he considered. "The settlement," he mused. "It's certainly been a long time."

Farrin waited, holding his breath. At last, Lurgl's eyes returned to his.

"Do you acknowledge that you're requesting my assistance as a personal favor to you?"

"Well," Farrin hedged, "it's Bianca's safety which—"

"Farrin." Lurgl cut him off evenly. "Did she send you to ask me? Are you acting on her behalf, with authority to bind her to a promise?"

"No, of course not," said Farrin hastily. He sighed, fidgeting a little. "Yes," he admitted. "It's a favor for me. I'm the one who needs it, not her."

Lurgl nodded slowly, thinking this over. "I might be willing to assist you, but I require an exchange."

Of course he did. "What is it?" Farrin asked, much too wise in the ways of elves to blurt out something melodramatic and idiotic like, *I'll do anything*. He wanted Bianca to be safe, but he wasn't a complete imbecile.

Before answering, Lurgl climbed nimbly up onto a boulder, so that his face was level with Farrin's. The simple repositioning told Farrin that Lurgl was ready to bargain in earnest. Elves didn't like to negotiate from an unequal position.

"It's a very minimal requirement from your perspective," Lurgl began, stirring Farrin's incredulity. "I only require you to agree that if I ask you to keep any of what we might overhear to ourselves, you will comply."

Farrin frowned. "Minimal? Do you take me for a fool, Lurgl? I know better than to make such an open-ended bargain with an elf. How can I possibly promise to keep something a secret when I don't know what the something might be?"

"It will require a measure of trust," Lurgl agreed. "And although that goes against the nature of a bargain, you are a human, more used to making agreements by trust instead of according to terms. I would not have anticipated it to be a problem for you."

"Oh, you wouldn't, would you?" Farrin said dryly. "Don't think you can manipulate me, Lurgl. What if I hear something that affects Bianca's safety, and I'm not even allowed to tell her?"

"A valid point." Lurgl nodded sagely, then took a moment to consider. "How about this: my requirement cannot apply to anything relating directly to Bianca's safety, or to any matter personal to her. That is my counter-offer. My participation is subject to you agreeing to those terms."

Farrin crossed his arms, tapping one fist against his elbow as he thought this over. He knew there were still plenty of potential snares in this bargain. But he was asking Lurgl for help, and he'd never expected to get it for free. All things considered, it really was a minimal exchange. As long as he could tell Bianca what they overheard regarding her situation...well, it wasn't as though there was anyone else on this island he'd want to confide secrets in.

"Deal," he said abruptly, offering his hand. Lurgl shook it, and the bargain was struck.

"I did say tomorrow, didn't I?" Farrin asked in sudden concern.

Lurgl chuckled. "You did. Tomorrow it is. I assume you don't want to tell Bianca the details of the expedition?"

Farrin shook his head. "I'll tell her after. Hopefully we will have learned something worth telling. Can we meet outside the ward on the southern side at dawn?"

Lurgl nodded. "Barring catastrophe, I'll be there," he assured Farrin.

Satisfied, Farrin strode back across the clearing and into the jungle. He caught a flash of tan fur and whistled softly to Lottie. It was too late in the day to set out in search of aconitum, but he wasn't heading for the cottage, either. He knew a fairly safe place to make camp nearby. He wasn't quite ready to face those trusting, hurt brown eyes again.

<><><>

"We're getting close, aren't we?"

Farrin's whisper was barely a breath, but Lurgl still waved a miniature hand for silence. The elf leaped lightly from Farrin's branch to another, the jump impressive given his size. He leaned forward in a crouch, the tapered tips of his ears wiggling ever so slightly.

After a few minutes, which felt like hours, he nodded.

"That was a standard patrol," he murmured. "It passed not half a league from us."

Farrin rolled his eyes. "Half a league? That's why you made me crouch in silence all that time? They won't be able to hear us from there."

"I heard them, didn't I?" Lurgl pointed out.

Farrin closed his mouth, chastened. The point was unarguable.

"In answer to your earlier question, yes, we are getting close," Lurgl went on smoothly. Are you really not familiar with the location of the elven settlement?"

Farrin shook his head. "Not the exact location. I've just avoided the area altogether."

"Wise," said Lurgl.

It would certainly be ironic if the aconitum existed but was only found within range of the elves' settlement, Farrin reflected. But given Lurgl had spent most of his life there, and knew nothing of it, that seemed unlikely.

"Will there be a ward around the settlement?" Farrin asked.

Lurgl shook his head. "I doubt it. A ward that large would take far too much power. Besides, with no humans on the ground, what's the point? We know how to deal with the other jungle creatures. Let's move."

Farrin followed the elf silently, the two of them ascending so high into the canopy that Farrin felt a flicker of fear, accustomed though he now was to climbing trees. A fall from that height would almost certainly mean death. It was probably good they hadn't brought Lottie. Although the ocelot would probably be angry with him for a week for communicating how unwelcome she was on the expedition.

After another fifteen minutes, Lurgl paused.

"We are about to climb across the top of the settlement," he informed Farrin.

"Across the top?" Farrin repeated, surprised. "Isn't the settlement in a large clearing or something?"

"Of course not," said Lurgl disdainfully. "We are jungle elves. We live among the trees."

"So elves will be up here?" asked Farrin.

"Not *in* the trees, *among* the trees," Lurgl said, growing impatient. "My point is, you need to remain silent from now on. Their superior ears will hear any words you speak. I am familiar with this canopy, and I can direct us right above Acacius's dwelling. We will be able to listen from an elevated position, without exposing ourselves to their notice."

"*You'll* be able to listen," said Farrin. "I can't hear from that far away, remember?"

"Ah yes," said Lurgl. "I did remember." To Farrin's surprise, he drew a small vial from his pocket. "Bat wings, infused with magic. If you drink it now, it should last several hours."

"Bat wings?" Farrin repeated, taking the vial, but turning it over in his hand suspiciously.

"Bats have excellent hearing, Farrin," Lurgl said, definitely impatient now. It hadn't escaped Farrin's notice that the usually collected elf had grown more touchy the closer they drew to the settlement that had once been his home.

"I know that," said Farrin quickly. He frowned as his gaze flicked from the vial to Lurgl's face. "You weren't kidding that trust is required," he muttered. But he downed the contents without complaint. He'd expected it to taste foul, but it actually wasn't bad.

And the effect was immediate. Farrin had to clap his hands over his ears to muffle the cacophony as the sounds of the jungle suddenly overwhelmed him. He barely hung on to the vial in the process, and Lurgl snatched it back, muttering disapprovingly about human carelessness.

He turned to Farrin, the next words mouthed rather than said. And yet Farrin heard them, in a quiet but clear whisper.

"Now come on."

# CHAPTER TWENTY

# FARRIN

As they continued forward, Farrin's enhanced ears caught the sounds of the settlement hidden below the canopy. Elves called to each other, spoons scraped on bowls, artisans muttered the words necessary to process mined magic, feet padded against the wet earth...those and so many more sounds filled the previously still air.

Fascinated, Farrin listened to a dozen disjointed catches of conversation, until a name he'd heard before caught his attention.

"...just taking the meal to Acacius in his..."

Farrin saw Lurgl go still, clearly also having caught it. Moving so stealthily even Farrin's newly bolstered hearing couldn't catch a sound, Lurgl followed the direction of the voice. He looked satisfied, as though he'd received confirmation of where he'd expected to find the elf leader. After a short while, he stopped and motioned for Farrin to do the same. The elf settled himself into a comfortable crook where two branches met, from which Farrin inferred they were going to stay for some time. He found as comfortable a spot as he could, his interest spiking when he heard a commanding voice below.

"Just leave it there."

Farrin's gaze found Lurgl, and he raised a questioning eyebrow. *Acacius?* he mouthed, no sound actually escaping his mouth.

Lurgl nodded, his green eyes harder than Farrin had ever seen them, and his posture tense.

Excited at their success, Farrin leaned forward, ready to hear something of use.

Unfortunately, the leader of the elves didn't seem to realize that someone was eager to hear his thoughts regarding the missing princess at that moment, because he continued to go about his day with no regard to their mission whatsoever.

Lurgl had spoken the truth about the long-lasting effects of the potion, but by the time they'd been crouching in position for three hours, Farrin was about ready to give up anyway. Maddeningly, Lurgl didn't even look uncomfortable, his posture identical to how it had been when they'd first stopped, and his expression unconcerned. Increased exposure to the settlement seemed to have helped ease his tension, and he was now looking around the canopy below as if his ears allowed him to see the various activities he was hearing.

But then, finally, Farrin's ears caught something that made him tense on the branch.

"Good, come in," said Acacius's high, unyielding voice. "You have a report on the search for Princess Bianca?"

"Yes, Your Mightiness, but nothing of interest, I'm afraid," responded another elven voice. "No sign of her in the western pass."

Farrin heard a noise of frustration, presumably from Acacius.

"It's not good enough," the elf leader growled. "I want her found. That human queen thinks she can play us for fools."

"Is it possible her story is true?" the other elf responded tentatively. "That the princess is dead?"

"She's not dead," Acacius said dismissively. "I don't believe it for a moment. The queen isn't even confident of it—the mirror showed a trace of deception when she made the claim. The simple fact is, she made a bargain, and she failed to fulfill the terms. It's been three weeks since she promised to send us the princess. If we don't have results in one week more, I'll hold the bargain unfulfilled, and let the magic do its work."

Frowning, Farrin glanced at Lurgl, to see the elf looking very grave. Farrin didn't know what would ensue from breaching a bargain of this magnitude. What was about to be unleashed on the oblivious people of Sel?

But then, he reminded himself, the only way for the bargain to be fulfilled was for Bianca to be handed over to these elves as some kind of sacrifice.

Unthinkable.

"In any event," Acacius added, "it's clear that the queen's efforts to find the princess will yield nothing. She is as useless as the day she struck the bargain—thinking herself far above everyone else, but afraid of the very soil of her own kingdom. The initial tracks were clear—the princess did make it to the ground, and she survived as expected. She's down here somewhere, and the humans don't have the means to search for her. We need to double our efforts. And make sure every search group is armed with the special darts. If anyone so much as catches a glimpse of her, I want her incapacitated and brought in without any fuss."

"Yes, Your Mightiness." Farrin could imagine the elf bowing himself out, and sure enough, the patter of small feet sounded a moment later. He glanced up at Lurgl, who looked troubled.

Farrin's own thoughts were closer to panic. They were going to double the search for Bianca, and attack her on sight. No doubt the darts in question contained poison of some kind. Would it knock her out? Or incapacitate her in some more sinister, more painful way? He didn't care to find out.

One thing was for certain. It was no time for Bianca to go blundering through the jungle to get back to Sel. They were surely keeping that whole area under close observation. That was why Farrin had carefully avoided the city's surrounds. Obviously he also hadn't wanted the humans to catch sight of her and report it back to the queen, but they didn't concern him as much. They wouldn't stray far from their safe areas. The elves, on the other hand, were experts at tracking in the jungle. He had no doubt that it was only thanks to Lurgl's ward that she'd remained undetected this long. He'd been foolhardy, taking her out every day with only himself and Lottie. They'd been very lucky not to get caught the day before.

It was still quiet below them, Acacius presumably lost in his own thoughts. Farrin was just wondering whether they should start to edge away when a new voice spoke.

"You're doubling the patrol, Your Mightiness? Has today's mission failed, then?"

Acacius cleared his throat. "I've yet to learn how it went. I'm still hoping for success. But I don't want any other efforts to cease until we have her secure."

Fear trickled down Farrin's back. What was today's mission?

"Besides," Acacius continued, "I know for a fact that the patrols are getting lazy. I want a sense of urgency restored to the search. We must find the Snow Princess. This is the best opportunity we've had in my lifetime, and we may not get another like it for generations, for all we know."

"I know your hopes are high, Acacius." The dropping of the title told Farrin that the elf leader's companion was someone close to him. "But I think you overestimate what she'll be able to do. I told you, I've made a study of singing craft, and it's my belief that the volume of magic down here will overwhelm her."

"I don't care if she's comfortable!" said Acacius, sounding outraged. "I care if she succeeds in taming the magic."

Lurgl shifted infinitesimally, and Farrin's eyes flew to him. If the elf had looked troubled before, he was all the way to alarmed now.

Farrin didn't know what the elves meant by taming the magic, but clearly it wasn't good news for Bianca.

"Let me clarify," said the second elf. "When I said she'll be overwhelmed, I wasn't referring to her emotions. I meant the word quite literally, in relation to her physical capacity. The magic doesn't kill her on impact, because she's a singer and can channel it through her body. But you don't want her to just let it pass through. You want her to actually engage it, use it for a purpose and release it. But to actually make any progress on clearing the ground, she'd have to channel a hundred—no, a thousand—times what a singer on the mainland would use in their whole lifetime. If she tries to seize control of that much magic, it could well kill her. The human frame simply won't be able to withstand it for any length of time, if at all."

"Firstly, I don't need her to last for years and years," said Acacius coldly. "You're forgetting that she's royal. She might not realize it, but she will be stronger, and her frame will be more resilient to the passage of the magic than the average singer. I wonder if she knows how rare it is to have a royal who's also a singer," he mused. "I don't believe I've come across it before. The song must have come through her mother's line, I think." He cleared his throat. "But I'm straying from my point. Which is that whatever magic she can shift—and I anticipate it being a substantial amount—will be an excellent start. And then we can build on her work with any further singers identified in future waves of payment."

"If that is your first point, what is your second?" his companion asked, sounding unconvinced.

"My second is that she doesn't need to know any of this," Acacius said. "When she arrives, we can explain to her the benefits to the land of her taming the magic, and the benefits it would bring her people. She doesn't need to know that the task is greater than she can accomplish alone, or that it will likely kill her. We just need to motivate her to give it everything she has." His voice turned dismissive. "From what I've observed of her over the years, it won't be hard. She is trusting and generous to a fault."

In spite of the heavy heat of the day, fear lanced through Farrin like ice. He knew it was good to have the information—he'd finally discovered the elves' intentions for Bianca. But it was terrifying how accurately this Acacius had read Bianca, even from a distance. He was right—she probably would give everything she could, even to the point of it killing her, if she thought it would help her people and her kingdom.

Farrin couldn't let that happen.

He twisted on his branch, trying to catch Lurgl's eye. They had to leave, to warn Bianca without a moment's loss of time.

"Hopefully we will soon be able to discover whether you're right," said the unknown elf. "How many did you send to Lurgl's hideout?"

It was all Farrin could do not to gasp aloud. They knew where Lurgl lived? Was someone on their way to Bianca right now?

Lurgl also looked taken aback, although his expression was more angry than afraid.

"Only one," Acacius was responding. "Stealth is required, not force. If all goes to plan, no one will even have to drag her through the jungle."

"And you really think she's there? It seems so unlikely that any elves would take in a human without gain."

"I thought it unlikely as well," Acacius acknowledged. "When the thought first occurred to me, I dismissed it as an absurdity. But how else has she disappeared so completely? And you're forgetting a crucial detail, as I did at first—Lurgl always was absurd. His traitorous preference for humans is what led to his downfall, after all. And I have reason to believe that others who defected for the same reason have sought refuge with him. Perhaps together they are soft enough to take in a human fugitive." The elf snorted. "I still can hardly believe he thought we should ally ourselves with the humans. With humans! The most foolish of all creatures—we'd do better to ally ourselves with giants." He spoke scornfully, but perhaps his companion was shocked, because a moment later, Acacius sighed. "I speak in jest, of course. No self-respecting elf would have anything to do with giants, boorish beasts that they are."

The other elf spoke again. "If you believe Lurgl traitorous enough to give refuge to a human, and if you've known where he is all this time, why haven't you moved against him sooner? Why have you let him believe that he had succeeded in hiding himself from you?"

"I don't know what you mean by move against him," Acacius said disapprovingly. "I have no desire to kill him. He is my cousin, after all."

Farrin barely stifled a choke, his eyes riveted to Lurgl's face. The elf looked resigned. It seemed their bargain about silence would be activated. The reason for the peculiar exchange had now become abundantly clear.

"But he really was foolish to think I'd let myself lose track of him." Acacius sounded indulgent now. "I don't know the exact location, of course. But I've always been aware of the general area. I think my agent will find it, and then we'll see if the missing princess is holed up there as well."

Panic was rising in Farrin's throat, but he couldn't move, partly for fear of being detected, and partly for fear of missing some further crucial information.

"Lurgl will have activated a ward, surely," said the other elf.

"Perhaps," said Acacius, not sounding concerned. "But it's been three weeks. An absolute ward for this long would take more magic than Lurgl could have mined in all the years of his exile. It must be a limited one, and my agent has been well-coached in how to identify and exploit its weaknesses. She bears a revealing talisman as well as the talisman intended for the princess."

The talisman intended for the princess? Disregarding the risk of detection, Farrin shifted, reaching out to grasp Lurgl's arm. It was time to go. Bianca might be under attack even now, and they were still hours from the cottage!

Lurgl seemed to read his determination on his face, because he unfolded himself without argument, still moving in total silence. As they shifted, someone else approached the pair below them, and the conversation turned to less sensitive matters. But even if there'd been more to hear, Farrin didn't think he could have sat still for another moment. Not when he knew Bianca was alone and unprotected at the cottage, believing herself safe inside the ward Farrin had assured her would hold.

He could barely wait until they were clear of the settlement to let his thoughts burst out of him.

"Lurgl, this is so much worse than anything I thought!"

"It is certainly dire," Lurgl agreed, although he didn't sound excessively troubled.

"What was all that about Acacius being your cousin?" Farrin demanded.

"That was the matter which our bargain requires you to keep to yourself," said Lurgl calmly. "I am certain you will agree that it does not pertain directly to Bianca's safety."

"Yes, yes, fine, but why keep it a secret?" Farrin asked.

"Would you wish it to be known that your own cousin had driven you from your home?" Lurgl asked, a snap in his voice.

Farrin wasn't fooled. He knew there was more to Lurgl's reasons than that, but he let the matter drop. He had much more pressing concerns.

"Do you think it's true, about the purpose for which the elves want Bianca?"

"Undoubtedly," said Lurgl. "I recognized the other voice well. He is another cousin of Acacius—not on my side of the family—and is a close and trusted confidante. Acacius would have no reason to speak dishonestly to him."

"So if they get their hands on her, they'll use her up until she expires then throw her away, like a poorly designed talisman," Farrin raged. "It's despicable."

"It's self-serving," said Lurgl with a shrug. "Which is the way of elves." He caught Farrin's expression and gave a wry smile. "But it is a more than usually vicious example of our general philosophy, I agree. As my honored cousin intimated back there, my objection to Acacius's basic approach to elf-human relations is what ultimately forced me to leave the settlement."

Farrin frowned. "You didn't want them to force humans onto the ground to try to identify the singers," he said. "You took a stand on the humans' behalf."

Lurgl shrugged. "I'm not the only one. Several of the others at the cottage left the rest of our kind for the same reason."

"What about the other few?" Farrin asked dryly.

Lurgl laughed. "You are speaking of Dionysius, and you are correct. That was not his reason for seeking refuge. I believe it related to heavy losses in games of chance, or something along those lines. But we do not ask too many questions. None of us wish to speak of our past. We just want to live in peace and safety."

"But is it safe?" Farrin demanded, returning to the material point. "Acacius seemed to think his underling would be able to get through the ward, but she can't, can she?"

Lurgl looked uncomfortable. "I can't say that for sure. Acacius is right that it was necessary to build in limitations to make the ward sustainable. It doesn't keep everyone out, only those considered untrustworthy."

"And who does that include?" demanded Farrin.

"Well, given the nature of elves, it should really be everyone," said Lurgl reasonably. "We don't tend to give a lot of trust."

"But?" Farrin prompted, and Lurgl sighed.

"But when I cast the ward, it included as intrinsically trustworthy anyone who was within it at the time. Meaning any of those individuals have the power to choose to trust someone or not when they approach. They may not even know they're doing it, but the ward will respond to their instincts."

"Tell me Bianca wasn't inside when you cast the ward," Farrin said, horrified.

"Of course she was," said Lurgl. "What would be the point of casting it if she wasn't, given her protection is its primary purpose?"

Farrin groaned. Could there be any loophole more perfectly designed to exploit Bianca's good-hearted weakness? And on this of all days, he'd left her alone.

"We need to reach the cottage," he said grimly, increasing his pace. "As soon as humanly possible."

# Bianca

Bianca stretched, abandoning her half-hearted attempt to fix a broken windowsill and pacing listlessly across the room. She supposed she should be glad of the quiet morning after the terrifying near miss of the day before. But she wasn't. It was hard to go back to loneliness and inactivity after only one day of freedom outside the clearing.

She let out a soft groan, telling herself to be honest. The issue wasn't the boredom. It was the conflict with Farrin. She still felt upset over what had passed between them, her heart not sure whether to be defensive or ashamed in light of his well-meant criticism.

"Hello?"

The tearful voice jerked Bianca out of her thoughts, and she started toward the door. Who was calling? The voice sounded female, but she was fairly sure it wasn't Raella. But who else could it be? Who else would make it past Lurgl's ward?

When she reached the doorway, she realized that whoever it was hadn't actually made it past the ward. There was no one in sight, but the voice carried clearly through the trees.

"Hello, is anyone there? Please help me!"

Bianca hesitated in the doorway for only a moment. Her suspicions were roused, but she knew what it meant to be lost and alone in this jungle. She couldn't just ignore the plea.

Hurrying forward, she made her way through the trees, stopping short of the point where the air shimmered slightly.

"Please, if you're there, help me," the voice came again, and Bianca moved along the tree line in the direction from which it issued.

She drew up short as an unfamiliar elf came into view. The elf was female, as she'd guessed, but definitely not Raella. She had the same alabaster skin and glittering green eyes as all the elves Bianca had seen, but there the familiarity ended. She looked upset, tears glistening in her eyes as she searched the trees frantically.

"Anyone? Please, I'm in trouble!"

Bianca hesitated, torn. Her first instinct was to run out to the poor elf, but something held her back. She knew what Farrin would say, for one thing. But it wasn't just his warnings. Whatever he thought, she had learned caution from her experiences. She knew that the elves wanted to get their hands on her, and her ability to channel magic. She wasn't going to blindly trust a stranger. Cautiously, she moved forward, stopping just on the other side of the ward from the elf. Bianca could see the stranger clearly, but it was obvious that the elf couldn't see her. The ward was working.

"I...I can't let you in," she said, trying to sound sympathetic but final. "But if you wait, I can ask—"

She cut herself off. It was clear the elf couldn't hear her. Lurgl's ward must block sound as well as sight. Bianca bit her lip, thinking. Even if she'd known how, she wouldn't let the stranger in. That would be compromising everyone else's sanctuary as well as hers, and it wasn't her place to make that decision. The only way to communicate with the elf would therefore be to go outside the ward. But if she did that, she'd be at the mercy of any malicious intentions the stranger might have. If only she'd had more success learning to use her magic! Then maybe she wouldn't feel so vulnerable.

The elf was hiccuping slightly now, looking utterly woebegone, and Bianca's heart stirred in spite of her mixed thoughts.

"I, I don't know if anyone can hear me," the elf said. "But I'm looking for Lurgl. I don't even know if he's here anymore, but he told me once this was where I could find him." She drew a shuddering breath, a tear leaking down her cheek. "We were sweethearts once, and I know he's angry I didn't follow him when he left, but I was afraid. I didn't want to be alone out here. Only now they've found out what we were to each other, and they've cast me out. I have nowhere else to go."

Bianca drew in a breath. Was it true? If it was, Lurgl wouldn't thank her for casting out his sweetheart, come searching for him after years. Not to mention it would be unforgivably cruel to the elf before her. She took a half-step forward, on the edge of revealing herself, when the stranger pulled out a ribbon.

"If you don't believe me, give him this. He'll recognize it. He gave it to me when he left, and told me to get it to him if I ever needed help."

She held up the innocuous-seeming length of white ribbon, and Bianca frowned. Even through the ward, she could feel a strange, tangy flavor to the object. It must be magic, which meant the ribbon was a talisman.

All Bianca's suspicions returned, but still she hesitated. If Lurgl had truly given this elf the ribbon, he'd probably turned it into a talisman himself. Perhaps its purpose was to help her find him, or to help him find her, or something romantic like that.

Or perhaps it was a trap.

Bianca shifted her weight from foot to foot, in an agony of indecision. Oblivious to her wrestle, the elf spoke a final time.

"I don't know if anyone is there, or if I'm speaking to myself. But I don't know what else to do. I can tell he has a ward up—I wouldn't expect anything less. If I can't get through, I'll just have to hope he comes out. I'll leave this here. If he wants to find me, he'll know how. He always did."

With those words, she looped the ribbon around a narrow branch, swiping one sleeve across her wet eyes as she stepped back. Then, with a lingering look in the direction of the hidden cottage, the elf turned away, disappearing into the undergrowth.

Bianca stared after her, still totally at a loss for what to do. But in a moment, the elf was out of sight, and the opportunity to stop her from leaving was gone, anyway. As for the ribbon...well, she'd left it there for Lurgl, so the wisest course seemed to be to let Lurgl retrieve it. He would certainly know whether the stranger's story was true. And if it wasn't true, leaving the ribbon could be a trap, designed to lure Bianca from the safety of the ward.

She squirmed at the thought. It was uncomfortable to rate her own value so highly that she suspected the touching display of being a con designed specifically to draw her out. Was that really the type of attitude to life that Farrin admired?

After hovering for several minutes, Bianca turned back to the clearing. She would achieve nothing by staring at the ribbon all day. But the fluttering white strand haunted her thoughts as she went about her tasks, and she couldn't focus on anything else. She kept going back to check on it, wondering if she'd made the right decision. The night her father died kept flashing through her memory, as well as the first night of her exile. On both those occasions, she'd made a decision which had turned out to be wrong, and had led to great loss. Here she was, faced with another decision requiring wisdom, and she didn't want to make another mistake. But how could she know which was the right course? Which approach would lead to regret?

On one of her returns to the ward, hours after the unsettling encounter, she was just approaching the relevant place when she heard a deep, throaty call through the trees. To her dismay, she found a caracara perched on the branch, inspecting the ribbon.

"What are you doing here?" she scolded the bird. "Go forage somewhere else!"

The bird clearly couldn't hear her through the ward, because it gave no reaction to the sudden noise. Tilting its head to the side, it surveyed the ribbon, a look in its eye that Bianca didn't like.

"Oh, no, you don't!" she told it. "That's for Lurgl, not you!"

But the words had barely left her mouth when the caracara bent its head in an abrupt movement, picking at the ribbon with its beak.

For an anguished second Bianca hesitated, paralyzed by the fresh moment of decision forced upon her. But then she shook off her fear and charged through the ward. She knew the elf might have been lying, she knew it might be a mistake. But if there was any chance the tragic story was true, she couldn't let the bird carry the keepsake away. She would just scare the bird off, then retreat quickly back inside the ward, leaving the ribbon where it was.

The caracara froze, eyeing her for a tense moment. Then its claw closed around the ribbon as it spread its wings.

"No!" Bianca cried, lunging forward and grasping hold of the fluttering white strand just as the bird left the branch.

Instantly, Bianca knew she'd made a terrible mistake. The moment her skin touched the ribbon, she felt magic flare to life. The bird wouldn't have been able to sense the power, but it still released the ribbon with a screech, winging swiftly out of sight.

Bianca had no such escape. Her hand seemed bound to the talisman, unable to let go no matter how she tried to command it. Before her horrified eyes, the ribbon writhed and twisted with a life of its own, darting around her waist and securing itself with a painful tightness reminiscent of the ropes the guard had secured her with the night she'd been pushed from the platform.

"No!" Bianca gasped, trying to rip it off. But the more she pulled, the tighter it became, until she could barely breathe. She let go, her mind racing as she tried to think of another way out of the trap. If only the others were here, Lurgl would surely have some kind of magic in his stores that could free her.

But if the others were here, this would never have happened, she thought bitterly. Only she was fool enough to fall for such a brazen trap.

With or without the others, the cottage was surely the safest place to be. Bianca tried to move back through the ward, but to her horror, the ribbon had other ideas. When she tried to move, it pulled so tight that her vision spun. She stopped, trying to draw in a deep enough breath to satisfy the need for air, but even that wasn't enough for the ribbon. The pressure continued, unbearable and increasing.

Desperate, Bianca took a step away from the ward, and instantly the pressure eased a fraction. She tried not to move again, but the pressure was so powerful, she had no choice. It took only a moment to realize the terrible truth—the ribbon was leading her, forcing her to follow a set path. She tried desperately to resist, but she was powerless against the magic. Soon she was blundering through the forest, moving more quickly than she would have been able to on her own impetus.

She was being herded, and she had no doubt about the destination. It was taking her to the elves' settlement.

Panic rose, and she opened her mouth to scream for help. But she stopped herself. What if the elf who'd left the ribbon was hovering nearby, waiting for her? Or another party like the one she and Farrin had seen the day before.

Farrin. Her heart squeezed painfully at the thought of the Medullan. She'd justified his every fear regarding her trusting nature. She wanted to rage and scream at the heartlessness of the tactics used against her. No doubt the whole story had been a fabrication.

Defiance rose up within Bianca. She should never have left the ward, but she hadn't been completely thoughtless. She'd known there was the potential for danger, and she'd tried to be cautious. Wanting to think well of others wasn't the same as weakness, and she would show the elves that.

She was still moving through the jungle rapidly, crashing through undergrowth and falling over logs in the haste the ribbon imposed on her. At this rate, she'd get intercepted by a predator before she ever made it to the elves' settlement.

Trying not to dwell on the dangers she couldn't control, she focused instead on what she could do. She wasn't powerless.

Bianca narrowed her eyes, focusing on the magic that poured into her through her feet. She could feel it flowing through her and back out into the air, and she tried to hold on to as much of it as she could.

Lifting her voice, she sang a song of freedom, commanding the ribbon to release her.

Nothing happened.

Gritting her teeth in frustration, she tried again, with the same result. She tried singing to her feet to stop moving, and although her pace slowed slightly, she kept walking. Next she tried commanding the magic to leave the talisman, but there was no noticeable result from that. It was maddening. There was so much magic around and within her—she could feel it. Surely she only needed a fraction of it to counteract the talisman, but she couldn't seem to use any. It was like there was a bottleneck inside her, the magic blocking up completely when she tried to use it, only flowing free once again when she gave up and let it pass.

In frustration, she raised her voice, singing more loudly as she commanded the ribbon to release her at once. The ribbon didn't respond, but something else did. With a hiss, a small figure leaped from the trees. Bianca flinched, but it was only Lottie. She must have been hanging about near the cottage. The ocelot landed nimbly on the ground beside Bianca, who tried to stop moving.

She didn't manage it, of course, and Lottie followed curiously for a few paces, sniffing at Bianca's skirts.

"Lottie, please get help!" Bianca gasped. "Can you find the others? I'm in trouble!"

The ocelot regarded her out of unblinking amber eyes, then turned away, disappearing rapidly between the trees. Bianca watched her go, with no idea of whether Lottie was going for help or abandoning her. The jungle cat had never been overly fond of the interloper, after all.

Bianca kept singing, her words somehow turning to a mournful dirge, a Selvanan lamentation often spoken at funerals. As if in response to her words, rain began to patter gently through the leaves. It was a fine mist, but Bianca was still soaked in a few short minutes. Undeterred, she raised her voice, singing still.

"Enough of that racket. Do you want to alert every elf in the jungle to your presence?"

The surly voice made Bianca gasp, spinning around as best she could while still moving forward.

"Ulmer! Thank heavens! Please, can you help me?"

Five more of the elves trotted into view, Lottie slinking along beside them.

"Lottie, bless you!" Bianca declared, the words somehow coming out as song.

To everyone's surprise, something small and gray suddenly fell from a low-hanging branch, landing right in front of Lottie. The ocelot was the quickest to recognize it, snapping up the clumsy-footed mouse in a second.

The six elves all stared from the ocelot to Bianca, who winced.

"Sorry," she muttered to the departed mouse. "I didn't mean to do that." She couldn't quite hold in a sigh. As usual, the magic had worked when she wasn't trying to wield it, despite being useless when she desperately wanted its assistance.

Lottie purred, well satisfied with her reward for helping. With a flick of her tail, she leaped onto a branch and disappeared into the trees.

"What's going on, Bianca?" Raella demanded. "What's so urgent that Lottie scratched and prodded until we came? Where are you going? Why are you outside the ward?"

"I should never have left the ward," Bianca groaned. "I knew it, and yet I fell for the trap like a fool." Swiftly, she explained what had happened.

Raella clucked her tongue disapprovingly. "Pack of lies, for certain," she said. "Lurgl never had a sweetheart that I heard of. The rest of the elves are luring you to the settlement. We're headed the right way."

"What can I do?" Bianca asked desperately. "I've tried using magic myself, but I can't seem to wield enough to achieve anything substantial."

"A neutralizing talisman might do the trick," piped up Dakarai.

"Do any of you have something like that?" Bianca asked eagerly. He shook his head. "Nope."

Bianca kept her patience with an effort. "Any other suggestions?" she asked, her voice a little tart.

"I have some unformed stores of raw magic back at the cottage," said Arbor thoughtfully. "But I'm not entirely sure what to mold them into, and even if I could, it would take too long."

"No one's asking the obvious question." The voice was so irritable, Bianca didn't even need to look around to know it was Dionysius. "Which is, why is this our problem?"

"Oh, give it a rest, Dion," said Raella without heat. "This is the most interesting thing that's happened all week."

"So happy I could provide you with entertainment," said Bianca dryly.

"You need to remove the magic from the talisman," said Eason, as if it was the simplest thing in the world. "If you can mine the magic out of it, it should lose its power."

Murmurs of agreement passed around the awkwardly moving group, some of the other elves looking impressed.

"That's good thinking, Eason," Arbor said approvingly. "That would likely work. And it wouldn't require the use of magic to achieve. Just the right tools, and the right skills."

"Do any of you have those?" Bianca demanded.

Dionysius rolled his eyes. "What kind of idiotic question is that? We spend every day mining magic. We were doing it when that fool ocelot interrupted us."

"We all know how to mine static magic, yes," Dakarai said doubtfully. "But mining magic from a talisman actively in use is a much trickier thing. If it goes wrong, the magic could explode out and kill us all."

"Good point," said Arbor, and a few of the elves retreated several paces.

"Ulmer's the most skilled," Raella said, still trotting along stoutly beside Bianca. "He could do it, I imagine."

"Ulmer?" Bianca wished it had been one of the friendlier elves, but she still turned to him appealingly. "Do you think you can mine the magic out of the ribbon?"

Ulmer stroked a hand over his pale, pointed chin. "Most likely," he acknowledged.

"Will you?" Bianca asked. "Will you please help me?" She braced herself for the predictable reply.

Sure enough, the elf spoke. "In exchange for what?"

"Well," said Bianca desperately, "you can keep the magic you mine from the ribbon, if you have some way to store it."

"Not enough," grunted Ulmer. "Not given the risk I'm taking, and the effort required. I could mine magic from this boulder much more easily and more safely." He kicked a rock as he passed it.

"What do you want?" she asked, miserably certain she wouldn't have anything sufficient to offer.

Ulmer considered her thoughtfully, his green eyes as shadowed and suspicious as ever. "If I succeed in freeing you, you'll answer my question honestly."

"What question?" asked Bianca cautiously. The ribbon was still so tight around her middle, it was uncomfortable to speak.

"I'm not telling you that," Ulmer said shortly. "The question will be of my choosing, and you don't get to know what it is ahead of time."

Bianca bit her lip. No doubt there was some hidden purpose in it all, but it was her life on the line. She would have agreed to much more.

"Deal," she said, offering her hand.

Ulmer eyed it for a wary moment, then shook it. "Deal."

"Witnessed," chorused the other five elves.

Reaching into the satchel over his shoulder, Ulmer pulled out a monocle on a strap, putting it over his eye before frowning at her.

"This is going to be difficult with you still on the move like that. Everyone, see if you can hold her steady."

"In exchange for what?" responded five voices, most of them coming from a safe distance.

Ulmer grunted. "Never mind. I'll manage."

Without asking Bianca's permission, he leaped nimbly onto her back, twisting himself around so that he hung upside down—his feet hooked over her shoulders—as he examined the ribbon. Bianca twisted around in an effort to see what he was doing, and watched as he twiddled a dial on the side of the monocle, causing extra layers to clink out from the frame. It must be some kind of magnifying glass.

"Hmm," Ulmer grunted. "I see."

"What do you see?" Bianca asked nervously, her back protesting under his weight. She stumbled, returning her eyes to the path ahead.

"It's woven into the ribbon itself," Ulmer informed her. "Quite advanced manipulation of magic."

He retrieved a fine metal tool from his satchel and began to work on the ribbon. A glance showed Bianca that he was pulling a thread out from it.

"Careful!" she said. "If you try to pull the ribbon off, it gets tighter."

"I'm not pulling it off," he informed her. "I'm stripping the magic from it. Now be quiet and let me do my work."

Chastened, she said no more. She needed her eyes ahead, anyway, as she was navigating a particularly uneven stretch of the jungle floor. In a mercifully short time, Ulmer leaped off her, declaring himself finished.

"I think that's done the trick," he said. "Try to pull it off now."

Bianca noticed that he didn't make the attempt himself, and that he retreated several paces just in case. She pulled nervously at the ribbon, almost crying with relief when it fell away in her hand.

"You did it!" she cried. "Ulmer, thank you so much."

The elf gave no sign of having heard her thanks. "Now for my question," he said at once.

"Oh, all right," said Bianca, taken aback. "What is it?"

"Who, precisely, are you?"

# CHAPTER TWENTY-TWO

# Bianca

Bianca bit her lip, mastering her alarm. She'd made the bargain, fair and square, and Ulmer had just saved her life. She wouldn't have begrudged him the information even without the bargain.

"May I answer once we're back in the safety of the cottage?" she asked.

Ulmer considered her through narrowed eyes for a moment, then gave a curt nod. "Let's go, then."

The seven of them made their way quickly through the jungle, some in the trees, some on the ground. Although it had felt like a terrifying eternity that the ribbon had been pulling Bianca, she actually hadn't traveled very far from the clearing. In less than half an hour, they were all seated around the scrubbed wooden table, Bianca sitting on the floor in order for her legs to fit under the elf-sized furniture.

"Who are you?" Ulmer asked again without preamble.

Bianca sighed. "I am Bee, like I told you, but that's just a nickname rather than my proper name. My current title is still officially Crown Princess Bianca, at least as far as I'm aware. The day I came to you was my eighteenth birthday, and it was the day I was supposed to be crowned as Sel's queen. I am the eldest child and heir of the former king, King Octavio. Queen Marisol is my stepmother."

Six pairs of emerald eyes stared unblinkingly back at her, Ulmer's narrowed in thought.

"That's just great." Predictably, the sarcastic words came from Dionysius, who looked appealingly to the others. "You see what I've been saying all along? In sending her here, the huntsman landed us all in an absolute mess."

Raella frowned thoughtfully. "Maybe," she mused. "Or maybe it's an opportunity."

"That's why the queen was so ready to hand you over to the rest of the elves," said Arbor shrewdly. "She wants your throne, does she?"

"I suppose so," said Bianca quietly. "But you can see why I need to go back. I can't just let her get away with it. She's taken over the kingdom, but she has no right to it."

"Yes, good plan," said Dionysius approvingly. "You should go back today."

"Oh, enough, Dion!" said Raella impatiently.

Bianca rolled her eyes at the irritable elf. "I can't go today. I promised Farrin I'd wait at least until tomorrow. He wants to try to talk me out of it, I think."

"Of course he does," grumbled Dionysius.

Bianca ignored him, realizing that Ulmer was still watching her closely.

"It all seems strange to me," the elf said. "I don't follow human politics closely, but I know your father died two years ago. You weren't exactly a child then. Even if you couldn't be officially crowned, I would have expected you to be more or less running the kingdom well before you turned eighteen. And yet, your stepmother seems to hold absolute power."

Bianca flushed, shame washing over her. She caught the

knowing glint in Ulmer's green eyes, and knew he saw her weakness.

"If I had my time over, I'd do things differently," she said quietly.

"Who among us wouldn't say the same?" The new voice came from the doorway, and Bianca looked up to see Lurgl, looking tiny in the large frame, with Farrin towering behind him.

"Bianca!" the Medullan cried, hurrying forward. "Are you all right? What happened?"

"I'm fine," she assured him. She patted her hair self-consciously, finding a few twigs tangled in the white locks. "Why? Do I look a mess?"

"Never mind how you look," he said, concern clear in his brown eyes as they searched her face. "What happened? Did Acacius's agent manage to get to you?"

"Agent?" Bianca repeated. "Did you know about the plan?"

"We just overheard it," he told her. "And we raced straight back. I was afraid we would be too late."

"You were," said Ulmer, a touch of glee in his voice. "Her Royal Highness is indebted to me now, not you."

Farrin's eyes flew to Ulmer in surprise, although he didn't look nearly as astonished as Bianca expected. She grimaced. She'd known revealing her identity to the elves would mean Farrin finding out, but she'd hoped she might be able to tell him herself.

"You know about that?" Farrin asked Ulmer.

"Wait, *you* know about that?" Bianca demanded.

Farrin shrugged. "It was fairly obvious."

"Well!" exploded a few of the elves. It took Bianca a moment to realize they were offended not by Farrin's failure to share the secret, but by the implied disparagement of their intelligence.

Farrin's frown returned. "And you mistake my meaning. I

don't want Bianca in my debt." He moved closer to her, kneeling so that their eyes were level. "What happened, Bianca?"

She winced. "You'll think I'm such a fool," she said, the words coming out a little surly. Succinctly, she told him what had happened.

Farrin let out a groan, his face darkening. "I was afraid of something like that. They're devious, aren't they?" He turned to Ulmer. "Thank goodness you were able to mine the magic out of it. Thank you."

"Why are you thanking me?" Ulmer said. "I didn't do you any favors."

"Or Bianca, I imagine." Farrin's tone was dry. "I'm sure you required an exchange."

"It was a very reasonable price, from my perspective," Bianca assured him.

Farrin didn't press for details. "Are you sure you're all right?"

She nodded. "Of course I am. I just feel a fool."

Farrin still looked stressed. "I did tell you that—"

"*Don't.*" She cut him off with an upraised hand. "Don't say I told you so."

Farrin shut his mouth with a snap, seeming to realize he'd erred. "I'm just glad you're all right," he said quietly. "I wish that was the end of it, but..." He exchanged a glance with Lurgl. "We overheard some things you need to know."

Bianca sat up straighter, alarmed by the somber look on his face. "What is it?"

He told her, and her eyes widened at the account of the elf leader's cold-blooded plans for her.

"And if I did manage to...clear some of the magic, or whatever he called it, that definitely wouldn't be enough to make a substantial difference?"

"Of course it wouldn't," said Farrin, sounding alarmed all over again.

Bianca didn't respond to him, her eyes flying straight to Lurgl in a silent entreaty. The elf frowned thoughtfully for a moment before answering.

"I won't pretend to be an expert," he said evenly. "But I do not believe one singer, however strong, could make a significant difference to the unmanageable level of magic saturating the land."

Bianca nodded, satisfied. A frown grew on her face as she thought it all over. "Why do they care, though?" she asked. "Why do the elves want to clear the wild magic? I mean," she glanced around at her companions, "it doesn't kill you on contact."

"We never wished to be cut off from the mainland, living in lawless chaos," said Lurgl simply. "The jungle is dangerous on its own, of course, but it's much more dangerous since the magic went wild. We rely on the magic for many things, and it's already a struggle for us to manipulate it. It's too strong. Why do you think we're all so hardworking? All the elves are. We all mine magic all day every day in order to keep it barely under control. It's not supposed to be like that. Our brethren on the mainland don't live this way."

Bianca let out a sigh, overwhelmed by the state of her kingdom.

"So what are you going to do now?" Farrin asked Bianca, sounding uneasy.

Bianca shrugged. "I have to go home," she said. "I can't see any other way forward. Why delay? The elves clearly know where to find this place, and it won't be safe for me to stay here alone anymore."

"But without a plan you'll be just as vulnerable up there as you are down here," Farrin argued.

Again, Bianca looked to Lurgl. The elf nodded slowly. "I do

think you need more preparation before you take on your stepmother."

"What can I do?" Bianca asked helplessly. "She holds all the power—no amount of planning will change that. If I want to claim my rightful place, I have to show myself. Everyone presumably thinks I'm dead."

"She does not hold all the power," Lurgl contradicted. "Her limited mind can't even grasp the power at your disposal. I understand that you've had little success with harnessing your magic. I think it's time for me to take a hand in the process. I thought my ignorance of the craft of singers made it pointless, but perhaps there is something for you to learn from the magic of elves."

"I appreciate the idea," said Bianca wearily, "but in exchange for what? I have nothing left to give."

Lurgl chuckled. "No exchange this time. Think of it as a gift freely given, if it helps. Although of course I have a purpose of my own."

Bianca eyed him thoughtfully. "All right," she said. "I'll be grateful for any help you can offer me. I certainly wouldn't mind having a better grasp on my magic before returning to Sel." She glanced through the window in the direction of the out-of-sight ward. "But will it be safe here, given the elves know about it?"

"The agent didn't get past the ward, correct?" Lurgl said crisply. "As long as you stay inside it at all times, you should be safe enough. Not forever, but for the time it will take for me to help you train a little."

Bianca nodded, disheartened at being trapped once again inside the clearing, but knowing there was no other realistic option.

"And what about us?" Dionysius demanded. "We're in extra danger now, and our haven has been exposed. Not to mention we've lost half a day of mining thanks to having to rescue her Royal Foolishness."

"For which I'm grateful," Bianca said coolly. "But I've already negotiated the exchange."

"With Ulmer, yes," said Dionysius. "But what about the rest of us? Don't you think saving your life is worth more than an honestly answered question and a bit of excess magic? Don't you agree that we're all owed gratitude for what you've received today?"

Farrin shifted, a sound of protest and warning coming from his mouth. But Bianca cut him off with a gesture, her eyes still on Dionysius. She hadn't lived among elves for weeks now without learning a thing or two.

"It's neither here nor there whether I agree, because an agreement after the fact is no agreement at all," she said calmly.

Dionysius actually growled, turning away with a flourish and stomping from the building. Bianca couldn't help glancing at Farrin, and her cheeks dimpled in a smile at the sparkle of humor in his eyes.

Raella gave a crow of laughter. "Poor old Dion," she said. "He thinks it's criminal for humans to use elf logic against us. That's why he can't stand Farrin." Still chuckling, she moved off toward her hammock. "Sharing a sleeping space with a human princess," she commented to no one in particular. "Well, it's been a strange season, no doubt about it."

Bianca's eyes flew to Farrin again, self-conscious at this reminder of her status. He smiled back at her, although there was a definite shadow still in his eyes.

"Can I speak with you alone?" he asked quietly.

"Of course." Bianca rose, hurrying out of the cottage at his side. He led her a few paces into the trees, although still well within the ward.

"Are you really all right?" he asked, his eyes searching her form.

She nodded. "I really am. Just furious with myself. Another pivotal moment, another instance of terrible judgment from me." She dropped her voice to a mutter. "Maybe my stepmother is right. Maybe I'm not fit to rule."

"That's nonsense," said Farrin sharply. "Surely you don't believe that."

Bianca smiled painfully, unable to take comfort from his words when she knew the truth of his own poor opinion of her capabilities.

"Never mind," she said, forcing a light tone.

A flash of tan caught her eyes, and she watched as Lottie leaped from one tree to another above them, once again stuck to Farrin's side.

"Lottie's the one who actually saved my life," Bianca commented. She smiled more genuinely. "Although I'm trusting she won't ask for an exorbitant payment in exchange."

Farrin chuckled. "I'm sure she'll refrain." He was silent for a moment, his eyes roving over her face. "I'm sorry that Acacius has such selfish and evil designs against you," he said at length. "I was terrified when I heard them, and terrified today's attack would succeed."

Bianca shook her head. "It's a little alarming," she acknowledged. "But it's nothing so different from what we expected." She sighed. "My poor, vain, self-centered stepmother never really had a clue what she was dabbling in, I think."

"But she was aware enough of what she was doing to know that she was throwing you to the wolves," Farrin said, his voice hard.

Bianca sighed again. "Yes, she certainly knew that. I'm not making excuses for her, believe me. She was never going to see me as a daughter, I think. I doubt anything I did was ever going to change that."

She raised her eyes to Farrin's a little shyly. "I can hardly believe you knew who I was all along. You don't seem annoyed at me for keeping the secret from you."

"Oh, well, it didn't seem that big a deal to me," Farrin said vaguely. "Probably because I'm a prince myself."

Bianca laughed, but the sound cut off as she caught sight of his expression. "Are you serious?"

He nodded. "Prince Farrin of Medulle, to be precise. I'm not a crown prince or anything. Just a younger one."

"But...you...I didn't..." Bianca sputtered. "I—I don't know what to say."

"Your Highness, are the words I believe you're looking for," Farrin told her cheekily. "And a nice state curtsy wouldn't go amiss."

"No, that's definitely not it," Bianca said, unable to help laughing at the sparkle in his eyes. "Are you truly a prince of Medulle?"

He nodded.

Bianca could hardly make sense of it. Their many conversations passed back through her mind, and she raised troubled eyes to his. "You ran away and got on that ship in secret, didn't you? No wonder you feel guilty for what your family might be suffering."

Pain flashed across his face, and she hastened to explain herself.

"Not that I'm trying to criticize. I'm just understanding your reactions more now. Your brother must be in a dire state for you to decide it was worth taking the risk." Her voice turned dry. "I just hope your disappearance doesn't spark a war between our kingdoms, because between you and me, I don't like Selvana's chances."

Farrin laughed reluctantly. "A monarch should never make that kind of admission to foreign royalty."

"Yes, well, I'm not a monarch yet, am I?" Bianca said. Her voice softened. "And I trust you, as I've already told you."

Farrin's eyes were troubled as they met hers. "So you say," he responded quietly. "But back there, in the cottage, you didn't believe me. You kept looking to Lurgl to tell you the truth."

Bianca sighed. "It wasn't that I thought you would lie to me, exactly, Farrin. But when I say I trust you, I mean I trust your heart, or your intentions, or whatever you want to call it. The trouble is, you clearly don't trust me."

"Of course I do!" Farrin objected. "I'd trust you with my life."

Bianca paused, surprised and touched by the intensity of the declaration. Still, she needed to say this. "But not with my own life," she said gently. "The times I looked to Lurgl were the times I thought you might be withholding the truth out of fear I'd do something foolish and endanger myself. If you don't trust me to make my own decisions, then I can't trust you to give me all the information I need. In trying to protect me, you might hinder me."

Farrin looked anguished, and he took a step toward her, the movement seeming involuntary. "I didn't mean to withhold anything from you, Bianca, or to make you feel incapable. I just can't seem to help trying to protect you. When I started taking you out into the jungle, past the safety of the ward, I promised myself I wouldn't let anything hurt you." He gave a wry smile. "And while I know I have many faults, I do try to make a point of keeping my promises."

"Not all your promises," Bianca quipped. He looked startled, and she smiled, trying to show it was a joke. "You said you'd bring me back an apple, and I've yet to see a hint of one."

Farrin's features relaxed in a smile of amusement, but it didn't last long.

"I appreciate the impulse to protect me," she told him, responding to his renewed seriousness. "I truly do. But I'm not as incapable as you think. Even with Dionysius before, I could see you were ready to step in and fend off his manipulations. But I didn't need you to."

Farrin's eyes looked troubled, and his forehead was so creased, she wished she could smooth it with her fingers. How could she show him that while she meant what she said, while she needed him to hear her frustrations, she wasn't trying to drive him away? That was the last thing she wanted to do. She shifted closer, so that they were mere inches apart, and she had to tilt her head back to look up into his eyes.

"Like I said," she continued, "I trust your heart." In a rush of daring, she lifted one hand and laid it gently on his chest, over his heart. She could feel its steady, thumping beat. "But I can handle myself, Farrin."

His hand leaped to cover hers, and the warmth of his touch enveloped her, seeming to reach far beyond the point of contact to send heat rushing over her whole body. For a moment she started to shift, her weight going to the balls of her feet in an almost unconscious preparation to lift her face to his. Then she realized that his eyes looked just as troubled and conflicted as before.

He didn't believe her. He still thought she needed to be coddled.

With a sigh, she stepped back, dropping her hand and giving him a weary smile. "I'll just have to show you, I suppose," she said. "Until next time we meet, Farrin." She took a step toward the cottage, then cast a glance over her shoulder. "I hope it will be soon."

"Wait." Farrin moved toward her, one hand outstretched. "You're not going to leave for Sel immediately?"

Bianca shook her head. "I'll accept Lurgl's offer. If he can help me learn to use my magic, it will be time well spent."

"Will you be here for as long as a week?" Farrin asked.

She blinked. "I imagine so."

"And you'll stay inside the ward?" he pressed.

She gave him a look, and he raised his hands in a placating gesture. "I know, I know, and it's not that I don't trust you. I just need to know we're in agreement."

Bianca sighed. "Yes, I'll stay inside the ward."

Farrin nodded, apparently satisfied. With two more swift strides, he closed the distance between them, pulling her into a brief and unexpected hug.

"Thank you," he said into her hair, before stepping quickly back. "I wish I could help you more," he told her. "But I don't have a fraction of the power I once had. Still, I won't let you down, not if it's in my power to come through for you." There was no doubting the sincerity in those dark eyes.

Without another word, he turned and plunged into the jungle, leaving Bianca still dazed from his touch.

For Bianca, the next week passed in strange fits and bursts. When she was training with Lurgl, time moved far too quickly, her eager mind wishing it could string out every moment, make the most of each morsel of time the elf was willing to give her. All the rest of the time, each minute dragged interminably.

Once again, she was honest enough with herself to admit that it was Farrin's absence which made her feel listless. She'd told him she hoped to see him soon, but there had been no sign of him since he'd disappeared into the trees. Even Lottie had been absent, suggesting the two had gone on a journey somewhere. But where?

At least she was finally making progress with her magic. He might not be a singer, but Lurgl's training had proved much more helpful than Farrin's and her guesswork.

"That's it," the elf coached, as she held a quavering note that was keeping a twig suspended impossibly in mid-air. "Don't overthink it."

At once, Bianca's voice faltered, and the twig dropped. "As soon as you say that, you guarantee that I'm thinking too hard about it," she said, in mock exasperation.

Lurgl grinned, the dappled morning light filtering through the trees and illuminating his pale face. "The excessive suggestibility of humans is a bit of a barrier to this type of training," he agreed.

"I still don't understand why not thinking about my craft would help me do it better," Bianca said, rubbing her head as she tried to wrap her mind around the counter-intuitive thought.

She seated herself on a log, disregarding the dampness of the moss as it seeped through her gown. It was the same gown she'd worn every day of the last four weeks, and the white underlay was far from white now. Better for camouflage in the jungle, Raella had assured her.

Not that she and Lurgl were properly in the jungle. They were just inside the tree line, the tinkling of the waterfall in the clearing providing a constant background music to match Bianca's song. As she'd promised Farrin, she'd stayed inside the ward for the last week.

"Perhaps I'd better explain it to you as I would to an elf," said Lurgl thoughtfully, seating himself beside her.

Bianca noticed that he chose a spot on the upward side of

the log's slope, so his head was at a similar height to hers. Her lips twitched, although of course she said nothing. In their own way, the elves were as vain as Marisol.

"Through centuries of our own magical practices," Lurgl said, "we elves have learned an important lesson, one that defies human attitudes. We've learned that less is often more."

Bianca frowned. "What do you mean?"

"It means many things in many situations, in relation to the way we mine and process magic. I won't attempt to explain it all to you, as it would make no sense without a great deal of background understanding. I hadn't thought it was relevant for you—I truly know very little about singing—but I'd thought that the sheer quantity of magic in this land would make your song powerful, without you really needing to try. But now it's occurring to me that maybe that's the problem."

"What?" Bianca demanded.

"Well, it's what Farrin and I overheard that first made me wonder, although it took me a while to put it all together in my mind. Acacius's advisor said that he'd made a study of singing craft, and he thought the quantity of magic in the ground here might be too much for your body to handle if you tried to wield too much of it at once."

"But I feel fine now," Bianca said nervously. "Even though I can feel magic coming at me from the ground all the time. I've even grown more or less used to the pressure."

"I'm not suggesting contact with the ground is too much for your body," said Lurgl patiently. "We know that isn't true. But maybe it's too much for your *magic*. Or for your singing, I suppose we should say, since the magic doesn't come from inside you."

"I still don't understand," Bianca said, feeling stupid.

"I'm just guessing here," Lurgl said, "but I imagine that on the mainland, singers can grab as much magic as their ability can handle, and wield it. But it's different here. Here there's just so much magic, the land is overrun. And inexperienced as you are, I doubt you have the finesse to grab hold of only a little bit out of so much. You're probably grabbing at everything that's passing through you, except that's an unmanageable volume. I'm wondering if maybe when you try to grab too much, it just creates a blockage, as your singing capacity is unable to process any of it."

"Less is more," mused Bianca.

"That's right," Lurgl said, nodding. "When you managed to unwittingly wield magic up in the canopy before you came to us, your song was probably responding to the more modest amount of magic wafting through the air, or soaked into the trees. Well within the capacity of your song to manage."

"That makes sense," said Bianca, getting excited about these answers. "The same could be true of all the times I've managed to do something when I'm not really trying. I'm not grabbing at the torrent of magic, then. I'm just reacting instinctively, probably only accessing whatever magic is passing naturally through me at the time."

"Precisely," Lurgl agreed.

"Well," said Bianca, pleased. "That's certainly given me plenty to think about."

"Excellent," said Lurgl briskly. "It's time for me to join the others for the day's mining. But you can continue practicing without me, of course."

Bianca nodded, not feeling any great enthusiasm for the idea. She'd disliked being left alone before the attack with the ribbon. Now she dreaded it.

But she made her way back to the cottage uncomplainingly, waving Lurgl off as he hiked his satchel up his back and headed straight out into the jungle. Bianca sang softly as she wandered through the doorway, practicing as instructed. She glanced instinctively toward her own sleeping area to make sure it was tidy and stopped in surprise.

Something was glittering in her hammock. Hurrying over, Bianca saw a decorative comb sitting amongst the fabric. It was beautiful, the prongs a bronze color, and a flower on top formed from some kind of green gem, not unlike the elves' eyes. Lifting it carefully, Bianca noticed a square of paper underneath.

Her heart beating at double time, she read the simple message.

B,

For you, from a heart you can trust.

- F

Bianca's breath caught in her throat at the beautiful gesture, and the reference to her conversation with Farrin before he'd left. He hadn't forgotten her entirely during his unexplained absence, then. But when had he left it? It hadn't been there when she and Lurgl left for their training session. Had Farrin been here in the cottage that very morning, and she'd missed him? Surely he hadn't left again.

No, he must be planning to come back. His note didn't say anything about a goodbye. Striding over to the room's single looking glass, Bianca lifted the comb to her hair. It looked good against the stark white, she reflected. It was a well chosen gift. As she slipped it into her tresses, however, her senses caught something she'd missed before. It was lingering magic, but it wasn't from her own earlier song, as she'd unconsciously assumed.

Before her eyes, the familiar reflection in the looking glass changed. A horrible oozing blackness spread out from the comb, creeping over her head. She could feel the magic, corrosive and angry, paralyzing everything it touched.

She didn't even have time to wonder what had happened and how. The last thing she knew, before awareness fled, was a sensation of falling, falling, falling.

## CHAPTER TWENTY-THREE

# FARRIN

Farrin stilled, noting the rigid ears of the ocelot beside him. After a moment, Lottie seemed to decide whatever she'd heard was no threat, and she resumed her progress through the jungle. Farrin followed, content to trust the feline's superior senses. Something caught his peripheral vision, and he glanced up, surprised to see a wooden walkway above him. It looked rundown and disused, but it was still a manmade structure. He must be nearer the southern human settlement than he'd realized.

Moving more stealthily, he flitted from tree to tree, listening hard for any sound of human conversation. Before long, he caught glimpses of buildings up ahead in the trees, not clumped together like he'd seen in Sel, but in separate trees, connected by thin rope walkways.

Not for the faint of heart, life in Selvana's outlying settlements. Clearly those who chose to live here didn't do so for the sake of being social.

Farrin skirted around the settlement, taking care to keep to the denser undergrowth. From what Lurgl had told him, the apple groves would be due east, and not too far away. Sure enough, after about an hour of ground travel, he and Lottie found themselves at the edge of a relatively cleared area. Even the pressure of the magic was lessened as the space opened up.

It had obviously once been a planned orchard, but the apple trees were now growing wild. Many had self-planted between the orderly rows, and apples of various types hung in profusion from the branches. They also littered the ground, but Farrin hadn't come all this way to grab half-rotted fruit from beneath his feet.

No, he told himself dryly, as he vaulted up into a tree. He'd come all this way in a vain attempt to prove to himself that he wasn't such an imbecile as he must seem. He'd promised Bianca he wouldn't let her down, but he'd failed not only to keep her safe, but to teach her anything of use relating to her magic. He could only hope Lurgl was meeting with more success in that area.

It had stung, hearing Bianca's accusation that his lack of trust made him less trustworthy in turn. It had stung even more to realize she was absolutely right. And although she'd said she wanted to see him soon—showing the kindness of her heart, after her justified rebuke—it was abundantly clear that his presence was a hindrance rather than a help. He'd taken himself off to clear his head and sort out his seemingly disproportionate fears regarding her safety, but also to give her space.

Plus, she'd reminded him of a promise unfulfilled, which had given him an excellent excuse to make himself scarce while he wrestled with his own state of mind. For two years he'd kept himself going by force of will, and by determined, single-minded focus on his mission.

And now...he'd barely thought about the aconitum in weeks. Not only that, but he no longer had the blanket of detachment with which he'd protected himself all this time. Bianca had wandered across his path, cheerful and indomitable in spite of her sufferings, and completely destroyed every ounce of peace he'd had.

And, perhaps more confronting, she'd forced him to acknowledge that he'd never really had peace at all. He hadn't overcome his fear and anxiety—he'd just pushed them down, as evidenced by how instantly and uncontrollably they'd sprung up any time Bianca was in danger. He knew it was an overreaction—he had no real responsibility for her, and no logical reason to be so terrified at the thought of her being hurt. But he couldn't seem to help it.

Well, he reflected, as he slipped several juicy looking apples into his rucksack, at least now he wouldn't be going back empty-handed. The elves always received him better if he brought an offering. Surely it couldn't hurt with Bianca. Hopefully she would accept the token of his regard for the apology it was.

He glanced up at the sun. The overgrown orchard was a pleasant place, and he wouldn't have minded lingering. But Bianca had told him she'd stay with Lurgl for a week, and he didn't want to be away longer than that. What if she tried to brave Sel before he returned? The elves wouldn't ascend into the city with her, that was certain. They'd kept their existence secret from humans for generations. Which meant Farrin was her only option for a bodyguard, a role he fully intended to offer her.

He'd already been away almost four days. If he wanted to return within a week, he needed to start northward immediately. Swiping a final apple, he took a bite as he walked. It was a green apple, and he closed his eyes for a moment in appreciation of its tart juiciness. It had been far too long.

The next three days passed uneventfully. The rain was only sporadic, making travel easier. He and Lottie moved with their usual caution, avoiding predators with practiced methods, and finding safe camping sites before nightfall each day. On the last morning, Farrin rose before the dawn, eager to reach the cottage, which was only a couple hours away. He didn't usually travel before daylight, but as the terrain had grown more familiar, he'd felt himself relax.

He'd be seeing Bianca in about two hours. The thought made him feel both nervous and relieved. It made no sense.

"Just over that way is the clearing where we first saw her, remember?" he commented quietly to Lottie, when they were less than an hour from the cottage. "Kneeling in the undergrowth in that fancy gown." He shook his head. "Imagine if we'd just left her there. That would have been the worst mistake of my life." His tone turned wry. "And that's saying something."

Lottie flicked her tail irritably, leaping into a tree above Farrin's head and running forward with a speed he couldn't hope to match.

Farrin rolled his eyes. Lottie always got like this when he talked about Bianca. The ocelot's jealousy of the Selvanan girl was absurd, although also a little endearing.

He must have gotten more lax than he realized at being so close to his destination, because without Lottie's enhanced hearing, he was taken completely by surprise by the sound of voices from the undergrowth nearby. They were high, and a little cold, identifying them as elvish. Farrin froze, wondering whether to take to the trees or stay still and hope they passed far enough away not to detect him. He'd avoided being exposed to the settlement of elves for two years, and he didn't fancy gaining their attention now. But the next words he overheard drove all thoughts of caution from his mind.

"I still think the exchange was too beneficial for him."

"Well, you're wrong," responded another voice, shortly. "Poisoning the human princess is no small matter."

Poisoning the human princess? Farrin's heart leaped into his throat. They must be speaking of Bianca. But she'd promised to stay inside the ward! Surely no one could get to her in there.

His certainty disappeared rapidly as he realized the simple but significant fact that the elves were moving away from the clearing, not toward it. The attack with the ribbon had proved that they knew the location of the cottage. Had they found some way to get inside?

Without thinking it through, Farrin surged into motion, leaping across a patch of scrub to intercept the elves.

"Who are you?" he roared, bursting into their path with his sword already raised. "What have you done to the princess?"

The half dozen elves all came to an abrupt halt, one of them letting out a high-pitched squeal of surprise before clapping a hand to his mouth in embarrassment.

"What have you done to her?" Farrin demanded, his blade extended toward the closest elf.

For a moment, everyone was motionless. Then the elves exchanged one meaningful glance before scattering. Farrin tried to snatch at one, but they were too quick, their small forms darting into the undergrowth as nimbly as rabbits. He did catch the frantic protest of the one who'd squealed as he zipped from sight, however.

"A human on the ground! Are we already too late, then?"

Farrin had no idea what the elf meant by that, but he didn't much care. He hovered for only the briefest moment of indecision. Underneath his fear and anger, he was aware of great surprise—he hadn't expected the elves to flee instead of fight him, and his first instinct was to chase them down. But who knew if he'd succeed in catching any, and how long that would take? If they'd come from another attempt on Bianca, she might not have that long.

The thought decided him, and in less than a moment, he was back in motion, tearing through the undergrowth without regard for stealth. He didn't even bother taking to the trees as he approached the ward. Clearly there was no more point trying to hide the location of the clearing.

No one was in sight as he emerged from the trees, and no sound intruded on the idyllic scene other than the usual tinkling of the waterfall and the call of birds.

"Bianca?" Farrin cried, fear rising when there was no reply. Sword still drawn, he sprinted along the water's edge, his eyes on the cottage ahead. "Bianca? Are you there?"

He skidded to a stop in the doorway, horror washing over him at the sight of Bianca's form. She was collapsed on the floor in front of the looking glass, her arms splayed, and her face still. A horrid black substance oozed from her head, covering her face and torso, and stretching partway down her arms.

Disregarding any potential danger, Farrin threw himself down beside her, pulling her into his arms.

"Bianca!" he cried desperately. Her eyelids fluttered, and his heart leaped at this sign of life. But she didn't reply, or show any other indication that she could hear him.

A hiss from outside brought Farrin's head snapping up.

"Lottie!" he cried. "Help!"

The ocelot appeared in the doorway, looking as reluctant as the night they'd first encountered Bianca.

"Please," Farrin begged. "Get the others. She's still alive, but I don't know for how long, and I don't know how to save her. I can't work magic, and I don't know what they have in their stores—I need their help."

Lottie blinked once, staring uncomprehendingly at Farrin.

He let out a groan of frustration. "Get Lurgl and the others," he said. "Please!"

Her eyes on Bianca, Lottie gave a discontented mewl and flicked her tail. But after another moment she seemed to relent, because she turned and shot away into the trees.

"Thank you!" Farrin called after her, almost too afraid to hope.

His heart in his throat, he returned his gaze to the limp form in his arms. Bianca looked awful, the warm brown of her skin all but invisible under the glittering blackness of the substance oozing over her. Hesitantly, Farrin touched it, but his hand came away clean. The substance wasn't what was killing her. It was just some physical manifestation of the poisoning magic.

But how did he stop the magic?

"Bianca," he muttered. "Bianca, please wake up. Please come back to me."

His eyes searched her face frantically, but there was no response. He realized with a shudder that the black ooze was still moving, now past her elbow and inching toward her waist. It was definitely traveling downward. He followed it with his eyes, trying to ascertain the source. Last time she'd been tied up with a ribbon. Was the magic tied to a physical talisman again this time?

Farrin's eyes narrowed as they fell on the decorative comb nestled in Bianca's hair. It was a striking piece, and he didn't remember ever seeing it before. Surely she hadn't been wearing it the night she'd fled Sel, and she'd had no opportunity to acquire any other jewelry since.

Keeping one arm firmly around Bianca, he pulled the comb out with the other hand. It felt burning hot to his touch, and he dropped it onto the earthen floor with a cry. But no ooze appeared on his own hand. His eyes flew back to Bianca, and to his amazement, he saw that the dark substance was retreating, moving back up her body. His arms shaking with tension, he watched as it withdrew all the way back to her hair. When the last drop disappeared, Bianca let out a shuddering gasp and opened her eyes.

"Bianca!" he cried, his voice choked with relief. Unthinkingly, he gathered her properly into his arms, crushing her against him as he buried his face in her hair, which was once again pure white.

"Farrin?" she said, her voice coming out muffled against his chest. She sounded confused. "What...what happened?"

"I was hoping you could explain that to me," he said darkly. He squeezed her one more time before releasing her, a little reluctantly. She just felt so good in his arms, warm and safe and apparently quite happy to stay there. "I think it has to do with that comb."

Bianca's eyes, still looking a little dazed, followed his to the jewelry lying on the floor. She gave a gasp, another shiver passing over her.

"It was the comb," she confirmed. "I remember now. I put it in my hair, and then this horrible sludge started to race out of it, all down my face, and..." She shook her head. "I don't remember anything more. I think I blacked out."

"I don't think it can have been long," said Farrin. "I found you in front of the looking glass, and the black ooze was only halfway down your body." His voice shook a little, and the arm still draped supportingly around her tightened. "I think if it had made it all the way down, there wouldn't have been anything I could do."

"I think you're right," said Bianca softly. "And I wasn't expecting the others for hours. It would have been too late."

She raised a glowing face to his, all the color back in her cheeks. Not to mention those rosy lips. Farrin shook his head, trying to clear the foolish thought. What a detail to fixate on in a crisis!

"Thank goodness you came when you did," Bianca was saying. "Farrin, you saved my life. I have nothing to offer in return but my thanks."

He shook his head. "I don't want anything in return. I just want you to be safe."

Her expression softened. "Thank you for a gift freely given," she murmured. Involuntarily, Farrin started to pull her against him again, but then her forehead creased. He paused, searching her face cautiously.

"Bianca? Is everything all right?"

"But the comb," she said. She struggled to her feet, gently freeing herself from his arm. "I forgot."

She hurried across the room to her hammock, which Farrin could currently see. Clearly Raella's ward wasn't activated. Bianca retrieved something from the hammock, and moved back to Farrin's side.

Clambering to his feet, he received a small white square of paper. He sent Bianca a questioning glance, and saw that her expression was grim.

"It was with the comb, in my hammock. Read it."

Farrin did so, going still as he took in the simple message.

B,

For you, from a heart you can trust.

- F

"Bianca," he whispered. "I...I don't know how...I didn't leave—"

"Of course you didn't leave it," she said impatiently. "If you wanted to kill me, you could have done so lots of times, and much more easily than through some convoluted talisman. But do you see the message? It's like they're referring to our conversation last week. How could the elves know what we said?"

Farrin frowned. "It does seem that way," he said. "But it

could also just be a general statement of affection, and...well, faithfulness."

Bianca flushed a little, and Farrin pushed on.

"What concerns me more is how someone got past the ward to leave it here."

"I can't answer that," she said. She wasn't looking at him, but at her fingers as they fidgeted with a fold of her crimson gown. "And I have no idea why they didn't just kill me if they wanted to, because there's no one here but me." She swallowed, her expression resolute as she met his eyes. "I suppose you think that I should have seen through the message. That I should have been more suspicious of it, and—"

"What?" Farrin interrupted, startled. "Of course not! Bianca, this isn't your fault. How could you possibly know that someone had gotten through the ward? You're supposed to be safe as long as you stay inside it." He looked down at the note in his hand. "And this...well, it's convincing," he said. One side of his mouth quirked up in a rueful smile. "I only wish I had thought of a gesture this special."

"Don't be silly, I don't expect lavish gifts from you," said Bianca quickly, her cheeks once again heating.

Farrin studied her face, a smile tugging at his lips again. Say what she might, she'd obviously believed he'd given her a lavish gift. And it certainly didn't seem as though she'd been inclined to reject it. But that cheerful thought was soon eclipsed by the alarming reality of the situation. And in addition to wanting answers, he was troubled by the fact that she was still avoiding his eyes.

"Bianca," he said softly, reaching for her.

He cupped her chin in one of his rough, calloused hands, so different from how they'd been when he'd landed on Selvana fresh from his pampered life. Tilting her face gently up, he searched her eyes.

"Did you really think I'd blame you for this? That I'd be inclined to criticize *you* for someone else trying to kill you?"

"Is it so unreasonable?" Bianca challenged. Her clear gaze caused guilt over their last encounter to squirm through him again. "Last time we spoke, I told you I could handle myself, and you didn't believe me."

"I did," he protested.

She shook her head gently, not attempting to dislodge his hand. "I could read the conflict in your eyes, Farrin. You didn't believe you could leave me alone—you didn't think I could be trusted."

"That's not it at all," he said, horrified by this interpretation of his demeanor. He could see she was unconvinced, and he dropped his hand from her chin to grasp one of her hands. "Bianca, let me explain. You're right that I was conflicted. But it wasn't because I didn't believe you. I knew you were right as soon as you challenged me—I knew I'd been wrong to treat you like you couldn't be trusted. I meant well, but all I did was insult you, and I'm truly sorry."

"It's all right," she whispered, her hand warm in his. "You don't have to—"

"Yes, I do," he disagreed firmly. "You've proven yourself capable lots of times—you've surprised me, if I'm honest. But even if you hadn't, I have no right to dictate to you, or restrict your actions based on what I think will keep you safe." He swallowed. "It was that realization that troubled me so much. I knew you were right, and it was perfectly fair of you to ask me to step back and stop interfering. But I was conflicted because I couldn't bear to stand back—even if my fears aren't reasonable, I'm so terrified of something happening to you, Bianca." He drew a breath. "I didn't think I could stop trying to protect you, but I knew I had to try. That's why I went away for a bit. To try to get myself under control, and to give you space."

Bianca's smile was a little exasperated. "I didn't want space, Farrin. Not from you. And..." She lowered her eyes, then raised them to his, their expression a little shy. "I don't want you to stop trying to protect me. I just don't want you to think you have to protect me from myself."

"Bianca, I'm sorry I ever made you feel that way," he said earnestly. "Can you forgive me?"

"Of course I can!" she said readily. Her voice turned a little rueful. "Can you forgive me for being trusting when I should be suspicious?"

"I don't think that's an offense," said Farrin, half-laughing. "And if it is, it's not mine to forgive."

Her smile grew. "Well, I'll still endeavor to be appropriately jaded from now on," she said solemnly.

"Bianca, that's not what I want!" Farrin protested. "I love your trusting nature, I love that you—" He cut off as he saw the twinkle in her eyes. "You're teasing me."

She just grinned, and Farrin gave a long-suffering sigh. "You're impossible."

But he couldn't help smiling as he looked down into her glowing face. Clearly he'd gotten the comb out in time, and there were no lasting effects of the dark magic. It was an unspeakable relief.

"How about this?" he said. "If I want to give you a gift, I'll give it to you from my own hand, all right?"

Bianca's hand twitched in his. "You really don't have to give me any—"

"Maybe I want to," Farrin interjected. He shifted closer. "Maybe I want to give you the world."

"That's just silly," Bianca said, but her voice was a little breathless.

"It is silly," Farrin agreed. "Because I have basically nothing to give you, let alone the world. But that doesn't mean I can't want to."

Bianca's eyes were locked on his as she pulled her bottom lip between her teeth.

"Bianca," Farrin whispered.

"Yes?"

But he didn't seem to have words. His years of being a hermit were catching up to him.

Then again, maybe he didn't need words. He shifted his hand, sliding it up her arm, then slipping it around her waist. She made no protest—on the contrary, she took a step closer, lifting her face to his.

Heart hammering, Farrin lowered his head, his eyes on those impossibly red lips. They were only a whisper away—he could feel the heat of her breath. He felt her hand steal to his chest, and his muscles tensed under her touch. Pulling her the rest of the way against him, he lowered his lips to hers.

The door banged open, an irate voice causing them to jump apart just as their lips brushed.

"What is it this time? Why were we—"

Dionysius's angry words cut off abruptly, his gaze flying from Farrin's irritated expression to Bianca's guilty one. The elf groaned.

"Well, this is a fine mess."

"Go away, Dionysius," said Farrin, more annoyed with the grouchy elf than he could ever remember being before. "You're not wanted."

"Not wanted?" Lurgl's much milder voice joined the conversation, as the elf inched around Dionysius, who was blocking most of the doorway. "So you didn't send Lottie to fetch us all?"

"Oh..." Farrin blinked stupidly. "Yes, actually, I did."

"Are you telling me we've lost all this mining time for a false alarm?" demanded Eason, sounding annoyed. "Maybe Dion is right, and she really should compensate us!"

"Thank you!" said Dionysius, although he still didn't sound pleased.

"It's not Bianca's fault," said Farrin quickly, placing the slip of paper into Lurgl's hand as the rest of the elves filed into the cottage. "No, Raella, don't touch that!" he added sharply, as the female elf reached for the comb. "It's a talisman, and it almost killed Bianca when she put it in her hair. I sent Lottie for help, but then I took the comb out, and as it turned out, that was enough." He looked back at Lurgl, who was scanning the note. "That was with it. A forgery, obviously."

Lurgl raised troubled eyes to him and Bianca, who'd moved forward to join them. "This is...concerning," he said.

Bianca nodded her agreement. "I didn't even get to put any of our lessons to use, Lurgl," she said regretfully. "I had no opportunity to use my magic. The poison acted too quickly."

"So you've been making progress?" Farrin asked eagerly.

She nodded. "A little."

"How did someone get it in here?" demanded Arbor, who'd sidled up alongside Lurgl and read the note.

"That's the question," Lurgl said thoughtfully. His expression was confused as his eyes moved again to Bianca. "In addition to the obvious one, of course."

"What's the obvious one?" Dakarai demanded from Lurgl's other side.

"Why were they trying to kill her?" Lurgl explained calmly.

Bianca frowned. "Yes, that's a good point," she said. "It definitely didn't start pulling me away anywhere. I'm fairly certain it was trying to kill me."

"It was," Farrin agreed darkly. "No question."

"So are Acacius and the others trying to kill her, or trying to get their hands on her for her song?" Dakarai demanded.

"Maybe it wasn't the elves who sent it," said Raella. "Maybe it was her stepmother."

Farrin shook his head. "It was elves," he said grimly. Briefly, he explained the encounter in the jungle that had sent him running for the cottage. When he repeated what he'd overheard, Lurgl's expression became even more thoughtful.

"I'm not sure what's going on here," said the elf, "but I think I'd better strengthen the ward. No one who doesn't live here will be able to enter without express permission." His eyes fell on Farrin. "That'll include you, I'm afraid, Farrin. It's too complex to work you in as an exception."

"It doesn't matter," said Bianca suddenly. "Enough is enough. I need to go back to Sel. I need to face my stepmother. I said I'd stay a week and train with you, Lurgl, and I've done that now. I won't pretend to be a master with my songcraft. That would probably take years, and I'm not hiding here for years."

"I should jolly well think not," grumbled Dionysius audibly from across the room.

Bianca ignored him, still speaking to Lurgl. "If my presence is going to endanger everyone, and require you to use all your magic stores on a ward that's only necessary for me, it's all the more reason for me to go back sooner rather than later."

"Maybe you're right," mused Lurgl.

Farrin wanted to protest, but he bit his tongue, remembering his determination not to be overprotective. Bianca seemed to sense his tension anyway, however, because her eyes moved to his.

"I have to do this, Farrin," she whispered. "I've made the wrong decision way too often, but this time, I have no doubt about what I should do. If you could go home and right your wrongs, wouldn't you jump at the chance?"

He swallowed. "Yes," he admitted, even as part of him realized the truth was more complicated than that. For the first time in two years, he'd be reluctant to leave Selvana even if the opportunity was offered. "Do you mean to go right now?"

Bianca shook her head. "I feel very tired," she said. "The effect of the magic, I think. And it would be better to start out first thing. I'll get a good night's sleep and leave tomorrow."

Farrin nodded. "I'll go now," he said curtly. He raised the white parchment. "Can I take this?"

She nodded, and he slipped it into his rucksack. He wanted to consider the handwriting further.

"I'll be back before you leave," he told Bianca. "If not tonight, then by dawn tomorrow." His expression turned fierce. "It doesn't matter how capable you are, I'm coming to Sel with you."

Bianca's smile was so glowing, he could feel its warmth.

"I would love that," she said softly. Reaching out, she found his hand and squeezed it.

He returned the pressure, trying to say with his eyes what their audience of seven prevented him saying with his lips.

But thoughts of lips were anything but helpful. When he found his eyes straying down to Bianca's rose-red ones, he knew it was time to leave before his emotions got the better of him in much too public a way.

"I'll see you soon," he promised, releasing her hand and making for the door without so much as a glance at the others.

# CHAPTER TWENTY-FOUR

# FARRIN

Farrin strode through the jungle with confident steps, making no attempt to cover his tracks as he headed southward. He wasn't hiding from either humans or elves today.

Lottie appeared from nowhere, weaving around his legs in a way that almost made him fall.

"Hey, girl," said Farrin, not slowing his pace. "Thanks for fetching the others. Even if they turned out to be in the way more than anything."

Lottie gamboled ahead by way of response. She seemed pleased they were out in the jungle again. She probably thought Farrin was done with his distraction with Bianca, and ready to go aconitum hunting again.

Farrin almost smiled at the thought. Done? He would never be done with Bianca. As long as he lived, he would be bound to that generous heart, that beautiful face, those trusting eyes.

It wasn't precisely a surprise to him to discover that he was in love with Bianca. It had been growing for a while—if he was honest, it probably started the first day they spoke, when she thanked him for saving her with such warmth in her eyes. But he had been taken aback by the strength of the emotion when he'd held her in his arms a short time before. He'd fallen harder than he realized.

His heart squeezed at the memory of her words. She'd doubted his good opinion of her, and that was entirely his fault. He could hardly bear to think that she'd spent a week believing he thought her unable to be trusted on her own. It was him who couldn't be trusted. He'd criticized her trusting nature so many times, but why would he ever want to change one of the most beautiful things about her? It was hypocritical of him, to say the least, because he had benefited so much from it. He remembered the warm way she'd looked at him when he'd left a week before, telling him she hoped she'd see him soon. And that had been in the belief that he still thought her too weak to handle herself! Even when she was doubting him—and not without reason—she'd been kind and generous.

His face hardened as he made his way further south. Much as he might have been brought to realize that his fear over Bianca's trusting nature was his problem, not hers, he still had no intention of letting the false queen exploit it. If Bianca was determined to return to Sel the following day, Farrin would do more than go with her. He would ensure she knew what she was walking into.

As the first walkways of the treetop city came into view above him, Farrin began to scale the nearest tree. His satchel bumped strangely against his leg as he climbed, and for a moment he wondered why it was so heavy. Then he remembered the apples. He'd forgotten all about them when he was with Bianca, his thoughts completely taken up by her near miss. Not to mention the fact that they'd almost kissed.

"Stupid, interfering Dionysius," Farrin muttered to himself.

It didn't matter about the apples, at any rate. He would be seeing Bianca in a few short hours, and they would keep that long. It was a poor gift compared to a jeweled comb, but at least it wouldn't poison her. A shudder went over him at the thought of how close he'd come to being too late.

But how had the elves gotten inside the ward? He shook off the thought as the walkway came into reach above him. It was a problem to be considered when he returned to Bianca. With Lurgl there, and the reinforced ward, she'd be safe in his absence.

The walkway he hoisted himself onto was one of Sel's outermost ones, and didn't appear to be frequently used. It was in reasonable repair, but Farrin saw no one for about fifteen minutes, by which time he was well and truly within the grouped buildings. He kept his face impassive as he passed regular Selvanans going about their day. Those living on this outermost fringe of the city appeared to be Sel's less affluent residents, but they still seemed fairly well cared for.

On any Medullan street, his tattered garb and wild appearance would have ensured he had the attention of everyone he passed, but here he barely merited a second glance. These people were too used to the rough lifestyle required to survive in the jungle. Probably they thought he was a huntsman returning from an unsuccessful hunt, or a harvester who'd been separated from his group.

It was strange, he reflected, as he crossed with feigned confidence from one tree to another by way of the public walkways. He'd avoided this city ever since he arrived, choosing instead to keep the company of elves. But it was here that he could blend in. These were his own kind. Perhaps he should have tried this earlier. Maybe he could have eked out a more comfortable life among them up in the canopy, hiding his origins.

But no. Sooner or later someone would have realized he could walk on the ground, and that would have set him apart, and made him the object of suspicion.

Was that going to be Bianca's fate when she returned? If so, was there anything he could do to protect her from it? He chastised himself for the thought. These were Bianca's people—she was their rightful queen. Meanwhile, he knew almost nothing of their ways. The last thing Bianca needed was for him to shield her from Selvanans. Had he always been this overprotective? He was growing as bad as Emmett.

In a surprisingly short time, Farrin found himself nearing the center of Sel. He could tell from the increased bustle. He even passed a market platform, and at any other time he would have loved to have lingered to explore the wares for sale. Imagine if he found an aconitum flower there!

He knew that was nothing but a fantasy, however, and in any event, he had other priorities. Stopping to ask for directions from someone who looked very bemused at his ignorance, he continued toward the palace. It wasn't hard to spot. The impressive wooden structure was wrapped around the largest tree he could see, its conical shape embellished by the odd turret topped with a pennant.

At least, he assumed there were pennants on those poles. He couldn't really tell, as no wind stirred the leaves at present, meaning any flags lay flat and lifeless.

He'd expected to have to find a way around some kind of security, but the guards stationed at the entrance to the palace were chatting cheerfully with passing city-dwellers, and gave him no more than a cursory glance.

Bianca had told him that the culture of the palace was relaxed, and she hadn't been exaggerating. He couldn't imagine anything like that ever happening to a stranger trying to enter the castle at Port Dulla. He'd even had to fight hard for the girl from the beach to be taken in, mute and lost as she'd been after washing up on the shore.

He spared a thought for the girl. How old would she be now?

Nearly grown, probably. Had she stayed at the castle all this time? Unlikely. Emmett had probably been kind enough to find her employment somewhere.

A servant bustled past, looking busy and important, and Farrin followed her as unobtrusively as he could. A few people glanced at him as he traversed the corridor, but he walked with confident steps, trying to look like he knew where he was going, and no one challenged him. His eyes were drawn to the intricate carvings along the tree trunk, but he didn't stop to examine them, knowing that would mark him clearly as an outsider. No doubt anyone with legitimate palace business had seen them a hundred times and no longer considered them of interest.

When he ascended a ladder into what appeared to be the royal wing, he was challenged at last.

"What's your business here?" asked one of the guards manning the entrance.

"I'm here to report on the hunt," said Farrin, keeping it as vague as possible.

"Report to whom?" asked the other guard, his eyes narrowed.

Remembering the two guards he'd encountered when Bianca had first arrived at the clearing, Farrin paused. One of them had been named during the part of the conversation he'd overheard—the one who'd seemed more senior, and more confident. The silence stretched for an uncomfortable moment as Farrin searched his mind for the man's name.

"Horace," he said, the memory surfacing at last. "I'm to report directly to Horace."

The guard grunted. "Go on, then. He's at his usual post."

Mercifully, the man's eyes flicked unconsciously to his left, and Farrin took that as a guide. Painfully aware of his limp, he strode down the corridor, hoping that the royals were to be found in the same general area as this Horace. He squinted in concentration as he tried to remember the details of the conversation all those weeks ago. He was fairly certain Horace had said he was one of the queen's own guards, so that was promising. Of course, Farrin didn't want to actually run into Horace. He just wanted to get close to Queen Marisol.

Luck was with him. As he rounded the corridor, he heard a voice up ahead, giving a curt order.

"The queen isn't to be disturbed. That report will have to wait until later."

Farrin stilled. He was almost sure that was Horace's voice. He must be close to the queen's rooms. Footsteps approached—no doubt the repelled servant with the report—and Farrin sprang into action. He vaulted through the nearest window, landing lightly on the other side with his feet braced against the outside of the building and his hands gripping the sill. Due to the design of the building, there was another story not far below him, so he wasn't in danger of a catastrophic fall.

He couldn't use the roof as a platform though—it was too far down for his purposes. He shifted his hands to the branch below him, moving swiftly as the footsteps passed his window. Edging along, he followed the curving line of the corridor, staying low enough to avoid the windows. He continued past where he thought the guard who'd spoken must be, and kept going. A glance up showed an open window, perfumed smoke wafting out to keep the insects at bay, and a gauzy covering fluttering in any hint of breeze. He hadn't seen many windows with such fine material for curtains as he crossed the city. With any luck, that was Queen Marisol's chamber.

Farrin climbed nimbly through the branches, positioning himself just below the window. Maintaining a place that was close enough to eavesdrop but didn't expose him to sight required him to stretch awkwardly across an impractical space, and within minutes his muscles were protesting. But he ignored the sensation, focused instead on the high, feminine voice he could hear issuing from the window.

"What do you mean, I didn't deliver? I sent her to the jungle floor—it's not my fault if she got loose and was eaten by a predator before you could catch her."

"Do not attempt to fool us," responded an angry voice that Farrin realized he recognized. It was Acacius, the leader of the elves. Farrin's eyes widened. Was the elf truly in the queen's chamber at that very moment? No wonder she'd given orders she wasn't to be disturbed. But then he remembered something Bianca had said about the queen speaking via a talisman. "Princess Bianca is not dead," Acacius went on. "My agents confirm it. You agreed to provide her as part of our exchange, and the onus is on you to get her to us."

"Not dead?" The queen sounded nervous. "She must be dead."

"You know that she is not," Acacius said with obvious impatience. "Because this mirror will not communicate deception. I speak the truth when I say my agents have confirmed that she lives. She has sought refuge with a group of outcasts of our kind. I am even willing to provide you with the location. It's not far from your city. But you must retrieve her."

"How can I possibly do that?" demanded Queen Marisol. "I can't even go on the ground!"

"That is not our concern," said Acacius, bored. "You promised her to us, and I'm sick of waiting for you to fulfill our terms. You will provide her by sunrise tomorrow, or we will descend on Sel to claim the rest of our payment—and you can be sure the magic unleashed by the breach of our bargain will assist us."

"What do you mean the rest of your payment?" the queen asked, her voice shrill.

"I've already told you," said Acacius. "We require more humans."

"But you can't!" the queen protested. "You agreed to accept Bianca as a substitution for the others you requested."

"I did not," contradicted Acacius lazily.

"You did!" Queen Marisol cried. "You said you'd accept her as a substitute!"

"Have you still learned nothing of dealing with elves?" scoffed Acacius. "Do you truly not understand the importance of precise wording? What I said was that we would consider her as an interim measure."

Farrin could hear the panic in the queen's voice now. "But that's not fair."

"Bargains are not dictated by what is fair," said Acacius smoothly. "They are dictated by what was agreed upon. Now will you provide us with Princess Bianca as promised, or will you not?"

"I would if I could, truly," said Queen Marisol. "But I swear to you, it's beyond my capability."

"If you insist upon delegating—" Acacius began, but the queen cut him off.

"I can't entrust this task to anyone else. No one else is aware of…well, it must stay between us." Her next words sounded like they came through a clenched jaw. "Last time I gave the task to someone, he failed it completely. It would have to be me. And I can't do it. I don't know how to free climb. I can't just walk there —I'll die. And even if I didn't, one look at me, and she'd flee."

Acacius didn't respond immediately, and when he did he sounded irked. "I see that you speak the truth," he said. "Very well. I can see I will need to increase my investment. I will provide you with powerful magic. It will allow you—and you alone—to traverse the jungle floor for a limited time, and to disguise yourself, among other things."

"If you can disguise yourself, and you know where she is, why do you need me to do it?" the queen asked petulantly. "Bianca is trusting to a fault—if you can get near her, it shouldn't be hard to lure her into a trap."

"Do you know nothing?" spat Acacius. "Magic has limits. It cannot disguise elves as humans or humans as elves. We have tried exploiting her weakness. But she is too well protected. This task requires a human."

The queen was silent for a moment. "And you're sure whatever you're going to give me will protect me from the wild magic on the ground?"

"For a limited time," said Acacius. "It won't last long. Not that it needs to, as my deadline will not be extended. You have until sunrise."

"But that's less than a day away!" the queen protested. "How will you even get this magic to me?"

"We are nearby," said Acacius simply. "One of my agents will provide it to you within the hour, with instructions for its use."

Queen Marisol was silent for a moment, probably digesting this unpalatable statement of the elf's invisible infiltration of her city.

"You said the magic can do other things, too," she said at last, and Farrin could hear the cunning edge to her voice. "Will it give me a way to protect myself, if necessary? To attack anyone who might wish to harm me?"

"It can do so," Acacius agreed, and his wariness made Farrin think he also had noted the change in the queen's tone. "But take care, false queen. Do not think you can shield the girl, or spirit her away where I cannot reach her. Remember that I hold your kingdom at the end of my leash."

"Shield her?" Queen Marisol repeated, sounding outraged. "Do you think I care for her? I have no desire to protect her."

Farrin's blood boiled. Even without all the information, it

was clear to him that Queen Marisol's willingness to undertake the task was motivated less by fear of the elves' threats and more by her determination to deal with Bianca herself. And hopefully without anyone else learning how grossly the queen had deceived them regarding her stepdaughter. And this was Bianca's only remaining parent? His hands clenched conclusively where they gripped the branches. His involuntary motion caused him to slip slightly, and his arms strained with the tension of holding himself in position. He couldn't last much longer like this.

"Be that as it may," Acacius said coldly. "I do not give you magic without condition. Know that if you deceive me in its use, I will strip away and expose every ounce of magic you have ever used. And that is a promise."

Even Farrin felt a chill go over him at the threat in the words, and he had no doubt Queen Marisol would tread with care. Sure enough, she hastened to reassure the elf that she truly had no intention of trying to protect or hide Bianca.

The moment the queen broke whatever connection was allowing her to communicate with Acacius from afar, Farrin began to ease himself down.

Unfortunately, he'd left it too late for his cramped limbs. Just as he tried to shift his hand, his weak leg gave way, and he lost his hold, his leg slamming against the wooden wall with a thump. Instinctively, he grabbed at the windowsill above him, but that was a mistake. His hand had barely grasped the sill when another closed over it, its nails as sharp as talons.

"Guards!" the queen screamed. "Intruder!"

Farrin tried to pull away, but he was dangling now, helpless. Before he could blink, someone had charged into the room, and much stronger hands seized him and hauled him up. He found himself face to face with Horace, the older man's grip as unyielding as iron.

"Bind him!" cried the queen. "Then leave us."

"But, Your Majesty," protested Horace.

"You have your orders!" she cried, sounding almost as alarmed as she had when speaking with Acacius.

Looking reluctant, the guard complied, then bowed himself out. As soon as he was gone, the queen rounded on Farrin.

"How much did you hear?" she demanded.

He stared back at her, defiance rising in him. Perhaps she was beautiful to some eyes, but he saw nothing but poison when he looked at her. He refused to bow to her in any way. "Enough to know you for the treasonous viper you are," he said, doing his best to mimic Bianca's accent.

Quick as lightning, the older woman slapped him hard across the face. "You dare to say such things to your queen?" she gasped.

Face still stinging, Farrin glared at her. "You are not my queen," he said.

She reeled back as if she had been struck, not him. After a moment, her eyes narrowed.

"Who are you?" she asked curtly. "What's your purpose here?"

Farrin remained silent.

"Let's see if your belongings speak for you," she said, yanking his rucksack from him. He struggled, but the guard had bound him well.

The queen upended the bag, and the apples rolled in all directions.

"What fruit is this?" she mused, picking one up and sniffing it. "Where did it come from?"

"From a grove to the south," said Farrin reluctantly. He'd planned to give her no information, but he'd rather tell her that than have her guess that he'd come from outside Selvana, however long ago.

The queen was barely listening, continuing to rifle through his belongings. To Farrin's horror, she lifted the square of parchment, one chiseled eyebrow rising delicately.

"What is this? A love note? How touching. You must be F, I assume." Her eyes widened slightly as she read back over it. "And who is B?" Her gaze moved slowly to him, danger in its depths. "Not Bianca, is it? Is that what brings you to my window, Sir F?"

Farrin's face was hard, but he kept his lips sealed tightly shut.

"It is her," the queen breathed. "You know where she is." Her gaze turned thoughtful. "Not that I need your assistance to find her, as you've no doubt heard." She lowered her gaze to the crisp green apple in her hand. "And this is the gift to go with the note, is it? An exotic delicacy—I've heard of the abandoned groves near the southern settlement."

She turned the apple over, her expression thoughtful.

"Now, how can I turn you and your gift to good account? If the elves' magic is as powerful as that insolent fool Acacius claims, it shouldn't be too difficult to poison this in a manner that will be untraceable."

"Poison it?" Farrin repeated. "Are you out of your mind? I heard what the elf said. The magic is intended to capture her. If you use it to kill her, the elves will come after you."

"Do not think you can manipulate me with your fear-mongering," the queen snapped. "I don't know who you are, or how you ingratiated yourself to my stepdaughter, but I won't be spoken to that way. I am the queen, and you're an imbecile if you think I'm afraid of either you or a load of paltry elves."

"You're not the queen," Farrin growled, incensed by this confirmation of the queen's true motivations. Her hatred of Bianca had overcome her sense if she was finally willing to get her own hands dirty. "You're nothing but an imposter."

She ignored him. "Bianca certainly kept you quiet," she mused. "I never heard so much as a whisper of her having a paramour."

She tossed the apple into the air, catching it smoothly. "Yes, Bianca must be disposed of. It is unfortunate...I know it will grieve Ilse to have her sister's death confirmed. But her survival is too great a threat to me." She gave a decisive nod. "I think I'll poison it and have you present it to Bianca."

"I will never do that," Farrin said passionately. "I'd rather die."

The queen's smile was cruel. "Careful what you wish for, my dear boy," she purred. "And don't be so confident of what you'd never do."

Farrin gave a hollow laugh as he thought of the last two bitter years. "I don't know what torment you have in mind, but whatever you can think up, I've endured worse."

"But haven't you heard, Sir F?" the queen cooed. "Magic can make people do all kinds of things they never thought they would."

"Don't you dare touch her!" he snarled.

The queen ignored him, raising her voice over his threats. "Horace!"

The guard appeared quickly. "Your Majesty?"

"Take this prisoner to the dungeons," said Queen Marisol. "But gag him first."

"No!" Farrin shouted. "She's a murderer! She'll kill Bianca if—"

His words were cut off as the guard efficiently carried out his orders, and the next thing Farrin knew, he was being hauled from the room. Horace dragged him through some kind of lavishly furnished receiving room, while Farrin raged at himself for his folly in getting caught.

"Horace!" The breathless voice startled Farrin, who'd

thought the room was unoccupied. "Who's that? What's going on?"

Farrin stilled, his eyes falling on a lovely young woman whose eyes were strikingly similar to Bianca's. The resemblance wasn't strong otherwise, not least because of this girl's thick, dark hair.

"Not for me to comment, Your Highness," Horace said, his voice toneless. "Just following Her Majesty's orders."

"But did I hear him say something about Bianca?" she pressed. "Has there been news? Is she alive after all?"

Seeing the hope in her eyes, Farrin began to struggle afresh, trying to shout through his gag.

"That's enough," said Horace sharply, pulling him roughly from the room.

They traversed several corridors before Horace marched him out along a thin wooden walkway without rails. Unlike the rest of the palace, this walkway jutted out away from the safer conical shape. Farrin was forced to stop struggling, or risk both of them plunging to their certain deaths. Looking ahead, he saw a cell suspended at the end of the walkway, perched on a lonely branch. Clearly in Sel, a dungeon wasn't necessarily found at the bottom level of the palace.

As soon as they reached the cell's platform, Farrin started to thrash again. But the guard who'd been standing watch over the currently empty cell sprang to his fellow's aid, and they soon threw Farrin inside.

"If you take my advice, my lad, don't do anything rash," said Horace gruffly, as he locked the door. "Better to live to fight another day."

And with those cryptic words, he turned on his heel and strode back across the walkway, leaving Farrin to his panic.

# CHAPTER TWENTY-FIVE

# Bianca

In spite of the dangers to face her on the morrow, Bianca couldn't seem to settle to any kind of rest after Farrin left. She wasn't even rattled by the near miss with the cursed comb—at least, not as much as she should have been. Instead, her mind was consumed by the kiss she and Farrin had almost shared.

If only Dionysius and the others had been a little slower racing to her aid from their mining site!

She smiled at the absurdity of the thought. Of course she didn't really resent their swiftness in coming to save her. They'd been generous—more than she deserved, when all she'd brought on them was trouble. But she couldn't help reliving Farrin's words all the same, remembering how it had felt to be in his arms, pressed against him, his lips a breath from hers.

She sighed, banishing the appealing thoughts with reluctance. Daydreaming was the last thing she should be doing. She was returning to Sel to confront her stepmother the following day—she needed to practice her magic.

For the rest of the afternoon, she tried half-heartedly to work on her songcraft, following Lurgl's training. *Less is more* was the mantra she repeated to herself over and over, as she tried to mold just the quantity of magic that was always coursing through her from the saturated ground. It wasn't exactly a tiny amount.

As it was still early in the day, the elves had returned to their mining. Bianca stayed dutifully inside the ward, not intending to take any chances. Not that she had full faith in the ward anymore. She didn't think Lurgl had strengthened it before going back to his work, given she was intending to leave in the morning. Still, it seemed unlikely the elves would mount another attack so soon after the failure of the comb plot.

When evening drew near, the elves returned. But Raella soon kicked Bianca out of their area, unable to take her fidgeting. Bianca strode out of the cottage, finding a place by the pool to sit and wait. Surely he'd be here any minute.

But night descended rapidly, the jungle falling into the hush of dusk, then coming alive with all the sounds of darkness. And still there was no sign of Farrin.

Bianca wasn't prone to worry, as Farrin seemed to be, but she still found herself feeling anxious when she at last gave up and retired to her bed. Something hadn't happened to him, had it? Surely not. He was so capable, such a master of the harsh environment of the jungle. He'd said he'd come back for her. She knew he'd keep his promise. He always did.

<><><>

Bianca woke abruptly in the darkness, a cool breeze lifting the heaviness of the air in the cottage. She shifted, for a moment just letting the sway of the hammock lull her as she tried to identify what had woken her.

A glance through the window revealed that the sky, while not yet light, was beginning to show signs of gray. It must be nearing dawn.

Moving as quietly as she could, Bianca slipped from her hammock, her bare feet padding across the earthen floor as she made for the door. She collected her boots and continued outside to put them on, letting the other seven sleep. A quick glance around the room had showed that Farrin hadn't arrived in the night.

Bianca sat on a boulder near the water's edge, her thoughts heavy as she pulled on her boots. He might still come—he'd said if not the night before, then before dawn. There was still a little bit of time. What should she do if he didn't arrive? Should she start for Sel without him, or wait? He'd been so determined to accompany her, but if something unexpected had delayed him, she couldn't wait indefinitely.

"Bianca?"

The familiar voice wafted through the trees, and Bianca shot to her feet. Farrin!

She hurried past the tree line, following the sound of his voice. Why was he lingering out so far?

"Farrin?" she called, as she neared the ward.

"Bianca?" His tone suggested he hadn't heard her, and she frowned as he came into sight. It was him all right, his tawny hair tousled, and his expression confused. Why wasn't he coming through the ward?

"The ward!" she muttered, slapping a hand to her forehead. Lurgl must have strengthened it after all. She needed to let Farrin in. She bit her lip. But how did she do that?

"Come in," she tried lamely. "It's not supposed to keep *you* out." The idea was laughable. There was no one in all the world she trusted more than she trusted Farrin—certainly not any of the seven elves currently inside the ward with her, fond as she'd grown of some of them.

She'd barely thought it when the air shimmered a little, and Farrin's face suddenly lit up in recognition.

"Bianca!" he cried, although he didn't move.

"You made it," Bianca breathed. "I was worried when you didn't show up last night."

"I'm sorry I'm late," he said.

She shook her head. "No need to apologize. You're here now. Come on," she beckoned, "come inside the ward. I'm not supposed to leave it, remember? Although I suppose that's less meaningful now that I'm about to leave for good."

Farrin moved forward, swinging something around from behind him as he walked. Following the movement, Bianca saw that it was his rucksack, the same one he'd been wearing every time she'd seen him.

"I brought you something," Farrin said, his voice not quite natural.

He almost sounded nervous, which Bianca found endearing. Her eyes widened when the Medullan pulled something round from his pocket.

"Is that...is that an apple?" she asked. She raised her eyes to his, a laugh creeping into her voice. "You kept your promise. Farrin, you shouldn't have gone to so much trouble! How could you have reached the southern grove since yesterday?"

"I didn't," he said smoothly. "I already had it, but I forgot to give it to you." He held it out. "Try it."

Bianca took it, smiling as she remembered how he'd told her that if he ever gave her a gift, he'd give it to her from his own hand. It was all she could do not to catch hold of that hand and kiss it, but she told herself to stop being so sentimental.

"It's not like I expected," she commented, raising the apple to look at it.

"How so?" Farrin sounded a little nervous again, and she hastened to reassure him.

"It's not that I don't like it! On the contrary. I just didn't expect it to look like this. I remember you saying apples can be either green or red, but I assumed you meant different varieties. I didn't realize one apple could have both colors."

"Oh yes, it's fairly common," said Farrin airily.

Bianca admired it again. It was certainly an interesting fruit, one half of it bright green, and the other a deep red.

"Are you sure it's safe to eat?" she asked. She cast him an apologetic look. "No offense, or anything. I'm sure you know your fruit. I'm just...a little jumpy given recent events."

"Of course it's safe," he said. He gave her a winning smile. "Don't you trust me?"

Bianca's heart warmed at this reference to their earlier conversations. "You know I do," she told him softly.

"But still you won't try it," Farrin said, his cheerfulness sounding a little forced. Was he truly hurt by her hesitation? Bianca opened her mouth to reassure him again, but before she knew what he was about, Farrin swiped the apple back from her. Taking a small bite from the green side, he wrinkled up his face. "The red side is sweeter."

Bianca laughed. "Yes, I remember you saying that. All right," she added cheerfully. "Here goes!"

She raised the apple to her lips, taking an experimental bite from the recommended red side. It *was* sweet, the juice tangy and delicious in her mouth. But there was another taste, too. Something not entirely pleasant. It stuck in her throat as she tried to swallow it, like her body was striving to reject it.

"It's not quite what I expected," she commented, trying again to swallow it down. It wasn't blocking her air, but it was an unpleasant sensation nonetheless. Her vision started to spin, and she raised a hand to her head in alarm. "Farrin, I don't feel right. Something's off."

"Nonsense, you're fine," he said soothingly. "Have some more. It'll help."

"No," said Bianca. "No, I don't think so. I think maybe it had gone bad after all."

She stumbled a step forward, feeling strangely unsteady on her feet. She expected Farrin to reach for her, but instead he shifted back, as if afraid to touch her. That, more than anything, told Bianca that something was terribly wrong.

"F-Farrin?" she stammered.

It was him, wasn't it? It had to be him! And yet, he would never behave this way. He was still staring at her with a wary expression, and he'd made no move to help her. Bianca tried to focus on his face, but everything was unsettlingly blurry. She felt the apple drop from her nerveless hand, and felt a stinging in her knees. Her mind had barely comprehended that she now knelt on the jungle floor when darkness began to creep in at the edges of her vision.

She slumped fully onto the undergrowth, the dampness of the foliage in the early dawn seeping through her clothes.

At last Farrin approached her, but he made no offer of help. Instead he leaned down, his face twisted in a sneer she'd never seen before as he spoke, his words a low rumble.

"Who's legitimate now? Who's the most beautiful? I was never blinded by you, and now no one else will be, either."

Bianca blinked stupidly at Farrin's familiar face. Another wrong decision, and this time she hadn't even recognized it as momentous until it was too late. It should be a bitter realization, but she had no energy for either emotion or words as she slipped once again into blackness.

## CHAPTER TWENTY-SIX

# FARRIN

Farrin leaned his head against the wooden bars of his cell, a low moan caught by his gag. What time was it? The night must be nearly spent. It had been the longest, most miserable night of his life, and he didn't think he could stand many more minutes of it. Everything ached from how tightly he was bound—was this how Bianca had felt, the night he'd found her? And instead of freeing her at once, he'd led her to the cottage then disappeared, leaving her to the dubious ministrations of the elves.

She'd suffered from his lack of trust, and still she'd trusted him from the start. He didn't deserve her kindness, but more to the point, she didn't deserve what was coming to her. Because although he was hazy on the exact plans, he'd grasped enough to realize that the queen intended to exploit Bianca's trust for Farrin, then betray her.

And not to capture her. To kill her.

The thought was unbearable, and Farrin's impotence was almost enough to drive him past the edge of sanity.

A low hiss sounded in the darkness, and Farrin's head shot up.

*Lottie?* Farrin swiveled as silently as he could, looking for her. There was only one guard on duty, and Farrin couldn't see the man from his position, but it would still be wise not to take chances.

The ocelot's familiar face appeared between the bars, mewling her displeasure at his situation.

Farrin tried to shush her with his eyes, glancing toward the obscured walkway. Could she get through the bars? Could she free him from his ropes?

The feline apparently had the same idea, because she tried to push her head through the gap. But the cell had been well designed. It was too small. Farrin was just trying to think of another way to put the ocelot's presence to good use when he heard the unmistakable sound of footsteps approaching along the narrow walkway. Another guard change already? It had only been an hour since the last one.

He strained his ears, but he couldn't catch the content of the murmured conversation. A moment later, he heard footsteps receding, and let out a breath, his mind returning to his task. Then Lottie's ears pricked, her posture tense as she stared toward the walkway. Farrin heard the sound of a key in the lock, and scrambled to his feet as best he could, bracing himself for attack.

But it wasn't an armed guard who appeared in the doorway. It was a teenage girl in a richly embroidered dressing gown, looking nervous but determined. The same girl from the queen's personal receiving room.

"You know Bianca?" she asked.

Farrin nodded.

"I'm her sister, Princess Ilse," said the girl. "Have you seen her since she left Sel? Is she alive?"

Again, Farrin nodded, and the girl drew a shuddering breath.

"She's in danger, though, isn't she? Something…" She swallowed. "Something to do with my mother?"

Robbed of his voice, Farrin could do nothing but keep nodding, the movement growing frantic.

Princess Ilse hesitated for only a moment before stepping in, a small knife clutched in her hand. She removed his gag, then stepped back.

"Do you know where to find Bianca?" she asked. "Can you protect her if I let you go?"

"I know where she is," Farrin said quickly. "And I'll protect her with my life. Do you know what's planned for her?"

The younger princess shook her head. "Mama won't tell me anything. She denies that you even mentioned Bianca, but I heard it. You said something about someone killing her." She bit her lip. "It sounded like you meant Mama, but I know she'd never do that. She and Bianca haven't always gotten along, but—"

"I don't have time to listen to you try to convince yourself," Farrin cut her off brutally. "What time is it? Where's your mother now?"

"It's almost dawn," said Princess Ilse. "She left a short time ago. I don't know where she was going, but it's definitely not normal for her to wander around the city in the night. I've been lying awake most of the night, worrying about Bianca, and I'd just made up my mind to wake Mama, and make her tell me who you are, but when I went to her rooms, I saw her sneaking away, like some kind of thief."

"What did she take with her?" Farrin demanded.

The princess shrugged. "A rucksack. Dirty old thing, actually. I don't know what was in it."

"I have to go," Farrin pleaded. "Right now."

The girl hesitated for only a moment before stepping forward again. In a few minutes, she had his bindings severed.

"I hope I'm not making a mistake in trusting you," she murmured.

"You're not," Farrin promised her. He gave a soft whistle. "Come on, Lottie."

The princess stifled a shriek as the jungle cat slunk into sight. "Is that an ocelot?"

Farrin ignored the question. "Thank you," he said. "For helping me. I'll tell Bianca you're not part of her stepmother's schemes against her."

Princess Ilse opened her mouth, clearly ready to once again protest her mother's innocence, but Farrin didn't stay to hear it. He was already running lightly along the walkway, Lottie streaking behind him.

As soon as he could do so safely, he leaped onto the roof of the next level down. A swift sprint across it led him to the next, and the next. He descended rapidly, no longer caring if he was seen. His only thought was to reach Bianca before her step-mother did. How much of a head start did the imposter queen have? At least the route was more familiar to Farrin.

He raced through the jungle more rapidly than was safe in the darkness, taking several tumbles, but always jumping straight back up. By the time he neared the ward, the sun had properly risen, the well-known terrain visible on all sides. He raced straight through without a check, meaning Lurgl hadn't strengthened the ward as he'd contemplated doing. Farrin groaned. Did that mean the queen had found a way past it?

He catapulted through the last of the trees, emerging into the clearing with his heart in his throat.

"Bianca?" he cried. "Bianca!"

"In here!" The voice that issued from the cottage was high, definitely belonging to an elf. Farrin sprinted the final distance with his lopsided gait, throwing himself through the doorway.

"NO!" he shouted, despair gripping him at the sight of

Bianca laid out on the low wooden table, her hands folded over her chest in a funereal pose. "No! She's not dead! She can't be dead!"

"She isn't yet, but she will be soon." It was Lurgl who spoke, his voice sounding weary more than anything. "I don't know how they got to her this time, but she's definitely been attacked with dark magic again."

"It wasn't the elves," moaned Farrin, dropping to his knees beside the table. "It was the queen. Well, she was empowered by the elves, I suppose. Acacius provided the magic. I'm pretty sure she used it to impersonate me, so that Bianca would trust her and take the bait."

"So he is trying to kill her instead of capture her now!" Dakarai said, sounding pleased to have an answer to this riddle.

"No, he's not," Farrin spat. "The queen was supposed to capture Bianca, but she betrayed the elves. She was too obsessed with getting rid of Bianca to even realize how afraid of them she should be."

Murmuring passed around the group. "That's bad form, that," said Raella darkly. "There's going to be trouble in the city before many days have passed."

"I don't care about that!" cried Farrin. He took one of Bianca's hands in his, a dry sob rocking his body. She couldn't die. He wouldn't let her die! "There has to be something we can do!"

"We've done the only thing we can," said Lurgl simply. He pointed to one side, and Farrin followed the gesture to see a strange looking apple. One half of it was green like it had been when the queen had held it in her chamber. The other half was a bright, unnatural red. Each side had a bite from it.

"The apple," Farrin whispered, horrified. Bianca would never have thought to question that particular gift, not after he'd promised to bring her one.

"We found Bianca out in the jungle," Lurgl explained. "She

was alone, and that apple was beside her. Clearly she ate some, and that's what poisoned her. I found the piece still in her throat and extracted it." He sighed. "But it seems the poison is the magic itself. The apple was only the vehicle. This isn't like the comb, where the magic was spreading across her body. She's ingested it now, and it's inside her."

"Can't you stop it?" Farrin pleaded. "Don't you have some salve or something?"

"This is well beyond any salve," said Eason impatiently. "It's beyond the skill of any one of us."

"I don't know if I'd say that," Raella interjected. "Lurgl might have the skill."

"It is immaterial," said Lurgl simply. "I do not have access to sufficient stores of magic to counteract an attack this strong, even if my skill turned out to be enough."

"Who does?" Farrin demanded. "Who has that much magic?"

"Would anyone?" Arbor sounded doubtful.

"The leader of the elves always carries great magic on his person," Lurgl said. "As do the guards who follow him around."

"Acacius, you mean?" Farrin pressed.

Lurgl nodded. "Yes, Acacius is the leader. And even though he wants Bianca alive, I don't think even he would be willing to spend the incredible volume of magic it would require to reverse the death already taking hold of Bianca."

"I don't care what he's willing to do," said Farrin fiercely. "We'll find him, and we'll take his magic."

"It doesn't work that way," Lurgl told him. "Besides, the settlement is too far away. She'll never make it that far. I know it's hard, Farrin, but you have to let her go. She won't survive this."

"She will!" Farrin insisted. "I'll save her, if it costs me my life! And we don't have to go to the elves' settlement. I know where they'll all be. Acacius told Queen Marisol that if she didn't provide Bianca to them by sunrise, they would descend on Sel to claim the rest of their payment. The idiot thought she'd settled her debt when she sent Bianca down to them, but Acacius said he'd only ever agreed to it as an interim measure."

Several of the elves snorted at Queen Marisol's stupidity, but that was the last thing Farrin cared about. His eyes seared into Lurgl.

"Don't you see? Sel isn't far. She can make it if we hurry! The sun has already risen, which means Acacius will be there. The city is probably under attack already. I know he won't show any mercy, not after what Marisol has done with his magic. She was supposed to capture Bianca, and instead she tried to kill her to cover her own crimes. Acacius promised retribution, and he didn't sound to me like someone who'd hesitate to follow through."

"He isn't," Lurgl agreed dryly. His eyes narrowed. "What was the retribution he promised, precisely?"

"I don't remember!" said Farrin impatiently. "Does it matter?"

"It might," said Lurgl, speaking calmly. "Try to remember."

Farrin let out a grunt of frustration, but he screwed up his eyes, trying to remember what he'd overheard. "He said there were conditions to the magic he was giving her. That if she deceived him, he'd strip away and expose all the magic she'd ever used. Or something to that effect. He said, *that is a promise* —I remember that part for certain."

"Hm."

Lurgl looked very thoughtful now. He was silent for so long, Farrin could barely hold in his impatience. Bianca's hand was so cold in his. He couldn't bear to look at her face. If he did that, he'd fall apart, and he couldn't afford to fall apart. Not while she was still breathing. Not while there was still hope.

"There might be a chance," Lurgl said abruptly. "Perhaps the very chance I've been waiting for."

"What do we do?" Farrin demanded, uninterested in whatever personal concerns were behind Lurgl's extra comment. He didn't care what Lurgl was hoping to get out of the bargain—he'd give everything if it would save Bianca.

"We go to Sel, interrupt whatever fight is happening between the elves and the humans," said Lurgl. "And we carry Bianca with us. We'll need her to be present if there's any hope of using Acacius's magic to reverse the poison."

"I can carry her," said Farrin. "I'll sling her over my shoulder."

"Like a deer carcass?" Ulmer muttered.

Farrin ignored him, his eyes on Lurgl.

"Yes, that will be best," the elf agreed, pushing to his feet. Somehow his height—notably taller than the other elves—was especially prominent in this moment.

"Best?" The word exploded from Dionysius, who had surprised Farrin by so far remaining silent. "You think it will be *best* to carry that nuisance all the way to Sel and save her, when it's well past time we let her reach the end she should've met the night she first blundered through the jungle?"

Farrin found himself on his feet as well, towering over the elves as he leaned menacingly toward Dionysius.

"Don't. You. Dare," he said, breathing hard.

"Don't *I* dare?" Dionysius shouted. "You're the one out of line! You have no place here, huntsman. You're a homeless shipwrecked waif, yet you strut around like you own this cottage." He rounded on his fellows. "And the rest of you are no better! You can't even see what calamity this stupid princess has brought on us!" He gestured angrily at Bianca's still form. "Thanks to her, the rest of the elves know where we are, and breach our haven at will. Raella's treating her like a pet, Lurgl has delusions of grandeur, and everyone else turns a deaf ear to her insolence. I had things handled with the comb—I would have solved all our problems. But you all had to go and ruin that plan, and now that the human queen has brought us this neat solution to our problem, you're going to go and ruin that, too!"

"WHAT?!" Farrin didn't remember moving forward, but he somehow had the elf's throat in his hand. Dionysius's legs dangled two feet from the ground, his alabaster skin turning slowly red as he squirmed. "YOU were responsible for the comb?" Farrin roared, over the top of Dionysius's furious squeaks of protest.

"Let him go, Farrin." Lurgl's voice was so commanding, Farrin's grip slackened of its own accord. "I do not tolerate violence against any elf in this house."

Farrin's eyes were furious as he rounded on Lurgl, but the uncompromising look on the elf's face sobered him. If he wanted any hope of saving Bianca, he needed Lurgl's help. Resentfully, he dropped Dionysius, who spluttered as he clutched at his throat.

"You little worm," he gasped at Farrin.

"Dionysius, what have you done?" Lurgl demanded. He frowned. "And for whom? I know you've never liked Bianca, but I don't believe you came up with such a devious plan to kill her. With whom did you strike a bargain, and for what payment?"

"That's no affair of yours," said Dionysius resentfully.

Lurgl shook his head, his expression hard. "You bring shame on yourself."

"I do no such thing!" Dionysius cried, clearly stung. "I have broken no promises—I had no obligation to the girl."

"Indeed," Lurgl agreed coldly. "And I have no obligation to you, now or in the past. You are no longer welcome in this house. You will leave immediately."

For a tense moment, Dionysius just stared back at Lurgl,

apparently struggling to comprehend what he seemed to consider a gross overreaction to his conduct.

"As you wish," he spat out at last, stomping over to his own area. Within minutes, he'd gathered up his belongings and stormed out the door.

"I can hardly believe it," said Raella, dazed. "I thought we'd all grown fond of Bianca."

"Speak for yourself," grunted Ulmer, in his usual surly way. Farrin would have been angry at the elf's attitude, except that he noted Ulmer had shown no sign of sympathy for Dionysius.

"What's done is done," Farrin said, his voice uneven. "We can't change the past. We've wasted enough time on this already." Kneeling down once more, he drew Bianca's cold arm gently over his shoulder, tugging until the rest of her slight form followed. Then he stood up again, one arm keeping her securely in place as he turned for the door. "Let's go."

# CHAPTER TWENTY-SEVEN

# FARRIN

The trip back to Sel took twice as long as the trip out, but it felt at least five times longer. And that was in spite of Raella generously offering some of her personal reserves of magic—as *a gift freely given*—to lighten Bianca's weight substantially. Even without any great physical discomfort, every minute was agony, as Farrin felt Bianca's form growing steadily colder. The only thing keeping the panic at bay was the warmth of her breath on his back. She was still breathing, which meant she was still alive.

In spite of Raella's intervention, or perhaps as a sign that it was weakening, climbing high enough to get onto one of the walkways was a challenge with Farrin's load. But he managed it without dropping Bianca, which was the main thing.

He expected considerably more resistance than the previous time, given he was now accompanied by six elves, and carrying an unconscious Crown Princess Bianca over his shoulder. But the walkways were utterly deserted, not a soul in sight.

It was eerie.

As the group neared the palace, however, they began to hear the sound of conflict, screams mingling with angry shouts, and even the odd clash of a weapon. Something was definitely happening, and the palace was at the heart of the action. Long before they reached it, the city's residents finally came into sight, many people clogging the path ahead.

"Let us through!" Farrin shouted desperately. "We need to get to the elves!"

His cry attracted attention from those nearest, and fresh screams rent the air as people caught sight of his companions.

"More elves!"

"They have us surrounded!"

"No, these ones are friendly," said Farrin desperately. "Please let us through!" He heard Ulmer's grunt at the exaggeration, but this was no time to be pedantic.

He shoved his way past a family who looked utterly terrified as they shuffled closer to the palace. Using his elbows, he managed to make painful progress, the palace looming into view ahead.

"Hey there! Halt!"

The commanding voice made everyone in the area freeze. Everyone except Farrin and the six elves, who took advantage of the distraction to gain a bit more ground.

"You there, with the elves, stop!" A guard shoved his way through the crowd, intercepting Farrin in the middle of a crowded walkway. "Who's that over your shoulder? Where do you think you're—"

He cut off, just as Farrin finally took his eyes from navigating the crowded walkway and looked up into a face he recognized.

"You're Horace," he said.

"And you're the prisoner I tried to spring from the cell this morning, only to find you already gone," the guard said blankly.

Farrin blinked in surprise, before shaking his head. "Even if that's true, it doesn't matter now. We have to get the princess to the leader of the elves before it's too late. Is he here?"

"The princess?" Horace asked, starting forward.

Farrin turned slightly to show his burden, and the guard's pale face drained of all color.

"Princess Bianca," he muttered. "So she is alive."

"Not for long she isn't," Lurgl interjected. "Unless we get to the leader of the elves. So let us ask again: is he here?"

"Yes, I think so," Horace said. His gaze hardened as it passed over Farrin's companions. "There are many elves here, and none of them have come in peace."

"Except these ones," Farrin said firmly. "Please, if you want to help us save Bianca, take us to the elves."

Horace didn't hesitate. Turning around, he bellowed an order, clearing the path before them with astonishing efficiency. In minutes, they were ascending the palace itself. The higher they climbed, the harder it was to make progress, even with Horace's assistance. People jostled them on all sides, men, women, and children vying for position as they all headed toward the upper levels of the palace.

"Oi, watch it!" Raella told one woman, as she elbowed her way past the elf.

"I can't help it," the woman gasped. "I have to go upward."

"What do you mean you have to?" Farrin asked sharply.

The woman's eyes were desperate as she looked back over her shoulder at him. "Can't you feel it? We're all being drawn to the palace, whether we want to or not. It's some kind of dark magic—it must be!"

Farrin stared at Horace, and the guard gave a grim nod. "Half the city seems to be feeling it. That's why they're all crowding like this."

"When did it start?" Lurgl asked, his voice so calm that the guard threw him a suspicious look.

"At sunrise."

"When Acacius saw that Queen Marisol had failed to meet the terms he'd set," Farrin said grimly.

Lurgl nodded. "The bargain is officially breached, and the magic attached to it has therefore been activated."

"Did you say Queen Marisol?" Horace asked sharply. He looked between the two of them, his expression fierce. "Is she behind this?" His eyes shifted to Bianca's limp form. "Was it her who attacked the princess?"

"Of course it was," said Farrin impatiently. "She used the elves' magic, but her agreement with them was to hand Bianca over, not kill her. So now they're getting their revenge."

"It's not a matter of revenge," piped up Eason, sounding disapproving. "They made a bargain, and a bargain with an elf carries magic of its own. If you breach the bargain, the magic reacts—it's all perfectly above board."

As the elf spoke, they emerged onto a huge wooden platform, about two thirds of the way up the palace. It was crowded with people, most of them looking terrified. Marisol was nowhere to be seen, but at one end of the platform stood Acacius on a raised dais, other elves lining the platform below the dais. The elves seemed to be separating the humans into groups, examining them as one might look over a horse at market, and muttering to one another as they directed movement.

"Above board?" Horace repeated furiously. "To herd people like cattle? Look how many are being affected! How can the magic of one bargain be that strong?"

"It wouldn't normally be," Lurgl said fairly. "It's because of who made it. She wasn't royal when she first struck the bargain, but by the time the terms were fully set, Marisol was queen, with authority to bind her kingdom. Not to mention she made the bargain directly with the leader of the elves. That's a powerful promise, and the magic tied to it is correspondingly strong."

"Imbecile," said Arbor scornfully. "Any real royal would know better than to strike a bargain with the leader of the elves and commit their kingdom."

"But *why* is everyone being herded?" Horace demanded. "What is the magic doing?"

"It's enforcing the fulfillment of the bargain, on terms favorable to the one who didn't break it," Lurgl informed him. "The imposter queen promised the elves payment. They named Selvanan residents as payment, so now that she's failed to deliver on her end of the bargain, the magic is rounding up what was promised."

"If they think we'll all stand by while they kill our people for some petty—"

Farrin cut off the guard's furious words. "They don't want to kill them outright. They want to send them to the ground, to see if there are any other singers among them, like Bianca, who might survive. But you're right that most of them will die, and you're right that the elves don't care about that." He groaned. "This is a mess. We don't have time for this—we have to get Acacius to reverse the magic that's killing Bianca!"

"Well then," said Lurgl briskly. "We'd best begin." Seizing the arm of a nearby human, he used it to vault nimbly onto the shoulders of the nearest elf—Dakarai. He then ran on light feet across the shoulders of the other four, leaping finally onto the railing that ran around the whole platform.

Farrin watched in astonishment as Lurgl stared across the crowd from his elevated position, his eyes locked on Acacius on the dais.

"ACACIUS!" he roared, his high voice achieving a surprising volume. "Cousin and traitor! I challenge you for leadership of the elves!"

An instant hush fell over the whole scene, every eye turning to the elf on the railing. Fury raced over Acacius's face—which Farrin noted was a greenish-gray color rather than the pale white of the elves he knew. Glancing at the rest of the elves, he realized they were the same.

"Why are their faces like that?" he muttered into the stillness.

Raella grunted. "They paint it for camouflage sometimes, or when they want to look intimidating. I imagine they wanted the humans to be more afraid of them."

Glancing at the crowd, Farrin reflected that it seemed to be working.

"Be gone, Lurgl," Acacius growled. "I am leader here. You have no position among our kind."

"On the contrary," said Lurgl calmly. "I have a greater right to the position than you do, as well you know." The hint of a scowl appeared on his face as he scoured the group of elves. "As you all know." He cleared his throat, and his voice took on a formal tone. "By the succession laws of our kind, the mantle of ruler passes to the eldest grandchild of the outgoing monarch. Our last leader—her spirit be at peace—was my grandmother, and Acacius's also. I am her eldest grandchild."

"My father is older than your mother," spat Acacius. "The line passes through him to me."

"Incorrect!" Lurgl cried, his voice still carrying clearly over the throng. "That is a foolish human tradition, and it has never been followed by the elves. It is of no relevance which of our parents was born first—only which of us! And I am older than you by three years, Acacius. I am the rightful leader of our people."

The elves shifted uncomfortably, and Acacius's glower grew.

Lurgl's lip curled. "The humans are not the only Selvanans who have become cut off from the rest of their kind through the isolation brought on us all when the magic went wild. But have we really forsaken our ways so thoroughly? Do we truly wish to embrace the ways of *humans*, in our traditions of succession or anywhere else?"

A rustling passed through the elves again, many pairs of emerald eyes flicking between Acacius and Lurgl. Personally, Farrin thought the scorn in the tall elf's voice when he said the word *humans* was a little overdone, but that was neither here nor there. The real problem was that Lurgl was making a play for power when he was supposed to be helping save Bianca's life.

Farrin started forward, but Lurgl forestalled him.

"I have the right to the mantle," he called across the crowd. "But I recognize that, rightly or wrongly, that mantle has been given to another, who will not just hand it over. Acacius, I challenge you to a duel for the right to leadership."

Now it was Acacius's lip which curled, and Farrin could see why. Lurgl might be tall for an elf, but he didn't look like much of a fighter, whereas everything about Acacius was menacing.

"So be it," Acacius said, his eyes glittering.

"Enough of this," said Farrin, shoving his way through the crowd. Abandoning Lurgl, he made straight for Acacius. "You can indulge your stupid feud later!"

He emerged into the empty space at the front of the crowd, laying Bianca's still form gently down on the dais.

Mutters passed through the crowd of humans as people got a glimpse of the girl now stretched out on the wooden boards.

"The Snow Princess!"

"Is she dead?"

"Princess Bianca!"

Straightening, Farrin looked Acacius in the eye. Dais or not, the elf was still looking up at him. "The magic *you* gave Queen

Marisol is killing the princess," Farrin said furiously. "I know you want her alive. So lift it!"

"I do not answer to you, human," said Acacius coldly. He looked down at Bianca, his expression indifferent. "I see the fool queen's report was accurate. The princess is dead."

"She isn't dead!" Farrin cried. "She's dying, but you can still save her!"

Acacius laughed, the sound harsh and unpleasant. "I do not intend to waste my magic so lavishly." He gestured around at the masses of people crowding the platform. "If there was one singer, there will be others. I have no more need of her."

Fury rose up in Farrin at this callous disregard for life. Bianca was so still, her skin so cold. He didn't have time to find a way to convince the heartless elf.

But before he could speak, Lurgl once again made himself heard.

"Actually, cousin, you're required to waste your magic on the task. You're bound by a promise you've left unfulfilled."

"I beg your pardon?" Acacius's voice was deadly as he turned to the elf still perched on the railing. "How dare you accuse me of failing in an obligation?"

Moving with perfect balance, Lurgl strolled across the railing, all the way around the platform to the dais.

"Farrin," he said pleasantly. "Did you not overhear Acacius speaking with Queen Marisol yesterday?"

"I did," said Farrin, itching with impatience at the elf's calm manner.

"And do you remember telling me that you overheard Acacius say the precise words, 'and that is a promise'?"

"Yes," Farrin said slowly, his attention on Acacius as the elf went unnaturally still. "I do remember telling you that."

"Would you please tell everyone present what words preceded that vow?"

Farrin took a breath, trying to remember. He knew that precision was very important when it came to these matters. "That if Queen Marisol deceived him in the use of the magic he was giving her, he would strip away and expose all the magic she'd ever used."

"Thank you," said Lurgl, with a formal half bow to Farrin. He cast a glance over the elves nearest Acacius. "And is there anyone here compelled to bear witness that Acacius is so bound? That the queen agreed to use the magic to capture Princess Bianca, and that in using it in an attempt to murder the princess, she deceived the one who gave it to her?"

A few of the elves shifted, clearing their throats reluctantly. "I am," they said in a chorus, none of them looking at Acacius. Clearly their honor bound them to the sanctity of a bargain more powerfully than to any leader.

"Well then, it is a simple matter," Lurgl said. "Acacius, your promise is activated by the queen's deception. You offered her a bargain—the use of magic on certain conditions—and outlined the penalty for breaching those conditions. She accepted the bargain, and she then breached its conditions. You are as bound by the bargain as she is."

Lurgl once again looked over the group. "This is why a wise leader does not make threats. It gives the person being threatened power to bind you."

A few heads nodded sagely, tapered ears wobbling.

Lurgl flashed Farrin a smile. "Of course, Acacius would never have thought himself in danger of being bound by his ill-advised bargain—he didn't think Queen Marisol would know how to invoke it. But he didn't count on you overhearing."

"I'd say I was happy to help if I had any idea how this will save Bianca," Farrin growled. He was kneeling beside her, once again holding one of her hands in his. It was like ice, the sensation shocking in the humid heat of the morning.

"Ah yes," said Lurgl, turning back to Acacius. "You are bound, cousin, to do as you promised—namely, to strip away and expose every bit of magic Queen Marisol has ever used. Including the magic currently poisoning Princess Bianca. The quantity of magic it will cost you to complete this task is immaterial."

Acacius opened his mouth, then closed it without a word. This process happened three times, as everyone watched in stunned silence. The elf looked absolutely furious, but he clearly knew he was bound. Farrin could practically see his mind working, trying to find a way out. Evidently none came because after a prolonged moment, Acacius threw himself down beside Bianca, rage marring his features.

He pulled a pouch from his pocket and placed it on the ground. When he loosened the string, every elf in the vicinity began to murmur. Clearly its contents were something powerful, although the sight meant nothing to Farrin. Acacius pushed his thumb into the pouch, smearing some of the contents across Bianca's throat. Nothing visible remained behind. He did the same on her forehead, and again on her stomach. Then, finally, across her heart.

"Excellent," said Lurgl, apparently satisfied. "Now, I believe you will need to similarly strip the magic from Queen Marisol's necklace, not to mention that mirror. And don't forget that you promised to also expose every bit of magic she'd used. I'm sure all her subjects would love to hear the details."

Farrin ignored this smug speech, his eyes fixed on Bianca. She was so cold...surely it wasn't too late. He could hardly breathe as he watched her face for a sign, any sign.

Then, so abruptly it made him start, she drew a gasping breath and opened her eyes.

# CHAPTER TWENTY-EIGHT

# *Bianca*

Awareness returned suddenly to Bianca, her mind instantly alert. Her eyes flew open and she struggled to sit, noting that she was lying on wooden floorboards, not the springy undergrowth she'd collapsed into. She remembered pain, followed by numbness and paralysis. And creeping darkness. But she felt absolutely fine now.

"Bianca!" Farrin's cry jerked her eyes to him. He was kneeling beside her, his expression nothing short of frantic. "Bianca, are you all right?"

Bianca didn't immediately answer, her gaze passing in astonishment around the crowded platform. She knew this place well. It was in the palace. It was the platform where official functions were held—where her coronation was supposed to take place all those weeks before. How had she gotten back to Sel?

And why was the platform so crowded with people, and—

She gasped. "Are those elves?"

"Not the brightest princess, is she?" muttered one nearby.

Bianca ignored him. "Why have the elves shown themselves?" she asked, her eyes flying back to Farrin. But she suddenly lost interest in the answer, the sight of his familiar face bringing full memory rushing back to her.

"Farrin," she whispered, pulling back slightly. She saw the pain in his eyes, but he made no attempt to reach for her. For an agonizing moment, Bianca searched his eyes carefully, every muscle tensed.

Then she relaxed, letting out a breath of unutterable relief.

"It's the real you," she said, smiling up at him. "I can tell by the worry in your eyes. I don't know how I didn't notice it was missing last time."

Farrin's mouth fell slightly open, his chest rising and falling with the rapidity of his breathing. "You believe it wasn't me? Just...just like that?"

"Of course!" Bianca said, a little shocked by his reaction. "Did you expect recriminations? Farrin..." She laid a hand on his chest. "Whoever that was back near the clearing tried to kill me. Of course it couldn't have been you. I know you'd never do that, not for any payment, or any motivation. It was clever of them, to use the apple. I don't know how they found out about that."

Farrin drew a long, shuddering breath, looking completely overcome. "Bianca, I..." He swallowed, reaching a tentative hand out to cup her cheek. "I could never deserve a heart as generous as yours."

Bianca's smile softened, her hand coming to rest over his. "All the same, it's yours if you want it," she told him simply. Her smile grew. "And I don't ask anything in exchange—it's a gift freely given."

"Well that's a relief," said Farrin, leaning forward so that his breath was warm on her face. "Because I don't have anything that could come close to matching the value of that gift. All I can offer is my own heart, which seems to me a poor exchange."

Bianca didn't try to reassure him with words. Instead she

pitched forward, pressing her lips fully to his at last. Farrin's arms closed around her, and he pulled her flush against him. Everything else spun away—Marisol's deception, the elves' invasion, her own foolish decisions—none of it mattered. Nothing mattered except Farrin, the feel of his arms around her, the warmth of his breath mingling with hers, the indescribable safeness of him.

"Oi!" Raella's outraged voice broke into their moment. "We don't want to see that!"

Bianca and Farrin broke apart, Farrin looking as self-conscious as Bianca felt at the reminder of their large audience.

"Sorry," she gasped. "I sort of...forgot about everything else."

Heat leaped in Farrin's eyes as he smiled back at her. "I know what you mean." He clasped her hand. "Bianca, when I saw you laid out in the cottage...I thought you were dead."

She squeezed back, speaking bracingly in an attempt to banish the anguish in his eyes. "Not today."

The intensity wasn't gone from Farrin's voice. "I knew in that moment that I can't live without you, Bianca. Even if I could go back to Medulle, I wouldn't. This is my home now, and I won't leave your side, not if you want me here."

Bianca held his gaze, trying to let her eyes say what her mouth couldn't find words for. "I will always want you here," she whispered, overwhelmed by the enormity of his promise to make Selvana his home.

Remembering their audience, she raised her gaze to the elves and humans surrounding them on all sides. "Does someone want to explain what's going on here?"

"A number of things," Farrin told her, the touch of humor in his voice showing that he also realized the need for a change in focus. "It's a little hard to know where to start. If you're asking about the elves, I gather they're here to round up as many people as they can and force them onto the ground to test for singers."

"Your Highness!" The palace steward bustled forward from the crowd. "Thank heavens you're alive! I can't imagine where you've been all this time! We all feared you'd fallen to the ground."

"I did," said Bianca, struggling to her feet. "The ground is exactly where I've been all this time. It's not deadly for me, it turns out. I'm a singer."

"A singer?" the steward repeated, looking shocked. "I remember the old tales...but I thought they were no more than legends of the past."

"Just like elves," said Bianca dryly, her gaze hardening as it fell on Acacius. "So you're the one who's been plotting with my stepmother to get your hands on me, are you?" She glanced around. "Speaking of my stepmother, where is she?"

Horace appeared from the crowd, bowing low. "I believe she and Princess Ilse are hiding in the queen's chambers, Your Highness."

Bianca's brow darkened. Marisol had created all this mess, and she thought she could hide away, leaving others to deal with the consequences of her treachery?

"We can't have that," Bianca said firmly.

Closing her eyes, she extended her arms, feeling the magic that flowed all around her, boiling under the surface of the ground far below, but also seeping in more manageable quantities from the trees, the leaves, the wind. She could feel the difference—it was nothing like the irresistible tide that flowed through her when she was touching the ground, that would overwhelm her untrained ability as soon as she tried to grasp hold of it. This was a tamable volume of magic, and she knew she could mold it.

She pulled it into herself, bottling it up so that it pooled in her awareness, unable to escape her control. Then, when she'd gathered enough to herself for her purpose, she let her voice fly, clear and confident above the murmurs of the crowd.

*"Expose what's hidden,"* she sang. *"Break what must be broken to bring in the light."*

With the words, magic flowed out, targeted and controlled. It surged in an invisible flood, pouring through the crowd and into the side of the building, which it rent with a crack. The wooden walls splintered, a magical battering ram passing through several rooms until it broke open a final chamber. Marisol and Ilse were exposed, staring in astonishment at the trail of destruction left by Bianca's magic. At the same time, another stream of power shot diagonally upward, splintering an upper branch of the enormous palace tree so that the morning sun slanted downward and flooded the platform.

"Oops," Bianca muttered to Farrin out of the side of her mouth. "I should probably be more careful with my choice of words. The branches were an accident."

Farrin snorted on a laugh which he quickly disguised as a cough.

"Bianca!" The scream came from Ilse, who threw herself forward, tripping over the debris Bianca had left as she sprinted for her sister. She emerged onto the platform and carried on without a check, until she thudded into Bianca at full force. "You're alive! You're alive!"

Bianca's arms snaked around her sister, tears in her eyes as she laid her head on top of Ilse's. "I knew you couldn't be part of it," she whispered.

"Me?" Ilse pulled back, her eyes horrified. "Of course I wasn't! I would never try to hurt you, Bee." Tears pooled in her dark eyes. "Are you saying Mama was behind it? That's what he seemed to think," she jerked her head toward Farrin, "but I can't believe it, Bee. There must be a mistake."

"She's not exactly rushing to express delight over my survival, is she?" Bianca asked gently.

Ilse followed her eyes to where her mother still hovered in the exposed bedchamber, looking both afraid and angry.

"Bring her out, Horace," said Bianca sadly.

The guard gave a sharp nod, calling a few others to him as he jogged into the ruined building.

"If you're the princess, why did you break your own palace?" Dakarai asked from nearby.

Bianca couldn't help laughing at his conversational tone, but the sound soon turned into a sigh. "It was already broken," she said heavily. "I just exposed it."

She extricated herself gently from Ilse, turning to Farrin. "There was obviously something in that apple. How did you get rid of the poison?"

"Acacius did it," said Farrin, pointing at the elf, whose ear-tips were still quivering with irritation. "Although not because he wanted to."

Bianca frowned in confusion, but Farrin wasn't done.

"That reminds me," the Medullan said grimly. "Isn't there more for you to do? I believe you promised to expose every bit of magic Marisol has used."

"I hadn't forgotten," snapped Acacius.

"Princess Bianca." Horace's voice drew everyone's attention, as he emerged from the wreckage with Marisol in tow.

"Unhand me at once!" the queen spluttered. "How dare you accost your queen? I'll see you hanged for this!"

"Enough," said Bianca wearily. "It's time to be done with deception, don't you think? Your attempts to kill me have failed. Did you think I would keep quiet, cover up what you've done?"

"You're the one trying to deceive everyone!" blustered Marisol. "Kill you? That's preposterous! I never did any such thing—why would I?"

"I don't know, maybe to get her throne," someone from the crowd shouted sarcastically.

Bianca raised an eyebrow as she searched in vain for the speaker. She hadn't realized others doubted Marisol. But it made sense—she couldn't have been the only one to notice the queen's overly suspicious nature. She'd just been the last to understand what Marisol's lack of trust for everyone else meant —that she herself wasn't trustworthy, and she expected others to be like her.

"As for claiming that you never tried to kill Bianca, I believe Acacius has something to say about that. Don't you?" Farrin stared expectantly at the elf, who looked furious at being ordered about by a random human, but didn't seem able to refuse.

"Remove her necklace," Acacius said stiffly.

At a nod from Bianca, Horace obeyed, tossing the jewelry to Acacius.

"And she'll have a small mirror in her pocket. I need that, too."

Horace retrieved it, and Acacius snatched it none too politely. The little elf used something from a small pouch— powerful magic, judging by the tang it released into the air when the pouch was open—to smear across the blood-red gem and the surface of the mirror. He then threw the items to the ground as if they were worthless rubbish.

Climbing back onto the dais, he cleared his throat. To Bianca's astonishment, he proceeded to explain to the crowd the nature of the necklace he'd just stripped magic from, and its role in Marisol's marriage to the king. Tears stung Bianca's eyes as she realized how her father had been manipulated. At least he'd been happy, she thought miserably. And it hardly mattered now. He'd gone where no one could use him again. She listened in growing tension as Acacius—spitting out each word like it cost him pain—described the bargain he'd made with Marisol, and her use of the mirror to communicate with him. Finally, he described the magic she'd used to impersonate Farrin and poison Bianca.

It struck her that there were many holes in the tale—he described the specific instances where Marisol had used magic, and nothing more.

"He's bound by his own promise to Marisol—a promise he meant as a threat—to expose every ounce of magic she's ever used," Farrin whispered in her ear, and she nodded gratefully at the explanation.

When Acacius fell silent, Bianca stepped up onto the dais, even her unimpressive height towering over the elf.

"Is there anyone here who doubts or contests this evidence?"

The platform was silent, only birdsong meeting her words.

"Do you have anything to say in your defense?" Bianca asked her stepmother, her heart heavy as she looked at the furious queen.

"You are nothing more than a naive child," spat Marisol. "You think you can rule? You will be cheated by everyone, and the kingdom will fall apart in months. If you think your fair face will buy you goodwill forever, then you—"

"You are wrong," Bianca interrupted her calmly. "But I have nothing to explain, or to prove to you." She regarded the queen's livid face, the features still undeniably beautiful. "And my beauty or otherwise never had anything to do with it," Bianca added. "You're the only one who ever considered that of relevance to who was fit to rule."

She turned away from the older woman, her eyes falling on Horace, who sprang into a salute.

"Your orders, my queen?"

Marisol's gasp was audible. "You traitor! You're supposed to be the head of my guard!"

"Traitor?" Horace's voice was a deep and furious rumble. "I have never been a traitor. I have always served and guarded Sel's queen, and I will until the day I die, or am ordered to stand down. My only treachery was in failing to speak up about my conviction that you ceased to hold that position when King Octavio died. By no argument can you be considered to hold it now Princess Bianca has come of age, as every Selvanan is well aware." He glared around the crowd as if they'd all challenged him, but Bianca couldn't see anyone protesting.

"Thank you, Horace," said Bianca, touched by the loyalty. "Take her to the holding cell for the moment, and see she is well guarded. I will consider what to do with her at a later time."

The guard nodded and escorted Marisol from the platform, four others accompanying them. Bianca watched them go with another sigh.

"What are you going to do with her?" The tearful question came from Ilse.

"I won't execute her or anything," Bianca reassured her quickly. "But I can't just let this slide, Ilse." She ran a hand through her stark white hair. "I'll sleep on it before doing anything drastic, but I think she should be sent to the southern settlement. Perhaps a few years harvesting the outlying groves might help cool the fire of her greed and vanity."

"A wise decision," Farrin said gravely. Bianca wasn't sure whether he was speaking of the suggestion of exile, or the reluctance to see Marisol killed.

"Well, this has all been very entertaining," said Acacius irritably. "But we were in the middle of something. We are here to collect our payment, and we will not be denied."

Bianca drew herself up, turning to him. "Payment? Is that what these souls are to you? How dare you come here, to my palace, and threaten my people? What gives you the right?"

"I have every right," Acacius said coldly. "As you've just

heard. I made a bargain with your queen, and I will have my satisfaction."

"I am queen in Selvana," said Bianca, drawing herself up. "And I made no bargain with you."

"The change in ruler is immaterial," said Acacius shortly. "The bargain must still be honored. The magic demands it."

As he spoke, Bianca felt it. She narrowed her eyes to slits as she tested the air, sensing a darker and less familiar thread than the magic she'd come to recognize since she first touched the ground. That magic was flexible, dynamic, like an ever-tumbling brook—or torrential flood, in the case of the ground, where it had gone wild. But this magic felt entirely different. It was more like steel—unyielding and solid. It reached across the space, holding most of the humans on the platform in its grip.

It was strong, and for a moment Bianca felt daunted. But she clenched her fists in determination. She was the queen of her people, and she was the first Selvanan singer in generations. She was mistress of a land where magic had grown so wild it saturated the very ground. There was no lack of it, and its power couldn't be measured.

"The magic demands it, you say," she told Acacius. "Do you speak for the magic? Because it seems to me that the magic of the bargain is not the only kind of power in Selvana."

As she spoke, she drew magic into herself, pulling from the air, from the very wood of the floorboards, from the palace tree itself, a great, living, growing beacon of Selvanan power. This magic wasn't out of control like that which saturated the ground, but it was strong. It was enough. It would have to be enough.

"The humans have cowered in fear up in the canopy for too long, while the elves have roamed free on the ground below," Bianca said, still collecting magic. "But Selvana doesn't belong solely to the elves. We have a place here, too. Your people invited us here, and we've built a home. Selvana needs humans."

"I don't deny that the land needs humans," said Acacius angrily. "That's why we welcomed your kind in the first place. We could tell the magic was growing too wild with no singers to help tame it. We wanted humans to take up residence here, to keep it under control. But the singers were too few, and the magic already too strong."

"And I'm sure you warned our ancestors about the risks," Bianca said, her voice cold. "I'm sure you were honest about what you were asking of them."

"We had no obligation to warn you!" spat Acacius. "We owe your kind no loyalty. And you showed yourselves unworthy of any respect. A few deaths, and you all fled into the trees like cowards, leaving the magic to ravage the land and erode all hope of the singers fighting back. You should have stayed and fought for your land!"

"Maybe you're right," said Bianca calmly. Her vision was spinning a little from the quantity of magic collected within her, but her mind clearer than it had ever been. "Maybe we should have fought harder back then. But I'm no coward, elf. And I don't owe you any more loyalty than your ancestors owed mine. I will fight for my land, and more importantly, I will fight for my people. I refuse to acknowledge your hold over us."

With that challenge, she thrust her hands outward, lifting her voice in a song. She gave no great thought to the words, her energy all focused on directing the magic itself. Only one phrase came out, in a rising crescendo that released all the magic she'd gathered, sending it speeding toward the solid power of the elves' bargain.

*"We are free."*

Like a taut bowstring suddenly snapping, she felt the other magic give way, the Selvanan power overwhelming it. All around her, people dropped to their knees, or drew in gasping breaths as they clutched each other. They were released from the compulsion.

"No!" screeched Acacius. "You cannot do that!"

"I just did," Bianca told him, no compromise in her voice.

"You can't just overpower the magic of the bargain!" the elf raged. "The promise was still made, and it is still not kept!"

"If you intend to appeal to my honor, save your breath," Bianca told him frankly. "My conscience is not troubled in the least. You made that bargain in bad faith, intending from the beginning to exploit my stepmother and my people. Your actions were neither honorable nor reasonable."

"That's not how it works," snarled Acacius.

"Isn't it?" Lurgl leaped lightly onto the dais from the railing, where he'd been standing all this time for some reason. "She outmaneuvered you, Acacius, just accept it. You intended to use her powerful magic to improve life in Selvana—she's done precisely that, but according to her own terms. There's nothing you can do to undo what she's done. I suggest you retreat with what dignity you have left."

"Well said," Bianca agreed. She frowned. "It is not the beginning I would have chosen between my reign and your people."

Farrin's presence was warm at her back, and she felt bolstered as she glanced out at all the Selvanan humans, many of whom were calling out their gratitude and delight at her appearance. Raising her voice a little, she spoke to her people.

"For the last two years, I haven't been the crown princess you deserved," she started, and silence instantly fell. "I've second guessed myself, and let you suffer for my lack of confidence." She gave a wry smile. "Perhaps in the future there will be times when you suffer for my lack of experience. But I hope those times are few. I've had plenty of time to think these last weeks, since my stepmother had me thrown to the ground. Ghosts have risen up to reproach me, of all the moments of decision I've failed, when I haven't taken the action a wise queen would have."

She paused, her eyes flying back to Farrin, apology in their depths. "The first was the night my father died, when I failed to intervene in the pointless loss of life when the ship bearing the Medullan flag was sunk."

Farrin's eyes softened, and he reached for her hand, the pressure of his grip reassuring. She hadn't really thought he'd be angry—his heart was too kind for that—but it was a relief to express her regret, all the same.

"I've been torturing myself over that moment," she told the crowd, "and others that followed it. But I've come to realize that life isn't defined by a handful of moments, no matter how significant. Every breath we take brings with it a new moment of decision. A fresh challenge, a fresh chance." She raised her voice even further, hoping it carried all the way to those at the very back of the platform. "And my promise to you is that I will endeavor to make good decisions not just in the significant moments, but in all the little moments of my rule from now on."

She grinned as she glanced back at Farrin. "Although one decision *is* fairly momentous. I intend to form an alliance with Medulle through marriage to Prince Farrin." She dropped her voice. "Assuming he'll have me."

Farrin's eyes were alight with something much warmer than the humid air, and he looked like it was all he could do to stop himself from seizing her in his arms once again in front of their interested audience.

"I've already offered you my heart," he said simply. "You must have known I meant forever."

Bianca smiled. "I did," she assured him.

Turning back to the crowd, she raised their clasped hands, and the platform erupted in cheers. "I'll order construction to begin on a seafaring vessel at once. I know we have plans in our records, from the days we had a fleet, back before the magic grew too strong. It won't be easy to build it in the trees, but I know my people are capable. Then we'll be able to go back to your home and seek your parents' blessing for our marriage, and hopefully a proper alliance."

Farrin drew in a sharp breath, seeming too overwhelmed to speak. He obviously hadn't put it together that her ascension to the throne would give her the power to find him a way back to Medulle. But Bianca didn't waste a moment in worrying that he would change his mind about staying with her based on that information. She trusted his word too much for that.

Thoughts of trust turned her mind back to the elves, and she frowned at Acacius, who'd made no move to leave. Clearly he was still trying to figure out how to reactivate the magic of the bargain.

"Speaking of decisions," she said, her voice loud enough for the nearby elves to hear, but not carrying over the still-cheering crowd, "another I'd be wise to make is not to give any trust where it's manifestly not deserved. As the leader of the elves, you've shown that you—"

"Actually," Lurgl interrupted her smoothly, "Acacius is no longer the leader of the elves. I am."

# CHAPTER TWENTY-NINE

# Bianca

Acacius turned to his cousin, his green eyes glittering in anger. "Do not speak out of turn, Lurgl. You agreed to hang your claim on a duel. A challenge has been issued, but its outcome is yet to be decided."

"No, actually," Lurgl corrected him calmly. "The duel is done. I won."

Bianca stared at the elf in amazement, wondering what she'd missed while she was unconscious. Had Lurgl really fought with this fierce-looking elf leader? It was hard to imagine. Acacius was as unconvinced as she was, apparently.

"Don't be absurd," the elf leader said sharply. "No time or place was set for the duel."

"Precisely," Lurgl agreed. "You've grown careless of our ways, Acacius. If you accepted the duel without specifying the time or date, you left yourself open to my interpretation."

"I didn't accept the duel," said Acacius, although he sounded a little uneasy now.

Lurgl ignored his cousin, turning to the cluster of elves standing below the dais. They'd trickled in from around the platform, and there were probably three dozen now.

"I appeal to you all," Lurgl said formally. "Am I not correct that all the elements of a traditional duel are present?"

A portly elf bustled his way to the front, puffing his chest out and speaking in a slightly pompous voice.

"You have claimed success in a duel, and your opponent has contested your claim. Let the resolution of the matter be witnessed."

"We are witnesses," chorused all the other elves present.

The unknown elf cleared his throat importantly. "The first element of a duel is that one party declares an intention to challenge the other."

"I did so explicitly a short while ago, at this very gathering," Lurgl pointed out. "I believe you all heard me. My words to Acacius were, *I challenge you to a duel for the right to leadership.*"

"So witnessed," murmured many of the elves.

"But you never said a time—" Acacius snarled, but the pompous elf cut him off.

"That element is incontestable," he said sternly. "We are all witnesses. And as Lurgl has said, if no time was specified in the challenge, it was for the challenged to set a time, or to leave himself at the mercy of the challenger's discretion." He paused. "Providing the second element is satisfied, that is."

Turning back to the rest of the elves, he raised his voice again. It was quite unnecessary, as every person on the platform —both elf and human—was avidly watching the display of elf culture.

"The first element is satisfied. The second element required for a duel is some acknowledgment of the challenge by the one who was challenged."

"And I never did," said Acacius quickly.

"On the contrary," Lurgl told him sternly. "You are forgetting, cousin, that your lies only thrive in secrecy. You cannot imagine they will succeed here, where so many are witnesses. Your precise reply to my challenge was, 'so be it.'"

The crowd shifted, a few of the elves frowning in memory. Bianca saw one nod, then another.

"Witnessed." This time the confirmation came in more scattered, as everyone cast their minds back to whatever confrontation Bianca had missed while unconscious.

"That wasn't intended as formal acknowledgment of the duel," Acacius said quickly. "Merely that I understood your intention, however foolish I thought it."

The pompous elf frowned, his eyes searching the crowd. He beckoned imperiously, and a few other elves pushed their way through the throng. They all bent their heads together, muttering furiously.

At last, the first elf raised his head with a satisfied nod. "We are in agreement," he told the gathered elves. "The distinction Acacius has attempted to draw is immaterial. To acknowledge the challenge without explicitly rejecting the duel is to acknowledge the duel. The second element is satisfied."

He cleared his throat again.

"The third element of a duel is that one party outwit the other such that the outwitted party finds themselves bound to do something that will expose them, cost them something valuable, or humiliate them publicly."

Bianca blinked in astonishment. Judging by the surprised murmuring sweeping across the platform, she wasn't the only human to be taken aback by this definition of a duel.

Lurgl stepped forward and bowed low to the speaker. "On this element, if I may speak?"

"Go ahead," the elf nodded.

Lurgl addressed himself to the elves as a whole. "I submit that through the events we have all witnessed involving the removal of the magic poisoning Princess Bianca—a magic originally provided by Acacius—and the exposure of the other magic he had given to Queen Marisol, Acacius has suffered all three of the options listed. That is, the actions to which he was bound exposed his shameful dealings with humans, cost him valuable magic he expressly stated he did not wish to use, and humiliated him by forcing him to undertake an action he had refused with scorn to undertake when asked to do so freely. Not to mention he was forced to give an account of his affairs publicly in front of humans," Lurgl added as an afterthought.

The elves considered this speech for a moment, then many pointy-eared heads began to nod sagely.

"Witnessed," everyone agreed, including the elves who had gathered on the dais to discuss the last element.

Acacius was positively quivering with rage now, his green eyes shooting sparks, and his ears wiggling.

"You little—"

"The third element is satisfied," interrupted the officious elf. "All that remains is to satisfy the fourth and final element— namely that the party claiming victory prove to the satisfaction of the witnesses their own hand in bringing about the exposure, cost, or humiliation of the third element." He nodded to Lurgl. "On this point, it is again appropriate for you to speak."

"Thank you." Once more, Lurgl bowed low. "I would be glad to do so." He turned to the assembled company. "Princess Bianca was near my own dwelling when she was poisoned, and I was aware of her plight when I learned that Acacius was to lead you all against Sel this morning. It was my intention in coming to this place to orchestrate a situation in which Acacius had to undo the magic Queen Marisol had used against Princess Bianca. My companions can bear witness to that fact, given I declared my intention to them."

"So witnessed," said Arbor, Dakarai, Eason, Raella, and

Ulmer in unison. Catching up a moment behind, Farrin repeated the line.

The pompous elf looked them over before nodding. "Five witnesses," he noted.

"I don't think you count," Bianca muttered to Farrin, her lips twitching.

He just grunted.

"I trust their witness will be sufficient. There are no witnesses to my further information, but I wish to offer it for those who might have questions as to my motivations. I knew Princess Bianca's identity almost as soon as she crossed my path. I have sheltered her in my home for weeks with the specific intention of using her position to unseat Acacius from the role of leader which he stole from me."

A pang went through Bianca's heart at this calculating explanation for Lurgl's hospitality. But she saw many heads nodding among the elves, approval in each pair of green eyes. They seemed to like this cold-blooded motivation for the kindness shown to the human princess.

The elves on the dais bent their heads together, and this time their conference was brief.

"The fourth element has been demonstrated to our satisfaction." He looked over the crowd. "Is there anyone who can say with full honor that they are not satisfied?"

No one spoke. Bianca noticed that a few of the elves didn't look happy—surely some of them stood to lose from Acacius being replaced—but they made no argument. The laws of their kind regarding duels seemed to be as absolute as those regarding bargains. She supposed a duel was a bargain, of a kind.

The elf adjudicating the duel turned to Acacius, his voice cold. "It seems you have indeed grown careless of our ways, Acacius." He addressed the crowd. "The duel is complete, and

Lurgl is the clear victor. The stakes were Acacius's relinquishment of the leadership which once belonged to his and Lurgl's grandmother. Lurgl must now be formally recognized as our sole leader."

"Just like that," said Bianca, dazed.

"Just like that?" repeated Arbor, indignantly. "Do you think Lurgl just made all this up on impulse? It took some doing for him to orchestrate everything just so. He's been waiting for an opportunity like this for years."

"Well," said Bianca firmly, her eyes on Lurgl, who was now being swamped by applauding elves, "one ruler to another, I should be one of the first to congratulate him."

She muscled her way forward, reaching the dais just as Lurgl nodded serenely to an elf who was assuring him that Acacius had been a terrible ruler, and they'd all been sorry to see Lurgl go. Heroically, Bianca refrained from rolling her eyes.

"Congratulations, Lurgl," she said. "Perhaps we should consider a joint coronation."

She spoke jokingly, but Lurgl looked shocked. She was fairly certain the reaction was put on. Thanks to the dais, and his own height, the elf's eyes were almost level with hers.

"Certainly not," he told her sternly. "Elves conduct our ceremonies on the ground, not hiding up here in the trees with humans."

Approving murmurs passed around the nearby elves.

Bianca ignored Lurgl's tone, smiling at him. "So it seems you're the leader of the elves now, Lurgl." She paused. "Well, I suppose you were always the leader, even if you were in exile."

"I was not," said Lurgl with dignity. "I ought to have been, but when my grandmother died and my cousin dishonorably convinced our community to bestow the title of leader upon him, it ceased to belong to me. It is mine again only now that I have reclaimed it in all formality."

"Is that so?" Farrin's voice came from behind Bianca, his tone dry. "I would have thought you always considered yourself the leader, given your status as heir. I seem to recall you saying that ceremonies mean little to you elves, and that since Bianca was her father's heir, she was Selvana's queen, regardless of what Marisol might claim."

Lurgl gave him a pitying look. "Your memory fails you, Prince Farrin."

His slight emphasis on the title told Bianca that he was a little irked not to have guessed Farrin's real identity. Not that he or any of the other elves from the cottage had shown any sign of being greatly impressed or even unduly interested when she'd announced it to the crowd.

"My precise words," Lurgl went on, "were that *human* ceremonies mean little to us. Our own ceremonies are of great weight. They are binding."

"Of course they are." Farrin sounded unimpressed, and Bianca couldn't help laughing.

"This day has certainly held many surprises," she said. Her smile dropped as she took in the aloof and regal way Lurgl was holding himself. "So you were using me all along," she said, a little sadly. "I suppose I shouldn't be surprised."

Lurgl's face softened a little as he regarded her. "I'd grown fond of you, too," he said, his voice lowered. "But I was also using you, yes. And I advise you not to wait for an apology."

Bianca gave a dry laugh. "I may be too trusting, but I'm not a complete fool," she said.

"You're not too trusting," Farrin interjected, laying a hand on her shoulder from behind. "On the contrary, your generous heart puts the rest of us to shame."

She sent a smile over her shoulder at him, but it was Lurgl who responded.

"It might shame humans, perhaps, but a generous heart is

not something that is valued among elves." His voice was even quieter now, so as not to carry to the elves nearby, who had turned to gossiping among themselves about the dramatic change in leadership. "I didn't 'use you' as you put it out of any desire to do you harm. But it was necessary for my purposes to be able to demonstrate another reason for taking you in. My kin find my softness to humans incomprehensible. It will be much more comfortable for them to follow me as leader if they think I had a selfish reason for assisting you to reclaim your own position."

"That seems very backward to me," Bianca complained.

Lurgl laughed. "That's because you're not an elf."

"Is that why they got behind Acacius, and let him take your place?" Farrin asked. "He said something like that, the day we eavesdropped on the elves' settlement."

Lurgl nodded. "That was one reason. The other, of course, is the more obvious."

Bianca and Farrin waited, but he didn't elaborate.

"What's the more obvious reason?" Bianca pressed, bewildered.

"You don't know?" Lurgl asked, seeming genuinely surprised. "It's my height. I'm too tall for the ideal elf. Tall elves make everyone uncomfortable—it makes them seem too much like humans."

Bianca stared at Lurgl's unnaturally bright eyes and clearly tapered ears. Then her eyes traveled down his form to where his feet were planted on the dais, level with her hips.

"You don't look like a human," Farrin said bluntly, speaking her thoughts. "More likely most elves don't like others being tall because it makes them feel short."

Lurgl's lips twitched. "Perhaps. But in any event, it added to the general impression that I was too sympathetic to humans, I think. That and the fact that I was outspoken against the plan already in place in my grandmother's time—to lure humans to the ground to test for singers, regardless of how many died in the process." He glanced at the five elves from the cottage, who were standing together nearby, eyeing their fellows warily. "A few of the others left for the same reason, actually."

"Hang on," Bianca said, still trying to wrap her mind around the bizarre ways of elves. "So you're saying you were cheated of your right to rule because you're too tall?"

"No," said Lurgl, with a snort. "I was cheated of my right to rule because my cousin is power-hungry and deceitful. But my height—not to mention my softness toward humans—didn't help in terms of popular opinion."

"I see," Bianca said. "So it helps your reputation to throw me to the wolves in the process of reclaiming your position."

"That's hardly an apt expression," said Farrin, a defensive edge to his voice. "I thought there weren't any wolves in Selvana."

Bianca stared at him, utterly bemused by the strange reaction. "There aren't," she said. "But we still use the expression."

Farrin just shrugged, already looking like he regretted his odd outburst. "Of course."

Casting him one more astonished look, Bianca returned her attention to Lurgl, whose eyes now rested on the Medullan.

"So you are royalty," he said thoughtfully.

Farrin nodded.

Lurgl's emerald eyes were narrowed in thought. "In the direct line?"

"No, my brother is the crown prince," Farrin said quickly.

"But the current ruling monarch is your parent?" Lurgl pressed.

Farrin nodded. "My father is King Johannes of Medulle."

Lurgl shook his head slowly. "I ought to have guessed it,

probably," he said. "But I confess, it didn't occur to me to consider it."

"I don't know how you could have guessed it," said Farrin, a touch defensively. "I took care to keep my identity to myself."

Lurgl smiled. "Be that as it may, the information seems obvious to me in hindsight. It is the missing piece that explains the puzzle of your survival on the ground—I ought to have realized that you had magic of your own, to counteract the power of the wild magic. I think it very likely that is the reason you could withstand the lethal magic of Selvana."

"What?" Farrin looked startled. "I don't have magic! I swear, I'm not a singer. My situation isn't like Bianca's—my people haven't forgotten the ways of magic. I'd know if I was a singer."

"Of course you're not a singer," said Lurgl impatiently. "I spoke not of the ability singers have to wield the magic in the land. I spoke of the magic that is actually contained *in* your royal blood. The magic that ties you to your land."

Farrin stared at the elf, looking as confused as Bianca felt. "Royals don't have magic in their blood."

Lurgl sighed. "How little humans know of magic," he mused, his tone a touch pitying.

Bianca and Farrin exchanged a long-suffering glance, but thankfully the elf seemed inclined to elaborate.

"It is an area of magic largely left unstudied by humans," said Lurgl. "But among elves, the magic of royal blood is widely recognized to exist. We do not claim to fully understand it, of course. I must say, I am amazed to learn that even in a kingdom not your own, it worked so powerfully on your behalf. I would have expected it to have power only on your own soil." His pale forehead furrowed a little. "You are sure your royal blood is Medullan?"

"Quite sure," said Farrin firmly.

"No Selvanan ancestry?"

Farrin shrugged. "Not that I know of."

Again, the elf shook his head thoughtfully. "It is a most fascinating phenomenon."

"Does that mean that I have some kind of magic in my blood as well?" Bianca demanded. "That even if I hadn't been a singer, I would have survived the ground?" Her eyes lit up as a sudden thought occurred to her. "That Ilse can as well?"

"It's very possible," said Lurgl. "But I cannot tell you with any certainty—no one can. I imagine your sister might be reluctant to test the theory with her life."

"That's definitely not happening," said Bianca, shuddering at the idea.

Putting the strange revelation to one side, she cast her eyes over the assembled elves. It was a little overwhelming to bear responsibility for navigating the relationship of her people with this newly discovered species. Especially given their complex history.

"Well," she told Lurgl. "I suppose I can't resent that you used me. We both achieved our aims today, and neither of us could have done it without the other's help. I'd like to think that's a reasonable basis for more harmonious relations between our two peoples going forward."

"I would like to think so as well, Your Majesty," said Lurgl, with a half bow.

Bianca held up her hands, although she couldn't help smiling. "Not yet," she told him. "They might not mean much to you, but human ceremonies are pretty significant to us. My coronation got a trifle delayed, but I hope to see it carried out within the week."

"If I am welcome, I will attend," said Lurgl formally. "As a sign of goodwill from my people to yours."

"Of course you'd be welcome!" said Bianca, pleased. Her instinct was to throw her arms around the elf, but she doubted he would thank her, given the picture he was trying to paint for the rest of his kind. So she contented herself with a warm smile. "Whatever your motivations, Lurgl, you did save my life. And although I'm not making any offer of an exchange," she said quickly, "I will remember it."

Lurgl chuckled. "Nice save."

"I'm learning," said Bianca ruefully. "Slowly, perhaps, but definitely learning."

"Not slowly at all," Farrin contradicted, spinning her gently to face him. "You're amazing, Bianca. Don't you realize what you just did? You fearlessly confronted the leader of the elves—at the time," he added for Lurgl's benefit, "and called him out on his deception and dishonor. You even challenged your stepmother, and showed her how wrong she'd been about you. And as if that wasn't enough, you used magic—something no Selvanan has been able to do in generations—to break the hold the elves had over your people! And the best thing is, you did it all in front of your subjects, who know now just how strong a queen they're gaining."

He squeezed her hand. "If you can't see how far you've come since the night you were abandoned to the jungle, the rest of us can."

"I guess the fly didn't just escape the web to die after all," said Bianca, with a tiny smile.

"What?" Farrin looked confused, and she laughed.

"Never mind. What were you saying?"

"I was saying that you're breathtaking, Bianca," said Farrin. He smiled, reaching out to tuck a strand of her white hair behind her ear. "And I'm not talking about your beauty, striking as it is."

Bianca felt a flush rising up her cheeks as she returned the pressure of his hand. His affirmation meant more to her than she could say. She knew she could do it without him if she had to, but she was still glad she would have him by her side in the daunting task of ruling. In addition to all the personal reasons she never wanted to be without him, his knowledge of the world outside Selvana could be invaluable to the kingdom, especially if they hoped to reopen diplomatic relations with the mainland.

"So you two are going to marry, are you?" Raella elbowed her way forward, her voice long-suffering. "Typical humans. Always thinking with your hearts instead of your heads." She considered their clasped hands dispassionately. "Although I suppose it might be beneficial to have your kingdoms allied."

"Definitely beneficial," said Farrin solemnly. "That's my main reason for wanting to marry Bianca, actually."

"Very sensible," nodded Raella, as Bianca spluttered a protest.

"Farrin!" She couldn't help laughing at the twinkle in his eye. "Lurgl is one thing—I didn't suspect *you* of trying to curry favor with the elves at my expense."

Farrin laughed as well. "With Dionysius out of the picture, I need someone else to bait, and Raella just offered herself."

"Where is Dionysius?" Bianca asked, looking around. "I haven't seen him."

Farrin's expression darkened. "Lurgl cast him out. He was the one who planted the comb in your hammock. He confessed to it while you were under the effect of the poison."

Bianca's mouth fell open, grief washing over her at this unpleasant revelation.

"I knew he never liked me much," she whispered.

"It wasn't about you," said Raella stoutly. "At least, not fully. He gained something from the exchange, no doubt. We just don't know what."

"What will happen to him now?" Bianca asked, her voice quiet.

Raella shrugged. "Nothing. I expect he'll return to the main settlement, if he can. What he did might be unpalatable to you, but he didn't breach any obligation according to our kind. Although none of us will have much warmth for him after what he did."

"Unpalatable?" Farrin repeated, outraged. "He tried to murder her!"

"I still don't understand that," Bianca said, frowning. "I thought the elves wanted to capture me, not kill me."

"It is strange," Raella agreed. She sighed. "Well, I suppose I'll have to move back to the main settlement now, too. I don't know if I can stomach going back to being the only female in the cottage, surrounded by this slovenly lot."

Bianca and Farrin exchanged a glance, each trying to stifle a smile. The elf wandered off toward a group of others nearby, and Farrin's expression softened again.

"Now you're restored to your kingdom, you don't need me, you know," he said, the familiar hint of worry in his eyes. "Are you sure you want to be burdened with an outsider?"

"I will always need you," Bianca declared, slipping her arms around his neck. "You said you'd stay, and I'm not letting you out of your promise, Prince Farrin. You're stuck with me. And I think you'll find life up here in the trees is more comfortable than the vagabond existence you've become used to."

Farrin smiled down into her eyes. "As you wish, my queen," he murmured, before lowering his lips to hers.

# FARRIN

*Three months later*

"That looks right to me," said Farrin, nodding approvingly. "An excellent mast."

The woodworker beamed as he turned away, shouting instructions to his fellows.

"It's coming together nicely. At least judging by the pictures in the old books."

Bianca's voice made Farrin turn, smiling as he held out a hand to receive her. Accepting it, she pulled herself up onto the viewing platform that had been specially built to allow oversight of the ship in progress.

Bianca drew in a deep breath, a look of contentment spreading over her face as she looked down the cliff which fell away immediately below them, its steep side descending straight into the ocean. "I love that salty smell," she said. "I've hardly ever been this close to the ocean. We should have built walkways here years ago. It's a shame Sel isn't right on the coast like Port Dulla."

"I can't wait to show you the city," Farrin said eagerly. "It's fantastic being so near the sea. We do a great deal of trade through the port, of course, but it's also just beautiful."

"You must miss it," Bianca said softly.

He smiled at her. "I do, of course," he acknowledged. "But I would miss Selvana if I left here forever. I suppose I'm doomed to belong to two worlds."

"You don't look doomed," Bianca pointed out, her gaze passing over the open smile he could feel growing on his face. "You look happy, actually."

"I am happy," Farrin assured her as he drew her close.

"I like how much you've relaxed since I ascended to the throne," Bianca told him, nestling delightfully into his side. "You don't seem to expect an attack around every corner anymore, which I take as a big improvement." She snuck a look up at him. "And even better, you don't even seem nervous that I'll get myself into trouble whenever you're not with me."

"Of course I'm not," said Farrin staunchly, squeezing her. "I figured out a long time ago that the problem was with me, not you."

"Well, I had a bit to learn, as well," Bianca acknowledged. "And I hope I'll be a better ruler for my misadventure."

"You already are," Farrin assured her.

For a moment they watched the progress on the ship in silence. "Are you nervous to get back on a ship, after the last two times?" Bianca asked.

Farrin shook his head. "Maybe I should be, but I'm not. Both of those voyages ended badly, but I've been on ships lots of times before those, you know. Most of my memories are positive." He squeezed her against him. "Not to mention we'll have a singer on board this time. They say the deeps are a source of limitless magic, so even if we get thrown overboard, I'll trust you to sing me out of trouble."

Bianca laughed at his cheeky grin. "I don't know how I'm supposed to sing underwater," she pointed out. "But let's hope it doesn't come to that."

"We should really widen those walkways." Ilse appeared behind them, sounding out of breath and looking a little traumatized. "I actually had to free climb over one section!"

"I told you it wasn't a proper walkway all the way to the building site," Bianca laughed, helping her sister up onto the platform. "And didn't I see one of your guards carrying you across the free climbing section?"

"It still counts," said Ilse with dignity.

Farrin grinned at the sixteen-year-old. She wasn't much like her sister, but he'd warmed to Ilse. She hadn't quite been able to shake the vanity that made such a contrast to Bianca's unselfish heart, but having gone through the pain of seeing where her mother's excess of vanity had led, she was certainly trying.

"Is that what a ship is supposed to look like?" she asked doubtfully, casting a glance at the creation before them.

"Yes, as you'd remember if you ever paid attention in our history lessons," Bianca said, shouldering her sister playfully.

"To be fair, that one is only half finished," Farrin said. "It will look much more seaworthy when it's done."

"I hope so," Ilse said, looking unconvinced. "I don't like the idea of you sailing off in that thing and leaving me here, Bianca. What if you sink to the bottom of the ocean?"

"According to Farrin, I'll sing my way up from the deep," said Bianca lightly. She gave her sister's shoulder a squeeze. "Don't worry, Ilse, we won't sink."

Ilse sighed. "If you say so."

"I'm glad you both made it to see the progress," said Farrin. "I was expecting you an hour ago, and I'd almost given you up."

"It was my fault, actually." Ilse's cheeks heated. "I was...well, I was writing a letter to Mama. I received another one from her last night."

Both Farrin and Bianca went still, exchanging the briefest of glances.

"I suppose you think me traitorous, to be corresponding with her," said Ilse, a hint of defiance in her voice.

"Of course not," Bianca said quickly. "She's your mother, Ilse. I never expected you to cut her off altogether."

"Well, that's what I have done," said Ilse matter-of-factly. "At least, for a while. I've told her I won't be writing back again until she can send me a letter that isn't full of complaints." She wrinkled her nose. "Unfortunately, I don't think she's learning much from her exile."

Bianca gave a wry smile. "If she is going to learn anything, I imagine it will take a lot more time."

Ilse sighed. "Yes, I suppose so. I think I'll have to go and visit her eventually, but I admit I'm not in any hurry to travel to the southern settlement."

"She's not being pampered, is she?" Farrin asked abruptly. He was less inclined to let the former queen off lightly than Bianca seemed to be. Of course the reality was that she should have been executed for her attempts on Bianca's life. But he understood why Bianca had shown mercy, given Marisol was her sister's mother. Family loyalty was complicated.

"Of course not, Farrin," Bianca said patiently. "She's being put to work with the harvesters. And she's under guard at all times." Her voice turned dry. "I'm confident it feels enough like a punishment to her to satisfy even you."

Farrin doubted it, but he let the matter drop.

"I actually wanted to talk to you about something in particular," he said. "It's why I asked you to come this morning."

"Should I make myself scarce?" Ilse asked darkly. "I like you and all, Farrin, but I do *not* want to see you and my sister mooning over each other."

Farrin laughed. "It's nothing like that," he said. "It's about the elves."

"What about them?" Ilse demanded, sounding nervous. "I thought Bianca said that Lurgl had won most of them over to our idea about the singers, and they're done trying to trick all of us onto the ground."

Bianca nodded. "That's right," she said. "They're on board about us asking Farrin's parents to send Medullan singers on a diplomatic mission." She frowned. "Lurgl seems to think we'll need a lot if we're going to clear the magic enough to make the ground inhabitable. But at least we have some Selvanan ones to help get us started now."

Her face glowed with satisfaction, and Farrin felt a surge of pride. He'd loved watching Bianca's excitement over the success of the idea they'd come up with together. With Lurgl's help, they'd identified areas of rocky ground which were especially saturated with magic. By chipping the rocks away and carrying them up into the trees, they'd gained a valuable tool—a source of magic strong enough to activate any hidden singing ability, but not strong enough to kill anyone who didn't have the capacity to wield magic.

Given the magic in the rocks wasn't dangerous, the method unfortunately couldn't tell them whether Princess Ilse would survive on the ground due to her royal blood. That remained a mystery. One neither Bianca nor Ilse wanted to test in the only way they knew of, and Farrin didn't blame them.

Ilse had been willing to test herself on the rocks from the safety of the trees, but they'd revealed no capacity for singing. They weren't forcing anyone to take the test, and many were still too wary. It would take time to win people over with education and patience. But they'd already identified half a dozen singers through the method, and Farrin knew it lightened Bianca's heart to have company in her efforts to learn her craft.

Lurgl had even agreed to share some of the elves' learning about magic with the budding singers, which would be a huge help for them all.

In fact, Lurgl had been a great help in a number of ways since Bianca's coronation. She'd confided in Farrin that she'd never dreamed relations between the humans and the elves would be so strong this quickly—they would never have been this strong under Acacius's rule. And best of all, Lurgl was convinced there would be many more singers once magic became more accessible. He'd announced—to Bianca's mingled delight and embarrassment, if Farrin's eyes were any judge—that with the help of the Medullans, he hoped to reclaim the ground for human habitation by the time Farrin and Bianca's first child turned ten.

For his part, Farrin felt no embarrassment about the idea of having children with Bianca. Only excitement. But it felt like a far off dream, given her determination to get his parents' blessing before they wed.

Farrin returned his gaze to the half-finished ship. The wood-workers couldn't build it fast enough as far as he was concerned.

"Oi!" he called, his attention distracted by a flash of tan followed by a startled scream from a woodworker. "Lottie, get out of there! Stop scaring the workers!"

He grimaced at a laughing Bianca. "She does it for entertainment, the little minx."

Lottie leaped lightly from the ship's shell onto the platform via a handy branch. Springing up from the platform, she landed hard on Farrin's shoulder, then draped herself around his neck with an unrepentant yowl.

"Menace," he told her.

Ilse watched the display with wide eyes. "Is she safe?"

Lottie raised her head and hissed.

"Ignore her," Farrin said, rolling his eyes. "She won't hurt you."

"Is she going to live in the palace once you move in?" Ilse asked, still sounding wary.

"I doubt it," said Farrin. "She doesn't like the restriction of buildings. But I imagine she'll hang around, making a nuisance of herself."

"Don't believe a word of it," Bianca interjected. "He's absurdly fond of that cat, whatever he says."

"Well," said Farrin tolerantly, tweaking Lottie's tail. "We've been through a bit together, Lottie and I."

"What was it you wanted to say about the elves?" Bianca asked patiently, recalling Farrin's mind to their earlier conversation.

"Oh yes," he said. He met her eyes seriously. "It's about the elves who gave Dionysius the poisoned comb."

"Is that what Lurgl wanted to speak to you about yesterday?" Bianca demanded.

He nodded. "They thought they'd found the ones responsible, and they wanted me to come and identify them, given I saw them on the way back from the cottage that day."

"And?" Bianca pressed.

Farrin nodded again. "It was them. And they definitely weren't acting under Acacius's orders."

"You mean there was a separate group of elves trying to get hold of me, other than Acacius and the rest of the settlement?" Bianca demanded, clearly startled.

"Not exactly," Farrin reminded her darkly. "These ones weren't trying to capture you—they were trying to kill you."

"Oh," said Bianca. "Of course."

Farrin squeezed her hand reassuringly. "They're in custody," he said. "They can't get to you now."

"But why did they want to kill Bianca?" Ilse demanded. "Were they...were they working with my mother?"

"No," said Farrin. "Not that we can tell. But they were working for someone."

"Dionysius?" Bianca suggested.

Farrin shook his head. "They approached him. He owed them a great deal of money, apparently, and they canceled his debt in exchange for his assistance. No, whoever these elves were working for was very much against Acacius's plan to tame the magic on the ground. And not because they were concerned about the humans' safety," he added dryly. "They want the magic to stay wild. That's why they wanted Bianca dead, for fear she'd help tame it."

"Why do they want it to stay wild?" Bianca asked.

"That, Lurgl didn't know," said Farrin heavily. "They've been refusing to talk in response to questioning. But one of Lurgl's agents managed to overhear something they said when they thought no one was listening."

"What was it?" Bianca demanded.

"One of them commented to another that their employers will be very unhappy, and they'll have to mine magic elsewhere when their current source runs out."

"What current source?" Ilse asked nervously.

"We have no idea," Farrin admitted.

"The main thing is that whoever it is no longer has anyone working on their behalf in Selvana," said Bianca firmly.

"If you say so." Ilse sounded a little worried, and she wandered over to her guards soon after, leaving the other two to watch the woodworkers.

"It must be surreal, though," Bianca said suddenly, as if there'd been no interruption to their earlier conversation. "To think of going home after so long."

"It is surreal," Farrin agreed. "I'm itching to introduce you to my parents, and to Emmett." He paused. "And our guest, if she's still there, of course."

"A guest?" Bianca asked curiously. "Would the same one still be there after two years?"

"I don't know," said Farrin. "But it's possible. As far as I know, she had nowhere else to go. It's a bit of a strange story, actually. I found her on the beach, looking like she'd been washed up from a shipwreck, but we didn't know of any ship-wrecks. She wasn't much more than a child, and she was all alone."

"How awful," said Bianca with her usual ready sympathy.

Farrin nodded. "That's what I thought. It wasn't long after my own misadventure falling off that ship, so I felt for her particularly. I took her back to the castle, and tried to make sure she was looked after."

"But who was she?" Bianca asked.

He shrugged. "I don't know. I'm not sure even she knew. She couldn't speak, you see. She was mute. And she never communi-cated anything when we asked about her history. I don't know if she didn't want to say, or if she couldn't remember."

"What became of her?" Bianca's eyes were wide.

Farrin grimaced. "I don't know. I sort of...ran off and boarded a smuggler's ship only days after she arrived."

"That poor girl," said Bianca, giving him a look. "I hope the others were kind to her."

"Me too," said Farrin. "I think they would be. They're good people." He smiled at her. "Which is why I know they'll love you. They won't be able to help it once they get to know you." His voice dropped. "I just hope they can forgive me for what I've put them through."

"Of course they'll forgive you," Bianca told him, placing a reassuring hand on his arm. In spite of her words, her expres-sion was a little hesitant. "But how do you feel about going home without the aconitum?" she asked gently. "Will your family be disappointed about that?"

Farrin sighed. He'd told Bianca the truth about his brother, so he knew she understood the desperation of his search now.

"They didn't know the details of my plan," he told her. "And I don't think they would have believed for a moment I'd find a solution. But I confess, *I'm* disappointed I couldn't find it."

"We won't give up just because we've been back to Medulle," Bianca assured him. "We'll keep searching the island when we get home. If it's here, we'll find it."

Farrin nodded, a lump in his throat. He appreciated her words, but he had a sinking feeling that it was time to accept what he'd known for some time. Guilty as he might feel about Emmett's situation, it wasn't his to solve. It was his brother's battle, and no one else could fight it for him.

"I am looking forward to going back to Medulle," Farrin said, turning fully to face Bianca. "But the honest truth is, I'm looking forward to coming back here even more. Hopefully with a horde of Medullan singers accompanying us, ready to seal our alliance by helping to reclaim Selvana." He slid one hand around her waist, pulling her toward him as his eyes drank in her beautiful features and that striking white braid cascading over one shoulder. "The point is, I can't wait to start a new life here, with you."

Bianca looked up at him, the warmth of her smile eclipsing the heat of the day. "Sounds like the very best kind of adventure," she said.

As she nestled in for a proper embrace, Farrin's eyes skated over the ocean and the partially completed ship, on toward the lush, deadly, beautiful jungle beyond. An adventure indeed. And he defied anything, magical or otherwise, to stand against him when he had Selvana's big-hearted, clear-headed, and magic-wielding queen by his side.

# NOTE FROM THE AUTHOR

Thank you for reading *Song of Ebony*. I hope you enjoyed this first glimpse into the new world of Providore. I would be so grateful if you would consider leaving a review on Amazon—it would really make a difference!

If you want to learn more about the silent girl Farrin found on the beach, and discover what happens when Farrin and Bianca make it back to Medulle, check out *Song of the Sea*, the next installment of *The Singer Tales*. You're sure to find more adventure, fantasy, mystery, and hard-won happily ever afters!

Join up to my mailing list at deborah gracewhite.com to be kept up to date on new releases, specials, and giveaways, such as bonus chapters. You'll receive some great freebies, too, including *An Expectation of Magic*, a novella which is a prequel to my completed YA fantasy series *The Vazula Chronicles*.

Plus, you'll receive *Dragon's Sight*, an 8,000 word prequel to my completed YA fantasy trilogy *The Kyona Chronicles*.

Again, thanks for entering the world of Providore! I hope to see you back again.

# ALSO BY DEBORAH GRACE WHITE

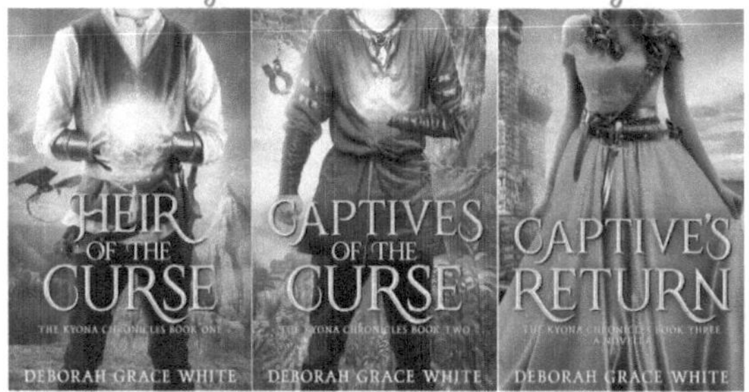

## The Vazula Chronicles: YA Fantasy

## The Kingdom Tales: Fairy Tale Retellings

# The Singer Tales: Fairy Tale Retellings
## (releasing throughout 2023)

# ACKNOWLEDGMENTS

As always, massive thanks to everyone who's helped make this new series happen. My husband, Ray, for listening through the book in its rawest form, and helping make it better.

My betas are fantastic: Mel W, Adrian, Mum, Andrew, Berri, and Steph. And huge thanks to Dad for developmental editing. Thanks also to Shae for the excellent job proofreading. Any remaining errors are definitely my own.

Thanks to Karri for bringing Bianca to life on this stunning cover, and to Becca for the gorgeous map.

To you, the reader, thank you for giving me the privilege of being an author.

And most importantly, to God, who brings everything hidden to light.

# ABOUT THE AUTHOR

I've been a reader since I can remember, growing up on a wide range of books, from classic litera-ture to light-hearted romps. The love of reading has traveled with me unchanged across multiple  continents, and carried me from my own childhood all the way to having children of my own.

But if reading is like looking through a window into a magical and beautiful world, beginning to write my own stories was like discovering that I could open that window and climb right out into fantasyland.

I cannot believe how privileged I am to actually be living that childhood dream and publishing my own novels. I do so from my hometown of Adelaide, Australia, where I live with my husband and our three little ones.

I've never outgrown my love of young adult stories, so the genre of young adult fantasy was always going to be my niche. Feel free to email me at deborah@deborahgracewhite.com and introduce yourself! Or subscribe to my mailing list at deborah gracewhite.com for free giveaways, sales, and updates.